KNOT OF STONE

Born in Cape Town of emigrant Dutch parents, Nicolaas Vergunst (1958) has worked as an artist, teacher, designer, curator and journalist. After a long-standing career with the national museums of South Africa, he resigned to write this novel and has since lived with his wife Ellen, a diplomat and historian, in Kiev, Kinshasa and Strasbourg. They have a house in Leiden where, eventually, they wish to return with their intrepid cats.

5 September

Dear Merces

A small gift of great tidings

Nicolaas

KNOT OF STONE
the day that changed
South Africa's history

Nicolaas Vergunst

ARENA BOOKS

www.knotofstone.com

First published in 2011 by Arena Books

Arena Books
6 Southgate Green
Bury St Edmunds
IP33 2BL
England

www.arenabooks.co.uk

Nicolaas Vergunst
Knot of Stone: the day that changed South Africa's history
1. Travellers – Europe – Fiction
2. South Africans – Europe – Fiction
3. Almeida, Francisco d', c.1450–1510 – Death and burial – Fiction
4. Cape of Good Hope (South Africa) – History – to 1795 – Fiction
5. Lisbon (Portugal) – History – Fiction
I. Title

ISBN 978-1-906791-71-1
Dewey Classification: 823.9'2-dc22
BIC categories: FFH, FJH, FV, 1HFMS

Concept, cover design, graphic artwork and layout by the author
Cover photograph by José Gomes Ferreira
Typeset in Baskerville

Printed and bound by Lightning Source UK

for Ellen

I am indebted to many and acknowledge their generous assistance: Rachael Clayfield and Laurence Oliver for their unpublished notes on the murder of Francisco d'Almeida, which inspired this novel. Ralph Shepherd and Helene de Villiers for their lucid research on the legend of Prester John in Ethiopia and Africa's own Grail stories. Malvern van Wyk Smith and Cyril Coetzee for their commentaries on the image of Africa in European literature, art and cartography. Johan Degenaar, for instilling a curiosity in all matters Aristotelian. Licínio Bingre do Amaral and João Perestrello for their insights into Portugal's overseas expansion and their interpretation of key texts. Larry Ferguson for his fresh ideas on reading the first draft, and Chris Thurman for his tireless editorial comments and astute advice on several later versions—a turning point in the book's slow evolution. To Greetje Lubbi and Harm Hazewinkel, my thanks for their input regarding plot, characterisation and dialogue. Finally, thanks to my publisher, James Farrell, for believing in this book from the start.

Preface

*Everyone loves a mystery story. When the mystery is not fictional
but is set in a real place, at a real time and with real people, then
the fascination becomes laced with the desire to know "the truth".*

Henry Lincoln, *Key to the Sacred Pattern* (1997)
co-author of *Holy Blood, Holy Grail* (1982)

I have seldom read or written fiction. I've tended to favour illustrated books with references and so, regrettably, have given scant attention to stories about crime, murder, detectives or spies. All that was before I began browsing around bookshops and saw how much modern fiction contributes to our pursuit for beauty *and* meaning.

Here I found novels about Plato, Galileo, Da Vinci and Napoleon. I uncovered mysteries riddled with secret symbols and sacred codes; adventures loaded with teenage magic and medieval legend; as well as thrillers bristling with immortal warriors and incarnate warlords… Then too, I also espied romances flirting with reincarnation.

So, I deduced that it is possible to publish a murder-mystery about the recurrent lives of historical individuals. My *histoire* (story) is not fictional but set in a real place, at a real time and with real people— people whose repeated interactions could solve a historical crime.

They are part of an unfolding human drama that has bound East to West ever since Alexander cut the Gordian Knot in ancient Turkey. I have tried to track their trajectory here.

The genesis for my story, however, is a massacre at the Cape of Good Hope on 1 March 1510; one hundred and fifty years before the first Dutch settlers arrived. Historians invariably describe how—on a windy summer morning when the tide ran high—sixty able-bodied men were slain by naked herders on a beach below Table Mountain. Most died defending a disgraced Francisco d'Almeida, ex-Viceroy of Portuguese India, then on his return to Lisbon. That afternoon, once the coast was clear, the survivors returned to bury their compatriots, leaving the despoiled body of Almeida in an improvised grave.

This became the first murder and first monument in South Africa's recorded history. There were no other witnesses, no other testimonies and—given all the other skirmishes along this coast—no alternative scenarios imaginable. And so it remained for five troubled centuries.

Until another version surfaced.

I came to hear about it from an itinerant priest, Rachael Clayfield, who mentioned an assassination plot involving the militant-religious Order of Santiago. This fraternity of armed knights—with its most powerful commandaries in Spain—jealously rivalled Portugal's rapid expansion during the fifteenth and sixteenth centuries.

It was an age of conquest, conversion, persecution and heresies. An era of neo-Templar crusades, African campaigns and broken vows. A time of lost reliquaries.

And the stuff of which conspiracies are made.

Sadly, the Rev. Clayfield died before her version could be verified. Frustrated by a lack of detail in her notes, I set out to find what facts or evidence still remained. As on a grail quest, my desire for the truth became obsessive—but my research led nowhere.

First, I had to learn that we interpret facts and give meaning to the evidence we collect; that *history* and the *past* are not the same.

We write our histories while the past can only be imagined. In fact, our actions and achievements need to be reimagined, reinterpreted and regularly re-evaluated. There is no indisputable "truth", only the truths we choose to believe in.

Yet, despite this, I chose to remain sceptical.

Then, some twenty years later, as 2004 drew to a close, a practising psychiatrist showed me a private, independent and still unpublished testimony confirming the role of assassins in Almeida's murder...

Enthralled by the concurrence, I reorientated my research, now as a historical narrative, sensing that those who were responsible for the murder mattered less than what lay behind the plot.

If such a plot even existed.

I have since used what material was available: recorded histories, official documents, private letters, diaries, oral testimonies, dreams and prophecies—including the clairaudient voices of our ancestors. Collectively, these provided the historical and karmic background for the story I offer here.

While *Knot of Stone* straddles different genres, it is first and foremost a work of historical detection. I chose the novel form over that of the travel journal, biography or monograph because it is better suited to "that willing suspension of disbelief". I hope readers will also suspend their belief when it comes to matters of faith and doctrine, just as I tried to avoid being dogmatic or coercive. My story is based on what I imagined, and now believe, happened that ill-fated Friday morning: Almeida was ambushed and killed, then ceremonially executed in a bizarre act of retribution—a death both real and symbolic.

Knot of Stone examines how an isolated murder (and others like it) can change the course of history. Furthermore, it investigates the lives of those who have redirected history's outcome on the world stage.

On the surface, *Knot of Stone* describes epic voyages of discovery, world trade routes and the ageless quest for a Terrestrial Paradise. On a deeper level, it examines the emergence of a mystic Christianity that came over the mountain—from beyond the forest or lake—and one that was meant to be independent of Rome.

Knot of Stone seeks to find a coherence between science and sorcery, rationalism and belief, philosophy and prophecy, as well as between European textuality and African orality. It traces Africa's recoverable past in relation to Europe's esoteric history—both the forgotten *and* the unseen.

To this end, *Knot of Stone* is a tale of entangled lives, legends and relics: from Aristotle to Averroës, from Prester John to Shaka Zulu, from Jason's Argonauts to Henry's Navigators, and from the sacred ark of Menelik to the blood-relic of Joseph of Arimathea. It weaves a tale around the lives of scholars, travellers, pilgrims, warriors, saints and sangomas. Ultimately, it ties a knot between the living and the dead; between our ancestors and ourselves.

These interwoven lives, including their karmic biographies, are like the strands of a Gordian knot that first appear to be intractable and unfathomable. Though we are unable to untangle the knot, its meaning is not beyond comprehension. On the contrary, from a bundled mess of historical, mythological and esoteric evidence an elegant story emerges; one that unravels with diligence and patience.

Finally, my reconstruction may not be the right one, but it is the only one I have to offer—for now.

In reimagining the events, I became as much a character of my own *histoire* as did those friends and colleagues about whom I wrote. As far as possible, their real identities have been retained in this story. Furthermore, the invaluable advice and assistance of several others is acknowledged above, and I apologise for any accidental omissions.

Lastly, I thank my three closest companions:

Stewart Young, for his compilation of Laurence Oliver's clairaudient karmic biographies, as yet unpublished, which proved germane to the formulation and outcome of this book.

Frans Lutters, whose boundless enthusiasm and resourcefulness has been indispensable. My narrative would be incomplete without his help and advice on the Grail research of Walter Johannes Stein. We corresponded throughout the process. Thank you.

Finally, I praise my beloved wife, Ellen Berends, for her generous encouragement, endless involvement and inspired insights. She once remarked: "Whatever you do, let it be worthwhile to others."

I thus hope my novel adds to our understanding of history and to our collective role in shaping the future.

Nicolaas Vergunst
Strasbourg

The massacre of Viceroy Francisco d'Almeida, 1510. From
Nauwkeurige Versameling... by Pieter van der Aa (c.1707)

*The [past] is like a very tangled knot which resists
untangling; but the fact that you cannot untangle it
does not mean you can't understand it. There may
be an elegant [historical] description of the entire
knot even if it is physically messy.*

Douglas Hofstadter, *An Eternal Golden Braid* (1979)

Prologue

Sometimes I feel like an historical character myself.
Hella Haasse, interview, *de Volkskrant* (20 February 1998)

'You saw the executioner,' blurted Sonja over the phone, 'we both know he aimed for the throat.'

Jason remained silent, the webcam's impassive eye monitoring each gesture in halted steps: his shrugging shoulders, the averted gaze, a face pinched with jaundice.

Sonja could still see the mountain's sombre silhouette behind him. Table Mountain slumbered: long, low and unmistakably flat.

Back in Leiden it was cold and dark.

'Can you hear?'

She fiddled with the Skype settings.

His reply was terse: 'Sure, and see you too.'

They knew it was staged to look like an error of judgement, a freak accident, one which none were prepared for yet everyone expected. After all, it had been predicted and, uncannily, like the prophecy itself, the message was explicit.

Now she'd received another.

'It says we were both there, Jason, together.'

'Nonsense!'

'Well, you asked me. D'you want to know or not?'

He hesitated. So much had happened to them in six months—and now this?

'Dunno. I don't recall anything, no ritual killing at all.'

His indifference was all too familiar.

She continued impatiently:

'The new message says we saw what happened, hiding in the dunes. Don't you think that's reason enough to know if—?'

'—if it *really* happened?'

He shrugged again, the blurred transmission exaggerating his face.

'Then why don't I remember anything?'

Silence. She lent in:

'Hey, I've asked myself that too, over and over, ever since we found that damn skeleton…'

Her retort was unnecessarily sharp. She should apologise, but her focus shifted as yet one more email popped up on her screen.

'Wait, I'll skype you back later.'

She hung up and opened her inbox. It was Thursday 16 December, the Day of Reconciliation in South Africa.

ARRIVAL

I travel the world and the seven seas
Everybody's looking for something...
Eurhythmics, *Sweet Dreams* (1983)

The infamous Cape of Storms was no myth. Sonja had witnessed its wrath half a year ago, when north-westerly gales and torrential rains battered the Peninsula. It was already the second week in June and she'd seen a heavy swell roll on the horizon, a tumultuous sea surge into the bay and windswept waves pound the beach below Table Mountain. It was a winter's tempest, a real Adamastorm.

Once it cleared, a jubilant sun vaulted over the Bergen van Afrika while the moon's disc dipped into the bay. Sonja was out for a brisk walk beneath the mountain's brow and, catching her breath, peered at the glistening city below.

Cape Town lay in its scalloped bowl, like a pearl, silent and still. It was the gem of a bygone era and the crown jewel of a former empire. It was the seafarer's Tavern of the Seas, a colonial Gateway to Africa, and the Mother City for generations of white South Africans.

Looking toward the city-centre she saw the Company's Gardens with its tree-lined avenues, ornamental lawns and formal footpaths— including the old white-washed Slave Lodge at the lower-end of the gardens. One by one she singled out the other buildings: parliament, the library, the national gallery and national museum. The last was easy to recognise with its conspicuous copper-domed planetarium.

Here, as Head of Anthropology, her hiking companion had spent the last three decades examining pre-settlement cultures at the Cape.

Professor Joshua E Mendle was a man with a flare for largesse, for grand gestures and, from his mother's side, endowed with an erudite mind. In appearance he was all too large for life. His enquiring nose bent against the breeze, his beard parted like a bow wave across his chest and, under a balding forehead, his eyebrows struck Sonja as the bushiest she'd ever seen. Blowing his hands for warmth, he resembled the vagabond pirate of local mountain legend.

Sonja and he nestled in a deep gorge used for reaching the summit. The first recorded ascent was made by Portuguese seafarers who—as hunter-gatherers had done for generations—climbed the same route to espy the environs. The interlopers were lost, Mendle explained, and from high above the Land of the Red People they offered their prayers while the gods of the Quena-ku whispered back on the wind.

No doubt the young men enjoyed the exercise too.

Not so the ageing professor who, catching his breath, spoke slowly:

'All roads lead to Rome, even caravan routes for circus animals, which is why old Pliny said: "Out of Africa always something new". Now taste our spring, it doesn't get any better, only in Paradise!'

He lent forward and cupped his hands, drawing a mouthful of clear water. It was cold and sweet. Though stiff, his body felt refreshed.

'Bedankt, but I have my own,' said Sonja, delving into her bag for the bottle she always carried with her.

Mendle was visibly disappointed. She'd declined the best he had to offer, even during the driest months of the year. It was a little miracle in his paradise, where the source literally flowed from the rock.

Sitting beside him, she swung her legs over the ledge, surprised how heavy her boots now were. She wore splash covers to keep her socks dry and woollen mittens against the chill. She leant in to retrieve the bottled water, her Persols dropping loose on their strap.

'With respect, Prof, it sounds like a conspiracy when it was merely an accident of history, a fortunate mistake, really, as the Dutch only set up a refreshment station after they'd been shipwrecked here. They never planned to settle, not permanently, no, as they far preferred Mozambique with its foot in East Africa's infrastructure. They even tried taking the island, twice, but the Portuguese beat them back.'

'True, had the Portuguese clung to the Cape the outcome could've been very different. South Africa would be another Brazil. We'd be Catholic and eating a lot more rice and beans. Oi-vey, how different!'

'How so,' she teased, twirling her bottle, 'whether Portuguese or Dutch, the natives would still be buried in a Christian graveyard?'

'Ah, master and slave, side by side,' he said with a raised eyebrow, 'including those who could conceal their traditional beliefs. Some had gold coins put over their eyes, as was common for the time, yet kept symbols of ancestral worship hidden under their clothes.'

'They were laid facing up?'

'Yes, but not the indigenes. They were buried in a seated position. Their remains are often exposed when storms gnaw at the hardened dunes along the beach,' he paused, wiping his wet brow with a sleeve. 'The unconverted were taken to a site farther away. The city is built on isolated burial sites that once surrounded Cape Town.'

'Isolated cemeteries and hospitals are a consequence of hygiene and wealth,' she noted pragmatically, 'like the old *isola Tiberina* of Rome. Moreover, the rich have always enjoyed better sanitation, better food, and the best cosmetics or medicine money could buy. Personally, I can't imagine life without flushing toilets, hot baths or clean sheets...'

Her gentle smile, Etruscan-like, evoked memories of his late wife.

'We all die in the end,' he replied, his face now drawn with sorrow.

For a minute neither spoke. They looked toward the Waterfront where, several years earlier, he'd uncovered a thousand skeletons: adults, infants and the elderly; slaves and free citizens; Europeans, Asians and Africans—including those born at the Cape itself.

As the SA Museum's senior anthropologist he'd supervised the dig amid much debate in the press. He was accustomed to controversy.

His career had been marred by Apartheid authorities and the new bureaucrats of democracy. While some had welcomed arguments for pre-settlement encounters, others now denied any foreign contact. He was among the few independent academics still prepared to challenge notions of origins, ownership and inheritance in southern Africa.

'There were originally two cemeteries: a site for Christians and an unmarked one for pagans, slaves, and those unable to pay the grave-diggers' fee. In the first we found a slave girl with a pendant around her neck—a tiny carved idol made of cowry shell. We suspect she was a heathen at heart when she died.'

'Perhaps,' suggested Sonja carefully, 'perhaps symbols and pagan rituals were tolerated as long as Christian beliefs weren't threatened. Or concealed, as Jews had to do in seventeenth-century Amsterdam.'

'Or, as we did here, initially. Lutherans too. We weren't allowed to display signs of worship outside our homes. Nor allowed to have our own church or synagogue.'

'Y'know, today, in Amsterdam, they say Sinterklaas can't parade with a cross on his mitre as it may offend others.'

Again neither spoke, taking in the view of the Mother City resting in the crook of the mountain's arm. The foreshore lay open to the Atlantic, a restless silver-green, as the Indian sprawled away, unseen, behind the mountain.

Out to sea the occidental and oriental currents collided: one born among Antarctic icebergs, the other coming from Equatorial waters. The upwelling, salt-laden Atlantic lumbered up the barren west coast while the shallow Indian swept down the lush eastern seaboard.

Over the millennia the cold Benguela and tropical Agulhas had influenced the temperature, rainfall and vegetation of southern Africa —as well as the movements of its coastal inhabitants.

'Indeed, the Cape is a natural wonder where East meets West and the southerlies flow northwards,' Mendle said, waving his arms out to sea. Out on the smudged horizon, amid the swirling ocean currents, lay the wind-flattened Robben Island.

'I know it was uninhabited, serving as a refuge for sailors,' she said, 'or, at least, I recall that it became a pantry, a post-box and a prison for the next five centuries.'

He raised his leg to tighten a boot lace.

'Ah, Robben Island's history as a high-security prison was inspired by the isolation of political prisoners during the Anglo-Boer War... Ironically, it's also where Mandela spent two decades.'

'But Apartheid prisoners weren't the first?'

'No, all manner of depraved and damned outcasts were sent to the island: runaway soldiers, convicted criminals, lunatics, lepers—even kings and princes. Mandela's great ancestor, king Makhanda, was there. So was imam Moturu, a prince from Indonesia. The most unfortunate, however, were the sick and diseased. As you said, this was our Tiber Island. Anyway, few fuss about these miserable lepers today, having left no descendants, unlike those British convicts sent to Tasmania—'

'—but what about the Portuguese', she interrupted, rubbing her slender shoulders for warmth, 'didn't they leave sailors on the island?'

'Ah, I remember something about mutineering seamen before the Dutch arrived... but my memory isn't what it used to be.'

He tied the other lace, pleased with his new boots.

Her face was cold and her hands numb. She spoke quickly:

'They say our memory is like a dog that lies down where it pleases; yours just seems a bit restless. What more about the Portuguese?'

The rotund scientist could sense her youthful enthusiasm. She was a colleague from the Institute for History at Leiden University and a specialist in European Expansion and Global Interaction. She'd been elected guest-curator for a forthcoming exhibition on colonial Dutch history at the Tropenmuseum, Amsterdam.

Now, here, at the Kaapse Vlek, she hoped to investigate disparities between official court records and the informal oral testimonies of the ordinary burgher. More specifically, she wanted to examine tensions between VOC officials and their dissidents, between the Companje's rule of law and their day-to-day treatment of convicts. It would be a brief visit, so her time was limited.

Fortunately for her, the Dutch were meticulous record-keepers and, after two long centuries, from 1602 to 1799, Cape Town's archives provided scholars with invaluable material—including climatologists studying El Niño's changing weather patterns.

Mendle continued:

'I think it was a Dutch historian, Pieter Kolb, who noted that early Portuguese sailors were afraid of cannibals and so sought refuge on the island, around 1500, allegedly, sheltering in a cave while feasting on fried penguin eggs and roasted seal breasts. The indigenes were neither man-eaters nor war-mongerers, of course, but would retaliate savagely if provoked—'

Mendle was cut short by the familiar ring of his mobile.

After fumbling in his trouser pocket, he began: 'Hello, Mendle?'

'Prof, Jason here, sorry to call, but last night's storm exposed a mass grave in Woodstock's railway yard—and it's no traditional burial site. The skeletons are laid out on their backs, arms folded, with heavier bones than we've seen elsewhere. The associated material suggests they predate any foreign settlers. You'd better come look yourself...'

Rising, his body stiff with fatigue, he sighed: 'I say, there is always something new in this far-flung corner of Africa!'

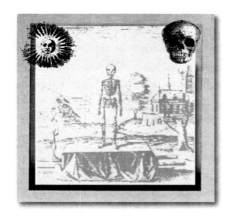

2

Bestow earth on unburied bodies.
Dig not up the tomb of the dead,
nor show to the sun things unseen
and thus call up divine anger.
Pseudo-Phocylides, *The Sentences* (1stC CE)

Mendle's dull blue Landi lurched to a halt on the loose gravel. He cut the rattling engine and manoeuvred himself over the passenger seat, clambering out on Sonja's side of the cab. His door was jammed.

The empty railway yard was located seaward of the Castle of Good Hope, along the old Esplanade, where rusting tracks traced the curve of a forgotten shoreline. Haunting street names—Beach, Tide, Spring and Marine—recalled what lay under tons of landfill.

The midday sun now sloped across the sky as Mendle set off, Sonja by his side, between piles of sleepers and tracks choked with weeds. He led her past a disused warehouse with its derelict loading bay, and then on beyond a platform strewn with splintered packing crates and old pallets. Everything was broken, barricaded and abandoned. This corner of his paradise looked grim and grey.

A prime location for a murder, he mused, recollecting what a once sober Inspector Morse had said: "The last to see the victim alive is usually the murderer."

Mendle did have a John Thaw-look about him—pale, ageing and inebriated—as if he too carried some unrequited sorrow. In her view, however, he was too talkative for a man with a silent past.

They passed a bright red gazebo where several student-volunteers sifted through a tray of clammy artefacts. The excavators huddled together, sheltering from the fresh sea breeze, surrounded by bundles of twine, coloured pin flags, plastic buckets and trowels.

A weather-beaten Caterpillar crawled away, like a pitbull sent to its corner, after digging under the defunct railway line. Unfettered tracks and scraps of tarmac lay scattered to one side, while red-and-white marker tape cordoned off the dig area ahead.

A young man in khaki shorts and matching veld hat stepped up to greet them. He was lean, sunburnt, and wore mud-spattered boots without socks. He also had conspicuous tan-stripes around his thighs and ankles.

'Jesus, here at last! I was about to remove—'

'—hello Jason,' proceeded Mendle politely. 'Sonja, my esteemed colleague, Dr Jason Tomas, also from the SA Museum…'

Jason shrugged, dusting off his hands.

Was that a greeting, she wondered?

Mendle whispered back, smiling: 'Jason does like to talk, a lot.'

'*Really?*'

'Indeed, as my associate he's never without an opinion. He's our most talented archaeologist but, alas, also our least gifted bachelor. He loves the solitude of field-work, especially on weekends.'

Jason drew closer, taller than Sonja estimated. Turning to her, he replied with feigned indifference: 'As a Gemini, I'm one part alter ego and one half his Doppelgänger. Prof M explores while I discover, and that's usually on Sundays…'

'Exactly, we were below Platteklip Gorge and about to unpack our breakfast when you so rudely interrupted. I should have known not to answer my phone. Anyway, show us what you've found?'

'Well then, come, follow me.'

Jason scrambled into the dig-area, his boots sinking to his ankles at the bottom of the pit.

'Right here, up here above me, is where the old tracks used to be. The trench was dug to lay a storm-water pipe, but the unprotected walls collapsed overnight. There, you can see where the rain washed the loose ground away. It was the machinist who first saw the bones, and his foreman who alerted the museum this morning…'

Sonja stepped up and peered into the gaping wound of earth.

The pit was deeper than expected. Lying in a bed of hardened sand were several skeletons, set neatly in a row. Jason looked up, pointing his picking-tool at the rough sidewall:

'The trench cuts through two distinct layers. The upper section is mere landfill, dumped before the tracks were laid a century ago. The lower consists of sterile sand-deposits, suggesting the area had once been a beach or estuary.'

Mendle knelt beside her, bending his good knee. She lent forward, like a curious spaniel, auburn hair drooping over one shoulder. Her glasses swung forward on their strap.

'The legendary Ma-Iti or abeLungu?' proposed Jason wryly.

Mendle clambered in for a closer look, his new boots sinking into a soup of sand, clay and water. She stood where it was firm and dry. Jason proceeded, waving his pick in the air:

'So far I've found a dozen skeletons lying side-by-side, orientated East-West. I'm not sure how many more there are, but then I guess we may never know. Not if Capetonians hear about another mass grave on their doorstep; even though there are no women or children this time—'

'—no women?'

'No, only men, and with variations to suggest differences in age and status. Looking at this man's dentures, I'd say he was over fifty when he came ashore. Healthy too.'

'Do y'know where from?' asked Sonja.

'No, not yet, as none resemble any local type. Physically, they're all much heavier than our Khoisan. So I reckon, overseas. Perhaps.'

Perhaps Indian or Phoenician, pondered the Professor. *No, too far off to be from Malabar or Carthage. Ah, and too large to be either Chinese or Arabian?*

Turning to Jason:

'Perhaps they were already dead and brought ashore to be buried?'

'Unlikely, at sea bodies were simply dropped overboard.'

'Aha. Then it may have been a massacre. Even a mutiny?'

'Or disease,' said Sonja, stepping back abruptly from the gaping wound, 'but why, why would the public want to interfere?'

'Because scientific endeavour and popular opinion don't mix,' said Jason, picking grit from under his fingernail. 'Historical evidence and public memory are like brandy and coke: never suitable in good company, yet always popular.'

Mendle chuckled, tracing a fractured jawbone with his forefinger. He'd been through it all before, at the Waterfront, when families stepped forward claiming they'd suffered enough indignities and—with all due respect—their ancestors deserved to be left in peace.

'Descendants want these sites covered in fynbos and transformed into memorial gardens. That's what they demanded last time—'

'—but can't you examine the remains first?' pressed Sonja.

'Who actually cares what we can prove today?' cut in Jason. 'With advances in bio-genetics, we're able to determine where individuals came from, who their parents were, what kind of diet they had and even how they died. Empirically, we know more about our past than ever before—'

'—but it's a loss to have them reburied,' she said, clearly agitated, 'future generations deserve to see this evidence.'

Mendle made it no easier:

'It's a futile debate, Sonja, a useless argument, actually, as one side favours scientific rationalisations, the other emotional justifications. Here it goes from one extreme to the other. Anyway, who are we to say what's best for the Dead? Who speaks for their Ancestors? More so, who'll listen to an old Italian Jew like me?'

'Europe has its own unwanted war memorials,' she volunteered, 'some citizens vandalise the monuments of their Soviet and Fascist oppressors, trashing the graves of unknown soldiers as if the dead were foreign football fans.'

'Sure, they may be foreigners,' cut in Jason, 'but not exiles, slaves or convicts. No, these were soldiers.'

Mendle swung round: 'Ah, why so?'

'Because I found metal clasps, buckles, riveted plates—and that dagger over there. Portuguese or Italian, I think.'

He pointed to a cross-shaped object under a sheet of clear plastic. Beside it lay several lumpy, mud-encrusted items of foreign origin. They were well preserved, considering their age, having been sealed beneath a layer of undisturbed topsand and, much later, under tons of building rubble.

Until now.

Energy surged through Mendle's body. He felt animated:

'If that's so, Jason, then I'd say we're looking at victims of the first pitched battle on our southern shores. See the scarred bones—here, and here, there too—these marks are made when weapons penetrate flesh and strike bone underneath.'

Sonja felt enthralled, but Mendle had other issues to deal with now. He stood up, adding decisively:

'Jason, put a gypsum jacket on this one, he seems to have a ball of leather wedged in his mouth—or something equally distasteful—and bring him back to the museum. We'll find out more about this riddle in our Lab, not here in the backyard of town. We don't want another *Sunday Times* sensation. We need uninterrupted time to do this, and fast, so keep it quiet…'

After all was said and done, the Professor returned to his dented Landi and unpacked their breakfast. Behind him scraps of torn plastic fluttered in the stiffening breeze, like the flags of a forlorn sailing ship. Beyond the barbed fence lay the Old Grey Father, Table Mountain, the ever-silent witness to many a by-gone age.

3

They sleep in the mountain's shadow
And depart from it no more.
Lance Fallaw, *The Watchers of the Cape* (1906)

Mendle cut away the plaster cast with surgical precision, revealing the fragile remains of a once sturdy and mature male. He and Jason then laboured overnight preparing the skull of what appeared to be a fully articulated skeleton. They found no sign of dislocation or injury —except for several missing teeth and a severely scarred jawbone.

Ah! Struck in the mouth from below, pondered Mendle, setting aside his titanium toolset and slumping into a chair, exhausted. He rolled his aching shoulders for relief.

It seemed to him that a long flat blade, probably made of steel, had struck the victim under the chin. Although only further examination could confirm this. Or show otherwise.

'I say,' he teased, looking up at Sonja, 'our good Doctor may have found the honourable remains of Viceroy D'Almeida—'

'—unlikely,' stepped in Jason, 'wasn't Almeida killed at Saldanha.' Unprovoked, he continued dusting the delicate bones with a fine hairbrush.

'Not so,' Mendle clarified, 'as the *Aguada de Saldanha* changed its name to *Tafel Baai* only after the Dutch started calling. In fact, they took the name from the Portuguese.'

Amused by this historical paradox, he added a footnote: 'The use of two names caused endless confusion until each, in turn, was applied to a separate shipping station. Even today, tourists don't realise that modern Saldanha lies 90kms north of Table Bay.'

'Like the anthropology student who thought Saldanha Man first appeared on Table Mountain,' flaunted Jason, referring to António de Saldanha, the Portuguese captain who first climbed the mountain. 'He was lost and wanted to check if his crew had rounded the Cape. From the summit they saw our extreme corner of the continent.'

'Some only make history when they're lost,' added Mendle, peeling off his latex gloves, 'like Alexander on the endless Asian steppe, or Columbus in the unknown Atlantic.' He opened a cabinet of surgical instruments and retrieved a half-jack and a cut-glass tumbler.

Pouring himself a shot, he explained to Sonja:

'Linguists say the local Quena and Sonqua referred to this valley as the *Camissa* or "Place of Sweet Water".' He repeated the word, twice, for additional emphasis:

C a mi ssa

C am is sa

'The Portuguese,' he noted, 'changed *Camissa* to *Aguada de Saldanha*, thus transforming a "place of sweet water" into the "watering place of Saldanha". This was probably done with the help of an interpreter, and may be the first act of appropriation at the Cape.'

Men of the Word—creationists, linguists, taxonomists—men who name people, places and plants, she noted, *like Linnaeus and his Hortus botanicus in Leiden.*

Mendle resumed their discussion:

'An early travel-writer recorded the onomatopoetic *Hoerikwaggo*, a Quena word meaning "Mountain of the Sea", a word that sounded like surf rushing back-and-forth against the shore.'

She noted it down, phonetically, questioning:

'Evocative, yes, but also unfamiliar, visually, at least. But why use *Quena* or *Sonqua*—is *Khoisan* no longer the accepted term?'

'Jan van Riebeeck recorded their use at the Cape in the 1650s and, today, linguists say it's how they called themselves, so I do the same. But the matter is far from settled.'

'*Khoisan* was invented by a German anthropologist to combine two indigenous groups under a single generic term, as in post-colonial *Burkina Faso*,' added Jason, 'however, the term is inaccurate as it fails to reveal power imbalances between the Khoekhoen and San. Their relationship was similar to that between the Romans and Etruscans.

The term *San* is itself derisive and derogatory, like Gypsy, as it comes from "forager" or "vagabond". And yet, ironically, it appeals to the very tourists upon whom the Bushmen depend today.'

Mendle's mouth was dry. He paused for another sip of Glenfiddich, then beckoned mischievously:

'Do you realise your name has a curious phonetic quality too? Just listen to its resonance for a possible past life connection.'

She caught the glint in his eye as he leant forward, whispering:

S o n   q u a
S o n   j a

'A mere coincidence,' she said with interest and charm, 'you should know I believe in chance rather than providence...'

Despite an adolescent curiosity with past lives—typical for that age —she had no interest in it now. In fact, as a disciplined historian she avoided transpersonal theories. Even if Prof Mendle believed in that stuff, she was sure the cynical Jason never would.

Turning heavily in his chair, Mendle proposed a break:

'First, something more to drink, then I'll tell you what I know about Almeida's murder.'

They had locked themselves inside the Anthropology Department where Mendle and Jason shared a small laboratory. Their lab was well-equipped, spacious and secure; with its own dehumidifier, fridge and dual-function DeLonghi coffee maker. The lab was always cold in winter, too hot in summer, and drafty all year round. Up in the roof a defunct airduct released the Ancient Spirits after dark.

It was a restless night as another cold front drove in from the sea, lashing rain against Mendle's office windows. His door stood ajar and the hazy glow from his PC formed rotating patterns on the ceiling. Several service lights flickered down the passage, plunging elongated shadows into the inky abyss. The museum was a primordial sea of darkness where whale skeletons and fossilized dinosaurs kept watch, and mounted lion protected the effigies of the Ancestors.

Long, long ago, long before the First Ones came, the land had been swallowed by the sea. Even the mountain was born beneath the water before it rose, giantlike, against the jealous sea-dragon. In myth, the mountain personified a titan: Umlindi Wemingizimi, Adamastor.

'The legendary amaRire, the First Ones, are no more real than the Atlanteans,' warned Jason, 'a myth is a myth is a myth.'

He gulped down a cold coffee as Sonja reset the DeLonghi. Mendle refilled his tumbler.

'Ah, Cesaria Evora understood it all when she said: "Work is Work, Whisky is Whisky".'

'What about Almeida?' asked Sonja abruptly.

What about him? Jason winced at her impatience.

Mendle merely gestured toward a more comfortable seat.

'I say, let's not presume too much. Our skull is a skull is still a skull, for now. Be that as it may,' he added, casting a smile in her direction, 'Francisco d'Almeida was the first Viceroy of Portuguese India and a notable ambassador, admiral and administrator. Bartolomeu Dias, Vasco da Gama and António de Saldanha were among the few to round this sea-girt Cape before him. Following historical sources, Almeida and fifty-seven men, perhaps more, were killed when they came ashore, some say on the old beach below District Six. Sadly, the shore disappeared when a deeper harbour was built, around the time steam-ships began calling at the Cape.'

He sipped his drink as Jason continued their preparations, brushing out debris from between the bones.

'To make a long story short, a group of sailors and soldiers—no doubt unsavoury, sunburnt and unshaven—found some herders from whom they tried to obtain, or more probably, from whom they tried to steal a few head of cattle. However, the latter didn't want to barter as a fattened herd symbolised status, wealth and prosperity. In return, the seafarers gave away mere trinkets—felt caps, pewter rings and glass trade beads—unwilling to exchange their own swords, lances or crossbows. Obviously.'

Jason smirked: 'So, instead, our Khoisan pilfered a few knifes?'

'Exactly, until someone hurled abuse and they began to brawl. The outnumbered sea rogues—twelve in all, I think—fled to the beach where a longboat awaited them. One of these was Almeida's servant, who returned with a bloodied nose and his teeth broken.'

Mendle paused, inserting his own nose into a swirling tumbler.

'Once aboard the flagship, the humiliated men asked Almeida to go punish the villagers. Reluctantly, he agreed, and so early the next morning, probably before sunrise, he led an ad hoc party ashore. Several men ran ahead to raid the village where—as far as I know—the first white man was killed on our southern shore. An accident, they say, as he was stabbed by his over-zealous compatriots in the chaos. The other men returned with what cows they could steal—and some children they had kidnapped.'

'Children?'

'That is, men of small stature. It was common practice to educate abductees back in Lisbon and then, years later, to return with them as *linguas* or interpreters. However, after that, their lives were full of contradiction and confusion, as neither Whites nor Blacks would treat a lingua as their own.'

Mendle fell silent, momentarily distracted by his own experience as a marginalized academic: *Again and again, the eternal outsider.*

'Shall I go on?'

'Please do, Prof, while I wait for the pot.'

She held up a packet of Ethiopian highland coffee, a birthday gift, from friends in the Museum Café downstairs.

'No-well-fine,' he said, lifting his tumbler. 'Now, where was I?'

'The punitive party was ambushed,' said Jason, as the aroma of percolating coffee filled the Lab.

'Ah, yes, Almeida and his men made a forced retreat to the beach. Unable to flee, they fell back between the dunes and rising tide until about sixty more were dead—all victims of fire-hardened spears and slingshot-stones. According to eyewitnesses, Almeida died kneeling in the sand, his eyes lifted up to heaven, with an assegai through his throat. Jorge de Mello Pereira, a trusted officer, managed to flee and returned that same afternoon to bury the dead.'

Mendle wiped his lips, concluding gravely:

'I could lose my job if the authorities find out what I've got here. Concealing these bones is not only illegal, but also unethical, so I'd prefer to keep our work a secret, please.'

She knew that the illicit trade, collecting and exhibition of human remains was a sticky business—even diplomatically. The bottled head of Badu Bonsu, an Ashanti king from the 1830s, was a grim example. Like the Tropenmuseum, Leiden University had been returning its specimens for years.

It was the Barcelona Olympics that shook the museum world when black athletes threatened to boycott the games if a stuffed *El Negro* remained on view in a local museum. The "Bechuana Bushman" was most probably a moTswana whose body had been stolen after burial,

17

also in the 1830s, and then taken to the Cape Colony where it was prepared for exhibition.

Right now, she reflected, their *El Portu* could jeopardise renewed restitution projects in South Africa.

'Your secret is safe, Prof,' she added cheerfully, turning to Jason.

'Jesus, it's not like I'm going to tell anyone! That'd be professional suicide…'

Jason packed away his tools, ever so methodically, then flashed a rare smile: 'Alright then, no problem.'

Mendle was visibly relieved:

'By the way, there's only one historical depiction of the massacre, published two centuries later, by a certain Van der Aa,' raising an eyebrow, Mendle winked, 'and he's also from Leiden.'

Sonja had to laugh, saying: 'Well, I'd rather not assume any karmic connection.'

Mendle beamed back.

She knew the artist's *œuvre* and filled in: 'Pieter van der Aa was an entrepreneur who, rather rapidly, became the city's top printer, the university's leading publisher and the country's least liked bookseller. He had a shop on the Rapenburg—our most beautiful canal—and his travel books were renowned for their illustrations; especially those with random scenes of Africa.'

Jason was speechless: *Does she ever breathe?*

Mendle left to fetch a book from his adjoining office. Returning, he stopped to show Sonja a fanciful depiction of huts, palm trees and fighting men on an otherwise deserted beach—all viewed from the safety of the roadstead. The ships were not Portuguese caravels but Dutch galleons, she noted, which revealed more about the engraver than it did of the event itself.

'Ah, then this Van der Aa was not the actual artist?'

'No, nor was he an explorer or traveller. I think the farthest he ever went was to the Frankfurt Book Fair.'

Still beaming, Mendle proposed: 'As far as I know, the national military museum has the only other depiction of the event—a modest painting by a local artist, a woman, or so I recall. Say, why not visit the Castle tomorrow while I catch up on some lost sleep?'

4

I think history is more likely to be born on beaches,
those marginal spaces between land and sea...
Greg Dening, *Mr Bligh's bad language...* (1992)

The Castle of Good Hope was the oldest extant building in South Africa, a cornerstone of colonial history, and still in mint condition. Built on the beach in 1666 to defend VOC possessions, it had never been besieged—except by busloads of trigger-happy tourists.

Jason was there, as agreed, ensconced on the terrace with an empty espresso. His casual demeanour made even the cane-furniture look comfortable. With his leather satchel slung over a chair and an open notepad lying on the table, it seemed he'd been there all morning. She drew a chair while, with a confident flick of his fingers, he hailed the slim cinnamon-coloured waiter at the bar.

Sonja had been out for a brisk walk and, dressed against the cold, now wore a knee-length coat and knitted scarf with her favourite tortoise-shell glasses. The latter were fashionable any time of day— particularly after a late night in the Lab.

'It seems odd that one hundred and fifty soldiers,' he said, once she'd settled, 'of whom most were well-equipped and experienced, could be so easily overwhelmed by a group of angry pastoralists.'

'So then, how many lived in an average Quena village?'

'About two hundred, maybe three, including women, children and the elderly.'

'And fighting men?'

'One hundred, perhaps more, but their throwing sticks were useless against the crossbow, lance or sword. Headless spears were no match for weapons of steel.'

'So what chance did the Quena have?' She removed her glasses to see him better.

'Chance, against these odds? Only one. Oxen. They had a herd of trained war-oxen which, when driven together, formed a formidable battering ram or protective shield. Early writers observed how they leapt like agile dancers between their stampeding cattle.'

She listened as his hands mimicked the movements of men and beast, his expressive gestures revealing more than his face allowed... He was handsome, yes, but too nonchalant for her.

'So what's your point, Jason?'

'Almeida wasn't crushed in a stampede.'

'What?'

'The skeleton we found is undamaged. Almeida—or whoever the skull belongs to—was slain in close combat by a hand-held weapon. The point of entry was under his chin and made by a controlled thrust. The blade smashed out his teeth and was sufficiently flat to leave parallel scars along his jawbone.'

'Then wooden sticks didn't kill him?'

'Who knows, he may have had other injuries and bled to death, even drowned. Whatever, only his bones can tell us now...'

Jason rose to settle the bill. She watched him saunter over to the waiter, a rakish Indonesian boy, with whom he chatted while paying. He returned smiling. Rare indeed.

He led her across the manicured lawn, neat as a billiard table, until they reached the entrance to the Castle Military Museum. Here a security attendant directed them toward the painting.

It was a vivid and dramatic work. Hemmed in between the rising tide and falling dunes, the Portuguese defended themselves against the fearless herders and their frightened oxen. Two figures dominated the foreground: one with a raised assegai, the other drawing his sword.

Almeida, certainly. His face was obscured, as if the painter wanted to avoid a portrait. Perhaps no reliable likeness existed?

According to the accompanying text, the artist had been inspired by a local illustrator, one Angus McBride.

While most seventeenth-century artists never saw the Cape—a fact Jason was pleased to point out—this one probably stood on the beach himself. Or rather, *herself*, if Mendle's memory was to serve them well. Either way, the details were too specific for an outsider.

Jason came and stood behind her. She lent in to read the text:

'It says the herders whistled and shouted, driving cattle against the heels of their foes. The sixteenth-century chronicler, João de Barros, writes that Almeida's men were surrounded and fell in the soft sand, wounded and trampled, as few wore armour and for weapons had only lances and swords.'

She looked over her shoulder as he turned away, his voice derisive:

'Whatever, soaked in history, the chroniclers fail to convince me. Their facts don't add up…'

'Perhaps,' she suggested, 'perhaps our best clues are in the Lab?'

'Too late. Prof M asked me to re-seal the remains until the threat of confiscation passes.'

She looked puzzled.

'I agreed to do it on Saturday.'

'Then you really are his alter ego.'

'Only on weekends,' he said with a wan smile.

'So you *do* smile, after all?'

He avoided the implication, noticing how white her teeth were, and proposed they visit the military library upstairs.

He led her out, via Reception, and up the narrow stairs.

'I-i-if it wasn't an accident,' she stuttered, reaching the last step, 'if Almeida wasn't killed by oxen or fire-hardened spears, then he must have been murdered by his own men?'

It seemed to her that there was no marginal space where Africa's past and Europe's history did not intersect; no beach below Table Mountain where the footprints of both native and interloper hadn't overlapped. Furthermore, she realised, there was no reconstruction of Almeida's murder from which either party could now escape.

5

*This life as you now live it and have lived it, you will have to
live once more and innumerable times more.*

Friedrich Nietzsche, *The Gay Science* (1882)

'Francisco d'Almeida was born around 1450, in Lisbon, and served
the court as a diplomat,' began Jason, as Sonja browsed between the
over-laden bookcases, careful not to trip.

Excess books had been boxed, bundled and stacked along the aisles.
It felt like a cold storage room, not a book repository. The Castle had
been built against rough seas, not rising damp. A shivering archivist
sat in the corner, alone, guarding his oil-heater. From what she could
see, they were the only visitors in the library.

Checking the wall clock (they had less than an hour before closing),
she handed Jason a monograph: 'Here, start with this...'

He went and sat at the reading table, his fingers skipping through
the pages, plucking information at random. Reading aloud:

'According to the seventeenth-century royal historian, Manuel de
Faria e Sousa, Almeida was the son of Lopo, first Count of Abrantes,
and a knight in the Portuguese Order of Santiago... Almeida was
graceful in person, ripe in council, continent in action and an enemy
to avarice. He was liberal and grateful in service and obliging in
carriage. In ordinary dress he wore a black coat... though later it was
a sleeveless cloak or doublet of crimson satin, with black breeches
reaching from his waist to his feet.'

'Like the one we saw downstairs?'

'Possibly.' Jason skipped on: 'Almeida acted as an ambassador for the ageing king of Portugal, Afonso V, trying to unite him with the young Juãna la Beltraneja, a child-princess from Castile... He visited France to secure support for this alliance—'

'—but Afonso didn't succeed,' said Sonja, coming to stand by the table, 'the French favoured an alliance with Castile for themselves.'

'Thus the French supported Castile, not the Portuguese?'

'Yes, making it a financial setback for Afonso who needed France's backing for his North African crusades... He was called Afonso "the African" because of his success against the Moors, most of whom were Muslim Berbers, Islamized Slavs or Moroccan slaves. And he used the *Reconquista* to unite Portugal and Aragon.'

'Then it was Portugal and Aragon versus France and Castile... like a quarter-final in the UEFA Champions League?'

Sonja smiled, recalling what else she knew of Europe's expansion: 'Diplomatic relations floundered while neighbour states bickered over the spoils of war—especially all that gold from Africa.'

After an inevitable sea battle, Portugal and Castile split the world between them, pole to pole, East from West, with Portugal securing sovereignty over all African trade. The line was redrawn by Spanish-born Pope Alexander VI, Rodrigo Borgia, that "rapacious wolf", midway between the discoveries of Columbus and Portugal's existing possessions. Rome always devoured its prey like a wolf, but now it faced a New Troy—Lisbon had come of age.

Fatigued, Sonja eased in beside Jason, reading over his shoulder:

'It says Almeida was dismayed by all the bidding for Juãna's hand. Not because she was illegitimate, or still so young, but because he no longer felt national destinies should depend on arranged marriages. It appears he thought royal alliances were archaic and that Europe's future should be better served by its elite mercantile class.'

'Whatever he felt for national destiny or historical will, he was also engaged by Isabella and Ferdinand. He was their confidant too.'

'Right, the Catholic monarchs united Castile and Aragon to form a single Spanish state in 1492, finally, after the expulsion of the Moors. In short, Almeida served the kings of both Spain and Portugal, each with their own allegiance to Rome.'

'How d'you remember all this detail?' He looked at her askance, sitting too close to meet her gaze head on.

'Easy, I memorise the decade and year, the century is obvious.'

'Well, it clearly works for you,' he said, noting the time difference between European history and African archaeology. The clock ticked on as he ran his finger down the next page, reading rapidly:

'Francisco d'Almeida was an inspired strategist who took command of the sea and secured the oceanic trade route to the Indies... but was reluctant to spend limited resources on costly territorial footholds, unlike his successor, Afonso de Albuquerque—'

'—that's unusual,' she interrupted, 'as Europe's overseas expansion depended on the capture and possession of new lands.'

'Like the English, who rushed ashore on seeing a Dutch fleet enter Table Bay, shouting "For King James!" They claimed the Cape and all the land between it and their nearest Christian neighbour, Prester John, then several thousand miles away. That's in 1620.'

Laughing again: 'I see you do recall dates too.'

'Sure, I *do* dates, while you can be so brutally honest!'

'No, the Portuguese were brutal. Tristão da Cunha cut off women's hands to steal their bracelets...'

His smile faded, looking away: 'Colonialists always impose a culture of violence on those they conquer, convert or civilise—'

'—perhaps, but what about cultural or commercial exchange?'

She began paging through her own book.

'Same-same, but look here!' he said, prodding her with his pencil. 'Almeida commanded the most decisive naval battle in the history of the Indian Ocean, in 1509, when his fleet destroyed the Egyptian, Arabian and Persian navies at anchor off Diu in north-west India... This victory not only ensured Portugal's monopoly of the sea, but set the political stage for another five centuries...'

Jason became animated. She put a cautionary forefinger to her lips, adding quietly: 'The ocean was a vast neutral zone. At that time no one dared deny others the right to sail the seas.'

He shrugged, half-listening, half-reading: 'Sure. It seems more men died at the Cape than all those at the battle of Diu.'

'Diu repelled Islam from the East and not, as had been tried before, by advancing overland from the West—'

'—right, it was a culmination of eight centuries of conflict between Mediterranean Muslims and European Christians, an animosity that began with the invasion of Iberia in the eighth century. The first to set foot on Gibraltar,' he added, 'was the formidable free-slave from Morocco, General Gibril Tarik.'

'Hence the name *Gibral-tar*,' she acknowledged.

'Right. My favourite uncle told me how Tarik made his men burn their boats: "My beloved brothers, we have the enemy in front and the sea behind us. Now we can't go home. We shall either defeat the enemy or die like cowards by drowning. Who will follow me?" I loved that story, even if Uncle Noor made it up!'

'Wait, back to the battle of Diu, I see it was more than a military victory, it was an act of revenge. His son had been slaughtered—'

'—Almeida, a father?'

'Yes, which means there was a woman too—here, read it. Married or not, Almeida was probably in love at least once.'

It was her first insight into Almeida's private life—like looking at an unfamiliar Dutchman and knowing he had, if only once as a child, sat on the knee of Sinterklaas. Catholic or not.

With cold impartiality, the archivist announced the library would be closing in ten minutes. Jason hurriedly picked for more:

'Lourenço, an only son... killed a year earlier... in 1508. Husayn al-Kurdî, commander of the Mamluk fleet from Egypt, ambushed him at Chaul harbour... The Portuguese had the upper hand until, for a shrewd price it seems, support came from the naval chief and master of Diu, Malik Áyáz, a former Russian slave... In the end, a combination of extra ships, swelling tide and bad timing cost Lourenço an arm and a leg. Literally,' he grinned, 'as both his limbs were blown off by two successive cannon balls. The ship sank with him tied to the mast, leaving only a handful of survivors—'

Appalled by his humour, she cut him short:

'—and the rest of Lourenço's fleet?'

'They escaped. It was a devastating blow for Almeida who, finally, stepped down as Viceroy, but only after avenging his son's death...'

Despite all she recalled of European expansion around 1500, she knew little of Africa or India during the next century. Her area of specialization was Dutch seventeenth-century mercantile exchange with Indonesia and Japan—Holland's so-called Golden Age. Now, at this cornerstone of South African history, her own *histoire* was about to change.

777

GRANDES
PORTUGUESES

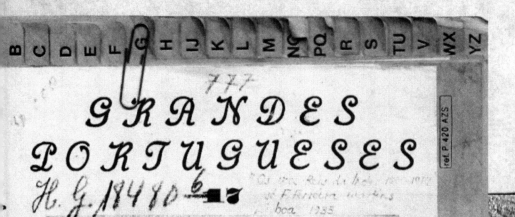

D. Francisco de Almeida

ALM YDA

DOM FRANCISCO D'ALMEIDA

Whosoever believes in the eternal recurrence
will die the same death, over and over
until the last is silenced forever

It began as an accident—like most scientific discoveries or inventions. Her feet felt clumsy, even stupid. Turning to leave before the library closed, her one shoe hooked the corner of a box and several books scattered to the floor. Embarrassed, she bent to retrieve them before the archivist could intervene.

Gathering the last items into her arms, a scuffed dossier fell open to reveal its contents: pictures, maps, notes, photocopied articles and some handwritten lists. Then, on a library requisition form, partially obscured, her eye caught sight of six blurred letters in faded ink:

A L M   Y D A

She checked again... had she begun to see his name everywhere, like the face of a beloved lost in a crowd? *Dalmeyda* definitely, yes, and among his portraits a scrawled note that warned:

Whosoever believes in the eternal recurrence
will die the same death, over and over,
until the last is silenced forever.

Sonja heard a heavy chair draw back, followed by approaching steps. There was no time to read more. Instinctively, she slipped the dossier from sight, under her coat front, as the Shivering Archivist came up to collect the books.

Flushing, she apologized, offering what books she held in her free arm. He brushed against her breast, accidentally, fumbling the pile with a frayed woollen glove:

'The box was left on our doorstep, unlabelled and unidentified, as if someone wanted it out of harm's way—like those Russian posters left on the front steps of the SA Library in 1960, the night before the ANC and Communist Party were banned. The stuff in our box is still unclassified. An expert was meant to sort it out months ago, which is why the box remains in the aisle. Here, let me clear it out the way.'

He shoved the box aside and returned to his desk, locking his top drawer and unplugging the heater. She heard him pocket his keys.

'Thank you,' she said, not sure of her next move, 'we'll be done in a minute.'

Check the dossier.

She turned away from the archivist, keeping the dossier flat against her tummy. Jason came round and stood behind her.

'What's this?' he hissed, aghast.

'Wait. Watch my back.'

'Whatever, he's busy. You're safe.'

She leant against Jason's shoulder, easing free the dossier, while the chilly bibliophile secured his filing cabinet for the night.

She peeped inside again.

There were pencilled comments in the margins, sepia photographs, souvenir postcards, an old Union-Castle Line calendar, a wire-ring notepad and some biographical tables, entitled *Tabula nomens*. Three embossed letters, WJS, appeared on the outside flap, presumably to identify a past owner. Sonja lent in, holding onto Jason as she read:

> On leaving Cochin the sorcerers, or astrologers, warned that Almeida would not pass beyond the Cape of Good Hope... it being the portal to the Estado da Índia and the border of his realm. Passing it in fine weather, he said to his attendants: "Now, may God be praised, the witches of Cochin are liars." A few leagues farther, after coming ashore, he was slain and buried at the watering place of Saldanha.

No matter how irrational it seemed—or however criminal it would appear to others later—Sonja knew she was going to steal the dossier. There and then.

The idea was as unexpected as it was reckless. She'd never done anything like it, not even a lipstick from the Bijenkorf. But this was neither the time nor the place to justify herself. She would tuck it under her coat, again, and simply walk out.

But wait, first another peep, a quick squizz at the prediction cited below. A curse, it seemed, by the same Manuel de Faria e Sousa:

'Hey,' she whispered over her shoulder, 'it says divine judgements are unfathomable... the superstitious talk of ill fortune and bad luck when Providence is really the only explanation. *O Providência*, I think Prof Mendle would like this!'

6

And if I ever lose my mouth
or my teeth—north and south—
'cause if I ever lose my mouth
I won't have to talk.

Cat Stevens, *Moonshadow* (1971)

Professor Mendle lived in a Victorian semi against the rim of the city bowl. It was a balconied double-storey with a secluded garden that slumbered in the mountain's shadow—like Mendle himself.

He had bought the house in the Seventies when everyone else was peeling enamel paint from their panelled-doors, sash-windows and trellised verandas. When back-to-nature was fashionable and truth-to-materials represented honesty and integrity—yet manual labour did nothing for the vanities of a serious academic.

Sonja and Jason now stood in front of the only house with gloss-white fixtures. Symphonic music muscled its way under the door and through the wrought-iron gate. A Wagnerian opera. Morse.

'Try again.'

Jason hammered at the door until a dishevelled Mendle let them in. Wrapped in a blanket, pharaoh-like, he led them to a darkened study where half-drawn drapes hid a pair of jammed sash-windows.

It was a cramped but comfortable mess.

A teetering bookcase held up the sagging ceiling while bundled journals stood like sentries at their posts. Mendle's desk was strewn with newspapers, crossword puzzles and a framed photo of his late wife. Her favourite cat slept on his flattened leather briefcase.

Mendle offered no excuses for his appearance, except to say that had Jason and Sonja not called, he may have looked more refreshed after a longer nap. There was no food in the house, either, not even a frozen meal, so perhaps they'd better go get something to eat?

'We came to show you this dossier—here, take a look—and to ask about the uncanny prediction concerning Almeida's death?'

They pointed to the reverse side of the UCL shipping calendar.

'Ah, I see you found the witches' prophecy,' he said cautiously, 'but we don't really know if it's fact or fiction. The *Lusíads* only appeared after the massacre. In fact, all in all, sixty years after.'

'Is that how long it takes to write an epic?' taunted Jason, recognising the title.

Mendle chuckled. 'Luís de Camões worked on it for over a decade and saw it published, finally, in 1572. It's the inspired history of a restless Portuguese nation who, as someone once said, were a "small people of big deeds". However, it's no history, but an allegory focusing on Vasco da Gama's historic crossing to India. *Os Lusíadas* simply means the "Sons of Lusus" and describes the adventures and fortunes of all who doubled the Cape... including the prophecy that Almeida would not pass this threshold on his return from India. But having safely done so, Almeida believed his curse was lifted or, at least, that it would not be fulfilled at the world's southernmost Portal.'

'So, what happened?'

'Ah, but he didn't pass *beyond* the Cape, did he? While we still don't know whose skull it is,' said Mendle, lowering his voice, 'we do know that Almeida was struck by his own men.'

'Jesus, not with that dagger we found next to the skeletons?'

'No, with a long flat blade,' he replied, before Sonja could ask:

'I thought he was ambushed when his punitive expedition failed?'

'Well, that's still true, but it didn't end like that,' whispered Mendle. 'I asked a friend for his advice, a psychiatrist who also happens to be clairaudient—a healer empowered by the Ancestors—like a shaman or sangoma, but one who doesn't trance and hallucinate. He's usually awake or conscious when the ancestral spirits speak to him, and hears the story behind a person's life, or the story behind a ring, a watch, a handkerchief and even, say, the story behind a photograph—'

'—or behind a rusty old dagger?'

'Aha, yes, even that rapier you found. I showed it to him yesterday, only to look at, of course. He doesn't only hear things, but voices also tell him about individuals and their past lives. He sent an email, just half-an-hour ago, to say that Almeida's murder was not an accident. It was premeditated. What happened remains true, yes, but not in the way historians have chosen to record it.'

'—and the dagger?'

'I have it back again…'

'I mean, was it used?'

'Ah, no, the rapier didn't kill him, it was used to defend Almeida. It seems to have belonged to one Gaspar das Índias, a skilled linguist, who first served Gama and, a decade later, died defending Almeida. Look at the message, here, I printed it for you.'

He handed them a page with two typed paragraphs:

Gaspar das Índias

Gaspar of India was a close confidant of Francisco d'Almeida and privy to his esoteric concerns. Almeida was well aware of those factions within the Catholic cabals that were antagonistic toward his secret commission to reopen channels of esoteric intercourse between East and West, and that they sought to destroy not only his work but also his life. They had already succeeded in having him displaced from his position as Viceroy of the Indies, and so on his final return to Portugal, unsure of anyone else in whom to trust, he confided in Gaspar that he was in peril of his life.

It was thus at the Cape of Good Hope that the conspirators struck and carried out an order of execution, disguised as a prophecy of doom, that Almeida should not pass beyond the Cape. The ambush was carefully orchestrated as an altercation between the sailors and the irate natives. Gaspar, the one officer who shared Almeida's anticipation of assassination, died defending his captain. The Viceroy was already dead, and his party wiped out, when the conspirators returned to seal their atrocity—ritually piercing Almeida through the throat with a lance of steel. Thus they silenced him forever.

It took Sonja a moment to process the revelation:

'So Almeida *was* assassinated?'

'More than that, he anticipated it—'

'—but how did he know about the prophecy,' she hastened, 'if it was only written sixty years later?'

'Aha, that's a good question. I always thought Camões invented the witches' prediction for dramatic effect. Now, indeed, it appears to have originated before Almeida left Cochin.'

'W-wh-which,' she stumbled, 'w-which is why Almeida rewrote his last will and testament before reaching the Cape?'

'Yes, like Camões, he believed in oracles and soothsayers.' Mendle pulled his beard, musing aloud: 'Both men were superstitious enough to take omens seriously and, as enlightened Christians, still believed in pagan prophecies. Let's just say they both sensed things weren't as simple as they seemed—'

Jason butted in: '—for which the restless Native had to be blamed?'

'Aha, the assassins had to cover their tracks, and so their crime was executed far from home and without witnesses. Yes, rather cruelly, it was the perfect execution.'

'But why,' she said bewildered, 'why, when he was an esteemed administrator and an acclaimed admiral?'

'Perhaps,' said Mendle, enrolling himself as her mentor, 'perhaps some thought him disloyal?'

She checked: 'How... y'mean disloyal to the Crown?'

'Yes, he could have betrayed a state secret or misused the spoils of war, and so deserved his punishment. I recall something about this in an essay I was given by a priest, which should be around somewhere. I'll have to look for it later. Anyway, the Portuguese nobility belonged to one of three militant-religious orders and competed for resources. Almeida himself belonged to the same Order that had once financed Prince Henry's endeavours. These knights also revived the Templar code and enjoyed spiritual and material privileges, but were severely punished for acts of disloyalty—paying the ultimate price for treason or mutiny. Say, Sonja, now show me the dossier...'

GREETINGS FROM CAPE TOWN

 # UNION-CASTLE
MAIL STEAMSHIP COMPANY LIMITED

GENNAIO - JANUARY - JANUAR - JANVIER 1971

LUNEDI MONDAY	MARTEDI TUESDAY	MERCOLEDI WEDNESDAY	GIOVEDI THURSDAY	VENERDI FRIDAY	SABATO SATURDAY	DOMENICA SUNDAY
25	**26**	**27**	**28**	**29**	**30**	**31**
MONTAG LUNDI	DIENSTAG MARDI	MITTWOCH MERCREDI	DONNERSTAG JEUDI	FREITAG VENDREDI	SAMSTAG SAMEDI	SONNTAG DIMANCHE

7

The Wild Fig Restaurant stood on the lower banks of the Liesbeeck
River, close to where Almeida's party had attacked the native village.
Nothing remained of their grass-huts or cattle-kraal, of course, only a
giant *Ficus macrophylla* planted two centuries later. On the same knoll
stood a seventeenth-century Dutch manor house; incorporating one
of Sonja's favourite courtyard restaurants.

A waiter with a long black apron swished them to a table near the
open fire, drawing a chair for Sonja. It was too cold to sit outside.

As soon as her companions were settled, Sonja told them how she'd
followed the course of the Camissa earlier that week:

'The Camissa drops off the mountain, flows beneath a canopy of
stone-pines and blue-gums, then disappears into a culvert under the
old slave-road. From there it's carried below the streets, beneath the
city, and out into the bay.'

Sonja pronounced the 'c' of Camissa with a click of her tongue, looking to Prof Mendle for confirmation. It was the same stream from which he'd drawn water when Jason called.

She rushed on, sparing no detail, until Mendle slowed her down, genially, suggesting he first study the wine-list while she attract the attention of a passing waiter. He also wanted to talk about the map in the dossier—if given half a chance.

Instead, Jason took the gap: 'During the summer grazing season the Khoisan built their huts beside the Camissa. It's the only stream left in Cape Town today.'

A waiter came to recite *Today's Specials*, doing so flawlessly, as if it were his favourite nursery rhyme, then left them to study the menu. Sonja resumed her meanderings of the tannin-brown Camissa:

'There's a boardwalk along the lower section, so it's easy to follow the stream from the weir down to the old wash-houses, now used for overnight bungalows on the Hoerikwaggo Trail.'

Both men knew this, of course, but wanted to hear how her story ended—less so the Swishing Waiter, who returned to take their order. To keep him occupied, Mendle changed the spicy cabernet to a flinty sauvignon blanc.

Sonja halted, grateful for his choice, then continued breathlessly:

'I visited a friend who lives near the stream, Patricia Schonstein, and stayed for supper. We met at the Book Lounge. She's an author herself, mostly novels, and married to the travel-writer Don Pinnock. Don mentioned a spring in the basement of old Milly's Bakery—now Kentucky or McDonalds—saying it was once part of the Camissa. It was apparently the first spring used by the Dutch and, also, the one shown to them by the Khoisan as a perennial source of fresh water. There was once—'

The waiter brought the sauvignon blanc and, halting mid-sentence, Sonja requested the roasted butternut salad, then continued:

'—there was once a pool, more like a pond really, from which the Khoisan drew sweet drinkable water. It seems this was the original Aguada de Saldanha...'

Mendle tasted the wine while Jason pursued her tireless digressions with increasing incredulity.

'Patricia wrote a poem about the homeless descendants who eke out an existence, drunk and oblivious, next to their vanished ancestral pool. Today, sheltering under Mill Street bridge with their shopping trolleys, they collect recyclable cans, bottles and old newspapers.'

Jason shrugged, preying on her liberal sentiments. He recognised the emotion—that sense of pity felt by a Stranger for the Native, the privileged interloper for the perpetually poor:

'What d'you know about people foraging on the fringes of society? Why should you bother about our bridge hobos, those disparagingly known as *Bergies*, Table Mountain's last hunter-gatherers?'

'R-r-re-renaming denies their history,' she stammered, taken aback by his terse response. 'Imagine an Indonesian renaming the Dutch, or calling Holland by another name today?'

'We all use derogatory names,' pressed Jason, 'the settlers called us *Hot'nots* because we smeared our bodies with fat and herbs; whereas we called you *Honkies* after your predilection for perfume and alcohol. Like taste, I guess, smell is relative.'

'Well, like a brandy and coke, your academic licence and my sense of poetic justice don't mix, at least not in good company.'

Jason flashed a rare smile.

Prof Mendle interceded: 'And I thought whisky and soda was a bad combination—now I know you two get worse!'

Clearly relieved, he raised his glass and proposed a toast: 'To Life, Friendship and the Fairest Cape.'

The wine, Springfield's *Life from Stone*, had a crisp finish, as dry as blackpowder. It had diffused a volatile situation.

The waiter brought her salad and, for the men, the grilled line fish. Mendle led their conversation back to the Camissa:

'I remember Jose Burman telling me, sometime in the Sixties, that the stream flowed under the city. He often wrote about Table Mountain's hidden charms, including its caverns and springs, and described the Camissa in his little blue book, *Safe to the Sea*. It's an informative and descriptive work, taking its title from Swinburne's poetic phrase that "even the weariest river winds somewhere safe to the sea". I say, Sonja, he's rather like Don Pinnock, always going off somewhere to find something unusual to write about.'

'Burman was nostalgic,' noted Jason, 'Don more succinct.'

'Ah, but Burman wrote fifty years ago. He wanted to describe the forgotten waterways of the Cape before they disappeared. He refers to the stream as the *Varsche Rivier*, after the Dutch, of course. Say, who ever thought of rehabilitating indigenous names back in 1962? We hardly knew they even existed!'

'Back then, Prof, even I didn't exist,' said Jason with youthful glee. 'I was only born in 1982.'

'Yes, I see that, but international conservation and environmental projects began with the Bambi-generation—my generation—back in 1942. As did an almost cult-obsession with prehistoric caves.'

Mendle beamed at his young colleagues.

'Sure, your generation also gave us vegetarian restaurants and the most famous rock-art sites in the world.'

'So what did Burman say about the river?' asked Sonja, wanting to pursue the matter before the conversation lost focus again.

'Ah, yes, Jose obtained permission from the City Council and was taken down a man-made tunnel—then known as *Capell Sluyt*—by an official guide whose support-team followed above, from manhole to manhole. Jose said it was pitch-black, except for the light from their mountaineering lamps. Crossing under Mill Street, the low drainage tunnel opened into a seven-foot conduit made of smooth brick walls with a roughcast floor. Vertical shafts rose to manholes at street-level, incorporating metal rungs for the ladders. Spider-webs hung from the roof while stalactites grew where lime leached through the cement. At one spot—and here I can only imagine Jose's amazement—the entire tunnel was covered with rock-flow formations, like a real cave.'

'As above, so below,' noted Jason, who'd explored the mountain's upper caves with his brother long before.

Jason digressed while their table was cleared. His brother now lived in London and was, to Sonja's surprise, a tax lawyer for an off-shore investment company. *How differently we turn out to be... as for my brother?* She pulled herself back when Mendle resumed:

'The crucial point came when Jose reached the sprouting fountain. Quick-drying cement can stop a leak; but if ignored, water pressure will rip an entire wall apart—'

'—what then?'

'Nothing.'

'What d'you mean, *nothing?*'

'Exactly that, they stopped the leak. The only other damage he saw was caused by summer fires and winter rains, causing rockslides that blocked the tunnel.'

'So, no flash-floods or collapsing walls?'

'No, nothing, Jose clambered on, further and further underground. The conduit continued sloping down toward the sea until it zigzagged around the foundations of the Castle. Jose thought it was the original course of the moat. The tunnel then passed under the railway tracks until, another kilometre-or-so further, it finally flowed into the bay... somewhere near the Yacht Basin.'

'And does it still follow this course?'

'I don't know, but it's worth finding out. Why not ask Don?'

Jason shrugged.

☩ ☩ ☩

Later that evening, dressed in pyjamas and slippers, the Professor retired to his study and re-read Burman's valedictory introduction: "The history of South Africa starts with a single natural feature—a river. Without this river there would have been no settlement at the Cape, no Republic of South Africa."

Mendle had always enjoyed this image, semiotically, as if a river and a republic were related to each other as *source* was to *outcome*—as the Tiber was to Rome or the Thames to London. Moreover, he was also pleased with himself for recognising the Aguada and Camissa in the dossier, mapped out below the UCL calendar. The sketch made sense, of course, but only when turned sideways.

Aha, so what of the skull, should I have turned that around too?

Mendle sighed deeply, wondering if the head had been struck from above, by someone standing over the body, that is, after Almeida had fallen to the ground?

It was too late. Jason had re-encased the bones that morning. The ash-grey skull now lay entombed where neither Stranger nor Native could find it. Unless someone talked. But only two other people knew about it—and they were still young enough to keep their word.

8

A knot tied with the tongue is never undone with the teeth.
Medieval English proverb

On Sunday, frustrated by developments, Jason initiated a rapid skype exchange with his brother.

J: Anton, are you free?

A: do I have a choice?

J: no, never, not with me

A: fine, so what's up, Boet?

J: I'm unable to sort out the bones we found, Almeida's death is like an entangled knot with suspicious loose ends

A: so are you trying to *unravel* or *tie up* these loose ends?

J: actually, I'm trying to sort out a messy historical affair

A: life is messy, Boet, our past all the more so

J: it was only five hundred years ago

A: so what's wrong?

J: Portuguese writers view this period as a spiritual-political matrix where myth, faith and history intertwine...
the victim was silenced forever, ritualistically, and left with his mouth gagged, his tongue cut and his teeth smashed

A: awesome, in Sicily the mafia have a way of doing this too... if a man talks too much he gets murdered and left with a stone in his mouth. There's an old Sicilian proverb that says: "The man who talks too much will ruin himself through his own mouth." Silence is what men of honour value most.

J: which is why the dead remain silent?

9

*Whatever the form, all divinatory practices reveal
the human quest for a larger context of meaning,
a means by which to understand and respond to
the many faces of suffering and uncertainty.*

John Pemberton, *Art and Oracle* (2000)

It poured again that Sunday morning as the stable yard turned into a mix of mud and manure. Even when the rain stopped, the paddocks remained cold and wet. Most horses were kept indoors, out of the snap sea breeze, while Sonja worked her mare in the covered arena.

It was her only weekly therapy.

Returning home, chilled to the bone, her first desire was for a long hot bath. Her second was to spend the afternoon reading quietly in bed. The rain continued, unabated.

With an XL T-shirt tucked around her thighs, she settled under the duvet and started to read. Mendle had returned the dossier with self-conscious satisfaction, drawing attention to the calendar with its map of Almeida's ill-fated advance and retreat.

He'd also given her two books on early callers at the Cape, before a permanent victualing-station had been established. Although well annotated, the commentaries were florid, the translations inaccurate, and the events somewhat exaggerated. Or so he'd warned her. She sensed his design: unreliable texts have things to reveal too.

The first was a publication for the 1952 tercentenary festival when white South Africans celebrated the founding of their nation. The historical date was 6 April 1652.

She was surprised to find that the book's author, Victor de Kock, then the country's chief archivist, had described Almeida's murder as "one of the greatest tragedies in the history of Portugal".

Why a tragedy? Because the Portuguese never colonised the Cape of Good Hope, but took Angola and Mozambique instead?

Yes, had it not been for this massacre, the Portuguese would have controlled the entire coast for the next 450 years—from the mouth of the Congo River to the Mozambique Channel.

But had Holland's bearded Sea Barbarians taken Mozambique's low-lying coral island instead, including the old Arab fort and store built there, then the Dutch would never have retreated to the wind-swept dunes of the Cape. *We'd have had a Dutch East Africa instead?*

Mendle had been correct on that point: possession of the Cape was an unexpected event, an unlikely and impractical choice for any great seaborne power. As for the witches' prophecy, was Providence really the reason for the arrival of the Light Ones—the so-called abeLungu, as Jason called them?

Absurd, she told herself, *there's no divination here.*

However, according to De Kock, Almeida was not the king's first choice. His compatriot, Tristão da Cunha, had already been elected; but was forced to resign due to a temporary blindness.

A fortunate inconvenience, or was this also Providência?

Almeida left Portugal in command of twenty-one ships and over fifteen hundred extra men, then the largest fleet to sail from Lisbon. He left for a period of four consecutive years—which, she deduced, should have concluded around March 1509—but only relinquished his powers to Albuquerque that November, several months later, and returned grieving his son's untimely death. After three months at sea he brought his meagre ships into the watering place of Saldanha to collect wood and water. Fresh meat was not mentioned.

According to De Kock, the Hottentots came to the beach as soon as the Portuguese dropped anchor. For recreation from the journey's monotony, Almeida allowed some men to trade while the rest of his company filled empty casks at a nearby spring.

The Camissa again?

Rattles, beads, mirrors, as well as iron and brass, were bartered on the beach. Once the natives became "familiar", Almeida sent several men to their village to fetch cattle and sheep.

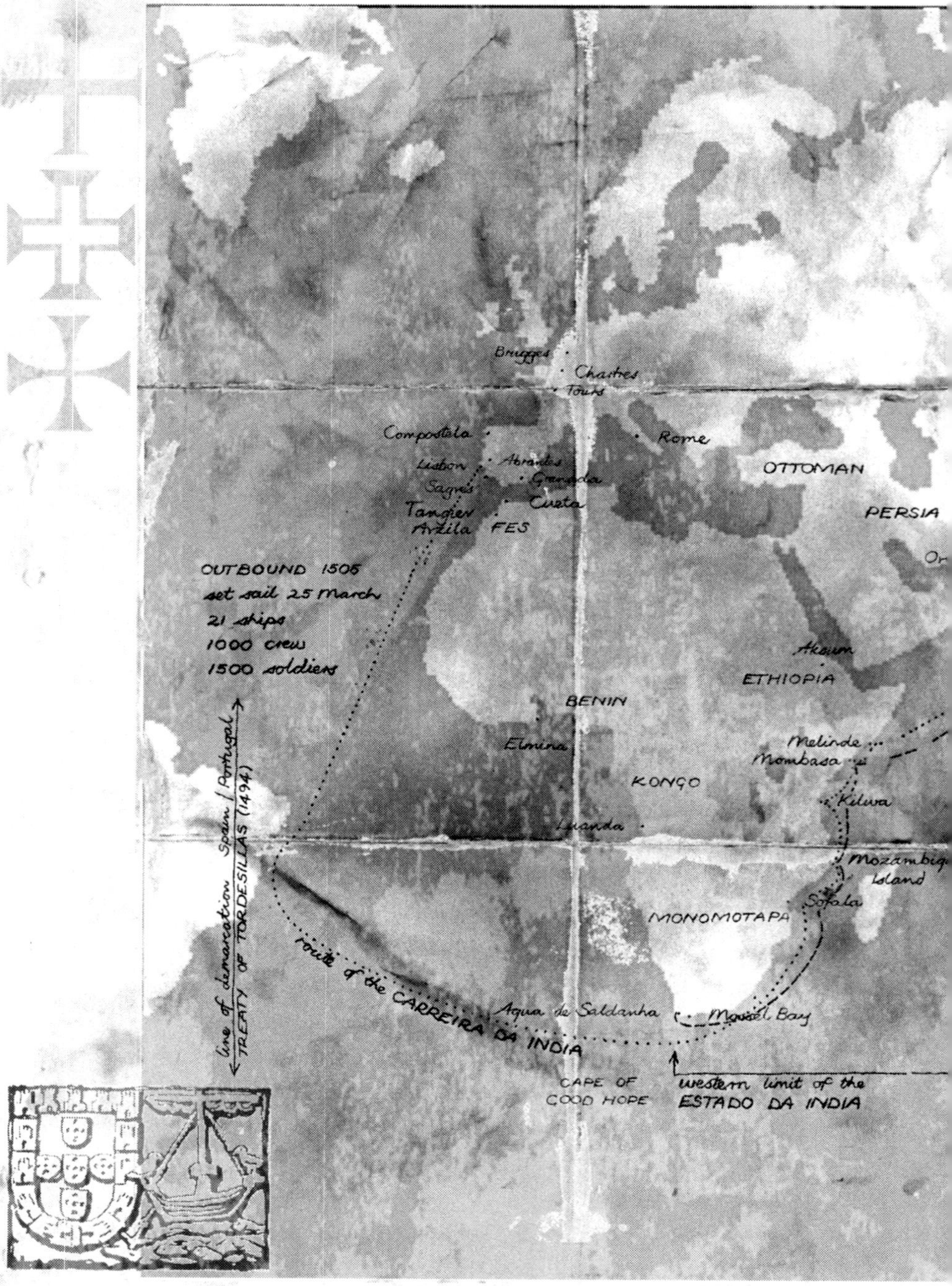

Brugges

Chartres

Tours

Compostela

Rome

Lisbon Abrantes

Sagres Granada

Tangier Cueta

Arzila FES

OTTOMAN

PERSIA

Or

OUTBOUND 1505
set sail 25 March
21 ships
1000 crew
1500 soldiers

Aksum

ETHIOPIA

BENIN

Elmina

Melinde

Mombasa

KONGO

Kilwa

Luanda

Mozambique
Island

MONOMOTAPA

Sofala

line of demarcation Spain / Portugal
TREATY OF TORDESILLAS (1494)

route of the CARREIRA DA INDIA

Aqua de Saldanha

Mossel Bay

CAPE OF
GOOD HOPE

western limit of the
ESTADO DA INDIA

CIPANGO

Deshima

HOMEBOUND 1509
set sail 19 November
3 ships
200 men?

GUJERAT
BIJAPUR

Goa
licut
Cochin

southern limit of the ESTADO DA INDIA

It was here that the scurvy-ridden sailors and herders first started to quarrel. And, as so often happens, their argument began without any apparent cause or reason. The records weren't clear.

Perhaps the sailors took a cow without offering a fair price for it?

De Kock acknowledged the discrepancies behind this incident too, saying that at least one chronicler recorded how certain companions were enraged to find their daggers pilfered; another deplored the way compatriots robbed the unsuspecting natives.

For whatever reason, this misunderstanding resulted in Almeida being induced, against his better judgement, to return and punish the herders.

According to contemporary reports, Almeida knew that some dire necessity awaited him ashore. He was filled with a sense of gloom and, on leaving the flagship, spoke as if foretelling his own death. Clambering into a longboat he allegedly said: "Ah, whither will you carry this infirm man of sixty years?"

Almeida wanted it known that he went against his will?

De Kock went on to describe how the Portuguese looted the village: emptying huts, seizing hostages and stealing cattle. Those who'd fled the first attack now fell upon the invaders as they ran back to the shore. Making haste, the Portuguese dropped their "miserable booty" and "stolen children" until, enraged by their audacity and cowardice, the herders attacked the main body of men—including the Viceroy himself.

The natives inflicted severe injuries with their spears, stones and knobbed sticks. As she'd learnt at the Castle, the Portuguese were ill-prepared, inadequately armed and overconfident. According to the ever-vigilant João de Barros:

> They sank in the sand of the shore and were entirely powerless and unable to move, and the natives came down upon them so light-footed and nimble that they appeared as birds, or rather, like the devil's executioners. They fell upon the nobles, who for love of the Viceroy offered some resistance, as the common men with the first booty that they gained had run off in front. The most pitiful occurrence was that some of the wounded, unable to take a step on the shore because of the loose sand, fled to the water to find more solid ground, and stained it with their blood.

Almeida's scarlet cloak made him a desirable target. He was struck in the throat by a spear and sank to his knees.

Before he died, or while he could still speak, Almeida committed the ensign to his nearest officer, giving him orders to save the flag. His last reported words were: "With all my years and sins, I end my life here since it is the will of our Lord."

Was Almeida loyal to both Cross and Crown until the end?

De Kock relates how the natives then threw themselves upon his abandoned body, quarrelling as they tore at his cloak...

What bold prose, she thought, to evoke the biblical scene of soldiers quarrelling over Christ's robe. *An innocent victim?*

According to Barros, sixty-five Portuguese men died that morning. These he describes as the "flower of the nation", as they came from the finest families back home. Those who managed to flee to the ships returned, but only after the last natives had left the beach. This time they returned heavily armed.

The next day, filled with sorrow, the ships set out to sea and sailed for Lisbon. When news of this disastrous occurrence reached king Manuel, the entire country fell into mourning. De Kock offered no more detail, unfortunately. She'd have to cross-check this with the dossier's *Tabula nomens*.

✝ ✝ ✝

Sonja moved to her north-facing kitchen, finding the sunlight there more pleasant than in her bedroom. It had stopped raining and drops of water wandered across the glass like grains of corn in a divination dish. Could such randomness reveal a coherent message? Even if it did, it was not something she could easily interpret...

She knew the baVenda used bowls to determine guilt or innocence. She'd seen their shallow-carved bowls at the SA Museum, including one that identified liars. She felt tempted to consult such an artefact, or a local sangoma, but quickly dismissed the idea as too fanciful and far-fetched. *I'm not going to become a cultural tourist in ancestral Africa.*

She turned to the other book and found the same source material and imagery. Ian Colvin not only drew on Camões's grandiose epic, but felt equally inspired writing his own *Cape of Adventure* in 1912:

And now the Viceroy saw the evil conjunction of his stars, for the boats were no longer there; they had sought refuge from the storm near the ships. In their panic some of the men rushed into the sea, others fled along the shore. The Viceroy stood alone, save for Jorge de Mello:

"Where are those to whom you have done honour now?" said the officer. "Surely this is the time to repay benefits!"

Almeida turned to him: "This is no time for evil-speaking. Those who owe me any favour lie behind me on the sand. Save the king's flag; it is being dishonoured."

He spoke no more, for an assegai pierced his throat, and Jorge de Mello left him there and saved the flag. There he was buried, and fifty more with him, the man who had given the king an empire and was Viceroy of the Indies, among those nameless sand-hills at the watering place of Saldanha.

The prose was overwhelming. Had Almeida's heroic death-speech been invented, or had his cloak simply become a symbol of sacrifice? How much of this was poetic invention, how much mere divination? *How much a mix of both?*

Almeida was presented as a man who believed in prophecies and—like Alexander at the Oracle of Sîwa—eventually succumbed to his own superstition. He'd studied the stars but believed they still foretold his destiny. As a naval commander, he understood the ocean currents and yet felt his fate was borne on a breeze at sea.

Almeida had also witnessed the use of divination at court, then still popular among cosmopolitan rulers of the Renaissance. Even during the Portuguese Inquisition, divination rites remained part of a meaningful universe where chaos and cosmos co-existed; where disorder existed only because it was defined by order; and where chance and uncertainty still had some role to play. A world where the Old Ways overlapped with the New.

Living between two worlds—medieval and modern, town and country—Almeida accepted Christianity and paganism as a means for enlarging his comprehension of the world. He blended his belief in a single divinity with that of the ancient diviners.

He straddled the Occident with its one God, an ineffable divinity, and the Orient with its plethora of spirits and deities. Like Camões,

Almeida blended religious rationalism with folk superstition, official doctrine and informal divination. It seemed that Almeida could fuse Catholic notions of grace with a sense of karmic justice.

Her insight seemed to fit like a keystone, a centre piece holding the overarching facts in place.

She tilted back her chair and watched the dusk-grey skyline recede, struck anew by the fallibility of historical writing and the uncertainties of biblical texts.

She had her doubts about the Gospels—each emphasizing its own peculiar facts yet omitting other details entirely. As for the crucifixion and resurrection, the New Testament was not only inconsistent, but also seriously incomplete; and for reasons not yet explained, entire books had been left out of the Bible. *So too with Almeida's histoire?* Here also, inconsistencies and omissions occurred. Some said he was struck by a slingshot behind the knee, others by a spear in the neck. Most said he was found on the beach, a few that his body lay too far inland and had to be abandoned.

De Kock was an archivist writing for students of early Cape history; Colvin an imaginative storyteller for young boys. While popularising history, each emphasized the unique aspects of the tragedy. De Kock stressed the Cape's geo-political destiny; Colvin that Almeida was a victim of fate and predestination. Moreover, the former described how Almeida's men fled like cowards; the latter how they fought with valour...

Interesting, neither mentioned Gaspar das Índias.

What happened to Almeida's other companions, she wondered, of which twelve were reputedly noblemen? At this stage she knew only of Gaspar. Perhaps the *Tabula nomens* would reveal more?

The light was fading as she set the book aside. In the street below she heard a car splashing passed, heading home.

The weekend was at its end.

She needed time to distinguish whose voice she heard: De Kock or Barros, Colvin or Camões? Each told what he wanted recorded for prosperity. It was a mix of archival research and bardic inspiration, personal opinion and public information. Inseparable, like mud and manure.

10

*If talented, linguas would frequent the antechambers of power,
share state secrets and, at times, fulfil a determining role.*
Dejanirah Couto, *The Role of Interpreters...* (2003)

Sonja re-read the clairaudient's message with meticulous care. The key phrase, if there was any underlying truth to it, alluded to a secret commission and clandestine execution.

In the absence of any particular evidence, however, there appeared to be only one other who knew of the Viceroy's fate and misfortune: Gaspar das Índias.

It seemed that Gaspar was privy to Almeida's esoteric concerns and shared his master's fear of entrapment. Moreover, he knew of the commission and may have played a part in re-establishing intercourse between Europe and the East. He may also have known who sought to destroy the life and work of his master.

So then, who was this Gaspar?

Was he a Jewish traveller, a Muslim merchant, or a Hindu trader? Perhaps a Buddhist monk or Christian convert? She knew about the travels of St Thomas and the Nestorian Christians of southern India. Well, yes, vaguely. There were also the Manichaeans who practised a blend of Christianity, Buddhism and Zoroastrianism in north-west India. Whatever Gaspar's religious convictions were, he was her only key. As with Camões, she'd have to uncover his connection...

It was a crisp, wintry morning and she'd risen early, before the char came to do her week's ironing. Her apartment in Victoria Street was conveniently located opposite the SA Museum, making it an easy two minute walk to work.

She had a temporary office in the Social History Department, with a window overlooking the Garden's Avenue. Besides a few resilient leaves still stirring in the breeze, the oaks were all but bare. Each day, from behind her desk, she could watch squirrels nibbling the crumbs dropped by passing schoolchildren.

Above her desk hung several posters promoting period portraiture, vernacular architecture and an exhibition of indigenous stone tools. Mounted on the opposite wall were two maritime charts, a modern topographical map and a big satellite image of the Cape Peninsula. Pencil sketches of a salvaged VOC shipwreck (drawn by the previous occupant in her office) were pinned beside a sepia print of a British ethnographer filming a Zulu woman. The most recent addition was a poster for the national *First Encounters and Lasting Legacies* conference. The SA Museum would be hosting the event that week.

Other than a postcard from the Algarve and a photo of her garden in Leiden, there wasn't much to show she'd been the sole occupant of the office for the past fortnight.

She sat with her laptop and typed in *gaspar das indias*, then pressed *search*. Scrolling down she found a promising source: Jewish Heritage. She nursed her mug while up-loading the site.

Gaspar's biography proved to be a fascinating tale of intrigue and deception. He was supposedly born in 1444 at Posen, Poland, and presented himself as a travelling Jew who'd come to Alexandria via Jerusalem. He was later taken prisoner and sold as a slave in India where, for his talents, he obtained his freedom and served the Governor of Goa—taking on the name of Yusuf 'Adil. His original name was not known.

In 1498, when Gama first reached India, Gaspar was there to greet him on behalf of the Governor. According to popular sources, Gama arrived with Ahmed ibn Majid, a master navigator or *mu'allim* whom he found at Melinde. Gama wasted no time purchasing Gaspar and promptly had him converted—baptizing him "Gaspar da Gama". Gaspar served as a pilot (probably after Majid fled) and guided the Portuguese through the treacherous Indian waters.

Years later, Gaspar found himself in Lisbon where king Manuel granted him a royal pension, including horses, which enabled him—or so Sonja guessed—to marry well, and was thereafter deployed for his linguistic skills in various naval expeditions.

In 1500 he accompanied Pedro Álvares Cabral on his epic voyage to India and, after crossing the Atlantic, was among the first white men to step ashore in Brazil. On their return they met the Florentine Amerigo Vespucci (after whom the continent would be named), and advised him on prevailing latitudes, trade winds and ocean currents. In 1502 Gaspar went back to India with Gama and, finally, in 1505, set off again with Almeida.

The website ended abruptly, much to her irritation, claiming that "he took part in the latter's expedition against Calicut in 1510, when he may have died".

So, killed in India? The clairaudient had clearly stated the Cape.

Despite his confusing biography, most other sources concurred that Gaspar was a talented pilot and gifted linguist. He was known as Gaspar da Gama, Gaspar d'Almeida and Gaspar da Índia—in short, he was recognised by the patronymical names of his various masters. Other than that, there wasn't a single reference to things occultish…

Nor anything about his relationship to Almeida.

Using *gaspar da gama* as her next keywords, she redirected to learn that he'd served as a lingua for the royal household. He was later sent to India with Almeida and two other interpreters.

However, her best find that morning came from a scholarly article on sixteenth-century linguas in Portuguese frontier societies, written by Dejanirah Couto of the École Pratique des Hautes Études, Paris.

From what she read, linguas were a rare and underrated ensemble of interpreters: converted slaves, captured natives, former renegades, adventurers, even concubines or exiles. They belonged to a marginal sector operating between milieus—something the nobility couldn't do themselves because of their own regulated social status and limited knowledge of other languages. In brief, linguas were the middle-men between East and West.

Interpreters thus led a double life, straddling at least two cultures, while seldom belonging to either. Despite their liminal social position, linguas occasionally integrated into the higher echelons of their host society, either abroad or in Portugal, as Gaspar had done.

According to Couto, Gaspar da Índia was an Ashkenazi Jew and one familiar with the carreira da Índia, the so-called India Passage. He mastered Hebrew, Arabic, Chaldean and a mix of Italian and Spanish. He also prepared his son Baltasar for the role of lingua, taking him to India when he sailed with Almeida.

Besides his son, little else was known about Gaspar or his family. He simply disappeared from the historical record, like a comet, briefly visible before vanishing.

Frontier societies were not merely unstable, Couto continued, but profoundly corrupt. What a lingua earned was insufficient in a fragile economy where everyone—from an administrator to a retired soldier or slave-trader—was set on making a private fortune. Corruption was a necessity, not a choice.

So, too, the exploitation of the rich.

Linguas were not only skilled in espionage, but knew their master's darkest secrets—including each and every vice and weakness. Their ambivalent status displayed a mistrust engendered by the master-class; a situation aggravated by the lingua's function during secret negotiations or spying missions. For instance, young Baltasar was sent to spy on Admiral Husayn al-Kurdî and his Mamluk navy.

Another spy was Sidi Ali the Twisted (nicknamed for his squinting), who settled in the Sultanate of Gujarat. He was a Moor from the Kingdom of Granada which—she now recalled—was where Islam, Judaism and Christianity had intersected in al-Andalus, then Moorish Spain. At the time Granada was the largest city in Europe.

Although Sidi Ali had no fixed relationship with the Portuguese, he acted as lingua for some naval officers imprisoned at Chaul, south of modern Mumbai. As a demonstration of political solidarity, Sidi Ali protected the captives—probably survivors of Lourenço's crew—and so prevented them from being deported to Istanbul. To acknowledge this act of service, Almeida had Sidi Ali rewarded with four hundred cruzados—then a handsome fee.

To honour his son's death, Almeida was indebted to a Moor?

Sonja double-checked the facts and found that it was Malik Áyáz —that Russian slave again—who released the prisoners, once attired and fed, before pledging himself to become a humble servant of the Crown. Known to be shrewd, Malik Áyáz was probably intent on becoming a spy too.

Jewish linguas rarely converted as Lisbon's elite wanted to distance themselves from their servants. The situation changed once titles or properties were obtained, even for Jews, as happened when Gaspar became a *fidalgo* at court.

However, it wasn't easy to distinguish an unconverted lingua from a New Christian, except for the patronymic name, typically that of a baptismal godfather.

So far as she knew, Gaspar da Gama was just such a convert.

Due to their knowledge of different cultures, linguas were suspected as having their souls contaminated by the constitutive Other. Knowing oriental languages not only implied they knew the thought of the pagan but, worse yet, that they also had access to a conceptual world which eluded their masters. Paradoxically, linguas were viewed with esteem and suspicion.

Gaspar too?

Acting as an interpreter or informer, a lingua could receive gifts, at times secret, for their part in concluding a successful transaction on behalf of their master. Following oriental custom, donations were also offered by a receiving king or warlord.

Gaspar's rapier, she guessed, *was such a gift.*

He certainly dined with governors, frequented their chambers of power and was privy to state secrets. He may even have fulfilled a vital role in Almeida's career as Viceroy, given that they spent their last five years together...

And yet she learnt nothing more of Gaspar's bond with Almeida, or of his own religious beliefs. Of one thing she was sure: as an esteemed lingua Gaspar moved with ease among Muslims, Jews and Christians —and had access to the arcane knowledge of the East.

11

O'er the great strange land I guarded,
Since ever the worlds were light.
Beatrice Bromley, *The Song of Table Bay* (1924)

Mendle had been given a new message and wanted to show it over lunch. He said nothing about it beforehand, only that he'd join them in the Museum Café.

When he came down, late as usual, Sonja was discussing Gaspar's life as a traveller, prisoner, slave, translator, navigator and advisor:

'I spent the morning searching for Gaspar and found he was also known as Yusuf 'Adil. It seems he took his name from the Sultan of Bijapur whose favourite residence was on India's west coast. Both Yusufs were in Goa when Gama arrived.'

'*Yusuf 'Adil* literally means "Joseph the Just",' said Jason, already a step ahead of the Professor.

'Aha, a man known by the names of others and, like the biblical Joseph of Israel, also sold into slavery, freed, and then elected as councillor. This may be why he took the same name or, at least, why he borrowed scenes from Joseph's life. It sounds like Joseph of Israel and Yusuf of India were both transformed by their experiences in captivity, both were trusted by the most powerful rulers of their day, and both played a determining role in their adoptive empires.'

A young student brought them fresh juice and asparagus quiche. Mendle decided the message could wait until after they'd eaten.

'According to local lore,' continued Sonja, 'Yusuf 'Adil Shah was the son of Murad II of Turkey, a sultan and a caliph. When Murad died, the eldest sibling ordered the customary execution of all the brothers but, with the help of his mother, Yusuf fled the massacre disguised as a slave and made his way across Persia to India. Here he was bought by the prime minister of the Bahamani Sultan and, later, became Governor of Bijapur province. Yusuf was clearly gifted and, following the decline of the divided sultanate, rose to declare his independence, thus founding the Adil Shahi dynasty in 1489.'

'What a tale,' beamed Mendle, 'how much of it is historical, how much legend?'

'Well,' she added carefully, 'Islam's rise to power in pre-Modern India was recorded by Muhammad Qasim Ferishta, a court historian from Persia who, already a century later, wrote that Yusuf 'Adil Shah was their unequivocal dynastic father-figure.'

'Aha, so Ferishta is the Bard of Bijapur?'

'No, *nota bene*, unlike Camões, Ferishta is an authorative historian whose history of India spans twelve volumes…'

She hesitated, recalling her Leiden professor who once remarked: "No historical work is ever complete or entirely consistent."

'Do historians give credence to this Muslim lore, or not?'

'Yes and no. Even if Yusuf's foreign birth was real, direct descent from an Ottoman sultanate is virtually impossible. There's no grand Turkish-Persian-Iranian birthright or Chinese-Mongolian bloodline, as was then fashionable, so I guess historians simply resorted to tales of special connections and secret origins. Yusuf probably came from an obscure family of low status and meagre means.'

'So what's new?' said Jason, eyeing the student with the roaming coffee pot. The nonchalance of the waiter's trailing hand appealed to him. 'Most dynasties legitimize themselves by reinventing history.'

Jason knew the Zimbabwean dynasty had done just that when they came to power in the thirteenth century, and that the invention of family ties was common among the Bantu elite. *We choose our friends*, he thought, *not our families*.

'Bijador survived as a separate realm,' Sonja continued, 'until the Portuguese were driven out five centuries later. Yusuf 'Adil Shah was killed in a conspiracy shortly after Almeida's departure, thus allowing Albuquerque to take advantage of the instability in West India.'

Mendle lent in, extending his elbows across the table:

'And now you're wondering if the two assassinations are linked?'

Restraining herself, Sonja suggested quietly: 'W-wh-whatever his origins—no, I'm not—whatever his origins, Yusuf was a cultured man who invited poets, artists and craftsmen to his court. They even came from Rome. He was an enlightened scholar, a tolerant ruler, an advocate of religious diversity and an accomplished musician. His legacy is best reflected in the art and architecture of his time—'

She saw Jason was restless, fiddling with his sleeves until the young waiter brought him a refill. Mendle requested another slice of quiche. Sonja ordered the same, reasoning aloud:

'As one translator said to the king of Portugal, "a lingua has to eat in proportion to the service he provides".'

Jason reacted tersely: 'Was it also part of Gaspar's service to dine with those who took no interest in the poor?'

Mendle smiled, accustomed to the vagaries of his colleague. Jason was the son of a minister and a very much younger mother—a once shy girl from the Cape Flats. His family spoke no uniform *taal*. He lived in a netherworld of different cultures and disparate histories: German and Afrikaans, Lutheran and Catholic.

Not that this excused his behaviour.

However, to save Sonja discomfort, Mendle explained the semiotics behind the name *Gaspar*.

'In the biblical nativity, as you both know, Gaspar was one of the Magi whose gift of gold became an emblem of wisdom. According to ancient lore, the Magi anticipated the rebirth of their patriarch Zend, father of the first Zoroaster in Persia—'

'—in the version I learnt as a child,' she called out, 'the three Holy Kings represented Europe, Asia and Africa.'

'Aha, the medieval archetypes for the three known continents, the three known world races, and the three known ages of mankind. You do realise, of course, that none of this is biblical. And yet it became a basic canard among ancient Mediterranean cultures.'

'I was told the youngest was a Moor from North Africa,' recalled Jason, feeling ambivalent about his seven years in a Catholic school, 'and that Gaspar was a young prince from Ethiopia…'

Sonja had learnt it from her Protestant teachers too. To her mind, Africa was a land of slaves and miners—not noble princes.

'One occidental tradition presents the ageing Gaspar as coming from Tarsus, Turkey, and hence a European,' said Mendle, adopting his rabbinical role again. 'The adult Melchior comes from Arabia and is deemed Asian. Young Balthasar is from Sheba in Ethiopia—not to be confused with the Arabian Sabea—and hence an African. Semiotically, Africa was seen as a continent in search of spiritual enlightenment and so, following the first crusades, Balthasar and the Queen of Sheba became the most popular allegories for the conversion of pagans—'

'—and ever since pagans were young, black and gifted?'

'—and beautiful?' she added.

'Ah, yes, always beautiful! "The Queen of the South came like the rising dawn to behold the wisdom of Solomon",' cited Mendle. 'Both Solomon and Sheba provide the founding myths for our two modern nation-states: Israel and Ethiopia.'

'Beautiful or not,' stepped in Sonja, 'I think it strange that the most famous woman in history has no real name?'

'But of course, elsewhere she's known as Azeb, Bilkis, Kandake or Makeda, even as Sibilla.'

'And Sibilla, this Queen of the Desert, is also a Rastafarian saint,' added Jason mischievously.

Mendle chuckled at the thought of a Rasta feast day in Rome, with reggae on the Piazza di San Pietro. He refocused:

'More so, Jason, she comes laden with gifts from a land of exotic wonders, rare luxuries and sensual pleasures. Gifted indeed!'

'An envied world, a world of pleasure and desire,' noted Sonja, 'at least until Edward Said exposed the myth of Orientalism.'

'Aha, and so we must ask ourselves why African legends have such an extraordinary afterlife—'

'—or why Africans always bear the gifts of others?' added Jason with a grin, 'and why Gama was sent without decent ones in the first place? It was probably Gaspar who asked: "What brings you here?" and Gama who replied: "Spices and Christians".'

'Aha,' appraised the Professor, 'Gama should have known better after Mozambique, where he'd seen dhows laden with pepper, cloves, ginger, rubies, pearls and rings of silver—all from the East—and your gold from Monomotapa, of course.'

'Zimbabwe?'

'Yes, here at Moçobiquy, Gama heard about Prester John and the coastal towns of White Christians who fought the Moors. In truth, they were probably the descendants of former Chinese seafarers or local Hindu traders.'

The waiter returned with three cups of black Ethiopian coffee, a gift from the kitchen. Mendle sighed approvingly, opening his brief-case and sliding the message across the table.

'Here, Sonja, for you, from the psychiatrist Dr Laurence Oliver.'

Gaspar das Índias

Gaspar das Índias or da Índia was known to the Portuguese simply as Gaspar. He was also called after Gama and Almeida, for he was an associate of both and accompanied them on their voyages—acting as their lingua and pilot. He was of uncertain background and knew little of his own origins, simply telling what tales about himself were suitable at the time. In fact, he was of somewhat mixed ancestry and a native of Alexandria, where he grew up as a homeless street child—learning to work rather than steal.

He led an adventurous life as a traveller and trader until, after settling in India, he rose to prominence in the service of the Governor of Goa—enrolling himself as a sort of minister of commerce. It was in this capacity that he first met Vasco da Gama and accompanied him to Portugal on his historic return. Prized in Portugal for his own skills as a navigator and linguist, Gaspar took part in several expeditions. Knighted by king Manuel and married to a Portuguese lady, he was then named Gaspar das Índias. He was one of the party with Francisco d'Almeida and killed by natives at the Cape of Good Hope on 1 March 1510.

*History, a complex mixture of opinions and viewpoints, is
dependent not only on what is recorded by whom, but also
on what information survives through chance or artifice.*

Janette Deacon, *Rock Paintings in the Cederberg* (1994)

While Mendle rushed home to watch the final Test between England
and the West Indies, Sonja and Jason went down to the SA Library.

The national library and national museum were both founded in
the 1860s as symbols of imperialist collecting and classification. They
had been modernized in the previous century and stood at opposite
ends of the historic VOC Company's Gardens.

Midway between the two stood the imposing statue of Cecil John
Rhodes, former prime minister of the British Cape Colony, with his
arm raised toward the interior. The emphatic inscription read:

Your Hinterland

is there

The Gardens offered a very fine overview of South Africa's diverse
floristic kingdoms—with acacias, proteas, fynbos and semi-desert
shrubs growing on their left and sub-tropical plants and trees to their
right. Even the day reflected this diversity, changing from a miserably
wet morning to a sparkling clear afternoon.

They proceeded to Special Collections; a spacious reading room
with shuttered windows facing the oak-lined Avenue. Sonja wanted
to know why Almeida's retribution had been so severe.

'What could have been their motive?'

'Corruption?' replied Jason, catching up with her on the other side of the desk. 'No man is beyond corruption. Or temptation.'

'Are we always corruptible?' she asked rhetorically. 'Most men were given a second chance out East, a second chance to prove themselves —as in *Second Life*—where they could assume new identities and fulfil old fantasies. However, diplomats are supposed to be beyond corruption and, as the carreira da Índia took about nine months, one way, from Lisbon to Goa, the period away from home became four years —including time to travel. That's why the average diplomatic posting is still four years today.'

She knew this from her own childhood. Her family had moved time and again before she went to university. They had an apartment in Den Haag but only stayed there for one term, before her brother's accident. As an ambassador, her father had been posted to diverse corners of the world—including Sri Lanka, Indonesia and Japan.

'What about mutiny?' suggested Jason. 'Perhaps they rebelled when matters got out of hand—over wages, rations, or whatever—and then dragged Almeida ashore to kill him?'

'Unlikely. There were too many, sixty-five in all. No, this was not a spontaneous act but a premeditated murder, one that may have been planned days, weeks, or even months before. Actually, we should be looking at Almeida's term of office at Cochin.'

'Where?'

Jason's geography was limited. Born in South Africa, he'd visited Zimbabwe and Ethiopia, but only because the museum sent him.

'Cochin, a fortified port-city in southern India, it's in the dossier.'

Instead, he took a book from the pile and hurriedly read:

'Almeida was appointed in 1505 and left Lisbon with instructions to "seize strategic harbours and islands around the Indian Ocean Rim." King Manuel ordered him to capture and construct forts, especially at the entrance to the Red Sea, and to blockade Muslim trade with Aden and Suez, as far as Cairo... But Almeida was reluctant to spend his limited resources on coastal fortifications and so took command of the sea instead.'

'His so-called Blue Sea policy?'

Jason nodded, turning the page: 'Look, in contrast, Albuquerque took one port after another, ruthlessly, until the kingdoms of Bijapur and Vijayanagar were cut off—leaving both isolated. Their armies always protected the mountain passes and river crossings, not the open sea, as traditional enemies usually advanced across the vast interior. They weren't prepared for a naval attack.'

'Well, after all, India is bigger than Europe—'

'—right,' he said leaning in, 'and I guess they hadn't seen a hostile fleet since Alexander the Great.'

The indoor air was stifling. Glass windows kept the freshness out, like a hermetically sealed flask. He read on:

'Manuel wanted Ceylon and Malacca, and so instructed Almeida to secure both and to stop rivals from entering these or any other ports Portugal controlled. Those who did were made to pay taxes.'

'So you paid to sail the seas?'

'Sure, if Arabs taxed overland caravan routes, then the Portuguese would do the same when fleets crossed the ocean.'

'Then the Estado da Índia was defined by sea, not by land?'

'Right, and Manuel the Fortunate was called the Sovereign of the Seas—'

'—a novel concept.'

Jason read aloud: 'Crowned at twenty-six... Manuel used the title "King of Portugal and of the Algarves on this side and beyond the sea in Africa, Lord of Guinea and Lord of the Conquest, Navigation and Commerce of Ethiopia, Arabia, Persia and India". In those days big men liked long titles.'

'As did Zaïrean President Mobutu, apparently, who called himself "The All-Powerful Warrior who goes from Conquest to Conquest, leaving fire in his wake", or something equally pyrotechnic. Anyway, the Indian Ocean thus became Manuel's pond, pricked with forts and churches along the coast.'

'Sure,' shrugged Jason, 'and Almeida protected Manuel's private monopoly, stopping others from using their new sea route. Someone else lost a lucrative business.'

'It was more than a business, Jason, it was the livelihood of entire families and cities: the Foscari of Venice, the Gujarati of Diu, the Mamluk warrior caste of Cairo and the Zamorin rulers of Calicut— even the Ottoman Turks. Their lives were all interdependent.'

He flicked his pencil against her book.

'Hence the battle of Diu?

'Yes, ultimately, it was Manuel who ordered the offensive. Even as a brilliant strategist, Almeida failed to satisfy his greed.'

Still flicking idly: 'But was that reason enough for murder?'

'Unlikely. Unless Almeida refused to execute his orders which—'

'—which Albuquerque and Cunha then did? I see they arrived in 1506 with a fresh fleet and captured Socotra island... the strategic gateway to the Gulf of Aden.' He drew an imaginary map in the air. 'But this was to be a waste of resources as Muslim ships continued to pass at night, trading with the Arabs and Egyptians up the Red Sea.'

'Wait a moment, I read that Cunha was elected first, but the onset of blindness compelled him to resign. Y'know, it intrigues me to see how some individuals make history in the absence of others.'

Jason stared back blankly. She explained:

'For instance, Vasco da Gama's father had been asked to find a sea route to India but died, uncannily, as the fleet was being prepared. Tradition has it that his eldest son then refused to go and so young Vasco himself was elected. He was twenty-eight and had only been as far as Guinea, I think, fighting French or Castilian pirates.'

'Then Almeida was not Manuel's first choice?'

'No, nor did he fulfil Manuel's ambitions. Jason, read the dossier!'

True, it was Albuquerque who captured Ormuz, the great mart at the entrance to the Persian Gulf, giving the Portuguese access to the Euphrates-Tigris Valley—and all the land beyond.

'Right, but that's not all, look, Albuquerque arrived in India with secret orders to replace Almeida, but Almeida refused to step down before the end of his term. He'd been appointed in 1505, which means he was Viceroy until 1509. Right?'

'Yes, but we don't know when his term of office actually expired,' she hesitated, 'his refusal can't be a reason for murder?'

'If you want a good reason, how's this?' Jason tapped the sentence, reading aloud: 'Here it says that Almeida harboured captains who mutinied after Albuquerque seized Ormuz.'

'—what?'

'That's what it says. He sheltered three insubordinate officers after they abandoned Albuquerque, and then gave them his protection.'

'Why, why mutiny?'

'Self-interest? The captains wanted to plunder Ormuz.'

'Is that what Albuquerque claimed?'

'Sure—'

'—so they fled? Come on, Jason, doesn't that sound dubious, why abandon a city once you've seized it?'

'Dunno, perhaps Almeida—'

'—Almeida doesn't seem to be one to harbour unscrupulous men. As we already know, he was an admiral, ambassador and an advisor to the most powerful king in the world. My guess is that they had good reason to disobey Albuquerque.'

'Well, outraged, Albuquerque was forced to abort Ormuz.'

Jason read on, quoting extracts here and there: 'Albuquerque sailed to Cochin where tension with Almeida intensified after the Mamluks killed his son Lourenço—'

'—Lourenço, oké, but what about Albuquerque's captains?'

'Among the deserters were António do Campo and Manuel Telles Barreto. There was a third—but I can't see who here—and together they persuaded Almeida to stop Albuquerque taking power as he'd failed to serve the king's interests. Jorge Barreto, the chief officer and a relative of Almeida, I suspect, recorded *ex parte* how Albuquerque wilfully disobeyed his orders in pursuit of self-gain. However, charges against Albuquerque were presented as a conspiracy—and here's the wicked twist—a conspiracy Almeida himself had instigated! Isn't that ironic? Anyway, allegiances shifted once it was clear that Albuquerque was to become Governor and Almeida would return, disgraced, on the next boat home. Albuquerque is today a great Portuguese leader in India and Brazil and without equal in Portugal's pantheon of heroes. Or so chance and artifice would have it. Now, Jason, doesn't that make you think?'

He understands that "greatness" is largely an
attribute of memory, not of men.
Verlyn Klinkenborg, Introduction, *Heart of Darkness* (1993)

From: jtomas@mweb.co.za
Sent: Tuesday, June 15, 19:03
To: awayfromhome@gmail.com
Subject: RE: Almeida and Albuquerque
Hi again Sonja, Wikipedia has a telling portrait (attached here) with a useful synopsis of d'A. The facts below may interest you:

Francisco de Almeida, known as "the Great Dom Francisco" (c.1450 – March 1, 1510), was a Portuguese noble, soldier and explorer... When Afonso de Albuquerque arrived at Cochin to supersede him, Almeida refused to recognise his credentials and had him cast in prison. Albuquerque was released after three months' confinement, on arrival of the grand-marshal of Portugal with a large fleet, in November 1509. Almeida sailed for Portugal the next month. He was killed in a skirmish with the Khoekhoen at Table Bay, near the Cape of Good Hope. See http://en.wikipedia.org/wiki/Francisco_de_Almeida

---

Look for yourself. Let's chat more tomorrow at 4. Jason

*And this same view, seen from thy brow by man,
has been before thy face since earth began.*

W Angus Kingon, *Address to Table Mountain* (1926)

It was the week of *First Encounters and Lasting Legacies*. A week in which the country's leading scientists, historians and curators assembled for their annual conference. The SA Museum hosted delegates from as far afield as the Atlantic-African states, the Indonesian archipelago and the former Soviet republics.

After attending a discussion on the controversial "origins" of the Russian people, Jason skipped the afternoon session to join Sonja in her office. She wanted to know more about Almeida's portrait, while he thought it best to be there in case she found something new.

And she had a knack for finding things too:

'Almeida's portrait belongs to the British Library,' she began, 'it's part of their Sloane Collection. Those in the dossier are all copies.'

He pulled up a chair for a closer look.

Dom Francisco Dalmeyda

The portrait was by an unknown artist from the sixteenth century and appeared to be based on secondary sources: testimonies, records and reports. It portrayed a sturdy figure with a square-trimmed beard —as was probably fashionable, she thought—and showed a receding hairline that elongated his face. There was one conspicuous detail: Almeida had a wart on his right cheek.

'It's him on the Escudo, but without that wart!' exclaimed Jason, waving a dull banknote in front of her.

The museum's collection manager had loaned him some notes and stamps. Though sealed in plastic, the resemblance was obvious.

'Isn't it ironic,' she noted, 'that Portugal dominated the mercantile markets of Europe, yet couldn't stay ahead of their competition?'

'Their risks were high—with shipwrecks, disease, superstition and piracy—sure, but why, why lose momentum?'

'Because it was a corrupt, debt-ridden family business based on an antiquated *modus operandi*—one which entrepreneurs exploited.'

True, while others introduced joint stock companies and risk management, Portugal failed to gear itself up for the burgeoning capitalist market. She summed it up neatly:

'The feudal Avis simply couldn't transform themselves fast enough, financially or morally, and so they collapsed two short centuries later, exhausted, their royal coffers depleted and the family outrun by their Dutch, French and British rivals.'

'Like the Afrikaners who lagged two centuries behind looking for the Promised Land, and so missed out on the Age of Enlightenment.'

He slapped a hand against his forehead.

'*Eish!* How stupid was that?'

She shared the irony but not his world-view. His world had too many rascals, cowards and jealous trouble-makers. Alexander Pope knew it well when he stated: "All looks yellow to the jaundiced eye."

'While Southern Europe was paralyzed by persecutions, Northern Protestants were able to advance politically and economically. The Spanish Inquisition prohibited secularisation, divination, witchcraft and bigamy. What's more, Portugal's own demise happened just as Holland liberated itself from its Spanish oppressors.' She lowered her voice, adding: 'Ironically, it took an exiled Portuguese-Jew, Spinoza, to start Holland's intellectual revolution and, as a result, the Cape submitted to the pragmatism, rationalism and jurisprudence of the North; to Roman Dutch Law, the German Reformation, the French Huguenots—who were themselves anti-Catholic—and, much later, to the grand mining magnates of British Industrialism.'

'And for that we should be grateful?'

Sonja was not to be ambushed so easily.

She'd pursue the portrait of Almeida tomorrow. At this hour, she reflected, MS Sloane 197 fol. 9 lay in a box, like a treasured pearl, buried deep in the vaults of the British Library.

Jason was keen to attend the conference reception in the museum's Whale Well. Mendle was there too, under the barnacled humpback, and so they waded out in his direction. The primordial pool was awash with feeding delegates. Mendle was delighted to see them.

'Ah, Sonja, this way!' he beckoned.

She tugged at Jason's sleeve, altering their course around a shoal of caterers.

'Oh-boy, look what we have tonight… samosas, pakoras, bambals.' Mendle swayed at a passing tray of snacks.

'The usual mix,' said Jason, 'never suitable but always popular.'

'Why always at receptions? After a long flight I'm too disorientated for raw, spicy or exotic food,' volunteered Mendle, without shame. 'Now, what did you find today?'

'First, what happened at the last session?' asked Jason. 'I'm sorry I missed it.'

'No matter, nothing was said that you don't already know, except that tempers flared and enraged panellists stormed out—'

'—why, Prof, you were supposed to convene that session?'

'Aha, some overseas colleagues challenged the old origin theory of Great Zimbabwe—'

'—the Exotic-vs-Essentialist hypotheses again?'

'Exactly. Imagine a hall full of Tomb Raiders and Relic Hunters debating whether the Phoenicians or Chinese fucked the locals before the Portuguese did.'

What did he say! Jesus, is he drunk?

Jason looked around for the waiter with the food tray. 'You need to eat something, Prof, here try this… then tell us about the fight.'

With his mouth full, Mendle replied: 'Ah, Ben Kune…'

'But I thought Ben had retired from the public-lecture circuit?'

Turning to Sonja, Mendle explained:

'Ben caused a storm with his speculations about Chinese-Muslims reaching the Cape—long before Apartheid was law—and having sex with the natives. Ben said DNA tests would confirm this one day—'

'—when he first said it, two decades ago, the archaeological society turned its back on him,' cut in Jason, grabbing some more samosas.

'Ah, but he should have known better. Never make professional statements about the racial or sexual proclivities of others. At least not in South Africa, where race and sex have been taboo for so long.'

'Ben said the East first discovered the West, and not the other way around,' continued Jason.

'Why?' she asked, 'because Fra Mauro's map shows that they were here first? Y'know the Chinese are still the world's top entrepreneurs and explorers—recolonising Africa and mapping the moon? But do you have proof that they were actually here beforehand?'

'No, not yet, but Jason found a Quena burial-site with a Chinese artefact—an opaque glassware bowl from the same period.'

'But that doesn't prove Zheng He sailed around the Cape?'

'Ha, it was then the Devil's Cape, because of its extreme relation to the known world,' interjected Mendle, lurching at a passing tray.

'Is that proof?' she asked, 'how do we know it isn't a trade item? Why else would the Chinese be so far from home?'

'We don't know, yet, but the absence of anything similar at coastal settlements or along inland grazing routes suggests it wasn't a trade item,' replied Mendle, adding something new: 'At Thulamela and Mapungubwe—the proto-Zimbabwean sites in the Limpopo basin— glass and porcelain have been found and are linked to Indo-Arabian gold-traders. They already had contact with the interior via Sofala, now Beira, since the first millennium.' He paused for another bite. 'We otherwise don't have enough evidence, not now. But Jason will test his thesis at next month's archaeology conference in London.'

'So, how do you know Jason has something of value?'

'Because I found it one Sunday—'

'—that's because you have no competition on Sundays,' declared Mendle. Like Morse, he'd be at home listening to *Tannhäuser* while Sergeant Lewis would be out doing the dog's work.

'*Natuurlijk*. Sunday is not only a lucky day for digging up skeletons but, I guess, the dead don't own their own bones...'

15

The Cape of Storms, which keeps his memory
Along with his bones, will be unashamed
In dispatching from the world such a soul
Neither Egypt nor all India could control.

Luís de Camões, *The Lusíads* (1572)

Angus McBride was a specialist in the rarefied art of war. As a gifted and prolific illustrator he had painted soldiers, cavalry charges and besieged castles for over sixty years. Angus's knowledge of combat uniforms, weapons, forts and famous battle scenes was encyclopaedic, and his artworks filled an entire house in Victorian Wynberg where he lived with his wife, Pat, and their Siamese cat.

Sonja tracked them down via the Castle Military Museum, having told the curator she wanted to interview the artist.

'Mr McBride may not recall Almeida, or that he even painted him,' warned the curator on the phone. 'The work was commissioned by a publisher decades ago, and only recently entered our collection when McBride himself donated it. You're welcome to visit our library—we're in the Castle, upstairs, next to the museum.'

She felt a twinge of guilt, their dossier still in her bag, as she drove out to see McBride early the next morning. She found him at home, dressed in a dark silk kimono, looking very much like one accustomed to a life of deadlines, late nights and the morning after tea ceremony. His entire household appeared to float on the fumes of painter's turpentine. Artworks cluttered the hallway, floor to ceiling, waiting to be shipped off for an exhibition. Or so she thought.

'They've been stacked against these walls for years,' he explained, 'ever since the picture-rails were full.'

He led her into a studio crammed with drawing boards, pencilled sketches, brushes and paints. Paper tissues were strewn about every-where—except on a tall Chinese tea table standing by the window.

She saw warriors from every period: gladiators, legionaries, samurai and crusaders. There was but one notable incongruity, a set of erotic paintings depicting woman warriors.

'Oh dear, yes, a fantasy series for an almanac in the Sixties, done to represent the twelve signs of the zodiac. That one's Virgo.'

He reached for the Amazon, but the busty warrior eluded his grasp, being set too high on the bookshelf: 'She's my favourite.'

'*Tsjonge!* I'm a Virgo too, but never looked like that—'

'—but you weren't born then,' he said with a mischievous smile.

'No, nor was I destined to be a woman-warrior, lush or not.'

'Yet you seem feisty enough to draw a sword from its scabbard,' he said provocatively. 'Tell me again why you came? Did you want to buy one of my paintings?'

'Thank you, no, I'm here about the Portuguese Viceroy, Francisco d'Almeida, who—'

'—Hmmm. I've done the Greeks, Romans, Gauls and Vikings, the French and English too, even the Spaniards and Moors, but not the incompetent Portuguese.'

'He was killed at the Cape.'

'A Viceroy, you say?'

'Yes, murdered, along with sixty-five others.'

McBride paced the floor like a restless dog, swaying in front of his books before halting. He scratched his head as if tickling his memory was going to help.

'Soldiers in combat?'

'Yes, including natives and their war-oxen.'

'Oh yes!' he cried, 'war elephants were used against Alexander the Great, blocking his cavalry and stampeding his infantry—like African cattle were also trained to do. The fear of more elephants across the

Hyphasis was the straw that broke the camel's back, if you pardon the mixed metaphor. War-trained elephants declined rapidly with the invention of new battle techniques in the Hellenistic period, although Hannibal still used elephants—'

'—sorry, Mr McBride, we're talking about war-oxen at the Cape.'

His face lit up.

'Yes, I remember now, a bloody difficult affair drawing half-naked men in combat. I'm better at rendering armour and uniforms, but the light, that beautiful morning light on Table Mountain! Actually, my wife and I went down to the beach at sunrise to capture the effect. Personally, I think it's the best part of the painting. Do I still have it? Well, you should have said so—'

'—I did, when we spoke on the phone yesterday. Your painting is now in the Military Museum.'

'Is it really? Well, I never remember details like that, and yet I can recall what I learnt at school fifty-odd years ago. Anyway, I'm glad I forgot about it,' he chuckled, 'or I may have turned my studio upside-down looking for it.'

Thinking practically, she suggested: 'Why not use a calendar?'

'I forget names and dates too. Bloody memory, y'know.'

'So what *do* you remember about the murder?'

'I'm afraid nothing, nothing at all. But then what more can *you* tell me about this Viscount?'

'Viceroy. Well, I think there was a clandestine order of execution,' she prompted, 'to ensure Almeida never returned to court in Lisbon. It was disguised as a prophecy of doom-or-something.'

She could hear McBride rummaging through his memory bank.

'Hmmm... why's that?'

'Because Almeida came from a leading family,' she laboured, trying hard to jolt his memory. 'Imagine the scandal if a Viceroy—literally the king's right-hand man—went on trial for protecting rebel officers and then imprisoned his successor, Afonso de Albuquerque.'

'Albuquerque!'

'Yes, Albuquerque—'

She'd found a charmed word.

'—of course, Albuquerque, that one-armed scoundrel. Come, sit, while I fetch a fresh pot.'

Albuquerque, a scoundrel?

It was not the response she'd expected. She dusted the draughting stool and reset its tired-looking cushion, then prepared herself for a long history lesson. He hurried back:

'You think Albuquerque ordered your Almeida killed?' he asked, twirling the tea leaves in the pot.

'As an act of retribution, yes, for being humiliated in India.'

'An intriguing idea. They were two embittered rivals who couldn't utter a word of respect in each other's company. Almeida called him a loose cannon while Albuquerque thought he lacked boldness.'

'Why, because Almeida didn't seize more land bases or, b-because,' she slowed down, 'because he avenged his personal losses? He seems to have been the wiser leader and a better comrade.'

'That may be true, hmmm, but history remembers him as making one critical error of judgement—'

'—which was?'

McBride poured the tea, now a perfect colour.

'As Viceroy, Almeida lent himself to a scheme of deception—'

'—deception?'

'Yes. Actually, you could say treason. After Ormuz, Almeida gave three insubordinate captains protection, safe escort and a fair trail.'

'But they'd plundered Ormuz, or so Albuquerque claimed.'

The accusation still sounded dubious.

'On the contrary, the rebel officers complained that Albuquerque kept their share of the spoils—without explanation or compensation. Customarily, each man was entitled to a portion of the loot. This was divided, like a salary, according to each man's station and service.' Angus shifted his weight against the shelves. 'Only one fact remains, Almeida believed them, unquestionably.'

'So what happened?'

'João da Nova, captain of Almeida's flagship, then joined the fray. Although not part of the so-called "mutiny of the captains", Nova supported their case against Albuquerque and, together, petitioned Almeida not to yield to Albuquerque's secret credentials.'

'Claiming he was the next Governor?'

'Yes, but the four captains persuaded Almeida not to submit. They argued that Albuquerque was unfit to govern and so, in due course, Almeida called a special council to hear evidence *in absentia*, before Albuquerque reached Cochin.'

'And?'

'It was like putting flint to gunpowder. Both commanders bristled with incriminations while their officers remonstrated. Albuquerque felt betrayed, particularly by João da Nova, who died shortly after the trial opened in Cochin. Hmmm.'

'And where did king Manuel stand in this whole affair?'

'Both commanders appealed for his support, discrediting the other.'

'But who did Manuel favour?'

'Almeida established a monopoly, Albuquerque a trade-empire… the latter, definitely.'

'Making Albuquerque the greatest hero in Portuguese history?'

'Yes,' said Angus, pacing up and down with his cup, 'but Manuel made sure he'd be remembered above everyone else.'

'But it was not as he would have wanted it,' she added. 'Isn't it ironic that historians now describe him as that "cynical autocrat who played one of the greatest games of diplomacy ever lost".'

McBride roared with pleasure:

'Well, we get what we deserve. Albuquerque fell into a depression when Manuel failed to acknowledge his grandiose achievements. As Governor, he'd carried out his orders with zeal, seizing ports and building fortresses around the Indian basin. But Manuel was a master at divide-and-rule and appointed Albuquerque's rival and personal enemy to succeed him. Albuquerque was consumed by resentment. Aggrieved, he became ill and ended his ignominious life bedridden. Severe sickness eventually killed the miserable old rogue.'

Albuquerque, sick?

'D'you know what he died of?'

'No, but for as long as Manuel lived, he stubbornly refused to allow the return of Albuquerque's remains. The king was superstitious— like the old folk from the back-country—and apparently declared that "as long as Albuquerque's bones are there, India is safe".'

So that's why Almeida's bones stayed at the Cape, she reflected, *to safeguard the southern Portal to India.*

16

God is angry, the elders have gone,
their bones are far, their souls wander.
Where are their souls?

Quena praise poem, *The Ancestors* (undated)

'Ancestral bones are sacred in traditional African societies,' began Prof Mendle, strolling along the beach. 'Bones are used for settling disputes, putting the deceased to rest, and for predicting the future.'

The tide was out and the sand felt cold beneath their feet. Two sets of prints trailed behind them, between the high-lying flotsam and the retreating surf. Ahead stretched Bloubergstrand, northward, as far as each could see, and across the jade-green bay rose the majestic form of Table Mountain: long, low and, as always, unmistakably flat.

'Bones are also used to call the Ancestors, like witnesses to a trial—'

'—as in a jury,' Sonja asked, 'to see justice served?'

'Exactly, but moreover, the Ancestral Spirits include witnesses from the North; from as far off as Tanzania and Kenya. Remember, too, that Camões says Almeida was killed to pay for the brutal plundering of East African cities, especially Kilwa and Mombasa, where his men butchered the Swahili and the Arabs.'

'But it didn't begin with Almeida. Pedro Álvares Cabral told the Sheikh of Kilwa, Amir Ibrahim, to face God's wrath or convert to Christianity. Kilwa was then the largest trade-centre in sub-Saharan Africa and the sheikh suzerain over most towns on East Africa's coast —thus an important ally. Two years later—I think it was in 1502— Vasco da Gama threatened to burn the city and kill its inhabitants, unless the sheikh swore allegiance to Portugal. After three years the enforced tribute of gold had not yet been delivered, and so it fell upon Almeida to extract payment—or attack the settlement. Almeida described the bay and its islands as something special: "Kilwa, of all the places I know in the world, has the best port and the fairest land that can be." Anyway, after driving out the sheikh he set in place a token ruler... But you're right, ultimately, as commander-in-chief, Almeida was responsible for all their atrocities.'

She recalled Colvin's colourful account of white-washed houses, flat-topped roofs and narrow streets; of shadowy harems and quiet courtyards; of pomegranate trees, hanging vines and cool fountains. She imagined the throng of spears and morions, the clamour of Moor against Christian, scimitar against sword, one in heavy armour, the other in gay silks. Then the rush of steel as men-at-arms burst open chamber doors, killing and plundering, grabbing rare stuffs in vessels of brass and silver. Finally, when all was wasted, Almeida's men piled silk and spices, ivory and ambergris, onto a huge heap and set the city ablaze. Safely on the beach, the monks raised their cross and chanted *Te Deum Laudamus*—and then on they went to Mombasa.

Lost in thought, she stopped when Mendle bent to retrieve a piece of bleached driftwood.

'For my garden,' he volunteered. Amused by yet another historical paradox, he added jovially: 'Today the island ruins at Kilwa Kisiwani attract about one tourist a day; unlike the white beaches of Zanzibar, the open plains of the Serengeti or the heights of Kilimanjaro and the Olduvai Gorge.'

'Seriously, Prof, we should relativize such acts of violence, including disembowelment and cannibalism. We tend to judge such atrocities through a lens that's been ground by our humanitarian conscience, a conscience sixteenth-century soldier-warriors didn't possess.'

'Ah, neither did the Swahili or Arabs. For instance, after severing links with other cities, the network fell apart so rapidly that Portugal abandoned Kilwa within a decade. With its trade links and fortunes plundered, the city met a gruesome end as the maZimba—a generic term for *marauders*—swept in from today's Zimbabwe or Malawi, and massacred the inhabitants. Little is known about them, other than that they were cannibals. I first thought they migrated north when the Portuguese took control of the gold mines in the Zambezi Valley, but now it's being suggested that they descended from the baMaravi, who came from the lower Congo basin fleeing war and disease.'

He halted, stooping for another plank. She stepped back to tie up her hair as he, straightening stiffly, continued:

'Anyhow, soldiers from Africa's forests and the deserts of Arabia don't have that same conscience today.'

'No, nor do gun-toting schoolboys or soccer hooligans. So much for theories of historical progress. Anyway, I only want to know who was murdered—besides Almeida and Gaspar—and what happened to their bones?'

'Aha, but are you sure they really *were* killed? Many men simply disappeared to start a new life elsewhere—'

'—wait, I never questioned that, I mean, I assumed the death-toll lay somewhere between fifty-seven and sixty-five—'

'—you just assumed,' nudged Mendle mischievously.

'Well, I know twelve were officers, three of whom had abandoned Albuquerque. So now what?'

'Perhaps you should look at who was *not* killed?'

He felt inspired. It sounded like something Morse would say.

'Start with those in the dossier. Almeida's Companions for instance. You can be sure of one thing, the *Tabula nomens* is there for a reason. And since you stole it, you're now responsible for its contents.'

'*Really?* Anyway, for now, I think the only survivors were Jorge de Mello, Jorge Barreto, Diogo de Unhos and—'

'—one at a time, Sonja,' he said, easing the pace.

'Oké, first Jorge de Mello, possibly a relative of Rodrigo de Mello. Rodrigo was married to Almeida's daughter, Leonor.'

'Ah, how tempting, a possible family connection. Who else?'

'Jorge Barreto, chief officer, who encouraged Almeida to go ashore, then marched ahead to sack the village himself.'

'Or didn't want others to know what he was up to. And?'

'Diogo de Unhos, master of Almeida's ship, the *Garça*.'

'Aha, who took Almeida ashore but left when the wind picked up.'

'Yes, then two years later, when Diogo touched the Cape again, he took Cristóvão de Brito to see the grave. According to the dossier—it's the last entry in the *Tabula*, I think—Cristóvão found it unmarked and had a cairn or cross erected nearby. It was the first defeat and earliest memorial built by white interlopers in southern Africa.'

'Locally,' added Mendle, 'it was also the first fatal encounter with a stranger from across the Great Water. The abeLungu came from the "nesting place of the sun", arriving in ships built like giant birds with wings of white. Their longboats swam ashore like fish with raised fins and flashing teeth. Reptile-like in scales of armour, they spat fire and attacked their prey with claws of steel. The seafarers, in turn, viewed the swarthy locals as skittish, untrustworthy and unreliable. From here on through the Portuguese called only out of necessity...'

'Well, Prof, that's poetic!' she said, 'but in reality the event merely perpetuated the black man's burden of blame in South Africa. It was conveniently used to accuse the hapless native of any misdemeanour, misfortune or mishap; especially since it happened so far from home. Anyway, sorry for that, I also think Cristóvão may have been related to Lourenço de Brito.'

'Aha, I see we have lots of relatives, and when blood is thicker than water, the plot always thickens...'

'Well, we also have Pedro Barreto and Jorge Barreto who, having led the march that morning, were among those that returned to bury the dead. Though elsewhere it says Almeida's body was never found.'

His bones are far, his soul wanders?

They returned to Mendle's Landi as the sun dipped into the sea. The mountain stood up like a cardboard cut-out against the plush skyline. It occurred to her that Almeida had never received a proper burial. Moreover, the Cape of Storms symbolised a forbidden threshold and a sacred portal between Iberia and India, the two far-flung peninsulas of Eurasia.

His soul wanders between West and East?

'Death at the Cape not only symbolised a psychological threshold,' added Prof Mendle, 'but also a transgression from the familiar to the strange, from the Self to the Other.'

They sat by the car brushing sand off their feet. She found her feet to be inelegant, as if they belonged to a different body, to someone far shorter than she felt herself to be.

'Camões says Almeida was killed in retribution for his actions along East Africa's coast,' reflected Mendle. 'Likewise, Credo Mutwa says Attila the Hun, Julius Caesar, Napoleon and Hitler—even Shaka Zulu—all had miserable, lonely deaths. Yes, indeed, I think it is time to look at that *Tabula* again. And to ask ourselves who WJS was?'

TABULA NOMENS

Almeida's Patrons

1. JOÃO I   1357–1433
Almeida's great forefather, Fernando Álvares, joined the battle of succession against Castile at Aljubarrota in 1385, putting João on the throne and establishing Portugal's independence. The victory formalised a long-standing alliance with England (known as the Treaty of Windsor, still valid today) which helped to found the Avis dynasty. As the new king of Portugal, João I initiated Europe's expansion into Africa.

2. AFONSO V   1438–1481
Linked to João I by an illegitimate son, Afonso and the Bragança family pursued the succession of Castile and the conquest of North Africa. Almeida's father Lopo fought in Morocco (1458, 1460–64 and 1471); and as a young *fidalgo*, Almeida himself served at the battle of Toro (1476). After the defeat, Almeida acted as Afonso's envoy in negotiations for the hand of princess Juâna la Beltraneja of Castile.

3. FERNANDO, DUKE OF BRAGANÇA   1430–1483
The Duke of Bragança was a diplomat at the courts of Afonso V and Manuel I, themselves from the House of Bragança. Fernando married the daughter of Infante Diogo, Duke of Viseu (Manuel's brother), and thus had rights of succession to Portugal's throne. However, when accused of treason, João II had Fernando executed (1483) and, the following year, murdered the Duke of Viseu himself. With their possessions confiscated, most of the Braganças fled the country to join the court of Ferdinand and Isabella in Spain. Many returned when João II's successor, Manuel, had them recalled in 1500. The Bragança would later rule for almost three centuries.

4. JOÃO II   1455–1495
Implicated in a plot against the new king, João II spared Almeida as he had already left for Spain in 1483. On Almeida's return from Granada in 1492, João made him commodore with orders to seize the New World discoveries for the Portuguese crown.

5. MANUEL I   1469–1521
Born Manuel de Beja, he unexpectedly became heir to the throne at João II's behest—and was henceforth nicknamed the "Fortunate". Almeida served as king Manuel's supreme commander in India, but fell victim to political intrigues back in Portugal.

6. FERDINAND I OF ARAGON   1452–1516
Almeida first fought against Ferdinand at the battle of Toro (1476) and, joining the Braganças in exile during the 1480s, fought for Ferdinand and Isabella at Granada (1492). The Catholic monarchs united Spain under a common Christian crown.

7. ISABELLA OF CASTILE   1451–1504
Ferdinand and Isabella ruled parts of southern Italy and commissioned Bramante's *Tempietto* in Rome. Almeida allegedly delivered a gift of gold on their behalf. His brothers, Pedro and Fernando, were sent to Rome by João II for the same purpose (1494).

Almeida's Compatriots

1. BARTOLOMEU DIAS   c.1451–1500
Dias was the first Portuguese explorer to sail around southern Africa (1488). He was sent to find Prester John—a legendary Christian priest and king—as well as the silks, spices and jewels of the Indies. Although his ships returned empty, Dias opened the way for navigators like Pedro Álvares Cabral and Vasco da Gama. While of modest standing, Dias was known to Almeida via connections at court. Dias died when his ship, and three others, sank off the Cape of Good Hope (29 May 1500).

2. PÊRO DA COVILHÃ   c.1460–1526
Covilhã also served Afonso V at Toro and, together with Almeida, went to Tours to seek an audience with Louis XI of France (1477). A decade later, in the same year Dias set sail for the Indies, Covilhã went via Egypt to find the realm of Prester John. Covilhã travelled as far as Calicut before returning to Cairo. From there he went to Emperor Eskender's court at Aksum, Ethiopia, where he was detained for thirty years. Covilhã was reputedly "the most famous secret agent of his day".

3. PEDRO ÁLVARES CABRAL
c.1467–1520   *Order of Christ*

Cabral crossed the Atlantic with Gaspar das Índias and Bartolomeu Dias, making landfall at Brazil for the first time in 1500. Dias went with to establish a trade depot at the gold-exporting port of Sofala, but sank en route in a violent Atlantic storm. Cabral was left to round the Cape of Good Hope with only half his fleet, running up the East coast to Sofala, Kilwa, Mombasa and Melinde. At Kilwa he demanded a tribute of gold and the city's allegiance, adding notoriously: "convert or face our sword". Cabral was the first European to set foot in America, Africa and Asia—binding together the trade of four continents. His appointment was made to counterbalance factions of the nobility and their competing orders.

4. VASCO DA GAMA
c.1469–1524   *Order of Santiago*

Gama captained the first fleet to sail directly from Europe to India (1497–98), calling at Mombasa and Melinde, Anjediva Island (where he met Gaspar das Índias) and then on to Calicut and Goa. He set off as a young *fidalgo* and returned a celebrity—quickly marrying Caterina de Ataíde, a cousin of Almeida. Tactfully, Gama had Cabral displaced as Manuel's nominee for the next voyage, going back himself in 1502 for further riches. En route he pre-empted war with Kilwa and Mombasa, a matter Almeida was compelled to settle three years later (1505). He later succeeded Afonso de Albuquerque as governor of Portuguese India, but died in Cochin soon after his arrival (24 December 1524).

5. CRISTOFÓRO COLUMBUS
1451–1506

Columbus witnessed the capitulation of Granada (1492) when Ferdinand and Isabella repelled the last Moors from Spain, thus completing the *Reconquista*. Here Almeida and his compatriots served under the banner of *Sant'Iago da Espada*, Saint James of the Sword. With the war finally over and the wealth of Granada safely confiscated, Columbus received the financial backing required for a westward voyage. However, on his return João II instructed Almeida to sail west and seize all that Columbus had discovered in the Atlantic.

6. FERNANDO MAGELLAN
c.1480–1521

Magellan was sent to install Almeida as Viceroy of India and captained a large nau at the battle of Diu (1509), helping Portugal secure its supremacy in Indian waters. He was subsequently demoted for his alleged absence without leave and for illegal trade with the Muslims. Although disgraced, the Spanish crown employed him to find a western route to the Orient's Spice Islands. A few years later, off in the Philippines, Mactan islanders killed Magellan before his dwindling fleet could complete the world's first circumnavigation (1519–22).

7. TRISTÃO DA CUNHA
c.1460–1539

Manuel appointed Cunha as Viceroy of India but, when illness affected his eyesight, had him replaced by Almeida. As compensation, Cunha commanded the next armada out from Lisbon (1506), operating off East Africa and West India. Although Cunha was never re-elected, his son Nuno succeeded him as governor of India (1528–38), until intrigues at court had João III recall Nuno to Lisbon. He was lost at sea off the Cape of Good Hope before a squadron sent by the king could arrest him.

Some sources claim he was shipwrecked and drowned, others that he was buried at sea?

8. AFONSO DE ALBUQUERQUE
1453–1515   *Order of Christ*

Albuquerque spent ten years fighting the Moors at Arzila and Tangier (1460–71), the Castilians at Toro (1476) and—when Rome itself felt threatened—the Ottomans at Otranto (1481). He returned to Morocco in 1489 and 1495. His first trip to India was in 1503, with a large fleet, to establish a fort at Cochin (taking Almeida's brother Duarte with him). Albuquerque thus "carved a foothold for Portugal's empire in the East". He returned to India in 1506, with Cunha, and succeeded Almeida as the second governor of the Estado da Índia (1509–15), laying the foundation for others; including Vasco da Gama (1524) and Nuno da Cunha (1528).

9. PERO D'ANHAIA

After Almeida's grand departure in 1505, Anhaia commanded the first squadron to sail for the Estado, with orders to build a fort and command the factory at Sofala. Although Anhaia and almost all his men died of disease, probably malaria, it was from Sofala that the Portuguese first probed the interior for the legendary *Mwanamutapa* (Monomotapa).

to pay for Indian silks and spices?

10. VASCO GOMES DE ABREU

Abreu was a captain in the great outbound armada of 1505, returning to Lisbon in 1506 to report on Almeida's Viceroyship. He commanded the next squadron to depart (1507), replacing Anhaia at Sofala. Falling out of favour with Almeida, Abreu requested that he be permitted to return. Almeida consented, sending him back to Lisbon with cargo.

11. ANTÓNIO DE SALDANHA

Saldanha sailed with Albuquerque's fleet (1503) and, after making landfall at the Cape, was lightly wounded in a skirmish. Although Dias probably set foot here before, Saldanha was the first navigator to identify the *Aquada*. He sailed on to become fort captain at Cochin until, under Almeida, he took command of the garrison at Sofala (1509–12).

12. ÁLVARO TELLES BARRETO

Barreto sailed with Albuquerque's second fleet of 1506, under Tristão da Cunha's command, serving as captain of the *Garça*. Already rotting and leaking, the *Garça* was given to Almeida for his trip home (19 November 1509). The nau and two other ships sailed in stark contrast to the armada of twenty-two that he had arrived with four years earlier.

Almeida's Companions

1. DIOGO FERNANDES LABAREDAS

Homebound with Almeida's small fleet, Labaredas sailed into Table Bay and went ashore to fetch fresh water (20 February). During the week that followed, Labaredas befriended a local herder and was granted permission to visit a nearby village in order to barter meat (28 February). He returned with a sheep, which he presented to Almeida, and was soon dispatched with twelve men to obtain more livestock—particularly cattle.

2. GONÇALO HOMEM + FERNAÕ CARRASCO

Homen was a servant of Almeida who joined the party of twelve sent back to the village. Returning to the *Garça* with a bloodied face, he tried to persuade Almeida to lead a punitive party ashore. He was supported by the servant of Jorge de Mello Pereira, Fernaõ Carrasco, who'd also been beaten. The two were known as "the ever bellicose fidalgoes". As a result, Almeida called a council of officers (*cortes*) to hear their views on making war against the natives.

3. PEDRO BARRETO DE MAGALHÃES

Magalhães went to India as captain of the *Santiago* which, being overladen, first sank in Lisbon harbour and could not sail with the great armada of 1505. Four years later (1509–10), he accompanied Almeida on his ill-fated voyage home. During their war council on the *Garça*, he argued for a punitive expedition, lending support to veterans like Manuel Telles Barreto and António do Campo (two of the mutineering captains). Magalhães led the pre-dawn raid on 1 March but, amid the men's disorderly retreat, died under a hail of stones and assegais.

4. JORGE BARRETO + FERNÃO PEREIRA

Barreto was a kinsman of Manuel Telles Barreto and co-led the march on the village with one of the twelve, Brito Lanças, acting as guide. The first victim was Fernão Pereira who, on entering a grass hut, was slain in error by a passing compatriot. When news of this blunder reached Almeida, still on his way, he had the attack called off. Jorge Barreto survived the raid and, later that same afternoon, came ashore with Mello Pereira to bury the dead.

a relative of Almeida's wife, Joäna Pereira?

Francisco Barreto led conquest of Monomotapa

5. LOURENÇO DE BRITO

Brito captained the fortified factory at Cananor and, under Almeida's instructions, guarded Cochin tower in which Albuquerque was held for three months (September–November 1509). Brito was a trusted comrade-in-arms and returned with the *Santa Cruz*, the second of three ships used to escort Almeida home. Asked if it was prudent to punish the natives, Brito advised against it, suspecting foul play. He did not land the next morning, saying he was ill, and on hearing the news later, grieved the loss of his bosom companion. He immediately went aboard the *Garça* and made an inventory of all Almeida's belongings, sealing the sea trunks and nailing down the cabins. Brito led a recovery party but was killed, along with Martim Coelho, when the enraged herders returned to the beach that same afternoon.

6. GASPAR DAS ÍNDIAS

Orphaned and enslaved, Gaspar rose to become the advisor and finance minister of the Sultan of Bijapur. After the Portuguese arrived in Anjediva, he served as Gama's pilot and as Almeida's lingua, spending his last years back in India (1505–09). He is mentioned in Almeida's final testament, written aboard the *Garça*, and died beside his master on the beach.

7. DIOGO PIRES

Pires served as a tutor to Almeida's son, Lourenço, and as ship's captain at the battle of Diu (1509). He took part in the punitive expedition of 1 March and, hearing that Almeida had been killed, cried aloud: "May God grant that I not live while the father and son are both dead." Pires refused to leave the beach and died beside Gaspar, protecting Almeida's body.

8. JORGE DE FIGUEIREDO

Figueiredo was Almeida's obedient servant who, once Lourenço de Brito secured the cabins, was ordered to guard the Viceroy's possessions and to provide all servants and slaves from his master's stores. Figueiredo may have shared Brito's suspicion of treachery.

9. MARTIM COELHO

Coelho sailed with Vasco Gomes de Abreu's small squadron of 1507, and later served as ship's captain at the battle of Diu (1509). He survived the ill-fated raid on the village but was killed after the skirmish, when he and Lourenço de Brito returned to recover Almeida's body.

10. JORGE DE MELLO PEREIRA

Mello Pereira commanded the first squadron out from Lisbon in 1507, aboard the *Belém*, which he also captained at Diu (1509). He took the *Belém*, the third of three ships, back via the Cape with Almeida. During their retreat, having helped the wounded into the longboats, he returned to fetch the fallen Almeida. Foreseeing his own end, Almeida entrusted the king's standard to him. That same evening Mello Pereira led a second recovery party, accompanied by Diogo de Unhos and Jorge Barreto, and was himself wounded in the arm. It was Mello Pereira who found Almeida's body, despoiled of all its clothing. However, the survivors elected Barreto as their new commander (not Mello Pereira) and so Barreto reported on this tragic event back in Lisbon, for which king Manuel declared a day of mourning.

11. DIOGO DE UNHOS

Unhos accompanied Almeida aboard his flagship, the *Garça*, acting as captain or "master of the ship". He took Almeida ashore before dawn, in a longboat, and watched the massacre from beyond the surf. He returned that evening to assist Mello Pereira with the burial. Two years later, in 1512, Unhos called again to show Christovão de Brito the unmarked grave.

12. CHRISTAVÃO DE BRITO

Brito touched at the Cape (1512) for fresh water and firewood, and asked Diogo de Unhos to show him the grave. Unable to find it, Brito had a stone cairn and wooden cross erected. At the time, king Manuel forbade ships from calling, unless in dire necessity.

a relative of Lourenço de Brito?

RAID	Fernão Pereira.
RETREAT	Manuel Teles Barreto, Fra Coutinho, António do Campo, Pedro Barreto Magalhães, Gaspar de las Indias. Francisco d'Almeida, Diogo Pires, Pedro Teixeira?
RETURN	Lourenço de Brito, Martim Coelho
RECOVERY	20 more killed?

I knew that I should have to die, of course, with or without your order. If it be soon, so much the better. Living in daily torment, as I do, who would not be glad to die? The punishment will not be any pain...

Sophocles, *Antigone* (c.442BCE)

From: awayfromhome@gmail.com
Sent: Thursday, June 17, 19:58
To: jmendle@sam.org.za
Subject: Almeida and Antigone

Dear Prof Mendle

Camões's prophecy claims that the Cape of Storms is destined to preserve Almeida's memory with his bones. Yes, but for how long, for how much longer must we keep our secret?

I feel like Antigone who cannot respect the dead without first disrespecting the living. To bury her brother she had to break the law and, by doing so, also defied her future father-in-law, the king of Thebes. Must we do the same and defy museum ethics and the dictates of two governments?

In the meantime, I need time to sort out my research priorities. I'll call you in a few days, after my return.

Till then, Sonja

Journey

18

It is good to have an end to journey towards,
but it is the journey that matters in the end.
Ursula K Le Guin, *The Left Hand of Darkness* (1969)

Cape Town's history was as much part of East Africa as it was part of South Asia—the geo-politics of all three regions overlapped. In fact, Egypt and India had a knock-on effect all the way down the coast, from Melinde and Mombasa to Kilwa and Sofala, ending up at the Cape of Good Hope. Almeida's murder demonstrated this.

However, these pre-colonial connections were not part of her VOC research project. In this regard she'd made little progress and would have to focus on Cape Dutch history again, and soon. Or withdraw from the exhibition, which wasn't really an option.

Despite this, she chose to spend her last weekend alone. Alone in the country, away from the dig, the museum, from Prof Mendle, and from any more talk of Almeida.

She'd return to the archives on Monday and work like the wind. *True journey is a return.*

It was irresponsible, yes, but she wanted to see the Garden Route— that Eden by the Sea—before she went home. The tourist brochures promised her a glossy, self-catering paradise with indigenous coastal forests, mist-shrouded mountains and unspoilt beaches. What more could she want for her final weekend—besides inspiration?

She'd drive up the coast to Mossel Bay, then cross the mountains at Oudtshoorn and return via the Klein Karoo. Promising herself time to relax, read, and write postcards, she soon had the local market, fishing harbour, lighthouse and maritime museum on her to-do list.

Museums are where past and present meet, she reminded herself, and the Dias Museum was dedicated to Portuguese captains who'd called at the Cape. They belonged to the Order of Christ, to its secret inner circle, so the museum should have information on…

She stopped herself rationalising the trip. No, she was not going to spend her last weekend delving into the death of a retired viceroy and his intrepid interpreter.

If the museum has material on Dutch galleons, then a visit would be justified.
And only then.

According to the web, Mossel Bay was a comfortable day trip and an easy place to find accommodation. Her plan included a detour via Cape Agulhas and a lunch-stop in Swellendam.

She set off around mid-morning, at leisure, driving through rolling wheat fields, terraced vineyards, and the beige-green folds of the Overberg. Reaching the coastal turn-off at midday, she followed the road down to the sea, to where one world ends and another begins.

The long drive was a dismal disappointment—her first for the day —as she found herself on a scrawny section of the coast without any point to mark the spot, except a lighthouse surrounded by low bushes bent oblong by the wind. Jagged rocks ran parallel out to sea, aligned like the teeth of a saw. If Cape Agulhas was the actual tip of Africa, then Cape Point had to be the symbolic "South End". On finding the lighthouse deserted, she turned the hired car and headed back to the national road, the sun crossing her path as she drove east.

Nostalgic Swellendam was a convenient place to stop for lunch. The open-air museum was located around the Drostdy and presented frontier life as rustic, simple and sublime. The town was named after Governor Hendrik Swellengrebel and his wife, Helena Ten Damme, a lady of notable accomplishments who—like Emperor Constantine's mother, also an Helena—had promoted Christianity in her realm.

Sonja knew that a mixed race had sustained frontier societies for both the Companje and the Estado, and that a shortage of women had been a common problem. Inevitably, the importation of young widows and orphaned girls signalled the transition from a temporary settlement to a more permanent society—as did their return to more conventional family values.

The Cape *mulato* were an entangled sub-group who also kept the settlement together when usual social bonds failed, or when regular relationships no longer applied. Today's descendents were dressed in folk costumes and played their master's role in the museum café, restaurant and gift shop. Swellendam had reinvented itself for the tourist industry. This proved to be her second disappointment.

Sonja drove back to the N2 and continued travelling east, listening to music once sung by pilgrims travelling to the Holy Land. She sensed her trip was part of a much longer journey, a pilgrimage in itself, with the Cape acting as her symbolic Jerusalem.

But first and foremost, she had her research priorities to sort out, or she'd be going nowhere slowly in future.

The Dias Museum was easy to find, being at the lower end of town, but had closed for the day when she arrived. It was situated above a sheltered cove where the Portuguese first came ashore during the feast of St Blaise, in 1488, to draw fresh water from a perennial spring. Unfortunately, before Dias could intervene, tragedy struck.

According to the authorative *History of Southern Africa* (which lay on the back seat of her car), the strangers were unlike any creatures seen before. They were large, pale, and covered themselves with garments of bright ornament. The curious natives kept themselves to a safe distance as the colourful strangers came ashore.

Sonja felt overwhelmed by the tangible traces of history around her. Sitting under a monumental melkhoutboom she tried to imagine the scenario five hundred years before. She imagined sailors dragging their longboats onto the beach while herders gathered inquisitively along the ridge behind her. Perhaps a few ventured closer, enticed by bells and mirrors, offering goods in exchange.

Before long, the seafarers made for the spring with their casks, but as the customary tribute for water-usage wasn't respected—by giving a suitable gift—an affronted herdsman hurled a stone at the tall ones. Others joined in as the intruders yelled back, incomprehensibly.

Then came a sudden rush of air—*whoosh*—followed by a dull thud as one of the herders fell to the ground, a crossbow bolt stuck in his throat. Fear spread like summer veld fire.

The herders fled, leaving the newcomers to what water they could carry off. And so the tragic episode became Quena legend.

The Song of the abeLungu, to borrow Jason's term again, was sung around the fatty cooking fires of the Gouriqua, then re-enacted by the neighbouring Attaqua and Hessequa, and later, retold among the clans of the southern coastal plain, including the talkative Chochoqua who lived between Table Mountain and Saldanha Bay.

From there the song spread up the West Coast to where, with the annual winter migrations, it was carried into the interior. Centuries later, in a rock shelter deep within the Cederberg, one of their slender descendants painted a sailing ship in red-ochre. Who knows what he knew of ships and sailors, or if he'd ever been to sea himself?

Perhaps he wanted to be empowered, or desired the power of the ship? If the eland represented a trancing shaman, as the lamb did the sacrificial Christ, then the ship may have represented the place from which the Light Ones came?

It could be a metaphor for some place across the Great Water; the place to which Autshumato—that half-brother they called Herry—had been taken a century-or-more after Almeida. It had all happened a long time ago, when the Dutch and English first arrived—but she couldn't recall those details now.

Sonja stood by the well, looking at the outgoing tide, reflecting on the tragic crossbow incident. She now knew of two men killed on these southern shores: both shot through the throat. One White, the other Black. Both bloodied and silenced forever. For Camões, she recalled, such encounters "put a tongue in silent stone."

She walked back to the car, reluctantly, following the last rays of light down the footpath. She'd be back in the morning.

Five centuries before, when Almeida's weather-beaten compatriots returned, João da Nova built a pole and cloth *ermida* for private prayer, making Mossel Bay the first place of Christian worship in southern Africa. Nova is also credited for the discovery of St Helena Island, having supposedly sighted it in the southern Atlantic on the feast day of Helena of Constantinople. The date was 1501–2 and the "African Century" had just begun.

19

The history of Portuguese expansion is at once very well known and hardly known at all.
Malyn Newitt, *History of Portuguese Overseas Expansion* (2005)

Sonja's third disappointment came while driving across town. Taking a wrong turn, she found herself on the outskirts of Mossel Bay and unable to find her way back in the dark, even with a road map. The one she had was waterproof, untearable, and supposedly child-proof —yet she struggled to fold the damn thing away. *Why*, she wondered, *why is this always harder than ironing a shirt?*

She drove on, into the darkening countryside, toward a lead-grey horizon until the first guesthouse appeared. A rustic setting was not part of her plan but, too bad, she wasn't going back before dawn. A beachfront B&B would have been nicer. Well, tomorrow then.

Her hosts were an Afrikaans couple who ran a modest guesthouse to help subsidise their family farm. The wife came from a long line of *melkboers* who'd worked the land for generations; her husband from a seventeenth-century carpenter who, shipwrecked and sick with fever, had been left behind when his co-survivors walked to the nearest trading station. The Cape was then several dangerous weeks away and, if you survived, Sofala a few months' trek. Four centuries later, the Pereira family still fell on hard times.

After a traditional casserole dinner, Piet Pereira invited Sonja to see his livery yard. He'd built the stables around a knarled old pepper tree, using local sandstone for protection against the hot dry wind. Now a retired horse-breeder, he kept a stallion called Abrantes and several schooled mares.

The mix of manure and fresh sawdust brought back memories of a playful but short-lived childhood. In her experience, stables offered a safe haven far from the regulated world of adults. But it was here that she first witnessed, with mixed emotions, the awesome chaos of male sexuality.

She wished she could return to that interior world of lost innocence, to the secret world she'd created as a child, to a world that was never supposed to change.

But she knew that wasn't possible. She could never step into the same river twice—as Heraclitus so well observed—since its water and its bed were forever changing. As had her life.

Sonja returned to find liqueurs being served in the library and was soon engrossed in books on horse breeding and shipbuilding. Here she learnt that Andalusian horses were taken by Portuguese explorers as gifts for African kings.

Furthermore, by the fifteenth century, horse ranching developed on the fertile floodplains of the Tagus where the ground was soft and the grass grew tall. The new shipyards were situated on the other bank, to the west, at Lisbon itself.

Lisbon was then a cosmopolitan centre for Genoese shipwrights, Jewish financiers and Venetian bankers; for Castilian mapmakers and spies, German traders and travellers; Muslim mercenaries and pilots, neo-Templar knights and Benedictine monks; Flemish court painters and, of course, for all those slaves from Africa.

As Europe's first modern nation-state, Portugal emerged against a background of political intrigue, rebellions and executions. The word *Portugal* itself came from the Roman *Portus Cale* or "hot harbour", today Oporto, the once beautiful port where the Douro greets the Atlantic. The Phoenician-Carthaginians introduced the inhabitants to the sea and, slow-slow, like the Douro, the famous Portuguese seafarer was born—first as a fisherman, then as a seaman.

Her host bade goodnight as he passed the library. She gathered a few books and retired upstairs herself. It had been a long day.

Her attic room was minuscule and bedecked in a pink floral print. The curtains, lampshades and upholstery were made of a demure fabric which, she felt, was unsuitably girlish for a Thirty-something visitor. Nevertheless, she had a flushing toilet, a hot bath and clean sheets—weekend trips could be worse. She undressed, washed, and slipped into her T-shirt, then eased between the sheets. Reading in bed was an indulgence she'd perfected since childhood.

She settled on Malyn Newitt's *History of Portuguese Overseas Expansion*, thumbing through it like a detective thriller, uncovering mysterious secret societies, political conspiracies, conflicting religious loyalties and perilous journeys—but no romance, sadly. The fortunes of the Avis (and the downfall of their rivals), had all the trappings of a great Sophoclean tragedy. Her thumb soon struck gold.

Europe's merchant-nobility was obliged to pay heavy poll-taxes for merchandise transported along Eurasia's millennia-old trade routes. These routes belonged to a hazardous caravan network using mules, camels and slaves to convey goods high in value but low in bulk—including Chinese silks and porcelain, Indian cottons and pepper, Indonesian cinnamon and cloves. Such trans-continental routes also served as conduits for trade, language, technology and ideas.

The main route ran from the Chinese capital of Chang'an, Xian today, via the Himalayan valleys and Afghan passes, and then across the Arabian Desert to the port-cities of the eastern Mediterranean. Exchange along this line of oases, once known as the *Khurasan* or "Old Silk Road", prepared the ground for varied beliefs; blending cultures and promoting religious tolerance. All the great conquerors of Eurasia—Alexander, Genghis Khan and Timur—used this route when crossing South-Central Asia.

With Islam's expansion came ever increasing transit costs; making the import of luxury goods unduly expensive. Moreover, ceaseless interference by jealous clans made it a risky journey for merchants, pilgrims and slaves.

As a consequence, Muslim traders established an alternative route over the *Bahr-al-Hind*, the "Indian Sea", so that most Mediterranean ports were soon receiving seaborne goods from Malacca, Cambay, Ormuz and Kilwa. They came via the port-cities of Basra and Suez and then overland to Baghdad, Damascus and Cairo. In return, Arabs offered wool, linen, ivory and amber. She knew the fragrant gum resins of Arabia—frankincense and myrrh—had been long used for perfumes and medicines.

Odd, she felt, *that such facts should stick in my mind.*

The centre of this vast commercial network was the Middle East, not the Mediterranean. Europe was of limited value, Portugal merely peripheral. The West had no raw materials or manufactured goods to offer India, China or Japan—except imported gold and silver.

Without Africa's gold there could have been no grand sea-trade in the sixteenth century and, subsequently, no modern world economy. According to Newitt, the adverse balance of payment was a decisive force in Europe's development.

She read on. With the fall of Constantinople in 1453, the bulwark protecting Europe from Mongolian, Arabian and Turkish invaders finally collapsed. Constantine's "New Rome" had given Western society a millennium in which to establish itself but, as the maritime empire fell, so did its command of the Mediterranean environment.

Built on both sides of the Bosporus, Byzantium-Constantinople-Istanbul was a strategic East-West link. Furthermore, once in Turkish hands, the Ottomans severed Europe's access to the land, sea and river routes of the east—including Poland, Russia, India and China.

The Ottomans' only challenge came from the wily Venetians who, now better placed than other city-bankers in Europe, were quick to monopolise the transit of oriental goods into the Mediterranean.

In response, Europe's Atlantic cities considered an entirely novel approach, the circumnavigation of Africa, although no one yet knew this would prove to be the world's largest continent. Their unilateral effort would put Lisbon at the helm of history.

African history had already entered a new phase in 1415, when Portugal seized the port of Ceuta, the "key to the Mediterranean".

Ceuta secured Europe's first foothold in Africa, as Rome had done with Carthage one-and-a-half thousand years before, and guaranteed Portugal's safe passage though the unpredictable Strait of Gibraltar. At its narrowest, the strait was only eight miles wide.

Sonja understood the need for expansion, that was the easy part, but what impact it had below the equator was unfamiliar territory.

So, did Portugal really push Africa into the modern age?

The capture of Byzantine Ceuta was a turning point in Portugal's own history since, on his return, Prince Henry established his famous school of navigation at Sagres—launching an era of modern global traffic. For this purpose the Avis family controlled the institutions of state, including the ever-powerful Order of Christ, and monopolised all African trade and exploration.

She paged on to learn that Prince Henry died in 1460, aged 66, and that his nineteen year old grandnephew, Crown Prince João, was made responsible for exploring West Africa's coastline. Burdened by the problems of succession, little progress was made until João himself became king and resumed the quest for an Atlantic passage. He immediately set about building a fort on the Mina coast to secure his source of gold. And so *El-Mina*, "The Mine", became Elmina.

Despite claims to the contrary, the young king was optimistic that Ptolemy—the great geographer and astronomer of Antiquity—had been mistaken when he described, firstly, the Indian Ocean as a landlocked Emerald Sea and, secondly, that Africa and India were connected by a bridge of land. Like his grand-uncle, João held to the classical idea of a Great Outer Sea surrounding the world. Greek and Arab geographers had seen this as a vast river, circular in form, encircling all Europe, Asia and Africa. Like Henry, João believed the Indian and Atlantic met below the southern pole-star and, by the mid-1480s, felt the terminal point of Africa lay within his reach.

To this end João elected Bartolomeu Dias, a schooled mariner and minor noble at court, to sail around Africa's southern extremity. Dias would open a sea route to the vast riches of the East...

Sonja went to sleep and dreamt of sailing toward a Stormy Cape in a caravel with torn sails. Her brother, Bart, was on deck and called to the herdboys along the beach. They, in turn, leapt about and shouted back in a language she couldn't speak yet understood: "Go home, you, or be killed!"

It was a recurrent dream, and with this scene she'd always awake. Wet with anxiety.

20

*O salty sea, how much of your salt
Are tears of Portugal!*
Fernando Pessoa, *The Portuguese Sea* (1934)

She rose to find the morning sun far above the horizon and, by dead reckoning, guessed the sun's arc would cross the bay until it reached the distant Outeniqua mountains—known to the local Quena as the "place laden with honey".

She had observed the opposite in Cape Town, where the sun rose behind the mountain and set over the sea. It felt as if she'd driven across an entire continent in one day. Her journey seemed to draw attention to the world anew, to a world as it was and not, not at all, as she had expected it to be.

Now, delivered from her dream, she prepared herself for an easier day and went downstairs. It promised to be a beautiful weekend.

After a lazy breakfast on the enclosed stoep, she joined her host for an outride to Smuggler's Cove. She rode a forward-going mare called Cintra, an honest Cape chestnut, and raced toward the rugged sea cliff. The fresh air and adrenalin rush was a heady mix, especially in gallop, and for a while she tried to forget about Henry's Navigators, the Knights of Christ, Almeida, and the tales of the abeLungu.

In the back of her mind, nevertheless, she thought about the things Portugal wanted besides sugar, salt, slaves or ransomed nobles—and all that gold from Africa.

✛   ✛   ✛

It being a Saturday, the museum bustled with children from the local community. It was also the weekend after National Youth Day, and she wondered what advantages today's youngsters enjoyed compared to Jason's generation. Presuming township life was any better now?

For these youngsters, as much as for herself, the most prominent exhibit was a full-scale replica of Dias's caravel. She first mistook it for a model, being so small, and feared for the sailors fingering their way around Africa's uncharted profile.

The museum was decked with coloured murals depicting famous ships and seafarers—most notably portraits of Dias and Gama. There was no mention of Almeida.

Wandering on, she saw how the Age of Discovery was shown as a period of naval reconnaissance and territorial acquisition, as well as one of technological and scientific invention. At the time, political boundaries and economic frontiers were redrawn while the latest maps reflected the bold onset of universal history. These so-called Discoveries marked a threshold in human history.

True, the *Descobrimentos* not only marked a transition in European societies, but for African, Asian and American populations too. Our world was one of intersecting histories or, as Greg Dening succinctly put it, "a world where no one escapes the history of the Other".

On her way out, feeling disappointed, she paused at Reception to ask if the museum's library was open to the public. Without a reply, the sullen-faced attendant phoned for help: '*Meneer s'n besoeker is hier.*' Sonja had no choice but to wait.

Minutes later a man in khaki approached, somewhat over-heartily, Sonja felt, as if he'd been expecting a visitor. Introducing himself as Henk Cloete, Chief Curator, he invited her for a behind-the-scenes tour. He was a colossal man with a coarse beard and curly hair.

He led her to a utility area behind the museum where doors were labelled *studio*, *store*, *classroom* and *kitchen*. The walls were adorned with cheerful children's paintings of white-sailed caravels amid calving whales, the name of each child emblazoned in proud letters. Henk's office was in the far corner, with a most spectacular view of the bay.

Here he offered her a plump leather armchair, near the window, and then went to fetch coffee from the kitchen. She heard him speak Afrikaans and, moments later, came back with two heavy mugs. She wondered how best to ask about the library…

Passing her a mug, he explained how their caravel was built for the fifth-centenary celebrations, having sailed down from Lisbon. He also thought she should know it weighed a hundred tons. In turn, she thought it better to let him talk. Which he did.

On his desk stood a model, a perfect miniature of the caravel.

While he elaborated, she scanned his office: model ships, nautical charts, marine photos and an antique sea clock. Henk was clearly obsessed with maritime exploration and, like her brother, she could imagine him mending toy boats built with sucker-sticks and entangled twine. Or drawing desert island maps with buried treasure.

However, unlike Bart, Henk talked incessantly and knew more than she'd ever find in the library. So she let her coffee stand (it was *oplos* anyway) and posed a question to help give him focus:

'What were the Portuguese looking for? Was Dias told only to find a sea route, no more, or was he searching for something else?'

'Gold to exchange for spices and Christians to fight the Moors,' laughed Henk, swinging his boots under the glass tabletop. 'Spices included drugs, perfumes, cosmetics and dyes; but the master spice was pepper, of course. A shipload of pepper made a man very rich, mega-rich, like a billionaire today.'

Henk's demeanour did not fit the role of curator. Not to her mind, not according to her experience in Holland. He looked more like an environmentalist or wildlife conservator.

'At that time the word "Indies" referred to all land around the Indian Ocean, from East Africa to South Asia. It was a source of great wealth and wisdom. Fat João II wanted both—'

'—both wealth and wisdom?'

'*Ag nee,*' he laughed, 'both trade and crusade! Dias left with the best charts and latest equipment, though all we know comes from a single source, a chronicle by João de Barros. It's a shame Dias's own log never survived.'

Sonja nodded. Henk's thick accent and occasional use of Afrikaans demanded extra concentration. Despite her Dutch.

'Anyway, Dias commandeered two caravels and a broad-bottomed boat for extra supplies. He took a padre, three stone crosses and, I think, four female hostages from Guinea. Dias was told none could be set ashore until he passed the furthest landfall made by his *voorganger*, Diogo Cão.'

Four abducted women? She knew he'd also taken eighteen of the finest horses as gifts for black kings, "so that they might think well of us and give us samples of their land's products".

'The hostages were dressed as messengers from João's court,' added Henk, 'and returned as interpreters, *vertalers.*'

Henk spoke confidently, mixing the museum's official version with his own. He had created a story that was both formal and colloquial. However, it soon dawned on him that she was not the journalist he'd been expecting.

'You're not from the *Herald*, *is jy?* Then you aren't here about the coin smuggling?'

'No, I'm a historian researching VOC documents at the archives. Sorry, did you have another appointment?'

'*Ja*, but they said she'd be here and now she's not,' he laughed, 'so you can stay. Let me talk to Reception.'

Henk reached for the phone and called Sullen Face, leaving Sonja to mull over the four abandoned hostages.

Those solitary women, left alone, now they had reason to be sullen.

Cão sailed up the Zaïre, twice, searching for Prester John in the Old Kingdom of Kongo, now northern Angola. His captains reached the Yellala cataract, over 180kms upriver, where they chiselled their names into the rock. Determined to succeed, they persisted overland by dragging their longboats behind, until it dawned on them that this Black Potentate was not the same as the one in Christian legend.

Cão then sailed back to the open sea and continued south, reaching present-day Cape Cross on Namibia's coast.

'It's a dangerous coastline with heavy swells, fogs and maddening doldrums. He died out there—I think from malaria, the *mal de mer*—though some have other theories about his disappearance. Anyway, after his death the crew turned their boats and sailed home. Already since the days of Hanno, the imperial Phoenician Argonaut, the West coast below the equator was known as "the white man's grave". And before that, as punishment for raping a Persian girl, king Xerxes sent a Carthaginian prisoner...'

Henk reached for his copy of *Dias and his Successors* and, finding the passage, read with the measured voice of a radio-announcer:

'Cão disappears entirely from history. It seems inconceivable that, had he returned to Portugal, no reference should survive in chronicle, document or tradition. The writer is Prof Eric Axelson,' added Henk, 'our best historian on Portuguese explorers in southern waters.'

Mendle had mentioned Axelson too, and so the hint of conspiracy caught her interest:

'Was Cão perhaps killed?'

'*Ja well*, it's what they say, but the surviving records are unreliable. They were written for Portugal's own pomp and glory.'

Raising his mug to salute Dias's portrait, he added:

'They kept their secrets *dig en donker*, recording things to mislead their rivals.'

'I'd heard these were distorted to confuse others.' She was tempted to ask more, but said instead: 'First tell me about Dias.'

'Dias counted four crosses as he sailed down the coast, further and further south into unknown waters.' Henk dunked a rusk in his mug. 'The proper word is *padrão*, but I speak no Portuguese.'

She found his honesty refreshing. He had no professional piety or pretensions, and pronounced foreign words with naive imagination.

'The Portuguese also used names like *Baia dos Tigres*.'

'But there are no tigers in Africa?'

'*Ag nee*, that's 'cause the wind forms tiger-striped patterns on the dunes. Dias came ashore at *Golfo da Conceição*, with its flocking birds, but it actually means "Bay of the Whales", *Walvis Baai*. It's where you find your diamond smugglers today—though that has nothing to do with our Smuggler's Cove.'

Sonja smiled, giving him a wide berth to continue.

'Anyways, Dias sailed on until he reached *Angra das Voltas*, that's Luderitz today.'

'Isn't that where a second hostage was left on the beach?' she asked, having read of their miserable plight the night before. Unknown women were better treated than men; or so their captors prudently reasoned. After which no one heard from them again.

'*Ja, reg*. The first was probably dropped off after the Kongo. All we know is that the third died before she could be put ashore. Anyhow, the ships sailed on, but even here historians are mistaken. Dias was not blown out to sea by accident. Instead, he got tired of beating against the wind and so set a course for the open sea.'

'Wait, did Dias make this passage seem more treacherous than it really was, or were his successors genuinely mistaken?'

'Both, and they were misled. The last stretch down to the Cape is dangerous, genuine, but they made it sound worse and then ended up believing their own propaganda—'

'—which is why Francis Drake called the Portuguese cowards and described the Cape of Good Hope as the most beautiful he'd seen on his entire circumnavigation?'

The clock struck. Her time was running out.

Henk continued:

'Dias tacked out to sea, *wyd en syd*, until he found favourable winds to take him back. He did not see the Cape, being then too far south, but reckoned it lay behind him when, after three weeks, he saw land again. The land now lay to the other side of their ships and followed an eastward trend. But it was only after he saw Table Mountain itself, on his return, that he renamed it *Cabo da Bôa Esperança*, the Cape of Good Hope.'

'I thought king João renamed it?'

'*Ja*, some say the king chose the new name—'

'—as you said, Portuguese history is a patriotic praise-poem.'

'Like that one-eyed poet who praised it from beginning to end.'

'Camões, yes, from the founding of a nation to the establishment of an empire. It's their foundation myth of social origins and political conquest.'

'Like our Groot Trek festival in 1988,' said Henk, 'when Afrikaners celebrated the origins of their *volk en vaderland*. My family didn't get to go as we were Coloureds—but the Nationalists made it across the country in a symbolic ox-wagon...'

'In 1988 Edward Said also claimed that "historical writing is, after all, writing and not reality". But wait, go back, what happened *after* Dias left Mossel Bay?'

'Dias was certain India lay before him and wanted to follow the coast. Already from the north-east came a warm sea-current...'

Henk fell silent. She waited, raising her mug for a sip. It was cold, but that didn't matter now.

The clock ticked on...

He reached for Axelson's book, saying the crew threatened mutiny after three days and refused to sail any further. Hungry and short of supplies, they returned to Kwaaihoek where Dias took leave of his last cross. Enrolling himself anew, Henk cited Barros:

Dias bade farewell with as much grief and sorrow as if he was leaving his own son in exile for ever, remembering with what peril to himself and all his company he had journeyed so far, solely to this end, since God had not granted him success in his principal design.

God wouldn't grant success when he came so close, why?

Henk wiped his mouth with the back of a hand. His creased palm looked like a parchment *mappa mundi*.

'Wait, what else did Barros say about this "principal design"?'

'*Ag nee*, Henry, Dias and João looked beyond the immediate riches to be found in Asia. They all shared one design—a *geo-political design*, says Axelson—to find this independent priest-king in East Africa.'

'So their first ambition was to counter the spread of Islam?'

'*Ja*, right, in a war fought across the Mediterranean—from Lisbon to Jerusalem—Prester John was their best ally.'

Saturated by the subject, she stared out the east-facing window, wondering what became of the last Negress put ashore at Algoa Bay. The grief-stricken woman had been left with instructions to enquire after a Black Potentate named John—and was never seen again.

21

'Say, have you ever wondered what we remember when we die?'

'Y'mean what we remember about those who die?'

'No, not *your* memory of me, but *my* memories of the life I lived? For instance, do my memories exist after death?'

'I don't think of dying,' said Sonja self-consciously, aware of their age difference, 'well, that's not entirely true, I'm actually obsessed with Almeida's death and what keeps his memory alive. Gaspar's too. But for now, all I want to know is what happened to Dias?'

'Ah, Dias, poor man, he felt humiliated. He never received the gifts lavished on his predecessors, nor was he promoted. Instead, he was told to confer with the royal mapmaker, Bartolomeu Columbus—yes, the brother of Christopher—and made to supervise shipbuilding for a new expedition. Faster caravels were needed.'

For all she cared, caravels were like castles mounted on a barge, a floating fortress sent to sea... When she drew her mind back, Mendle was talking about the dossier, adding:

'A decade later, demoted in rank, Dias served as a pilot on Gama's historic voyage, but he only sailed as far as the Cape Verde Islands. In 1500 he sailed across the Atlantic with Cabral's fleet, reaching the shoulder of Brazil in the company of Gaspar. Approaching the Cape a comet streaked the sky—a heavenly portent, they thought—after which a rogue wind sank four ships. Dias and his men were never seen again. Ironically, Dias died at the Stormy Cape he himself named Good Hope.'

'Then Dias never found this Prester John?'

'Ah, alas, no, but the quest for him began centuries before. Even if most serious scholars say he never existed.'

'It's only a legend?'

'You should know, Sonja, nothing is mere legend, fact and fiction co-exist in history.'

'But surely we should draw a line somewhere,' she blurted, 'aren't academics meant to distinguish between these two, as we do between belief and evidence?'

'Actually, yes, we need to find a synergy between them, as we do with imagination and experience. We need both to make sense of life, and to give meaning to the world in which we live.'

'Well,' she added, 'truth isn't about any observable correspondence or coherence with reality, as there's no consensus between knowledge and the world. Truth is constructed, we-make-the-world-so.'

'Whether constructed or not, we shouldn't believe in something we can't look at critically. Otherwise we have no way of giving value to a battle, a romance, a legend, a quest, or say, a Test cricket result. Ha, we should always test ourselves and the world around us.'

She brushed a loose strand from her face. He continued:

'To speak the truth does not assert anything significant about the world, but merely indicates that there is a general agreement about its nature, which we then accept as true. Take some maps of the world, say, where the Arabs or Chinese depict south on top. To us it seems as if Africa has been turned on its head. That's because we accept Ptolemy's projection of north above, with east to the right. In Judaic and Christian maps, however, east was on top to show the Paradisal source-of-the-world, with Jerusalem at its centre, hence the word *orient-ation*. We orientate ourselves by facing three things: the rising sun, the open sea, and the way forward. This is the result of ceremonial, conceptual and navigational necessity. Seen from outer space, of course, our planet has neither a top nor a bottom.'

She smiled, gently humoured by his explanation.

'Truth is something we only imagine,' he added slowly, 'it's what Coleridge and Keats called the "truth of the imagination". Truth is what we choose to believe in, not because of any accord between fact or reality, but because it comes from experience and imagination.'

'That's a useful definition for history too.'

'What, that history has no accord with fact or reality?' he teased.

'No,' she answered, with a broadening smile, 'that history offers a plausible accord between our experience and imagination.'

He beamed.

They were sitting at his favourite table in the Museum Café. Outside a couple of vagrants begged spare change from passing tourists. She'd heard Jason call them *bergies*, an historical term for those seeking overnight shelter on the slopes of Table Mountain. They too lived on the heath, like medieval *heathen*.

Sonja had invited Mendle for lunch, saying she wanted to discuss her research project.

He now waited, patiently, wondering when or even if she would raise the issue. She turned her attention from the homeless:

'No, visiting Mossel Bay had nothing to do with my VOC project. Well, maybe it did, in a r-ro-rou-roundabout way…'

It was a clumsy start. She stumbled on, about her mid-summer break and that she'd soon be going home.

'Ah, but you're in the southern hemisphere now?' he tested.

'I know, which is why my world feels upside down.'

She wanted to visit the coast of Algarve, where her parents had a second home, and then return to Leiden to rethink her project. Who knows, after reassessing her commitments, she may even visit Cape Town again. But for the moment, she'd lost interest in the VOC and had to be far tougher on herself if she was going to complete her research in time.

'I'd rather examine Portugal's expansion in Africa, providing I can find better sources. But that wouldn't interest a Dutch museum.'

'It depends on the purpose of your enquiry,' he said sageously, 'is it poetic or academic?'

'Purpose? I simply want to know what happened.'

She felt impatient.

He rephrased:

'But is your purpose poetic or historical?'

'Is there a difference? I thought poetry and history make the past intelligible,' she said, trying not to sound academic, 'aren't they part of the same evidentiary procedure whereby we narrate events?'

'Then you think fictional and historical writing are equal?'

'Yes, but only because they're both indispensable... equally useful and equally useless,' she stated, not sure of his argument.

'Aha, but for Aristotle poetry is superior as it tends toward the philosophical. For him poetry expresses itself in universals; whereas history deals only with particulars.'

'Oké... so what?'

'Well, if we understand this to mean that poetry is worthier than history because it speaks of what must be true, rather than what is true, then historical writing should be regarded in more poetic terms. Briefly, Aristotle's *Poetics* argues that poetry expresses our highest human values; whereas history only tells us what we once were, not what we may yet become.'

'Meaning?'

'Classical historians believed it was their duty to ennoble the world through poetry, and this assumption influenced how Western history would be written for the next two millennia.' He paused to rest. 'Say, shall I continue, or do you already know this?'

'It's good revision, Prof,' she smiled, 'so don't stop now.'

'Well-then-fine. Aristotle's philosophy of history shaped the entire concept and methodology of Western history from Antiquity to the Renaissance, even up to the early twentieth century.'

'Is that why Plutarch, Shakespeare and Woody Allen wrote death speeches for their heroes?'

'Ha! They all want a better world for the living. Likewise, Camões wrote for the purpose of improving the moral marrow of his people. His epic was supposed to teach people by way of good examples, but as Portugal's past included such sullied episodes, he had to recast these to support the assumption of divine historical purpose. Camões and his contemporaries thus welded fact and ideals to embolden the sons of Lisbon.'

'And so?' She knew there was a point to all this.

'If poetry speaks of what *should be true* rather than what *is true*, then the reasons for the embellishments around Almeida's murder become apparent. Historians wrote what they thought we needed to know.'

'In other words, the official chronicles don't include profound esoteric insights, unless these fitted a programme of moral development.
In short, bold histories maketh bolder nations?'

'Exactly! Camões—that alembic of a man—wrote about Almeida's
historical acts while not, take note, not mentioning anything esoteric.
Such things were kept secret, since it was dangerous to stray from
official Catholic values. Chroniclers only selected what was thought
beneficial to their patrons or to a willing audience.'

'But I thought Almeida was assassinated for disloyalty; because he
betrayed something secret or confidential?'

'Yes, but look at the events. Death by assassination or suicide is an
ignoble way to end a glorious career—it's an insult, as fighting men
prefer to die by the enemy's sword.'

'As a woman, I'd rather flee.'

'Heroes die on battlefields. Cowards are dishonourable.'

'Personally, I never thought of death as honourable, or heroic.'

'Almeida was denied an honourable death because he supported a
mutiny. Ah, alas, today he's remembered as the victim of an ambush,
killed by half-naked men with throwing sticks. But what they fail to
mention is the role of his assassins and how it stopped him gaining
power back in Lisbon.'

'You presume they knew?'

'Of course they knew! There was enough intrigue about Almeida's
succession to make even the most loyal chronicler suspicious.'

'Well, aren't the discrepancies suspicious?'

'No-fine, the best scholarship on the subject remains inconclusive.
Eric Axelson spent his life—from the early 1930s to the late 1990s—
uncovering old documents, presenting new insights and, ultimately,
lifting the veil of secrecy around the Portuguese mission in Africa.
Despite his research and the work of other experts, the subject is still
shrouded in mystery.'

'Well, to be honest, I don't know how to begin or where to start.'

Impatience stirs an endless restlessness.

'I believe your trip to the Dias Museum was a good start. But what
you really want to know is whether or not they had a secret mission.'

'No, all I want to know is *what* made it so damn important?'

'Aha, then start at UCT. The University of Cape Town has a fine
collection of rare books and manuscript maps. But don't expect any

primary material—lost or forgotten—as Axelson would have found it himself. The best you can do is follow his trail…'

She not only felt herself slipping between critical and conventional readings of history; but sensed her research had become an *à la carte* affair. She had already started choosing what to read and what to leave out…

'Always start at the source,' he suggested, 'start with the authentic artefacts, with documentary evidence, if there's any to hand. If not, make use of a good library. But remember, unlike the ancient tablets of Moses, African history is not carved in stone.'

She laughed at his banter:

'Well, as Einstein said, "why remember facts if you can make use of a good library".'

He loved their silly repartee. She was smart and shared an uncanny resemblance to his wife, Ruth, who'd been a linguist at UCT. The two of them played word-games during her illness, particularly when she could no longer walk.

'Well,' said Sonja spontaneously, 'I want you and Jason to come over for dinner, this Friday, before I leave.'

She reached for the bottled water in her bag. Plucking his beard, he uttered cautiously: '*Oi-vey.*'

'In fact, Prof, I want to cook an exotic dinner… that's if you're brave enough to try my Indonesian *rijsttafel?*'

He was fond of Sonja and wanted to say how much he'd miss her. Instead, the best he could manage was:

'As the ageing Einstein also said: "Our problems cannot be solved at the same level of thinking as when we created them!" Now go see what you can find at UCT.'

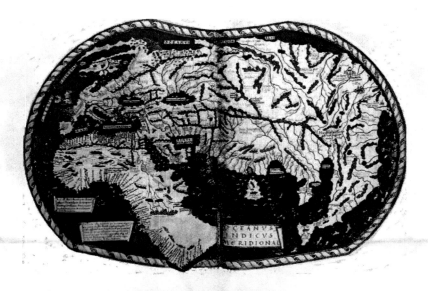

22

A map is not the territory...
A Korzybski, *Science and Sanity* (1941)

'A map is just a model for a place,' said Jason emphatically, entering the university in step with Sonja. They had agreed to meet in front of UCT's Centre for African Studies and, heading for the manuscript room, passed the Martellus Map on display. It was only a facsimile, he observed, as the original was in the British Library. She recognised the creamy parchment from the dossier, but still couldn't figure out why it had been included.

'It's the first map of the Cape after it was rounded by Europeans,' he added, 'showing places Dias named along the coast. It was part of a much larger *mappa mundi* by Martellus Germanus, a German pilot, who sailed for the Portuguese. Here, look at the legend.'

Grinning with satisfaction, he pointed to the faded brown text:

ultima navigatio Portug. AD 1489

Sonja stood behind him, reading over his shoulder, as a wave of students swept down the passage. Place-names were set inland so as not to obscure the bays and rivers needed to fix a relative position at sea. She followed the names down the elongated coast until, dramatically, the southernmost corner careered into the scroll-like frame.

The heel of Africa did not fit.

'What happened here?' she asked, incredulously. 'Was Martellus unable to adjust his measurements when Dias returned?'

'That's what I thought too, but knowing how well they kept their secrets, I reckon the distortion was deliberate.'

'Deliberate, why?'

'To mislead others, so they'd lose their way in the icy waters of the southern Atlantic.'

He flashed a wry grin.

'But wouldn't it endanger Portuguese ships too, unless the map was meant to be a fake?'

She looked about for a place to sit.

'Sure, breaking into the ornamental scroll was a deliberate act of forgery and intrigue—one done by Bartolomeu Columbus.'

'What? The one Dias had to confer with?'

'Yes. Some say João II told Bartolomeu to record Dias's sightings. Others say Bartolomeu was at court when Dias reported the latitude. Whatever, Bartolomeu was the king's confidant on cartography and had access to the royal treasury.'

'So he knew the true reading taken by Dias at the Cape?'

'Right, around 35 degrees, but given as 45 on this map.'

'But why, why exaggerate the distance?'

'It's no exaggeration, it's deception—'

'—to deceive who? Merchants from Venice? Flemish spies?'

'Actually,' he whispered, 'to deceive the Spanish!'

'You mean the Portuguese?'

'No, it was done to gain Isabella's support for a westward voyage. Remember, once Dias opened the Eastern passage, enthusiasm for an expedition across the Atlantic waned—so Columbus had to revive interest among his Spanish patrons. Look here, see, not only has Africa been extended south but Asia also enlarged to the east. Thus navigation around Africa appeared much longer and the Indies far farther than either really were.'

'Wait, how on earth did you come across this c-co-conspiracy?'

She stumbled, trying to find a way around the word.

'Not me, Arthur Davies, in the late 1970s, when he saw that details of Dias's voyage had reached Venice within a year—and were then used by Martellus in this map.'

'How, via the Columbus brothers?'

'Yes, Davies noticed that Bartolomeu had taken a tracing to Seville, where he and his penniless brother extended Africa 45 degrees to the south—thus breaking into the frame.'

'Speaking of size and scale, would a cartographer ordinarily make such a serious miscalculation?'

'Definitely not, at least not according to Davies, who regarded this as the essential evidence of deception. And then there's the date—'

'—date?' Her feet ached, she desperately needed to sit.

'The legend says 1489 when, in fact, Dias was already back that December. So within a few months the king had been betrayed and a Spanish queen deceived.'

'If it's a facsimile, then where's the original?'

'Dunno. Perhaps lost when Sagres was sacked—'

'—or destroyed in the great fire of Lisbon?'

'Either way, the one in the British Library is a fake.'

'Unbelievable, and you know I dislike conspiracies—'

'—but it's true, the BL map *is* a fake,' he lowered his voice, adding, 'and Yale University has the *original* tracings.'

'You mean Bartolomeu's tracings of the original map?'

'Yes, and they're four times the size. Martellus's map is only one-quarter in scale. So who has the best copy—BL or Yale?'

'Wait, did Martellus know Columbus?'

'Who cares,' he whispered confidently, 'Columbus's discoveries are far too over-rated, anyway. He spent five weeks at sea before sighting land, sure, but Gama was out for three months all in all. Now that's navigation!'

'It seems Columbus discovered something he wasn't looking for,' reflected Sonja, 'something Europeans didn't yet know existed, well, at least, not officially.'

Jason took out his notepad and flipped to a page of scrawled text. He spoke with the soft Nespresso voice of George Cluney:

'Columbus was a conniver, a rogue, an opportunist who Davies summed up best, saying: "Such alterations were all to the advantage of Columbus, unscrupulous no doubt, but they earn our admiration for the sheer audacity of the great discoverer." How damning is that!'

She'd be damned if she had to stand any longer.

✠   ✠   ✠

Seated at last, they studied the maps in comfort while the librarian carried their requisitions back-and-forth.

The first was a hand-coloured woodcut by Sebastian Münster, also a German, who's *Africa Nova Tabula* was one of the earliest separate maps of Africa. His concept of a unified Africa, including Arabia Felix, was heavily indebted to Ptolemy.

'Arabia Felix,' Jason explained, 'translates best as Fortunate Arabia or, simply, as Milton preferred: "Araby the Blest".'

'So Arabia and Ethiopia not only produced great coffee, but were part of the same region?'

'Actually, they were regarded as the same continent.'

Münster's map was also in the dossier.

'The Ptolemaic view,' he added, 'still dominated cartography after printed ones were reproduced and distributed.'

'Gutenberg, 1440s, and like Münster, also from the Rhineland?'

'Right,' grinned Jason. 'Furthermore, printed maps were made for collectors and so lagged behind manuscript maps used by explorers. Printed ones were often out of date by the time they went to press.'

She looked up from the folio, settling her gaze on him:

'Surely new information could be printed faster? How could a hand made map be more up to date than one hot-off-the-press?'

'Because these portolans were produced in secret,' deflected Jason, self-conscious under her stare.

'I see factual places co-existed with fabulous dragons, serpents and elephants.' She recalled her favourite lines by Jonathan Swift:

So Geographers in Afric-Maps
With savage Pictures fill their gaps
And o'er uninhabitable Downs
Place Elephants instead of Towns.

'It's a b-br-brief synthesis between reality and fantasy... Jason, sorry, you continue.'

Sonja knew she talked too much, especially when she felt nervous. She leant back, opening the space between them.

'Maps were regarded as state secrets,' he resumed, 'and mapmakers worked under pain of death should they lose or disclose anything.'

'Then translators and cartographers shared the same disposition— both were entrusted with royal secrets?'

'Right, now check this out,' he said, pointing to the map. 'The Cape of Good Hope was rounded decades before but is *not* identified here, and this edition was printed around 1545.'

'That's half-a-century later. Why?'

'Because decorative maps were theoretical, like this one, and not intended for practical use. They represent what collectors wanted to imagine, rather than what explorers already knew.'

'And?'

'Look, the Mountains of the Moon and the Great Lakes are there. So too is the source of the Nile and the realm of Prester John. Here, can you see it, between the White and Blue Niles?'

She leant in to read:

Hamarich Sedes

Prę te Johan

His realm was there, yes, so too were today's Morocco, Senegal, Mali, Guinea, Chad, Sudan, Somalia and Kenya. The furthest realm south was Quiloa—apparently an Old Portuguese name for *Kilwa*.

But something else caught her eye. It was a strange, seated giant on the West coast, above Cameroon, watching a ship sail for the Cape. A figure with only one eye, a monstrous giant, Monoculi?

'It's the one-eyed Cyclops from Greek mythology,' explained Jason. 'Camões recast him as Adamastor, the Guardian of the Portal and the one who challenged Gama when he reached the Cape. The name *Adamastor* means "untamed" or "wild" and embodies all the hostile and vindictive character of the Cape of Storms.'

23

Jason sat staring at the illuminated map on his liquid-crystal screen. There it was, *Ifriqiya*, crescent-shaped and without a southern tip.

African cartographers were indebted to Claudius Ptolemaeus, the illustrious scholar from Roman Egypt, whose *Geographia* was still the oldest surviving atlas of the world. Unlike his peers, Ptolemy filled his maps with mythical and theoretical concepts, including the fantastic inhabitants of a once fabulous and savage Africa.

Admittedly, the land beyond the sand-blown deserts existed merely as an idea, a concept, which from a Mediterranean perspective, had been merely imagined before it was explored.

For Jason, viewing it from the south, the continent's size and shape remained unimaginable. He knew that *al-Sahara* meant "the Desert" and Kalahari "land of Thirst", but what lay between them was something he knew little about. While born-and-bred in the South, his knowledge of the continent north of the Limpopo was embarrassingly limited—ancient Arabia included.

Jason lived downtown, alone, in a comfortable loft-apartment. The interior was designed around a glass wall, a tall Palladian window, through which the afternoon light now spilled. From here he could watch the sun sink behind the mountain.

Arranged against this view were three comfy Art Deco chairs and a matching low-back sofa on which Sonja now reclined. Along the far wall, stacked on sleek ashwood shelves, stood his music magazines, sound equipment and vintage vinyl collection. Suspended above the room were the coolest halogen lamps she'd ever seen. It was a perfect catalogue studio.

Located by the docks, the triple-storied building once served as an export warehouse and proudly retained its handsome wooden floors, timber beams and spacious interiors. The building had Union-Castle Line pedigree stamped all over it.

Sitting in front of the huge arched window, she paged through a book on the Zimbabwe Ruins while he travelled further back in time. Herodotus, he learnt, had said Africa was "washed on all sides by the sea, except where it joined Asia". Africa's name came from the Latin *Aphrica* (sunny), giving rise to the word *Ifriqiya* among the Arabs and, in turn, *Africa* among the Europeans. First applied to Tunisia, it came in time to refer to the entire continent.

Furthermore, the term had its distinct geographical and racial uses. First, it divided north from south, physically, setting pharaonic Egypt and the Maghreb apart from a Sudanic-Ethiopian interior. Secondly, racial stereotypes separated white from black; the lean, light-skinned Moors from their plumper Negro counterparts.

Related to this was a further division among the inhabitants of the narrow savannah; stretching from Mauritania on the Atlantic coast to Abyssinia along the Red Sea. According to Homer, this was where the "savage" and "fabulous" denizens dwelt, at opposite ends of the Sahel Belt, and where the sun set and rose each day.

Africa's ever-differing inhabitants were spread across the entire continent, west to east, and down as far south as they could multiply. Beyond this lay the infamous *Terra inhabitalis*.

Historically speaking, the continent was already split before the impact of colonialism. Before Francophone West Africa and British East Africa divided traditional territories between them. Previously, Arabic and Bantu expansion split the continent across the middle, into a Northern and Southern realm respectively. Africa, he reflected, was cut down the Rift Valley *and* across the Sahel Belt. Furthermore, the early human migration corridor—the "Out of Africa" passage—followed the lush Afromontane forest and grassland, especially along the shoreline larder of East Africa.

Conceptually, Africa was also split in the European imagination. Jason recalled how Professor Malvern van Wyk Smith had not only demonstrated this via the ethno-geographic clichés of Classical and Renaissance scholars; but showed how it became the most enduring concept dividing Africa itself—until well into the Apartheid era.

It was a concept that possessed Prince Henry and the explorers of Atlantic-Africa, a concept that transformed the Discoveries into a quest for individual spiritual enlightenment. The Cape of Good Hope was thus a threshold on the North-South axis; and the portal between a modern West and an ancient East.

Likewise the once impassable Pillars of Hercules formed a portal in the North, between the Old World and the New. These two portals —Gibraltar above and the Cape below—reproduced the concept of an intermediary Africa.

Jason decided to re-read Van Wyk Smith's essay on Adamastor, especially the section about Portugal's presence in Cape waters. The book lay at work and, given Sonja's interest, he'd pass it on before she left South Africa.

She now chatted to Mendle on her mobile, saying something about "complex plots as the hallmark of conspiracy theories".

He clicked for traces of the Terrestrial Paradise in Africa, only to discover that the maritime heritage of Antiquity had been lost in Europe for fifteen hundred years. The geographic renaissance began with the diffusion of Ptolemy's *Geographia* in the fifteenth century, earning him the reputation as "the Aristotle of Maps".

The first printed maps of Africa appeared after 1450 and were produced under Ptolemy's name for the next two hundred years. The Ptolemaic discourse prevailed well into the eighteenth and nineteenth centuries, long after explorers returned to contradict the existence of Ptolemy's fanciful rivers, mountains and tribes.

The notion of an earthly Paradise had its modern recurrence: Jason knew of Dutch Voortrekkers who, on their slow migration toward the Promised Land, used their bible-maps as travel guides. *Nylspruit* and *Nylstroom* were bitter reminders of their belief in having found the *Nilus*, that "Great River of Africa", although none imagined how far south they actually were or, more significantly, that their bibles could ever be wrong.

Moreover, the Nile was seen as coming from the "Mountains of the Moon", a mountain range considered to be the southern extremity of Africa. Here a high-lying lake, cut off from the world, became the chosen place of the exquisite priest-queen Makeda, known to all as the Queen of Sheba. Today the sacred mountains are identified as the Ruwenzori of Uganda.

Jason returned to the home page, then went to re-set his Nespresso machine. Sonja was on her mobile phone, strolling about aimlessly, intrigued by his eclectic lifestyle.

On the ashwood shelves were a row of locally made Dinky Toys, a set of Bitterkomix and Zapiro cartoons, as well as a collection of old Broadway musicals. Against the opposite wall hung a series of black and white torsos by Robert Mapplethorpe.

Jason brought her a *Decaffeinato Intenso* and mouthed, "drink now". She sipped while Mendle talked. True to its name, the coffee had an elevated acidity.

Once settled again, he saw how Ptolemy assigned zodiacal rulers to various countries: Egypt, the country most emblematic of all Africa, was under the influence of Gemini, a constellation governed by the twin Mercury—the "One who Mediates"—and had a dual persona like that of Hermes, the Egyptian Toth and, later still, the Christian Raphael.

Jason stalled. The young god was a two-headed bisexual and a symbol of unity? Such geomancy was too much for him.

He clicked to the next link: "Gemini and Mercury recreate unity, reconcile duality, counterbalance opposite principles and regenerate natural energy. They are variants of the Ouroboros and the Phoenix, twin symbols of change, continuity and recurrence in Africa."

This perspective had held Africa hostage to an alchemical-heraldic language. While Renaissance scholars reassembled the legacies of the Greco-Roman and Judeo-Christian world, Europe's intelligentsia did little to encourage an understanding of cultures foreign to their own.

However, the people of Africa saw themselves differently, of course. The legacies of Jenne and Timbuktu, including the court-universities of Mali, Meroë and Khartoum, demonstrated how different they all were. From the royal palaces of Benin to the rock-hewn churches of

Ethiopia, from Sîwa to Camissa, Africans had no more in common than did the Saxons and the Slavs.

While she ambled around on her phone, Jason followed a new link. According to Greco-Roman beliefs, the world's natural order was reversed below the equator. Traces of this remained in the ancient "Crossing the Line" festival at sea, when sailors swapped places with their officers. Anthropologists saw this as a re-enactment of the ever-popular Roman festival, Saturnalia, in which slaves and their masters exchanged roles for a day. As a rite of reversal at the winter solstice, it marked a transition from above to below and from light to dark.

Jason's head swirled with all the intricate, interconnected detail... geographical, historical, alchemical, zodiacal. He logged-off for more Nespresso and, glimpsing at his reflection in the window, thought to himself: *I'm a real Clooney on a bad hair day.*

24

The discovery of the New World marks
the end of fabulous geography.
Joseph Conrad, *Geography and some Explorers* (1925)

It rained all night, once more, forcing Sonja to cancel her morning out-ride. The horses remained in until it cleared, around midday, but by then she was busy in her kitchen. She had *rijsttafel* to prepare—the way her mother always made it.

Mendle had a bad start too. His Landi was towed away after both cab doors jammed, leaving him to face the rain afoot.

He was obliged to ask for a lift, so Jason dropped by before dinner, gleefully demonstrating his new GPS as they zigzagged across town. In the end three kilometres became thirty minutes.

Sonja's front door stood ajar, expectantly, as they trudged in with wet shoes and dripping coats. Mendle greeted her with a light kiss, affectionately, while Jason merely handed her their farewell gift. She stammered, awkwardly, hands full, as Jason followed Mendle to the oil heater, pressing mud into the old style Indo-Kelim. Oblivious, the men chatted as she took their dripping coats off to the bathroom.

Despite her apartment's northern orientation, with a timeless view of the mountain, the open living room required additional heating: not only against the cold but for those winter afternoons shortened by the Table's shadow.

'Shall we?' she beckoned, once they were warm and dry.

She'd decked the table with a liver-tinted cloth to offset the delicate lake-green porcelain hired for the occasion. Offering a Heineken with the meal, she explained the origins of *rijsttafel* and the ingredients of each accompanying dish.

Filling their plates, she explained how the Dutch procured China's secret recipe for porcelain while others guarded Holland's monopoly with Japan. Drawing on past experience, she added:

'The emperor of "Cipango", as Marco Polo called it, closed all his ports for fear the Sea Barbarians would disrupt Japan's stable society. Dutch merchants were permitted to settle on the artificial island of Deshima, where they remained for two centuries, supposedly without women, and connected to the mainland via a narrow wooden bridge. This was only possible after they displaced the Portuguese from the bay of Nagasaki. The discovery of Japan was, ironically, Portugal's last great maritime achievement.'

'Ironic, indeed, as the Portuguese also introduced our first world-economy,' added Mendle, reaching for the chicken sate.

Jason stretched across too.

Sonja's father had studied economics before entering the Foreign Service. His first three postings were to the embassies in Colombo, Jakarta and Tokyo. It was in Indonesia that he met and married an independent Dutch doctor, then barely thirty herself, who'd survived the Japanese POW camps as a child.

Sonja's mother never spoke about the war, not directly, well, except once, when she refused to drive a Japanese car on holiday. Then, after Sonja's father retired, she swore never to go back East.

'An eastern voyage symbolised one of spiritual enlightenment,' said Jason, helping himself to a large dollop of peanut sauce. 'For this reason Portugal's exploration from West Africa to East Africa, from the shores of the Atlantic to the Indian seaboard, was far more than a mere adventure in maritime geography. Dias found not only the end of a continent but crossed a great divide, breaking into a new world, from a savage West to a fabulous East.'

'Ah, exactly, it was Gama who provided the proof and Camões the symbolism. It was a profound rite of passage, from hardship to riches and, finally, from damnation to salvation.'

Serving herself, she asked: 'What happened to those who failed?'

'Sadly, fulfilment alluded many. The archetypal southern voyager, Ulysses, floundered in sight of his goal, as did Moses. In fact, the Italians compared Dias to Moses as both were "permitted to see but not enter the Promised Land". But to understand the Portuguese, we must first review the Mediterranean idea of a divided Africa where, for instance, Homer describes two sorts of Ethiopians: those who dwelt where the sun rises, and the other where it sets.'

'Is that why the Empire's Sun Never Sets?' tested Jason.

'Ha! no,' responded Mendle, much amused, 'not according to a young Kenyan schoolboy who thought the sun never sets because God couldn't trust the Englishman. According to him, "God needs to see what the white man is doing".'

'Quotable!' mumbled Jason, his mouth full of rice.

'Aha, and probably true. Such ideas are often rooted in reality and powerful enough to influence the experience of several generations. Homer's reference to Africa's dark-skinned inhabitants, for example, was no doubt based on what early travellers reported on their return. These ideas informed how Africa would be imagined for the next three thousand years.'

'The eastern inhabitants were associated with the Nubian Nile,' clarified Jason, 'while those beyond the Sahel were either dog-faced or had eyes on their breasts. Headless savages—'

'—yes, but we needn't labour the point,' said Mendle, setting a new course. 'Indeed, the fabulous highland inhabitants and savage forest dwellers are at the root of Africa's geo-ethnography. In East Africa, the reputation of Meroë was extended to include Aksum, Christian Abyssinia and the realm of Prester John; King Solomon's Ophir and Sofala; Zimbabwe and Monomotapa...'

Mendle paused for another sip of beer, wiping his beard:

'Ptolemaic maps depicted a paradisal kingdom between and, later, below the branches of the Nile. Accordingly, the Terrestrial Paradise lay within Prester John's realm and was accessible from East Africa's Barbaria Coast. The route started out from Massawa and Mombasa but was, over time, relocated to Zanzibar and Sofala. Remember, Mozambique was the southernmost limit of the Muslim world—an alarming prospect for Christians still fighting an African Crusade!'

✠　✠　✠

After dinner, and lots more beer, Sonja unwrapped their farewell gift: a beautiful illumination produced the year Dias rounded the Cape.

'The fabled creatures of Africa,' clarified Jason.

She looked again—beasts and wild men dwelt in primal bliss on a verdant riverbank.

'The *Nilus*,' he added.

Sonja nodded, if only because the crocodile and lion were emblems of Egypt and Ethiopia. As for dragons, well, she hadn't seen one yet. Although she had seen a chameleon, her biggest ever.

But it was the monstrous human that now transfixed her.

'Hey, the mythological Wild Man, that hairy giant from medieval European literature, art and pageantry. He mirrors our irrational fears—like the uncultivated forest dwellers—and embodies all that those of the Latin rite detest...'

Jason cut her off: 'With more and more voyages across the Atlantic, these fears were projected onto Africa and the Americas. Reports of cannibalism were far more an invention than a discovery.'

She held her tongue, not sure about cannibalism in Africa.

'Astonishingly,' he pressed, 'it was already evident in the invention of the Aethiops, that degenerate inhabitant of southern Africa.'

'Marco Polo—' she started, but he continued:

'The Aethiops embodied the attraction and revulsion felt for pagan and animist Africans, challenging conventional boundaries between male and female, animal and human, sexed and sexless—and even between fact and fiction.'

She tried again—saying that Marco Polo wrote—but Jason had too much momentum:

'The ever-growing popularity of printed travel books resulted in an exaggeration of local fact—reproducing the vulgar and reiterating the fantasies of a well-domesticated audience at home.'

'Marco Polo described the Wild Man as—'

She got no further.

'As Calvinists,' Jason drilled, 'most visitors to the Cape failed to comprehend the complexities and subtleties of an indigenous culture. In their view, the Natives had no redeeming belief in salvation or religion, and were therefore seen as animals. As animals, they could have no soul and were thus damned. As the damned they had no right to life, land or livestock—even to their own labour.'

'Ha,' interjected Mendle jovially, 'most visitors saw the Native as inhabiting two stereotypical worlds. First, he lived in Rousseau's Garden of Eden where life was pastoral, tribal and stagnant. Or, alternatively, he survived in a Hobbesian state where life was nasty, brutish and short. I say, even if things were new, all things in Africa are extreme!'

'Like Titus van Bengal,' she began, recalling his horrendous ordeal under the VOC, 'his life certainly was brutish and short.'

Her research into official records and informal testimonies had led her to the case of Titus van Bengal, a slave from north-west India, who killed his Cape master at the behest of a lover.

Reluctantly now, she explained:

'Titus van Bengal and his alleged lover, Maria Mouton, the wife of a Dutch farmer, were arrested and brought to the Castle for trial. Maria was half-throttled, scorched, and then strangled to death... Titus was impaled. First hoisted onto a pointed stake and left to die in the sun, his head and hand were then cut off. These were displayed as gruesome totems on a pole bordering his master's property.'

'Jesus, how perverse!'

She went on, although the violence sickened her:

'Companje officials took perverse pleasure in punishing dissidents. Punishment was not only brutal, but had to be symbolic—as with the murder of Almeida. Titus survived for two days, his ruptured bowels causing excruciating pain, yet humouring those offering arrack to dull his agony. When warned not to drink too much, in case he should fall, he replied that there was no danger of that as he sat fast enough. Titus died vowing never to trust a woman again, never, neither in heaven nor in hell.'

Jason grimaced: 'As above, so below. Below the equator is where the natural order was reversed and, here, cruelty countered virtue. That's why the ancient world invented the antipodes, so Africa could counterbalance Europe—'

'—so what are you, African or European, cruel or virtuous?'

'I'm your black-and-white-half-brother,' he said in jest, 'your Half-Blood Prince!'

THE

PORTUGUESE IN INDIA

ALM YDA

Being a History of the Rise and Decline of their Eastern Empire

FREDERICK CHARLES DANVERS

VOLUME ONE

John of Avis — Philippa of Lancaster
PORTUGAL — ENGLAND

Henry the Navigator
1394 - 1460

FRANK CASS & CO. LTD.
1966

Vasco Gonçalves de Almeyda
and Mécia Lourenço (wife)
were governors of Prince Henry
and donated a chapel at Tomar
for his private use (1426).

PRINCE HENRY
OF
PORTUGALL

CEUTA

DOM HENRIQUE OF PORTUGAL.
From an Old Engraving in the British Museum.

P.

Being

FR

Departure

25

The journey of a thousand miles begins with one step.
Lao-tzu, *The Way of Lao-tzu* (c.531BCE)

Sonja caught the first bus down to the sun-drenched Algarve, where fragrant coastal vegetation brought back fond childhood memories.

Her parents had bought a ramshackle cottage when property was still cheap, or more correctly, before local farmers realised the real value of their land. These foreigners were crazy, the old folk thought, to spend such well-earned money buying useless ground. That was all decades ago when Lagos, so-named for its lagoon, was little more than a lazy fishing village. Her parents now spent six months a year in their renovated *casa de campo* at Luz, just outside Lagos, in what was once a rustic village. Here she planned to catch up on her reading and, if time allowed, would visit Sagres. It was only 30kms away.

Prince Henry's School for Navigators, perhaps the first in Europe, had been destroyed in 1587 when Drake plundered the Algarve; after Queen Elizabeth had asked him to "singe the beard of the Spanish king". Almost every chart and manuscript—the correlated knowledge of Greek, Jewish and Arabian scholars—was either stolen or burnt. Drake, a zealous privateer, was intent on wrecking supply lines to the Spanish Armada, and so sacked Lagos in the process.

It was from Lagos, not Sagres, that Henry launched his expeditions to north-west Africa. It was from here, too, that he first sailed across the Strait to capture Ceuta. He and his brothers—that "Marvellous Generation" as Camões called them—used the conquest to prove themselves worthy of becoming armed knights. As a result, Henry became governor of the Land of Fès. He was then only twenty-one.

While the Moors praised Algarve for its hospitality toward travellers of other faiths, Barbary corsairs raided Algarve's coastal villages and sold their captives as slaves in Morocco.

In Islamic held cities, from Toledo to Jerusalem, the People of the Book were allowed to practise as fellow monotheists—providing they paid their taxes. But now the Algarve belonged to Henry.

Although there wasn't much left to see at Sagres, Sonja wanted to re-experience the place—like a pilgrim to a shrine—making the trip a symbolic gesture rather than a destination.

It would be telling, she felt, to compare Ponta de Sagres with Cape Point—the north-westerly *Promontorium Sacrum* with the south-eastern *Prasum Promontorium*—two of the world's most revered Capes. Situated at the extreme ends of their respective continents, they were seen as thresholds to the open horizon. Symbolically, the Algarve had been opened by the Knights Templar, the Cape by the Knights of Christ.

So, waiting for the bus the next morning, she closed her eyes and imagined the squalling gulls, the towering cliffs, the pounding waves and restless ocean where one world ended and another began.

✝ ✝ ✝

'Let's not forget,' said the well-built stranger across the table, 'that the title *o Navegador* was the invention of a romantic Englishman from the nineteenth century. Infante Dom Henrique was neither a navigator nor an explorer, but an ambitious and pragmatic baron of medieval Europe.'

'Well, I think the same Englishman said Prince Henry led Europe into the modern world. But I guess you see that differently?'

He returned her smile as he removed his navy jacket, adding:

'Dom Henrique's navigators replaced the knights of Charlemagne as the voyages of discovery replaced the crusades. In my view, yes, they shared the same vocation.'

'So Henry was not the ascetic scholar of historical writing? Not even a great visionary?'

'No, he has been many things to many people and his reputation a common miscalculation among those who saw British imperialism as succeeding the Portuguese overseas empire. Today his achievements are viewed more modestly by revisionist historians—'

'—revisionist?'

Her new acquaintance was fortyish, unshaven and heavy-set. His acquired demeanour blended seamlessly with the pousada's classical décor. They sat at the best cliff-top terrace in Sagres. He clarified:

'I mean those historians who have re-evaluated the Infante's role—'

'—and who say his role as the lone pioneer is over-rated?'

She was aware of the debate.

'Over simplified, yes, and exaggerated—'

'—and the role of Sagres?'

'They say Sagres was not responsible for the advanced research, technological innovation and systematic exploration that Henrique's enthusiastic biographers have us believe. Nor were the Discoveries done by individuals or families acting on their own. In short, Portugal and England did not make world history in isolation. The Eurasian seafaring nations ushered in an epoch of universal history *together*, yes, as part of a multinational enterprise that involved the East as much as it did the West.'

The pousada was hot, noisy and over-crowded. Sonja had met her companion by accident when an inexperienced waiter offered them the same table. The handsome stranger hung his jacket over a chair and beckoned her to stay.

Vladimir "Volodya" Vasilevsky was the youngest son of a naval officer, a former captain in the Black Sea Fleet, and one who grew up in the nostalgic grandeur of Sevastopol—then a closed city.

During the mid-1990s, when Russia's military presence relaxed and Ukraine's industrial privatisation soared, the family was quick to make its first millions. His disillusioned father, Dimi, had skilfully combined black-marketeering and the *blat*-system (an inconspicuous social custom where favours are returned for goods or services).

The five brothers played an elusive and entrepreneurial role in the region's pervasive shadow economy. They'd come of age as New Russians after stepping out of a shadowy past with a dubious fortune. As one of Moscow's wealthy *byznesmeny*, Volodya bought and sold real-estate—including a cliff villa on la Côte d'Azur which, he added casually, had once belonged to an Arabian sheikh. He was now on his way to view a luxury yacht in Lagos.

He'd been obsessed with maritime history since childhood, and the acquisition of a forty metre Parsifal would fulfil his dream of sailing the Mediterranean. He smiled, flashing three gold crowns, admitting he was no more a sailor than Prince Henry ever was.

To fit the part, however, he wore a French sailor's shirt with cream and navy stripes, rolled-back sleeves, and flashed a bulky gold watch the size of an anchor. Despite his arrogant trappings, Volodya was an engaging stranger with a maverick sense of history. He spoke fluent English (but with an affected French accent) and invited her to stay for lunch. The next bus was an hour away, so she agreed, if only for the seafood salad and one glass of wine.

After placing their order, Volodya explained how the Avis became Portugal's first naval dynasty and, with the capture of Ceuta, set out to control the caravan routes across North Africa. But the vastness of the Sahara and the ferociousness of the Berber tribesmen disrupted their attempts to reach East Africa.

'The Avis were obsessed with the idea of an independent Christian king, a potential ally who was neither Orthodox nor Catholic, nor had any allegiance to Rome or Constantinople. Dom Henrique's mother, Philippa of Lancaster, thus organized the siege of Ceuta and financed the first expedition to find this potentate, but died of plague before her ships could sail.'

The apologetic manager came with a gratuitous carafe of wine, and offered Sonja the first available table. But by then her companion was explaining how Henry's parents had united Portugal and England, and so she chose to stay to hear him out:

'If an alliance was to be secured, it would be below the Sahara, and Henrique's avowed ambition was to find this *Preste João*. As Administrator of the Order of Christ, he had both the opportunity and the means to do so. Not bad for a man of twenty-six.'

'I knew about his role and that he started young, but not that he was Grand Master for forty years.'

'A lifetime as perpetual governor and administrator of the Order. *Bon!* He submitted himself to the Benedictine code with body, mind and spirit. He practised celibacy and, occasionally it seems, adopted a hair-shirt and gravel bed.'

She noticed Volodya's voluptuous hands, sensual and heavy, with a ring of green agate beside a thin gold band.

'Did Prince Henry and Dias share the same "principal design"?'

'*Da*, both dedicated their lives to this quest. They were schooled in the Order of Christ and prepared themselves mentally and physically for their tasks—'

'—doing what, exactly?'

'Dom Henrique studied the works of geographers from around the Mediterranean. He was interested in foreign languages and distant peoples and, whenever possible, conferred with travellers on science, astronomy, mathematics, shipbuilding and, ultimately, the content, size and shape of Africa. This formed the basis of his library—'

'—so there *was* a library at Sagres, after all?'

'*Da da*. The Dom expanded the fishing village and built a school for navigation, preparing his captains for what they could encounter on their travels—outwardly and inwardly.'

'You mean their training was both physical and mental?'

'Yes. Portugal had been a nation of fishermen and merchants who hugged the coast of Brittany, Flanders and England, staying clear of the open sea. So preparations had to be psychological too—'

'—how then?'

'Well, it's not easy to say, as their training was shrouded in secrecy. We have to look elsewhere for examples.'

'Such as?'

'*S'il vous plaît*, first try your salad,' he requested, refilling her glass. 'A psychiatrist from Dornach, Dr Georg Unger, prepared American pilots for unknown conditions in Space during the 1960s. At the time, no one knew if we could digest or metabolize in outer space, let alone remain rational in orbit. His task was to train astronauts to control their thoughts in an environment without light, sound or gravity. Under these conditions our involuntary response is to sleep or lose consciousness. To this end, Dr Unger developed meditative exercises to prevent the loss of conscious control. Cosmonauts underwent the same training in our Soviet Space Programme.'

What Sonja knew was garnered from Algarve's travel websites:

'They say Sagres was as important to the early Age of Discovery as Cape Canaveral has been to the Space Age?'

'*Voilà*,' he replied smoothly, 'Dom Henrique taught his captains to overcome irrational fear and to trust their perception of reality. They had to prepare themselves for months at sea in a vessel no larger than a harbour tug—which is difficult to appreciate in a world of giant oil tankers and colossal skyscrapers, or today's NASA space stations.'

'I heard about a mission back in time to find the fossil-remnants of our solar system, to the asteroid belt billions of kilometres away. It must be the longest journey ever undertaken.'

He nodded, looking up from his local adaptation of *surf-n-turf*.

'It's all about making the right preparations.'

'Oké, but is there any evidence for this?'

'No, not that I'm aware of, although neurobiologists have since demonstrated how the human nervous system can be programmed, or rather re-programmed, by regular and repeated exercises. They've been able to show how the body can be taught to react *differently* to the *same* stimuli and, ultimately, how this can be made to induce an altered state of consciousness—'

'—as in chanting or a mantra?' inserted Sonja, recalling what she'd heard about trance-dance among the Bushmen of the Kalahari.

'Yes, though biochemical reactions are something else. There the danger of substance abuse is real, something you don't have with the repetitive physical acts of fasting or prayer.'

'And one for which you need a disciplinary code?'

He removed his signet ring, letting it roll across the table.

'Please, Mademoiselle, allow me a secret before you depart. I may call you Mlle Sonja, yes? *Bon*. While Sagres may not have produced any sophisticated science, it did serve as a school for a select group of neo-Templar initiates. Their studies were surrounded by secrecy as pre-Christian texts, especially those of Greek and Arabic origin, had long since been suppressed, officially. Books on esoteric philosophy were rare and, inspired by Templar ideals, anyone found withholding such knowledge had to be punished.'

'Yes, so I heard.'

26

Geography is the mother of history.
Nowhere in the world is this more
powerfully illustrated than in Africa.
Ali Muzrui, *The Africans: A Triple Heritage* (1992)

Why do men insist on talking louder when car radios have volume control? Sonja had difficulty hearing Volodya as his Lexus hurtled out of Sagres. It was an obsidian black monster with a dashboard fit for an astronaut. Yet it had the Goldilocks of Aircons; ensuring the cab was never too hot or too cold, but always just right.

She'd accepted a lift to Lagos, after all, when he offered to explain Prince Henry's devotion to esoteric Christianity.

'Some call this Grail Christianity. The Order of Christ was the semi-secret successor to the Knights Templar which, as I'm sure you know, had been founded in Jerusalem after the First Crusade.'

'Yes, under Count Hugues de Payen. They pledged themselves to a life of chastity, obedience, poverty—and to protect pilgrims visiting the Holy Land?'

'*Sine proprio*, properly translated, means to be without property or personal possession—*not* a life of poverty.'

'Yet they did become rich?'

'Their wealth belonged to the organisation, not to any individual. The Order of the Temple consisted of knights, soldiers and padres who were permitted to receive gifts: estates, credit papers and tax exemptions. Hence their fortunes. As warrior-monks they belonged to chapters spread over all Europe—including Portugal, where they received land and market rights. The founding of the Templars and the birth of Portugal were one and the same enterprise. The Order provided the inspiration and structure, the Avis its administrators. Thus to be Grand Master was a regent's duty and privilege.'

'Wait, did the Templars receive local support in foreign countries like, say, today's UN forces in Central Africa?'

'*Nyet*, they were never a peacekeeping force within a civil war, but a liberating army with its own geo-political agenda. However, rivalry between the new knights slowly eroded old notions of chivalry.'

Volodya's enigmatic reply raised new questions, but she thought it best to remain focussed. Other issues would have to wait.

'Following fierce opposition, the French monarch and French-born pontiff destroyed the Templars,' continued Volodya with a curled lip. 'They dispatched an Order of Dissolution and had the vast fortunes of the Templars confiscated. It was a night of bloody murders...'

He eased his Lexus through the bends.

'King Dinis, nicknamed the "Poet King", secretly supported the Templars and sent them into hiding; making a show of seizing their possessions. He then requested permission to form a new Order to protect his court and the church in Portugal. When his request was finally granted, Dinis reinstated his knights as the Order of Christ, returning their possessions. However, this merely deepened divisions between Roman Christians and Grail Christians.'

'I thought the Templars protected the pilgrim routes; particularly those overrun by bandits and mercenaries?'

'Partly. They also drove back the Infidel. Like a Jihad, the Crusade was a holy war.'

'Personally, I have difficulty with any war being just.'

'Justified or not, wars served to conquer, occupy and convert the Other, or to confiscate their land and wealth. The crusades were no different.' He revved the engine. 'On the other hand, pilgrimages were done for penance, pardon or patronage.'

'I'm not sure those distinctions mattered back then: war was war and religion was everything you could do in God's name.'

'Perhaps, but crusaders and pilgrims were away for years, travelling on often dangerous roads. They required safe transport, decent food, secure lodging and—like tourists today—insurances for their money. Remember, paper money was only introduced in the mid-1600s.'

'That's because leather money was edible. A century before, during the Spanish siege of Leiden, the starving citizens boiled their money to eat as food. Paper, obviously, was less tasty.'

He nodded, his lip curling into a smile: 'Paper itself was introduced via the Templars when they returned to France and, by 1320, was being produced for books in the Rhine Valley, first at Mainz, which prepared the way for the modern printing press. Europe's first paper books, however, were made two centuries earlier in Moorish Spain.'

Eager to hear more about the Templars before time ran out, she redirected: 'So how did they finance themselves?'

'Merchant-banking. They had contracts with Sephardic Jews who introduced techniques for accounting and granting credit. At their height, the Templars controlled thousands of depositories between Lisbon and Jerusalem and their commercial investments yielded vast profits—unlike voyages of exploration. An expedition to West Africa cost a fortune, and could bankrupt a family if the cargo was lost. Similarly, the Order of Christ financed the exploration of Africa's Atlantic coastline.' He pointed out to sea with his forefinger, leaving a blue smudge on the windscreen. His Lexus bolted down the N125.

'So the Crusades helped pay for the exploration of Africa?'

Nodding again: 'Trade, rather than exploration, caused the demise of the Order. The temptations were too great: gold, ivory and slaves yielded substantial profits abroad and secured generous grants back home—like land, status and access to court. They say Europe's first public auction of slaves was held in 1444, here at Lagos, though rampant abuse made the Infante forbid the kidnapping of blacks within a decade. Although responsible for the initiative, he failed to foresee the consequences of slavery—'

'—personally or historically?'

'Both, apparently. Astride his horse, Dom Henrique witnessed the separation of a mother and child when sold into slavery. He sat there without doing anything. They say he was impassionate; but then one Arabian horse was worth a dozen African slaves. *Tochno!*'

'So, he traded with West Africa to find East Africa's shores—thus making the Bulge pay for the Horn—but, but what did he hope to find there?'

Volodya squinted at the light glinting off the sea: 'The Infante's first and foremost ambition wasn't commercial, but mystical. His mission, you understand, was linked to the Sangreal legend and the quest for Preste João. He believed the empire lay in Abyssinia, later known as Ethiopia, and so sent explorers by land and sea. Alas, the alliance was never made. Instead, the Portuguese secured strongholds along the coast and usurped economic control.'

'They planted crosses to encircle a heathen Africa—like the Circle of Islam around Cape Town today.'

'What circle is this?'

'It's an invisible ring of shrines, or kramats, protecting the Cape.'

'Like the airborne icon above Moscow before the German retreat of 1941. Or the intercession of our Vladimir Madonna when it saved the city from Tamerlane and the Tartar hordes.'

'Anyway, I recall something about a trade depot in Benin, Nigeria, where locals said a paramount lord inaugurated chiefs by bestowing on them a helmet, a sceptre and a cross. Without these no one would accept the chief as a legitimate ruler. Yet none saw this Ogané as he was always screened by colourful silks and patterned bark-cloth; from behind which only one foot would be revealed during an audience. He has since been identified as the Oni of Ife—'

'—and since a similar story came out of Ethiopia,' cut in Volodya, 'they assumed he was the same potentate, in fact, that he had to be Preste João himself. And only twenty moons away to the east.'

'Why, why not the northern warrior-king of the Songhai Empire?'

'Sunni Ali? *Nyet*, he was Muslim, as were most rulers in the Niger crescent. No, they wanted this Ogané to be the true Prester John. So, studying their maps, Portuguese geographers calculated the distance to be around three hundred and fifty leagues farther, about another 1500kms inland. But navigating the vast rivers that flowed west until their boats could go no further, and then hiking through the endless rain forests to reach the mountain lakes in the east, was considered far too dangerous a way to travel. Instead, they thought it safer to start in Cairo disguised as a Muslim and, via local contacts, to follow the trade route down to Abyssinia.'

Seeing the Lagos turn-off and not wanting her companion to take her home, she hurriedly asked:

'Wait, you mentioned someone travelling inland?'

'*Da*. Tales of Ogané rekindled the hope of finding Prester John. So much so that the following year, 1487, when Bartolomeu Dias set off to round the Cape, Pêro da Covilhã left via Cairo to find an overland route. Years later, after a tiresome journey, Covilhã arrived at the court of Emperor Eskender in Yeha, near Aksum. Curiously, *Iskindir* is the local name for Alexander and taken from the Persian *Iskandar*. Eskender was a true Seeker of the World.'

He stopped to check: '*Ça va, Mademoiselle?*'

'Good, please go on.'

'Despite Eskender's majesty, Covilhã found little resemblance to the flamboyant legend. So, too, had Marco Polo two centuries earlier. After completing his travels in South Asia, Polo identified this *Praeti Jiani* as one of the magnificent Mongol Khans—with whom lived the Manichaeans and the Nestorians, the so-called White Christians of China.'

'So Covilhã travelled to India and Ethiopia, rather than China, to find this Christian Pope and Emperor?'

There was more on this "secret agent" in the dossier. She'd double-check his details later. For now, Volodya was still talking:

'Covilhã was well cared for but not allowed to leave Eskender's court. Three decades later, in 1520, when Padre Francisco Álvares arrived, he found Covilhã there with an Ethiopian wife and family. Covilhã was praised for his intelligence, wit, and his role as advisor— as too for being a skilled translator. He told the visiting padre that the nearby temple had once belonged to the Queen of Sheba. So far as I know, Mlle Sonja, some stone ibex heads are still visible there today. Covilhã died a few years later, having never seen his wife in Lisbon again, or the child she was carrying thirty years before.'

Volodya himself had not seen his ex-wife for over a year. Roxalena was a top fashion model from Kiev who now kept their apartment in Paris, supposedly pursuing a career as a designer. Rumour had it that her new *beau* was an Italian football star.

Reaching the Lagos bus terminus, Volodya pulled over. He offered to drive her back to Luz, but she charmingly declined, claiming that she preferred to walk as it was such a beautiful evening.

And so the Russian Bear and his Goldilexus disappeared into the balmy streets of Lagos.

27

And thus thou art a lasting monument:
To all who came and loved thee, and then went.
W. Angus Kingon, *Address to Table Mountain* (1926)

The sky was a pale coral-red and the air languid with the odour of
wild geranium. Now, back from Sagres, she joined her parents for an
apéritif under their giant cork tree. Beyond the garden, long shadows
traversed the weathered cliffs while, below, youthful waves eloped
along the beach. She felt like a child again.

As children, Sonja and her brother had spent their holidays playing
on the covered terrace, imagining ancient galleys passing out to sea.
Behind their renovated house was a derelict lime-kiln that served as a
white-washed shipwreck. Bart assumed the role of a peg-legged pirate
with stolen treasure (from their mother's jewellery box), while Sonja
played his pursuant, a sea-rover aptly called Captain Chase. She was
supposed to catch him, like the leaping herdboys in her dream, while
his limping leg would heal miraculously.

She'd ridden a school-horse on the Serra de Monchique that week,
up among the clumps of eucalyptus, from where she could view the
lilting landscape with its low horizon. She missed her brother now,
despite all that had happened, and decided to visit him in Holland.
She'd not seen him since Christmas.

A soft familiar voice brought her back to reality. Her mother was
talking about the drug-rehab clinic in Leiden:

'Bartold readmitted himself last night, but this time we won't help
him. Not again.'

They seemed to live in opposite worlds: one filled with darkness, the other with light. Her brother with depression and intense elation, her parents without indulgence or any self-pity. Oddly enough, Sonja had always been closer to her father.

'Wherever the posting,' he would say, 'people speak of Terrestrial Paradise as if it were somewhere in their own country. It was always beyond the desert, over the mountain, across the river or on the other side of the forest—but never where I went on tour!'

'But what if you'd found it?'

'*Mijn Zonnetje*, like any addiction, it's a quest for the sublime, one which evades those who seek it. I'm afraid there's no realm of joy in our world. Not even for Bart.'

Sonja could sense she was back in their world. Small things began to irritate her, irrationally and unfairly, from her mother's reactionary views to those irresponsible waves running along the beach.

Their house faced the arc of the sun, peering over Algarve's brow at a seemingly endless Atlantic. Perched on the edge of a continent, Portugal itself looked out to sea.

Ancient Phoenicia, which pre-empted the Discoveries, had faced west too. Likewise, the powers that succeeded Portugal also faced the Atlantic. The open sea was where the sun went each day and to the West, similarly, lay Holland and England's future...

She'd lost all sense of time, home and future, temporarily, at least. She now lived in the present, moment to moment, as on a journey, recalling a jolting bus with ragged fields and tangled figs, a forlorn fishing village with its sand-swept streets and white-washed homes; and, finally, the rock-strewn peninsula with its prisonlike Fortaleza. Here was a weed-ridden *rosa dos ventos*—for measuring wind direction, or so she'd heard—and a new auditorium. The latter once served as the stables, but was closed for the day, as was the tasteless cafeteria.

The most memorable moment was her walk to Ponta de Sagres where she stood, alone, except for some solitary fishermen, watching the gulls swoop over a swirling sea. She'd felt the same solitude at Cape Point. Both promontories were monumental in their rugged grandeur, and both were Holy Capes.

She was upset to find no certainty regarding the Sagres Academy, as virtually none of it remained. She'd stepped into a world where physical evidence scarcely supported the historical facts. What she saw provided no continuity with the past, nor any coherence with the present. Prince Henry's monastic home had recently served as a women's hostel. Apparently. As with the Dias Museum, past and present met in peculiar ways.

Oddly enough, she'd climbed Table Mountain only ten days before —to watch the full moon rise while the sun set, simultaneously—the moon over the Bergen van Afrika and the sun over the Green Sea of Darkness. Even more thrilling was knowing she now stood at the other end of that same circulating ocean. No wonder the *Sacrum* and the *Prasum* were revered as sacred Capes by the ancient interlopers, by those who came ashore, by those who lost their lives, and by those who never left.

Now, in the shadow of the great cork, she remembered Mendle's parting advice: 'Savour this book when the museums are closed. Historian Raven-Hart recorded the early callers, between 1488 and 1652, from Dias to Van Riebeeck.' On its very first page she read:

> Whenever India was spoken of, mention was always made of a very powerful king called Preste João of the Indies, who was said to be a Christian. Therefore it appeared to king João II that by means of him some route to India might be found... Also, it seemed to him that if his ships followed the coast which they were now discovering, they could not fail to reach *Prasum Promontorium* at the end of that land. Therefore... he decided to send both ships by sea and men by land.

Two Holy Capes—one above the equator, the other below—and both linked to the pursuit of Prester John. The same year Covilhã and Dias set forth was also the year in which the Camissa became entangled with the quest for Prester John.

As part of their three-pronged approach, the Portuguese also tried reaching the backside of Africa via the Congo River. But the East was not to be found by transversing the continent. A fact White explorers would only discover for themselves centuries later.

For now, if Prester John was linked to Almeida, she'd have to search for him herself. And alone, if necessary.

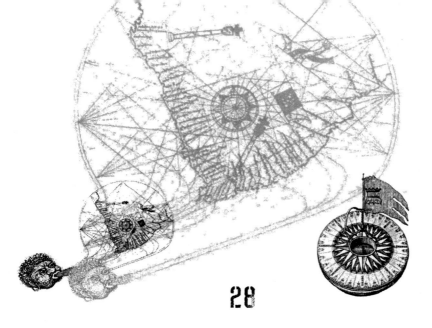

28

Landmarks passed on a journey are traces through space and time.

Martin Hall, *Negotiating the Past* (1997)

It was time to return. Well-rested and relaxed, Sonja set her mind on driving home in her brother's Volvo, a vintage coupé, which had stood idle in the garage since Christmas. As Bart's treatment usually took three weeks, she had the use of his car until his discharge.

Relieved, her parents thought it best if he came to stay with her too. *She had sabbatical for two more months, didn't she?*

Setting aside a few days for the trip, she chose Lisbon—that once sedate Old World capital—as her first overnight stop.

She bade farewell after breakfast and headed out onto the N125, searching for the northbound autoestrada. She passed the off-ramps to Portimão, Silves and Albufeira; names that recalled settlements of Phoenicians, Carthaginians and Moors. From *Lacobriga* came Lagos, recalling the legion of Romans once stationed there.

One of Rome's northern-most colonies had been Colonia, hence Cologne. Bart had been living there, she recalled, at the time of his accident, working for a contemporary art dealer. That was before the drawn-out court case with its verdict of manslaughter. She alone knew the dealer was drunk and that this was why Bart claimed to be driving. He'd spoken about it to her only after the inquest.

She tried not to dwell on the accident now.

Unable to focus, she began thinking associatively—from Colonia to iKoloni, from the Rhine to the Camissa—hoping for memories of a happier journey. Eventually she succeeded:

Driving to Mossel Bay she'd crossed the *T'kanna Ouwe* and *Koutima* (also known as the Pass of the Eland and the River of the Snake), then back via *Tradouw* and *Goudini* (the Pass of the Women and the Valley of Bitter Honey). Indigenous names revealed relationships to the natural environment that were as intimate then as they were rare today. The Dutch, on the other hand, were somewhat less poetic, as with *Mosselbaai*, simply named on account of the mussels found there. She thought back to Cape Town's long-lost beachfront and its pragmatic street names: Strand, Waterkant and Old Marine Drive.

Likewise, the Portuguese described places in terms of what they encountered, such as *Cabo Tormentoso* and *Terra da Fume* (Stormy Cape and Land of Fires). The latter was named for the smoke seen rising from the forest around Mossel Bay. As a result, maps of the region indicated: "Here be dragons". It was, of course, an invention rather than a discovery.

Yet there had been fires. Smouldering heather was used to smoke out beehives, making it easier to harvest the combs. The Gouriqua once made a delicious beer from fermented honey. Apparently.

She searched for more associations, hoping to keep her mind off what to do with Bart until her sabbatical ran out.

Unlike her Protestant forefathers, Catholic sailors named places after the saints and festivals celebrated when landfall was made. In practice, such place-names traced their journey in space and time. Their maps read like a Catholic feast day calendar. Place-names also recorded a host of Christian patrons. Gama named St Helena Bay to honour Constantine's mother, as she convinced the emperor to adopt Christianity as the official state religion.

The river emptying into the bay he called *Santiago* (after St James, patron saint of sailors), as Gama was himself a cavalerio in the Order of Santiago. The Dutch merely renamed it the *Berg*, as it flowed from the mountains.

Today a stone-hewn memorial marks the beach where Gama came ashore to draw water and where the Pater Noster was first recited in Southern Africa. To commemorate this act of worship, Gama named the next cove *Paternoster*.

Southern Africa's geography was thus defined by sea, and the land Christianized from its periphery to the interior.

She travelled inland too, trying to define her experience back in Portugal. She'd been to Lisbon before, of course, but never with such intent. And certainly not for its naval history. Now she wanted to visit the city's two most prominent sites: Belém's riverside tower and its neighbouring cathedral.

Like Bethlehem, Belém was where the long journey south began.

The Torre de Belém was a symbolic gateway to the world and the Mosteiro dos Jerónimos a rite of passage for departing seafarers. The cathedral was built beside the old city gates, over a chapel once used by Prince Henry, but only completed after Almeida's empty ship came limping back. It had the most beautifully proportioned claustro in all Christendom.

The Mosteiro dos Jerónimos was also the final resting place of both Gama and Camões. Yet despite their status as national heroes, Sonja had no time for men misled by cruel ambition or zealous pride.

Instead, she identified with Prince Henry and Bartolomeu Dias. Both lived and died searching for their grail.

☩ ☩ ☩

The long hand of Bart's car clock reached 12 as she drove across the Gama Bridge. It was here that she first saw Jason's cryptic sms:

> n-ruteLIS viaLON
> cu noon @ Arc d'V
> until wknd & bring
> nxt clu d'A murder

Sonja deduced that he was already en route to Lisbon, via London, for the archaeology conference at University College. He'd probably taken the BA night flight and, no doubt, would get an easyJet connection in the morning.

She was still thinking about him an hour later, unpacking her bags at a cheerful pensão she found.

That's tomorrow, at midday, under the Arco da Victória, until the weekend! How impractical. It was all too vague for her and, worse yet, he'd be staying three-or-four nights...

She began to fret, rushing about in haste, until she deciphered that Jason was bringing the next clue for solving Almeida's murder.

Although his presumption and timing unsettled her, she was too intrigued to care about any improprieties now.

Was it a message from the clairaudient? Had the Ancestors spoken again?

No, Mendle could have sent it by email.

Or had he found the essay that priest had given him?

No, Jason would have posted or phoned about that.

Maybe a manuscript-map from the library?

No, that too, he could have copied and sent by courier. Surely?

So it must be either bulky or heavy, even valuable, possibly something he couldn't send by DHL? Something he had to bring himself.

In that case, had he found a fresh clue at the dig?

Whatever it was, the promise of solving the riddle was all she could think of now—to the point of distraction.

She walked around Belém wondering where Jason was, how far he still had to travel, and what to do when he arrived...

She caught herself thinking too much about him.

Nou ja, we are drawn together by our mutual interest, natuurlijk.

But was there a closer bond? Surely not, Jason was a researcher, not a romancer. He was the South Pole to her North.

It was high summer and every second person on the street was on holiday. Reasonably priced accommodation proved scarce, especially with air-con and a private toilet. It seemed sensible to let Jason stay at the same pensão—if they had an extra room?

Sonja went to see the concierge, fearing the possibility that Jason may have to share the same room with her...

BLOCO

"Pioneer of the policy of sea power as the central strength of the empire, he was a just and fair governor, and defended the ideals of racial indiscrimination."

with a sculpture by Maximiano Alves c. 1930

100 FOLHAS

A5 XADREZ - 60Gr.

5 601645 301320

29

It was cold that year in Granada, fearfully cold, and
the snow was black with freshly dug earth and blood.
O, the familiarity of death! The imminence of exile!
How the joys of the past were painful to remember!

Amin Maalouf, *Leo Africanus* (1986)

The next clue wasn't bulky, or heavy, or even valuable—but it was a revelation! It consisted of six separate folios produced on a sticky typewriter with an inky ribbon, claiming Almeida's death had been a ritual murder. The folios were unsigned, undated, and seemingly still unpublished. A rusty wire-staple held the yellowing sheets together, the cover-page long since embellished by a ringed coffee stain. The first clumsy paragraph was littered with mechanical errors, typos and misaligned characters:

Francisco de Almeida

In the year 1510 took place a ritualistic death on the shores of Table Bay,then called Saldanha Bay,which was perhaps unique of its kind on African soil.It was the death of Francisco d'Almeida which one can read about in history books but where his death is usually attributed to the Hottentots.

Wait, a ritualistic death? To Sonja's astonishment, the folios stated that Almeida died because of his disloyalty to the Knights of Santiago. He not only betrayed Albuquerque, a member of the same Order, but had also failed to submit two relics obtained in Granada; a rare book and a precious stone, both brought there by the Arabs.

Also from Arabia, Sonja knew, came the decimal numeral system, astronomy, cartography and navigation. As did decorative gardening, canal irrigation and horse breeding. Arabic had served as the lingua franca in commerce, science and literature before Spanish became standard, and created a distinctive Andalusian consciousness, coupled with a long tradition of tolerance and separate rule. Local responses to stimuli—evident in the trade, warfare and poetry of al-Andalus—differed from the more uniform religious culture in the Middle East.

The Muslim empire had an East-West axis too, and a formidable navy that controlled the main trade routes from the Strait of Malacca to the Strait of Gibraltar.

The Nasrids believed that the Paradise of Muhammad was set in the heavens directly above Granada. This they echoed by creating a palace of tranquil courtyards, elegant fountains, luxurious gardens and deep shaded terraces. The Alhambra itself was filled with scented fruits, cool drinks, comfortable couches, silk embroidered robes and a host of beautiful *houris*—and yes, it was true, these virgins had dark alluring eyes, hidden like pearls in their shells.

Sonja sighed fondly, recollecting her backpacking days in Spain. She recalled gardens draped in pink bougainvillea and wrought iron balconies covered in jasmine. There were rows of silent cypresses, clipped myrtles and wild olives. The evenings hung with the scent of orange peel, dried fig and cherry blossom. Most memorable were the snow-capped peaks of the Sierra Nevada, visible in the distance, from which mules brought ice for making sorbet.

'I think some Moorish poet compared the Alhambra to a pearl set in emeralds,' she told Jason on the tram later, 'as the pink-hued stone was swathed in sombre-green.' She'd also seen slave cells, gypsy caves and the barracks once used by soldiers. Even stables for one hundred choice Barbary horses from North Africa.

From her historical studies she knew that Granada was part of an important trade network linking Andalusia to the Maghreb, and thus of strategic value to Castile. Granada's vassalage delivered slaves, mercenaries and corsairs from the fertile Niger crescent. The supply seemed endless—as was Castile's greed for gold.

Despite treachery and intervening wars, trade with the Maghreb persisted for two more centuries until the Portuguese (aided by some rogue Italians) established their own links with Senegal, Guinea and Benin. After 1479, the Treaty of Alcaçovas gave Portugal control of all trade with Africa.

Consequently, Castilian traders caught in West African waters were either thrown overboard to "die a natural death" or taken to Portugal and "burnt as pirates".

Like a disowned son, the Kingdom of Granada fell from grace and lost its allure as Castile's gateway to North Africa. Moreover, Queen Isabella had to secure her coast to compete for Atlantic territories. Somewhere to the west, across the ocean (or so Columbus told her), lay China and Japan. Marco Polo had described the wonders of the Orient, and Isabella was keen to secure her royal fifth of its wealth.

While the Nasrids assisted her in routing out rebels and renegades, even serving as spies, their co-operation was unreliable at best and dubious during times of internal strife. They were themselves divided, always bickering and seeking royal favours, and so Isabella decided they should all leave. And for this she needed to revive the *Reconquista*.

It took a decade to conquer the ports and surrounding fortresses, until Granada alone remained—landlocked, unstable and distracted. From what Sonja could remember, the citadel was a stone ship lying in the roadstead between the mountain and the coast; separating Castile from the Mediterranean Sea. Granada was a true frontier—remote, autonomous and corrupt.

As the last frontier of al-Andalus, Granada bristled with forts built to protect its mountain passes, river crossings, cultivated fields and hillside villages. The verdant plains were continuously watered by the springs, streams and melting snow of the Sierra Nevada.

The House of Nasrid was divided between those urging for war and those advocating compromise. "Fight," some argued, "rather than be enslaved, exiled or executed!" Others pleaded, "No, surrender, since they have Rome while we are abandoned by our brothers in Fès, Istanbul and Cairo." Sultan Abu 'Abd-Allah Muhammad chose to do both: *resist* and *submit*. Henceforth he'd be called Boabdil el Zogoybi, Boabdil "the Unfortunate".

As the Castilian troops advanced, the Nasrids prepared their fields and gardens for an ambush, turning every pavilion and tower into a fortress, each orchard or grove into a snare. But the Christian army could not be stalled. Isabella raised funds and forwarded supplies, then joined her consort at the front for the final siege.

Ferdinand led the campaign with vigilance, patience and prejudice (fuelled perhaps by the knowledge that he, too, had Jewish ancestry). Ironically, people of "impure blood" had produced Europe's most advanced society and now co-financed Spain's spectacular expansion overseas. Furthermore, if Granada had not fallen, Columbus would never have sailed West, not in 1492, nor for Spain. Probably not for Portugal either.

It begged a question: left alone, without outside interference, could Andalusian-Arabs have reached America first? They had the fleets, the skills and the technology—if not the will.

Imagine, a Muslim America!

The fall of Granada, which Columbus himself witnessed, ended in fervent feelings of nationalism; it symbolised the birth of a nation for Christian Spaniards. Unsurprisingly, Spain's National Day celebrates Columbus's discovery rather than Castile's victory...

Be that as it may, Queen Isabella's expulsions ended eight centuries of interaction between Muslims and Jews. The first Muslims arrived in the eighth century while the Jews, of course, had been sent during the Roman occupation. As a further irony, the latter were welcomed by Castile when England and France expelled them, around 1300. But now both had to leave. Thus, by an odd twist (and not Isabella's jewels), their wealth would finance the discovery of the New World.

Moreover, had Isabella not revoked the conditions of surrender— which were generous enough, initially—Granada would not be the symbol of Catholic intolerance and aggression it has become today. Had she not shunned the Moors and Jews, but given them a role to play in the consolidation of a centralised power, Western Europe and the Middle East may have developed quite differently. If so, relations between Tehran and Washington would be something else today.

Oi-vey, as Mendle would say, *how very different.*

Similarly, had the Cape not been abandoned, Portugal and South Africa would each have followed a different history too...

Sonja returned to the folios.

The anonymous writer stated that Almeida had been wounded and taken into camp, then nursed back to health by an influential Moor. *Whose camp? Which Moor?*

The clues in the folios were sparse. She suspected Almeida had been captured and held within the Alhambra's enclosure until the siege ended. The sight of Almeida, said the folio-author, so impressed the Moor that he asked to have this knight taken into his private care. As a commander in the Order of Santiago, astride his caparisoned horse, Almeida would certainly have made a striking impression.

However, after Granada's granaries were depleted, food shortages threatened man and beast alike. Horses were killed and eaten to feed the starving soldiers and civilians. Of the seven thousand horses that once charged into battle, only a few hundred now survived.

As for Almeida being wounded in battle, even this seemed unlikely. There were no pitched battles during the final two-year siege; only predatory expeditions, midnight raids and sporadic skirmishes. In fact, the final siege was characterized by acts of chivalry to display prowess and status, no more. These included parades, hand-to-hand combats, tilts and tournaments—all designed to boost morale while the battle-weary soldiers waited for a truce to be settled.

Most soldiers were homesick and wished to return before another harvest was spoilt. Some had not seen their wives and families for several years and had to be enticed with promises of more loot.

Ferdinand's plan was simple: he'd burn the farms, block supplies and starve out the enemy—winter's bitter snow would do the rest. And so, with patience, Ferdinand succeeded.

Within months Boabdil "the Unfortunate" capitulated—agreeing to deliver his city, intact, in exchange for a castle in Spain or, better still, exile in Morocco.

And so it came to pass that, on the first day of the Rabia Awal 897, 2 January 1492, a triumphant Ferdinand and Isabella rode up to the city. The campaign itself had taken twelve years, all in all, and, to honour the role played by the Knights of Santiago, the gracious monarchs allowed them to lead the procession through the streets of Granada.

The gate used to submit Boabdil's terms of surrender was sealed, as he'd requested. On his departure the royal ancestors were disinterred and taken with—so that none could be abused by drunken soldiers.

Popular lore has it that sultan Boabdil, reining in his horse to look back one last time, burst into tears. "You do well," spat his mother, "to weep like a woman for what you could not defend as a man." The bend in the pass is still called *The Moor's Last Sigh*.

Salman Rushdie's book—by the same title, she recalled—referred to Boabdil as the ancestral figure of his main protagonists. Another was Vasco da Gama. For Rushdie, Boabdil and Gama symbolised the complex social histories making up modern India.

As a scornful caprice of fortune, Boabdil el Zogoybi would be slain on a desolate battlefield in Fès, after which it was famously said that he died "defending the kingdom of another after lacking the will to die for his own".

She searched for more clues.

Whatever happened that winter, Almeida left Granada with an alchemical pearl and an Aristotelian treatise, a scientific discourse-or-other on the secrets of nature—or so the folios stated. Moreover, he concealed these relics from his comrades in the Order of Santiago.

While the inferences were vague and speculative, the last stole her attention: "Could one imagine that Almeida sacrificed his life in the place where East and West meet."

She turned to Jason:

'Hey, a sacrificial death, and Prof M asked you to give this to me?'

'Right. He found the essay among some old papers. Says it was written twenty-five years ago by a priest—a female priest, actually.'

'Oké, and he wants me to do *what* with it, exactly?'

'Whatever, you're the historian, he probably wants you to find the missing dates and footnotes?'

'Of course, but not now, or we won't get to the Maritime Museum in time. There's a tram leaving in five minutes.'

30

Tram 15 trundled by the Mosteiro dos Jerónimos with its adjacent museum of archaeology—which Jason vainly tried to photograph—and lurched to a halt before the CCB, Belém's Cultural Centre, itself a striking monument to design and architecture.

Sonja suggested they visit the CCB afterwards, if only for its roof terrace and restaurant. Her first visit had been with her father when the Centro hosted Portugal's presidency of the European Union. The 1992 development was then so unduly controversial (combined with the idea of a single EU community) that the CCB rapidly emerged as the performance-exhibition hotspot for all Lisbon. She'd visited the Centro on each visit but now, given the lateness of the hour, led Jason straight to the Museu de Marinha.

The Maritime Museum was stuck in an outmoded monologue with itself, she explained, and could scarcely have differed more in form and content from the Centro. It belonged to a by-gone era, revealing an inability to combine convention and innovation, revivalism and revision. Portugal's Age of Triumph appeared defiant in a world of relative sensibilities and the Museu reluctant to enter a discourse around first encounters and lasting legacies. While not her first, it would certainly be her last visit.

'If this is how they let the past and present overlap, officially, then the Museu has nothing new to offer, not now, nor for the future—except as a museum within a museum.'

He couldn't hear. A class of summer school students sauntered by, their voices reverberating down the great hall, drowning her out. Like football fans, they all wore coloured T-shirts with *Oranje Boven Tours* emblazoned on their backs. An amber-faced tutor hollered out orders while leading them on to the oriental room.

'The Sea Barbarians are still Dutch,' noted Sonja, amused, 'there's evidently no bridge too far.'

Taking Jason by his sleeve, she led him between the dusty cases and tacky information panels, hoping to find a fresh lead.

To his surprise, the hall was full of the paraphernalia seen in shop windows, publicity kiosks and hotel brochures. Here, too, were the phrases used by café owners and taxi drivers. Worse yet, he hurriedly observed, most exhibits were mere copies. He took the originals to be lost, destroyed, or simply kept elsewhere.

They paid scant attention to the Yellala Rock at the entrance and so, on impulse, Sonja retraced her steps, hoping the stone may revive some primitive contact with Africa. The inscription of Cão's captains was simple: "To this place came the ships of the Enlightened King João II of Portugal." It struck her that it too was a replica.

The real thing was still in the Congo? In this regard, Volodya had made a rather odd remark about the early seafarers, saying they returned as astronauts: 'Both the seafarer and astronaut explored the frontiers of their worlds,' he claimed, 'and after the historic 1969 moon landing, Neil Armstrong and his Apollo crew visited Kinshasa.'

She lost sight of Jason as a herd of adolescent boys stampeded in, following a beefy guide who bellowed: "Here is the statue that Prince Henry took to Ceuta. After the siege it was installed in the mosque and is now known as Our Holy Santa Maria of Africa."

Where's Jason now? She still couldn't see him, though she guessed he was well down the grand hall. She set off after him, shoving her way between the snorting bullocks, unaware of the man following her.

Built like a short-limbed ogre of Slavic legend, he wore heavy field boots, combat trousers and a black polo neck under a bulging leather jacket. He'd followed them from the pensão, although neither had given him a second glance, despite his conspicuous proportions.

She found Jason before a bright portrait of Almeida—a full-length painting showing the Great Dom in his black coat and doublet of crimson satin. She raised her voice, reading the caption:

'It says he was the heroic vanquisher of the Turks in the Persian Gulf who, by upholding a policy of the domination of the sea—sorry, it's a clumsy translation—by taking command of the sea, he checked the threat of a Mohammedian expansion towards Europe.'

A threat? An expansion towards Europe in 1500, nonsense!

They moved over to Albuquerque's towering portrait. It eclipsed all other exhibits. His caption was even more misleading:

'Albuquerque laid the foundation for the Portuguese empire with bases at Ormuz, Goa and Malacca—wait, it calls these milestones in his far-reaching vision of a Far East sea route—and that these three were later transferred to Aden, Bombay and Singapore…'

No, not true, what propaganda! The Afro-Asian Empire rested on foundations already established by the Arabs, Indians and Chinese…

It was a moot point. She read on:

'A pioneer of the policy of sea power as the central strength of the empire, he was a just and fair governor, and defended the ideals of racial indiscrimination.'

Indiscrimination? No, the Portuguese simply took local women for their own.

She led Jason toward the next gallery.

'Y'know the same quotation is in the dossier, handwritten, on that Bloco notepad. I assumed it referred to Almeida.' She looked about excitedly. 'D'you realise what this means, Jason? If the quote comes from this museum, then whoever put it in the dossier was here too!'

It was tantalizing to think they'd caught up with the dossier-owner, whoever he or she was. Distracted, neither noticed the ogre approach as attendants ushered the last visitors toward the exit.

He followed them out, toward the CCB, until Jason stopped to use the camera. Here he turned, surreptitiously, and hurried off.

Focusing the camera Jason suggested: 'We should let Prof M know what we've found, I mean, about the dossier-owner.'

'And you should skype Anton about your travel plans,' she replied, marching ahead, no longer sure of her own schedule anymore.

31

It is more important to acquire a good name than an estate,
because the name is eternal property.

João de Barros, dedication to Francisco de Almeida, *Década II* (1552)

'The Torre do Tombo is Portugal's most extensive archive,' said the woman behind the counter, 'and our oldest records date back to 1550 when the Church began recording births, marriages and deaths.'

'Jesus, we need them from 1450, a hundred years earlier.'

The librarian crossed herself devoutly, and explained:

'Our records were handed over when revolutionary zeal led to the abolition of religious Orders and the clergy feared their properties would be destroyed. After three feeble centuries, the Bragança family finally abdicated and militant nationalists established the Republic. These records now belong to the State and the biography of Joaquim Candeias Silva is, I think, the most authorative. I'll fetch it and the official genealogical indexes. Please use that table over there...'

She pointed to the row nearest the windows and withdrew behind her counter.

They went to their designated seats. Outside, leafy plants created a lush greenhouse effect behind a wall of curtain glass. The librarian soon returned with a pile of books.

Sonja still possessed a smattering of Portuguese (garnered from her holidays at Luz), and set about translating some of the key texts. She soon found anomalies in Almeida's family tree, making Jason check these against the two comb-bound pages in the dossier.

'Here, look at this,' she said, 'most claim he was born in 1450, but Silva's *Genealogia* puts him around 1457 and—'

'—his parents were married in 1442, right?'

'Yes, so—?' she could sense there was more.

'—so his father was away from home for a long time. Almeida was born ten-to-fifteen years later.'

'No doubt Lopo was off fighting the Moors. Look, he also went to Morocco after Almeida was born.'

'—and his place of birth?'

'Some genealogists list him as third, Silva says fourth, others as fifth, but this one has him as the last of seven sons... with two sisters.'

Jason lent forward, prodding her with his pencil:

'I mean *where* was he born?'

'O-oké, in the settlement of Abrantes.'

'Abrantes—their family seat?'

'Yes. Lopo was made Count of Abrantes after serving at Toro in 1476, remember. At the battle he and his eldest sons, including young Francisco, were defeated by Isabella and Ferdinand.'

'Imagine what Lopo would have received if they'd won?'

'Hey, Jason, not so loud!'

'Whatever, such entitlement isn't fair—'

'What's not fair? According to the dossier,' she said flatly, 'Lopo fought with Afonso in Tangier; Almeida's grandfather with Henry in Ceuta, for which he was knighted; and his great-grandfather with the bastard-son João I at the battle of Aljubarrota. If you recall, João was Henry's father, so that's three generations in succession. According to the dossier, Almeida's great ancestor was Pedro da Guerra which, I think, literally means "Peter the Fighter".'

'So what—Almeida came from a long line of fighting men?'

'They were all men who kept the Avis in power. They distinguished themselves in numerous diplomatic and military missions, for both Portugal and Castile. Lopo belonged to an illegitimate line of João I, so I'm sure he earned his title and deserved to be called "a just and reasonable man".'

'Sure, sure,' said Jason, nonplussed.

She sensed it best to steer their discussion elsewhere:

'In this book it says Pedro da Guerra was a natural son of João, himself born out of wedlock, which means the Sons of Lusus included royal *bastardos*. According to the dossier, Almeida's brother Pedro was named after his mother, as were Isabel and Catarina.'

AVIS

1385 – 1433	João I o de Boa Memória
1433 – 1438	Duarte o Eloquente
1438 – 1481	Afonso o Africano
1481 – 1495	João II o Príncipe Perfeito
1495 – 1521	Manuel o Venturoso

D. FRANCISCO d'ALMEIDA

*Foi Vedor da Casa do Mestre de Avis / D. Afonso V, que acompanhou a Toro
(1476); aio los Reyes Católicos D. Ferdinand e Isabella nas conquistas de
Granada (1492); Capitão-mor-do-Mar e
1.ª Vice-Rei da Índia (1505–09).
De D. Joana Pereira teve:*

|

D. LOURENÇO d'ALMEIDA

*Combateu em Tânger (1501); foi à Índia com paie em 1505, como Capitão-
mor-do-Mar; ele foi morto no combate naval
de Chaul (1508). Sem geração.*

|

D. LEONOR d'ALMEIDA

*Casou 1.ª vez Francisco de Mendonça, alcaide-mor de Mourão e irmão da
duquesa de Bragança, D. Joana. Casou 2.ª vez com (em 1511)
D. Rodrigo de Melo, Conde de Tentúgal e depois Marquês
de Ferreira, neto do Duque de Bragança.
Com geração.*

PEDRO da GUERRA = Peter the Fighter
|

FERNANDO ALVARES de ALMEYDA

*Foi Vedor da Casa do Mestre de Avis / D. João I, que acompanhou
a Aljubarrota (1385); aio dos Infantes D. Pedro e D. Henrique;
fundador da Casa de Abrantes e seu alcaide-mor.
De Leonor Gonçalves teve:*

|

DIOGO FERNANDES de ALMEYDA

*Participou na conquista de Ceuta (1415); foi Vedor
de D. João I, D. Duarte e D. Afonso V.
De Brites Anes teve:*

|

D. LOPO de ALMEYDA

*Participou na 1.ª expedição ao Rio do Ouro (1436) e nas conquistas
de Alcácer-Ceguer (1458), Tânger e Arzila (1460–71), Toro (1476);
foi Vedor de D. Afonso V; I Conde de Abrantes.
De D. Beatriz da Silva teve:*

*treasurer
to Afonso*

|

D. JOÃO de ALMEYDA

*2.ª Conde de Abrantes; colaborou na defesa da Graciosa (1480);
foi Vedor de D. Afonso V e João II.*

*treasurer
to Afonso
and João*

|

D. DIOGO FERNANDES d'ALMEIDA

Prior do Crato; participou nas conquistas de Arzila e Tânger (1471).

*governor
of João's
household*

|

He argued with Manuel
and promised
to leave for Spain on
Francisco's return
from India

D. PEDRO da SILVA

Comendador de Avis e embaixador de D. João II. Sem geração.

*ambassador
in Rome an
malta*

|

D. FRANCISCO d'ALMEIDA

1.ª Vice-Rei da Índia e comendador do Sardoal.

|

D. JORGE d'ALMEIDA

Bispo de Coimbra e II Conde de Arganil.

|

Sailed with Da Cunha
and Albuquerque
in 1503

D. DUARTE d'ALMEIDA

|

D. FERNANDO d'ALMEIDA

*Bispo de Ceuta, nuncio do Papa em França;
com promessa do cardinalato.*

|

D. ISABEL da SILVA

*Condessa de Penella, pelo casamento com
D. Afonso Vasconcelos e Meneses.*

|

D. CATARINA da SILVA

Freira no Convento de Jesus em Aveiro.

'And look, the boys are listed before their sisters.'

'Hey, you're right, then the sequence isn't chronological. Perhaps they're listed in order of importance?'

'Or according to inheritance,' volunteered Jason, 'some being more equal than others.'

She'd seen that pinched look before. No one could escape Jason's cynicism. She pulled the book closer:

'Whatever the rationale—entitlement, status or gender—there's no talk of Almeida's own involvement with the Order of Santiago. The dossier says he commanded the Order of Santiago at Sardoal, a town north of Abrantes—'

'—then Lopo's sons served the orders of Malta, Avis *and* Santiago.'

'Yes, but we still don't know why Almeida changed to the Order of Christ *before* sailing to India?'

'Perhaps,' Jason rapped the page with his pencil, 'perhaps as Viceroy he had to cut ties with the Spanish court?'

'But I thought the Order of Santiago was a multinational fraternity with independent headquarters? Even so, I guess the Portuguese were loyal to João II's successors, not to king Manuel's bitter rivals—'

'—sure, and what of France, didn't he also ask for help in Afonso's proposed marriage to sweet Juâna la Beltraneja, the child-princess?'

It didn't take her long to find a general reference:

'Here, the trip was undertaken after Portugal had been defeated at Toro. Afonso wanted the French to attack Isabella and Ferdinand, but Louis XI had no interest in supporting this affair.'

True, Louis was only interested in the military-political manoeuvres beyond his own borders, especially below the Pyrenees. Afonso felt deceived and returned disillusioned. Sonja continued:

'Among the dossier's biographies, under the Compatriots, it says that Pêro da Covilhã fought with Pedro and Francisco d'Almeida at Toro, after which he accompanied them to France.'

'Who's Covilhã?'

'Covilhã was a traveller, a linguist and a negotiator extraordinaire. He was sent to spy in Spain and served as ambassador in Morocco. Disguised as a Muslim trader, he left the same year as Dias by way of Alexandria, Cairo and Aden; taking a circuitous route to Cananor, Goa, Calicut and Cochin; then back via Ormuz before sailing down to Kilwa and Sofala. That's two thirds of the way to the Cape. I guess he was hoping to meet Dias on the far side of Africa; but they never saw each other again. Instead, Covilhã heard from an Arab or Hindu merchant that the sea beyond the tip of Africa lay open to the west— a fact Dias was discovering for himself, but in reverse. Some say this was the most important joint-venture in pioneer exploration...'

How does she recall all those places, he wondered?

'After returning to Cairo three years later, Covilhã received fresh instructions from João II and, once again, set off in search of Prester John. Now dressed as a Muslim pilgrim, he travelled on to Mecca, Medina and Sinai where, at the remote monastery of Santa Catarina, he heard mass for the first time in four years. He reached Ethiopia in 1493, finally. If you've read the dossier, you'd know he was still living with Emperor Eskender three decades later...'

'Then I reckon he found his Prester John?'

'That's what I thought too, when I heard the story.'

'You knew this before?'

'Yes, from a maverick Muscovite who collects of icons, maritime maps and luxury yachts... stuff like that.'

'Who?'

'Volodya Vasilevsky, a New Russian I met in Sagres.'

'Sure, sure, and I guess he's just a poor criminal trying to make a living? In Jo'burg, township slang for *nouveau riche* is Black Diamond, and they're the New Russians of Soweto.'

He looked at the clock and sauntered across to the security desk, asking haltingly: '*Olá... ong-de fee-kam oos la-va-boos?*'

The guard pointed to the toilets.

Sonja rummaged through the books, inserting green strips of paper to mark the relevant sections. He'd hardly been gone a minute when she found a list of New Knights in the Portuguese Order of Santiago —with a reference to Senhor Jorge, the natural son of João II, also born at Abrantes.

She raced on, looking for something new before Jason returned. And she found it:

The king presented his illegitimate son Jorge with a tutor, one Diogo d'Almeida, who immediately became the new prior of Crato. Then, two years later, João II sent an envoy to Rome with a request to have the teenage Jorge legitimized. To Sonja's surprise, she saw that the emissaries included two sons of Count Lopo—commander

Pedro da Silva and bishop Fernando d'Almeida—as well as members of the ducal Bragança. *So the Almeidas had close ties with both the Avis and the Braganças, albeit within or across the border?*

So close, in fact, that Pedro later promised to leave for Spain if his brother was given a safe return from India. *Why? Or, more importantly, why should the dossier-owner note this in the margin of Almeida's family tree?*

The Braganças and Almeidas had been loyal to Afonso and so, after his death, were reluctant to support young João's exploration of West Africa. Sonja could see these two families weren't alone.

Despite the status, wealth and fame acquired through crusading, the nobility were not united behind Portugal's expansion into Africa. This wasn't surprising as the Avis owned all trade in gold and slaves. Furthermore, to irritate his rivals, João rewarded Jewish and Italian financiers with tax concessions. In the end, the jealous nobles wanted these Jews sent overseas, rather than crusade abroad themselves.

One such financier was Isaac Abravanel—a Schindler-like figure who became a confidant of Afonso and the Duke of Bragança—and who saved the People of the Sabbath from the Spanish Inquisitors. Ferdinand believed the Jews should cover their own costs—as WWII deportees were made to do—and so Abravanel provided additional funding for Columbus's trans-Atlantic expedition. In 1492, merely three months after the fall of Granada, the Spanish monarchs issued the Alhambra Decree in which Jews were ordered to leave or face punishment—including death. Those providing shelter could lose their hereditary privileges or have their belongings confiscated. Most fled to Portugal, others made their way into Holland.

According to Simon Wiesenthal, Columbus sailed in hope of finding a new country for the Sephardim who, following the decree, were destined to live in the Maghreb. Columbus allegedly began his log: "After you expelled the Jews your majesties sent me with a fleet..."

All the more intriguing was the perennial rumour of a lost Tribe of Israel living peacefully in India or China; so finding them would solve the awkward problem of Jewish citizenry...

32

I wish that the earth does not weigh heavily upon your remains.
Ancient funerary altar inscription, Musei Capitolini, Rome (2ndC CE)

The low, white-washed church dated back to the thirteenth century, that is, to after the Moors were driven south. It was the only building left from Almeida's lifetime. The Igreja de Santa Maria do Castelo had a tiled roof, green azulejos behind the altar, and a parquet-like flagstone floor—worn smooth by the tears of countless generations.

It was at the heart of Castelo de Abrantes.

Admission to the castle itself was free, or so it seemed, as the tunnel gate hung ajar, unattended. Here Jason sallied forth into the blazing livery yard where virtually nothing remained of the original stables, stores or service quarters, except for some rough-hewn walls.

He marched instinctively toward the exposed summit where pollard willows grew around a roofless ruin. Sonja rested in the shade of an entangled willow while he clambered ahead to photograph the ruin, despite the midday heat.

'Both Juãna la Beltraneja, the girl-bride, and Afonso's daughter, left court to spend their lives in a convent,' she hailed after him, 'after which Afonso's daughter became known as Santa Joana.'

'Wasn't Almeida's sister sent to a convent, too?' he hollered back.

'Yes, it was a woman's best chance for an education. Every convent had a library and each nun access to books—'

'—didn't the nobility have their own?'

'Jason, you're smarter than I thought, though it doesn't look like that today.'

His face dropped.

'Not you, stupid. I mean this heap of rubble. It doesn't look as if there ever was a library here. It's hard to believe families once lived between these stones—in rowdy halls and smelly chambers, let alone with a mouldy library.'

Jason leapt down, grinning: 'It's not Camelot, only a model!'

The scrub-covered ruin was no more than a hollow shell filled with the litter of indifferent visitors: from Napoleonic soldiers to war-weary prisoners, from traders and lovers to occasional campers and passing vagrants. Even the Tagus sauntered by with equal detachment, while the sky turned a nonchalant grey.

The reinforced ringwall, first built by the Moors, served to protect Almeida's family tomb and private chapel. According to her research, the church now served as a museum. It stood alone; barred and shut.

Sonja had called the day before to ask if the chapel would be open at noon. Having scoffed at her overt organisation, Jason was now relieved to know a key was soon on its way. He checked his watch, 12:30, and the heat was getting worse. They waited by the church.

It was another half-hour before they heard a moped whine up the hill and a smoking Key Boy arrive to open the church.

Inside the chapel were the tombs of Almeida's father, Lopo, and his brother Duarte, who'd helped secure the King of Cochin's throne. In return, the Portuguese were permitted to rebuild the fort, thus laying the so-called Foundation Stone for their overseas empire in the East.

His mother Beatriz lay there too, next to her husband. The other tombs were not well marked, nor was the reported *sepultura improvisada* to be seen. Sonja had read that the latter was an ad hoc memorial made after Almeida's death. Perhaps it was in Evora, after all?

Besides the few sculptured prophets and a carved baptismal, there wasn't much else Almeida may have seen himself—except for two faded *tipo gótico* frescoes, of which one depicted a Templar knight slaying a dragon. The young knight wore a distinctive red cross on his white tunic (replete with red-white ostrich plumes) and rode toward a castle, lance poised, from where a king and ardent princess watched. It was as incongruent as that red-ochre ship in the Cederberg.

The Key Boy went out for a cigarette.

'What else did you read in the library yesterday?'

'Well, Almeida had been in love, at least once. He was married to Joanna Pereira, daughter of Vasco Martins Moniz, chief warder of João II and also a commander in the Order of Santiago.'

'Then both his paternal grandparents belonged to the same Order, binding him doubly to Cross, Crown and Country?'

'Yes, and by then the Order had acquired extensive possessions in Portugal, England, France, Italy, Hungary and Palestine. Abrantes was their first commandary in Portugal. The king donated the castle in the twelfth century, promising the Templars a third of all they conquered below the Tagus. Did you see the plaque outside, listing the recent renovations?'

'No,' Jason admitted, looking back at the open door. 'Anyway, we don't know how family alliances changed when the crown passed from Fat João to Big Manuel?'

She wasn't sure of these shifting alliances either, so confined herself to what she did know.

'It appears Almeida may have had *two* daughters.'

'What?'

She took a sip of water: 'Well, that's what I read yesterday.'

'*Olá*... now I get to hear about it.'

'Yes, now. Joanna Pereira was his wife and together they had two children. However, there appears to be another child, Suzana, who may have been from an earlier relationship, possibly a first marriage, as the Knights of Santiago followed a vow of "marital chastity".'

'You mean sex with a married woman was approved, but not with virgins or spinsters?'

'C'mon Jason, be serious, we all know they had mistresses. Even Prince Henry wasn't celibate all his life.'

He gave a wan smile. 'Like Queen Elizabeth I, not always a virgin?'

'Knights were allowed to marry. In her case, however, I think she desired virtue as a queen—not as a woman.'

'Like Catholic soldiers who abstained from sex on feast days—'

'—and while fasting—'

'—or during battle!'

'Y'know, Jason, soldiers couldn't have sex before 1486,' she teased, 'and then only because the Pope declared fasting unnecessary during war. *Natuurlijk*, making rape and pillage no longer a mortal sin!'

'How d'you know all this, if you're not Catholic?'

'I'm not an active Protestant either, Jason, I'm a social historian,' she smiled, 'or at least I was before my sabbatical.'

'Well, if I could choose, I'd rather be a martyr than a warrior.'

He strutted off, as if on horseback, making the sound of two halved coconuts banging together.

'Come on,' she called, reining him in, 'you'd have been court jester. Anyway, Almeida's first wife—if that's what she really was—probably died in childbirth.'

'According to Wikipedia, he only had Lourenço and Leonor.'

'So far I've found only one reference to this other woman.'

'So, possibly two wives, two daughters and one Lourenço?'

She smiled back at him.

'As we already know, Lourenço was killed at the battle of Diu. He was then twenty-eight and without issue. In the end, Almeida had no heir as women couldn't inherit property, only jewellery.'

'And Leonor?' he asked.

'Leonor was older than Lourenço, it appears, and married.'

'Jesus, the biographies are so inconsistent—'

'—perhaps those inconsistencies aren't as innocent as they appear. There may be more to these errors.'

'Like?'

'Like perhaps families wanted to reinvent their past? We should pursue Barros's connection next time—'

'—why, is there something else you want to do now?'

He could sense she had more to say.

'You said loyalties shifted between the reigns of Fat João and Big Manuel. Well, the ageing king thought the Crown Prince wasn't fit to rule, so he first promoted his natural son, Jorge de Lencastre—named after Philippa of Lancaster, I presume—as the future governor of the Order of Christ. The child was born in 1481, here at Abrantes, to the king's mistress, Ana de Mendonça.'

He burst into a grin, laughter echoing through the chapel.

'Seriously, Jason, what do these accidental deaths, retiring sisters and illegitimate sons have in common? We both know the Braganças and Almeidas descended from the bastard son of king João I, so we better think twice about their loyalties…'

Bastardos!

It was a sensitive subject for him, having grown up as a B-sibling where other children took pleasure taunting him because his hair was different.

'Jason, I'm only telling you what I found in the Torre do Tombo. Here, let me show you something...'

She led him out to the front steps, past the Key Boy, where she sat and translated the chronicles of Rui de Pina:

> It was the youngest son, Francisco de Almeida, who had the most chequered and interesting career: he was implicated in the conspiracy against João II, led by the Duke of Bragança, but let off lightly... he was linked to the equally ill-fated Duke of Viseu and spared, again, as he'd already fled to Castile for safety... he participated in the campaign against the Nasrids at Granada and returned to Portugal in 1492. Here, thanks to his family's connections to the Crown, he regained favour and, a year later, was nominated to lead a Portuguese expedition to see what Columbus had discovered. For diplomatic reasons the plan was aborted.

It had the desired effect. She'd found something extraordinary—like a rare and precious stone—and Jason knew it. He'd been outdone, at last, and so let her continue:

'When Columbus returned, claiming he'd discovered Japan, João II wanted to seize these new territories for the Portuguese Crown. Since the line of demarcation in the Treaty of Tordesillas had not yet been settled, he planned to send a fleet under the command of none other than Francisco d'Almeida. And that's in the dossier too, Jason.'

꘣꘣

Turn him to any cause of policy,
The Gordian Knot of it he will unloose,
Familiar as his garter...
                    Shakespeare, *Henry V* (1599)

Perched high on a wooded hill, the fortress glared over Tomar like a tawny owl, seldom seen at night or stirring by day. Sonja and Jason had driven up at dawn, when the air was still crisp and fresh, to see the Convento de Cristo and its Romano-Byzantine charola. Built to defend the Christian-Moor border, it served as the Templars' central oratory and as the headquarters of the Order of Christ.

They left their little Volvo in the shaded car park and strolled up to the gate, glad to stretch their legs again. It was almost noon.

Inside the ring-wall stood the royal palace, also in ruins, where she stopped to take in the sun-bleached view. Constructed on a narrow spur, the charola towered above its cloisters, battlemented terraces and long-dry cisterns. Dropping off to the creek below were scrubby groves and overgrown fields.

'So where did they keep their horses?' Sonja wondered, 'they must have had hundreds up here.'

'Recent excavations under Solomon's Temple unearthed stables for two thousand horses, though he supposedly had forty thousand for his chariots, all in all. And fifteen hundred camels.'

She knew each knight brought his own horse on joining the Order, which then belonged to the brotherhood: 'They themselves owned nothing and so couldn't be bribed. Their seal showed two men on a horse, apparently symbolising their renunciation of worldly goods.'

Jason took photographs while she continued:

'The demand for fresh horses resulted in the development of stud farms around Templar commandaries—all the way from Portugal to Palestine. A strong, well-schooled horse was important, so much so a knight was relieved of daily duties if his horse needed to be re-shod... Come, let's go look inside.'

She turned and headed for the weather-stained charola.

Had the dossier-owner been here too? And if so, what was there to see?

From the dossier she knew Vasco Gonçalves de Almeyda and his wife were governors of the young Prince Henry, and that they had donated a chapel for his own private use.

On finding his chapel—dedicated to St George the Dragonslayer, the patron saint of all Portugal—they entered a Piranesian labyrinth of hallways, stairwells and balustrades, before reaching the octagonal charola itself. The splendid interior spaces integrated light and form.

Its design was based on the Temple of Solomon, demonstrating the Templarist view that Jerusalem and not Rome, that "Eternal City of Despots", was the historical link between East and West. Their aim was to safeguard exchange beyond the Mediterranean environment: inspiring the Crusades, the Templars and the early Navigators. Below the belt of Islam, Henry had predicted, an alliance with Prester John would reunite East and West.

Tomar's entire architectural complex seemed cut from solid stone, like the rock-hewn temples of Ethiopia, observed Jason, transforming the site into an archaeological record in itself. He would've stayed to dig, if he could, but followed Sonja out to the grand Chapter Window behind the charola. Here she rested in the shade. Her feet hurt.

The sculptured ornamentation was stupendous and emblematic. They saw equilateral crosses, armillary spheres, marine cables, fishing floats, spiralled cords and, most striking of all, the Manueline knot with its coiled rope. What also struck them as new, or rather, what neither had seen before, were the massive buckles and girdles of carved yellow-grey limestone.

'There must be a strong link,' suggested Jason, 'between the Order of the Garter in England and Portugal's Order of Christ. I reckon this site binds the Portuguese and British empires.'

'All I know,' she added, 'is that the foundations of both are based on the same cult-heroes: Templar knights and Grail heroes.'

'Portugal and England are signatories to what must be the oldest diplomatic alliance in the West,' she recalled, 'dating back to when João became king and married Philippa of Lancaster.'

'The first Avis monarchs?' asked Jason, confused by the names as much as by the dates.

So, he'd still not looked at the dossier!

'Well, in 1386,' she said, leading him through the adjacent cloisters, 'the English supported king João at the battle of Aljubarrota, helping to establish Portugal's independence. The French, on the other hand, lent their support to Castile. This alliance—the Treaty of Windsor— is still valid today.'

'Why tell me? Because I haven't committed the *Tabula* to memory?'

'No, because of two coincidences I uncovered in the archives, two links to Almeida that are *not* in the dossier.'

Having passed the kitchen they came to stand before the refectory, below a triple-headed Trismegistus, carved into the vaulted ceiling above their heads. Here she added:

'First, the battle of Aljubarrota was led by the young and talented Nuno Álvares Pereira, a descendent of Charlemagne and a relative of Almeida's wife, Joanna Pereira. Secondly, when the French-Castilian soldiers fled the battle, many were pursued into nearby towns. Local tradition has it that one Beatriz de Almeyda, "the baker-woman of Alhubarrota", killed eight soldiers when they stormed her kitchen. It is said she was a giant and—like Goliath's brother—had six fingers on each hand. She bears the name of Almeida's mother. D'you think these are mere coincidences?'

They moved toward the dormitory.

On reaching the first corridor of cells she stopped, again, to rest her feet. Jason cheered her up:

'Hey, y'know Templar knights cut their hair short on top but left it long at the back? They must all have looked like Prof M: big, bearded and balding.'

Among the group that overtook them was a bald man—himself a goliath—whom Sonja had seen at the naval museum that week. She was sure of that, as he wore the same leather jacket over a black polo neck sweater. And dripped like the Swamp Thing.

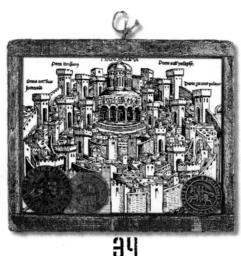

϶Ч

Solomon's Temple is a model of symbolic geometry.
Marie-Madeleine Davy, *Initiation à la symbolique romane* (1964)

From: jmendle@sam.org.za
Sent: Friday, July 16, 19:35
To: awayfromhome@gmail.com
Subject: Knights Templar

Dear Sonja

Thanks for your news from Tomar. I see you are pursuing the Knights Templar in Portugal. I thought you might like to read what Laurence has said about their role in medieval Europe. Some of it you may already know.

Knights Templar

A military-religious order founded on Christmas Day in 1118 by a band of French crusaders, led by Hugues de Payen, the first Grand Master, and under the patronage of St Bernard of Clairvaux, the monastic reformer of the Cistercian Order.

The headquarters of the Knights Templar was in Jerusalem, on the site of the Temple of Solomon, from which derived the name of the Order. Its purpose was to protect pilgrims in the Holy Land, ostensibly, but there is clear evidence of a more esoteric programme behind their activities. The original group of Knights Templar excavated beneath the Temple Mount and discovered there treasures of a mysterious sort. Legend has it they found ancient scrolls, similar to the Dead Sea Scrolls, and the lost Ark of the Covenant. They became the reputed guardians of the Holy Grail, the Turin Shroud and the esoteric knowledge of East and West.

While they swore allegiance to the Pope and were a chivalric monastic order—under a rule drawn by St Bernard—they had links with the Muslim military order of the Assassins and with various orders of Sufis. They strove behind the scenes of the Crusades for a religious and secular dispensation in Europe, trying in secret to topple and replace the imperial regime of the Church of Christendom.

During the two centuries of their existence, Templar knights distinguished themselves as Europe's greatest fighting force; noted for their chivalry, bravery and honour. They were the bankers of popes and the diplomats of kings, revolutionizing the fiscal systems of Europe and its economy of trade. Above all, they represented an esoteric religion heretical to Christian orthodoxy.

Eventually accused of heresy and sedition, the Templars were outlawed by Pope Clement V and King Philip IV of France who, in 1307, ordered the arrest of all its members. Officially, the Order ceased to exist when the last Grand Master, Jacques de Molay, and the leading knights were burnt at the stake in Paris in 1314. The movement continued underground, resurfacing in Scotland as the Freemasons, and in Portugal as the Knights of Christ.

From a karmic perspective, it is worth noting that Hugues de Payen was reincarnate as Henry the Navigator, and Jacques de Molay as Galileo Galilei. Both defied orthodox views of the world and explored the frontiers of our earthly existence. It is an irony of history that Pope Clement had been Pontius Pilate who, in his former life, was prefect of Roman occupied Judea.

In his own past life, Laurence Oliver had been the Victorian traveller, writer, spy and diplomat, Laurence Oliphant. For what it's worth, look him up on the internet.

JM

35

*The evolution of the doctrine of immortality of the soul was a
parallel and differing development in several Indo-European
cultures, and might originate from an earlier common belief.*

Peter Berresford Ellis, *The Celts* (1998)

The Universidade de Coimbra wrapped itself around the hill like a
coiled rope on the foredeck of a caravel. Here, near the old city walls,
Sonja and Jason found an internet café where they searched for *indian
christianity*. She remained hesitant on the issue of reincarnation, and
wanted historical facts.

It did not take long to locate a map revealing early Nestorian and
Zoroastrian settlements on India's west coast. These were found in
Goa and Cochin where Almeida himself had been. Both cities were
of strategic importance to the Estado da Índia, with Goa becoming
the centre of Portuguese influence for the next four centuries.

'The original message,' she reminded him, 'says that Almeida went
to India to re-establish esoteric intercourse between East and West,
suggesting it had been blocked, abandoned, or simply prohibited for
some time. So perhaps, perhaps he had a diplomatic role in renewing
liaisons between oriental and occidental schools of knowledge?'

He waited, sceptically, muttering under his breath.

'Jesus, this connection is slow…'

Sonja fidgeted restlessly until the site opened. A map revealed how
the first Christians were scattered across the Indies, from China to

Ethiopia, living in enclaves that pre-dated their presence in Europe. She listed three groups with whom Almeida may have had contact: the Manichaeans, the Nestorians and the Monotheists.

1. Mani, a third-century Persian prophet, blended Zoroastrianism, Christianity and Buddhism. His followers were the former disciples of Melchior, one of the biblical Magi or *Majusian*. The Manichaeans believed that the acts and teachings of Zoroaster, Jesus and Buddha emanated from the same source which, after the mass migrations from Atlantis, reintroduced the wisdom of the Ancients. Over time, Manichaean converts spread from the Middle East to South-East Asia, and from North Africa to Southern Europe—especially Spain and France. Although unable to survive the Middle Ages, their beliefs influenced the Cathars of Montségur. But more importantly, Sonja noted, they flourished on India's Malabar Coast.

2. Nestorius, a fifth-century bishop from Constantinople, blended Hinduism with Christianity. Nestorians believed in Christ's dual incarnation—that the man *Jesus* and the divine *Logos* were separate but shared the same body. Nestorians found support in Persia, Syria and Mesopotamia—flourishing on India's lush Kerala, all the way down to Cape Comorin. They reintroduced the Hindu concept of karma and reincarnation, as well as the ageless arcane knowledge of the Hierarchies; and assimilated local converts known as St Thomas Christians, after the apostle who first brought Christianity to India, around 50CE.

3. Ethiopian Christianity dates from c.330CE when Greek-speaking missionaries introduced the faith, a mere two decades after Emperor Constantine adopted it. Emperor Eskender of Lalibela (1471–94), blended the Abrahamic faiths of Judaism, Christianity and Islam, and kept council with Portuguese men like Pêro da Covilhã. Linked by legend to Ham, son of Noah, the Ethiopians acted as the custodians of the Ark. According to tradition the Ark, like the body of Adam, was taken to Egypt from Atlantis. After its confiscation in Israel, the Ark came to rest at Aksum, the old capital of Ethiopia. Menelik, the son of Solomon and Sheba, reclaimed the Ark and brought it back to Egypt, installing it on the island temple of Elephantine until it found sanctuary, allegedly, in the Chapel of the Ark at Aksum.

'The Manichaeans, Nestorians and Monophysites were condemned by Papal Rome as "those heretics from the other side of Jerusalem",' said Volodya breathlessly. 'The Pope was the sole and absolute head of the Church, *sans discussion*.'

Volodya had joined them for a drink, having called earlier to say he was in Coimbra on business. Coincidently.

He wore a linen jacket over a collared shirt, gold-plated cufflinks (to match the anchor), and straight piped pants with pointy shoes. His polished Gucci's gleamed with delight.

As did he, enjoying the afterlife of Sonja's embrace.

'In Russia the word *orthodox* means *right* belief or *right* doctrine,' he added, 'thus each church, East and West, Byzantine and Roman, believed they enjoyed sole rights before God.'

'Then why brand Eastern Christians as heretics?'

'Papal tradition restricted Catholicism to monotheism, claiming recognition of other divine beings to be heretical. Belief in the old sun-gods, the ancient light-bringers, was seen as an anathema.'

'First mutiny, now heresy!' chimed in Jason, recalling punishments endured by warrior-monks, knights and slaves: 'Our research turns out to be *A Shorter History of Punishment* and, like life itself, also appears to be nasty, brutish, and short on mercy.'

She sensed Volodya and Jason were vying for her attention.

The waiter returned with a shot of muddy espresso.

'Sagres, *s'il vous plaît*,' ordered Volodya, pulling his chair closer in. He continued:

'Fifteenth-century Catholics and their Lutheran counterparts failed to recognise the universality of Christ's mission. Christian teachings introduced a new humanism for what was meant to have been, from a new spiritual-historical perspective, the fulfilment and continuation of Zoroastrianism, Judaism and the Celtic religions.'

'Wait, they all had a Golden Age,' she replied, 'each matured and, like good Hellenists, laid the ground for other cultures.'

'*Da, da*, but this process was never completed. Nestorian Christians failed to bring about a new civilisation. Their efforts were aborted by Hellenism.'

'*Aborted?*'

'Yes, aborted.' Volodya turned his collar up against the slanting sun, like a lay preacher with a mouth of gold:

'According to Arnold Toynbee, an abortive civilisation is one which fails where another succeeds. When this happens, the former survives in the recesses of an emerging society. He claims that the Nestorians would have developed a civilisation of their own, but were unable to withstand the impact of Hellenism.'

She quizzed: 'Is this from his *Study of History?*'

'*Da*, and for their heretical beliefs the Nestorians were either forced underground or driven out of the East Roman Empire. Pockets of Nestorians survived in the monsoon swamps of the Indian peninsula. Similarly, Monophysite Christians survived on the remote rock at Roha, now Lalibela, in north-western Ethiopia—but, isolated from external stimuli and unable to meet their own socio-political needs, they eventually stagnated. Today's Monophysites are still the guardians of this ancient, undiluted religion.'

'You mean they just managed to maintain themselves?' challenged Jason, curling his fingers: 'Credo Mutwa says "Ethiopia was once the school of all Africa".'

Volodya scrutinized him for an indication of faith. There was none. He turned to Sonja, looking at her intently:

'Aksum is the result of Alexander's campaigning. Christians found fertile ground in Egypt, Persia and India—as they did among the Jews of Ethiopia—in fact, wherever Hellenism had made an impact. Alexander began this process of acculturation three centuries earlier, and it lasted until a hundred years after Christ. No doubt that's why he was called *Aléxandros*, the "Defender of Men". Some say Prester John held court with a sage from the days of Alexander. *Da*, the influence of Greek culture abroad was overwhelming—'

'—colonisation is supposed to be overwhelming. Like McDonald's, Microsoft and Reality TV.'

Volodya looked askance, noting Jason's hostility:

'I was talking about advances in art, technology and politics.'

They clearly annoyed each other. As for Toynbee, Sonja found his stimulus-and-response theory too linear. She refocused:

'You were telling us about Monophysite Christians in Ethiopia?'

'*Da*. Their role as the opponents of Roman Catholicism declined with Islam's expansion in Arabia and Africa. And so, struggling to preserve their own orthodoxy and independent dogma, Aksum's debate with Rome eventually fell by the wayside.'

'At the beginning of the eighth century?'

He nodded, sipping his cerveja. She waited for him to continue.

'When Muslim Berbers first made their incursion into France in 732, Western society was just establishing itself. After advancing like a deep ocean swell, the wave petered out as it reached the Loire Valley. Somewhere on the road between Tours and Poitiers, Charles Martel and his Frankish army halted their advance.'

He wiped his mouth, gold accessories glinting in the sun. She put her hand on Jason's knee to keep him quiet, rephrasing:

'The battle was not so much a turning-point in history, Volodya, as it was for the making of Europe itself. Like the battle of Diu, the tide changed and Europeans rose with it.'

'*Merci*,' he said, nodding heavily, 'the events that followed show how a nascent society can be stimulated to take action and then made to participate in larger political processes.'

'So the Muslims kick-started European society?' taunted Jason.

'France was the northern frontier in this Islamic-Christian conflict. Muslims also challenged Christians in far-off Abyssinia where equally fierce battles were being fought in the rocky desert.'

Volodya emptied his glass and ordered another beer. It was getting hot in the sun and he still hotter under his collar. He'd spare Jason a sermon. *Quel malheur pour Jason...*

'As sun worshippers,' she cut in, 'how did Zoroastrians compare to the Nestorians or Cathars?'

'*Pardon*, Mlle Sonja,' resting his hand on her arm, 'perhaps we can look at that next time. Let's stay with the Nestorians today, *ça va?*'

Turning back to Jason:

'After fleeing their persecutors in the East Roman Empire, they settled in Iraq and Iran—the Babylonia of the ancient world. As all archaeologists know, the ruins of Babylon lie just south of modern Baghdad. Over the centuries, Nestorians migrated further east until, in 1258, the ancient city was sacked. There had been two main impulses: the first went by sea to the Malabar Coast, sometime in the first century; the other to the oases of the Eurasian steppe from where they descended into China.'

Jason didn't reply, distracted by Volodya's hand on Sonja's arm.

'So that's how Christianity reached China?' she asked rhetorically, easing herself free.

Like a performing bear, Volodya made as if he hadn't sensed her withdrawal: '*Da*, the Peninsula Nestorians, or St Thomas Christians, tended to make a home for themselves in extreme environments— and like their Middle East ancestors, it was usually at the farthest ends of the earth. Continental Nestorians, on the other hand, were spread across South-East Asia and came close to creating a distinctive civilisation before Genghis Khan overwhelmed them. They became the official scribes, chroniclers and accountants of the Great Khan at Karakorum, keeping the state archives and acting as secretaries to a succession of so-called Mongolian "Prester Johns".'

'Hey, don't you see,' she said eagerly, 'that's why the Portuguese wanted to find the last surviving Nestorians in the Indies?'

Following Templar tradition, she understood, Almeida would have made contact with local Christians, Jews and Hindus. Was it a search for common ground, or a mutual spirituality, that had inspired him?

Is this what his secret commission was all about? If so, she guessed, *it was certainly not part of his official duties.*

What was known, with historical certainty, was that Almeida found two key rivals on the Malabar coast: the Zamorin of Calicut and the Maharaja of Cochin—both hereditary Hindu rulers. The Maharaja felt himself threatened and hoped the Portuguese would assist against neighbouring Calicut and so, with tact and diplomacy, the Maharaja welcomed Almeida, allowing him to re-establish the fort and factory built by Chinese traders eighty years before. Almeida thus founded the first European colony in India.

And yet whatever else Almeida achieved, privately or in pursuit of spirituality, was lost from record?

After him, under Gama, the Jews and St Thomas Christians were compelled to convert. Later still, Jesuit missionaries refused to allow any independent Nestorian enclave without an allegiance to Rome; forcing them to merge with the Latin Church. This created conflicts within the ancient Indian caste system, as Nestorians belonged to a higher rank, compared to the average Estado convert. Most of the latter were illiterate fishermen who, or so it was said, had descended from Chinese traders on the west coast. They were popularly known as *Chini-bachaquan* or "China-boys".

'Were there any Christian kings in India-China before the Jesuits?' pried Jason, clearly irritated by the vagaries of Catholicism.

'*Non*, but Prester John was linked to the Mongolian empire via a Buddhist-Chinese warlord,' he replied impartially. 'The warlord was Hulagu, brother of Kublai Khan, the one defeated by Muslim Turks. Marco Polo describes him in his *Travels*. As does Robert Silverberg, whose *Realm of Prester John* is still the best study on the history of the legend. *Da*, perhaps you want to know more about this priest-king? Tomorrow then, if there's time before you depart? Right now, let's not confuse the three *Indias* with the *Indies*.'

Agitated, Jason attracted the attention of a waiter:

'*Ahn-kohr, seel-voo-pleh?*'

Sonja borrowed his notepad for Volodya's summation:

'This potentate was known to legend as Prester John of India *and* as Prester John of the Indies—where *India* refers to a political realm and the *Indies* to its geographical location. The Indies encompassed all land around the Indian Ocean Rim while the three Indias included India, Arabia and Ethiopia. At the time, Europeans still believed the Indian Ocean was an inland sea.'

'Like the Mediterranean?'

'*Da da*, the Mediterranean divided the earth neatly in two, North and South; as the Indian did between East and West.'

'Then the Estado made this construction a reality,' she offered, 'since it stretched all the way from the Cape of Good Hope to Cape Comorin. At its best it was an empire of overlapping cultures; spread across the Indian Ocean from Sofala to Nagasaki.'

'Furthermore, our Indo-European heritage overlaps in language, law, weapons and religion. Many Hindu rites are similar to those of the Celts, Greeks, Romans and Christians; the oldest parallels being in Vedic and Celtic cosmology, astrology, numerology and linguistics. Most remarkable, however, is the doctrine of immortality and the belief that the soul dwells in our head, hence the cult of the skull as a trophy, cup or talisman. Another is that the body must be recovered for life on earth to continue, for further incarnations to recur.'

Sonja lost concentration. Something about Volodya's stare made her feel uneasy. He also bought too many gifts, gave her too much attention and, all too often, simply appeared out of the blue.

In short, he took too much interest in her.

To deflect, she led the conversation back to Portuguese India and, drawing a deep breath, prayed the bill would soon arrive.

'In 1668 the Portuguese Afro-Asian Empire finally collapsed,' she said, filling the gap, 'depleted by the machinations of Europe's Thirty Years War, the Anglo-Dutch Wars and the Franco-Spanish War—not to mention all the adverse effects of private trade under Spanish rule. The Portuguese were eventually driven out of Ethiopia, India, Sri Lanka—where my father was posted—the Persian Gulf and the Bay of Bengal. They had faced unprecedented local opposition, even in southern India, and were no match for their rivals—Holland and Britain. I think Malyn Newitt says: "Portugal failed to modernise its institutions or meet the challenge of the Dutch and English." While most bases were reclaimed, the Portuguese retained a foothold in Goa and Diu, incredibly, until the 1960s.'

The waiter came with their last round of drinks and the bill which, to keep the men from jousting, she insisted on paying. She wanted no tournament today, and let Volodya have the last word:

'Let's not forget that the transformations of the sixteenth century were brought about by the seafaring nations of both Europe and Asia —not by Portugal alone. The Eurasian world underwent a process of dramatic growth, through intrusion and expansion, bringing about more and more cosmopolitan and commercialized societies. *Da*, the Portuguese empire imposed itself upon a chain of well-linked trading centres already established in the East. Alas, this process was aborted by Europe's territorial empires in the nineteenth century.'

'Sanjay Subrahmanyam?'

'Mlle, exactly.'

ᴲ6

A moment comes, which comes but rarely in history, when we step out from the old toward the new, when an age ends, and when the soul of a nation, long suppressed, finds utterance.

Jawaharlal Nehru, *A Tryst With Destiny* (1947)

From: awayfromhome@gmail.com
Sent: Saturday, July 17, 14:32
To: jmendle@sam.org.za
Subject: Prester John

Dear Prof Mendle

Greetings from Coimbra, ancestral home of kings, poets and scholars. It is the traditional home of King Dinis, Camões, and the first treaty of friendship between Portugal and England. And good beer, as Jason discovered last night.

We found a map showing enclaves of Nestorians in southern India, including Cochin, where Almeida set up his main base. We think this was linked to his "secret commission to reopen channels of esoteric intercourse between East and West".

The word *reopen* suggests there had been some prior esoteric communication with the Nestorians—with those, at least, who practiced a mild blend of Judeo-Christian-Buddhist spirituality. Nestorians fused Western monotheism with Eastern polytheism—*ex oriente lux* with *ex occidente lux*—the source of which may have been Sufic.

Once Almeida left, Albuquerque moved his operational base from Cochin to Goa, signifying a renewal in political priorities. I think it also echoed a shift from the esoteric to the economic.

Almeida's commission was probably unofficial—a long-term strategy or *tempo longo*, as one source calls it—through which he hoped to re-establish dialogue between the Abrahamic and the Dharmic religions.

Experience teaches how important diplomatic ties can be, and how difficult it becomes when bound by treaties indefinitely. For instance, my father was in Colombo when Portuguese Goa and Diu were assaulted by Indian armed forces. I think, 1961. Ousted in 1947 themselves, the English stood by as their old ally refused to surrender its last enclaves in India. Symbolically, the only ship prepared for action was the *Afonso de Albuquerque*. The rest of the fleet had left.

It was not the first time England failed to adhere to the Treaty of Windsor. In 1890, during the scramble for Africa, England sent an ultimatum demanding the surrender of Portugal's Pink Map, its *Mapa cor-de-rosa*, which represented Portuguese claims to Angola, Mozambique and the territories in between, such as Zimbabwe, Zambia and Malawi.

Having lost in India, President Salazar threw himself behind a long and bloody war to protect Portugal's possessions in southern Africa. It was a hopeless war, as you already know, from your own experience in the old RSA.

We leave tomorrow. I go on to Leiden and Jason to London. So farewell, farewell from the little town that brought down Europe's last colonial empire and Portugal's last dictator.

Adeus Universitário!

Sonja

∃7

Saint, sorcerer, lunatic and romantic lover,
all alike are drawn to Brocéliande.

C S Lewis, *Arthurian Torso* (1948)

Volodya waited at the crowded little café overlooking the Jardim Botânico. The stepped terraces, rambling flower-beds and entangled footpaths had changed little since his last visit a decade ago—except for the exotic red squirrels he now saw everywhere.

Today, well travelled, overweight and estranged, he was back to see an auburn historian with connections in the museum world.

Sonja felt uneasy about seeing him one last time, and so took Jason along for lunch. While Volodya's voluptuous hands tended to drift, his tales of an African Prester John continued to seduce her.

He was immediately recognisable in his navy jacket, rising to greet her and offering a bottle of vinho verde as a farewell gift. He looked pleased she'd come to say goodbye. Jason too, he added, but without conviction.

The Russian Bear had a good nose for business ventures in Kiev; buying old apartments from impoverished owners, trading up with developers and then, via his brothers, selling on the property as glossy office-space to foreign investors. He also dealt in old icons that had, allegedly, been "salvaged from destruction" when Soviet authorities turned churches into archives, granaries or gymnasia. In return, he'd assembled a modest collection of old maps and rare manuscripts. Always dominant, he led the discussion:

'So you see, most stories surrounding the fabulous figure of Prester John are linked to the legends of Parsifal and King Arthur, to a quest for the Holy Grail and the Lost Paradise. Most appeared early in the thirteenth century when knightly orders and chivalrous virtues were at their height, and Latin Catholicism over-reached itself—'

'—y'mean when the oppressed rebelled?' began Jason.

Ignoring the remark, Volodya went on to explain how the Cathars were exterminated by the sword and the pyre:

'By then, Rome had institutionalized the Inquisition and its only threat, officially, came from the ever-defiant *Cathari*, the Perfect Ones. Hundreds, if not thousands, were murdered because they believed in Christ *and* the Grail. It was a tragedy that would be repeated in the next century, when the *Templari* were exterminated.'

'I thought they both defied Rome,' Jason interrupted, trying to bait the Bear, 'because the clergy had become too rich and powerful?'

'*Da, da.* Yes, it wasn't easy to understand the wealth and cruelty of the Roman Church, especially when it extolled the virtues of poverty. Understandably, stories about the Grail found a willing audience in a poverty-stricken and pest-ridden Europe; and for peasants and nobles alike, it was comforting to hear about the realm of a Perfect Prince where poverty, penance and the plague ceased to exist.'

'Only the poor and illiterate believe in a Realm of Righteousness,' taunted Jason, still setting his trap, 'it's their only comfort on earth.'

Volodya growled. *No, malheureusement, Jason had no faith.*

'These stories offer us more than mere comfort, Jason. We all feel a faint echo within because we sense King Arthur's garden at Camelot and Parsifal's forest of Brocéliande really do exist, if only long ago, or in a far-off land. It's an echo of our former life in Atlantis—'

'—like the Garden of Earthly Delights,' said Sonja quickly, before Jason snared himself.

'Yes, like the *hortus deliciari*,' nodded Volodya appreciatively, 'and in the Garden of the Grail even the squirrels have a proper home. It's as if we want Dante or Milton's Paradise to be real.'

'We cling to the notion of a terrestrial paradise in Cape Town too,' tossed in Jason. 'We've imported squirrels, trout, racing pigeons and track horses. Even hops for making beer.'

Volodya was in no mood for Jason's humour. Brushing him aside, he hailed a waiter, his gold teeth glinting in the sun:

'The idea of a paradisal kingdom spread as crusaders and pilgrims returned from the East, telling tales of a just and humble king who ruled the Indies. Some said he descended from the Magi, as he never seemed to age. Others thought he was the Evangelist, since Christ had said the Beloved John would live until he himself returned.'

Jason scoffed inaudibly: *And now we have an immortal ally!*

'His court was said to be so large that he ruled over seventy-two kings and their princes, bishops and nobles. However, his humility was such that he saw himself only as Christ's servant, and thus a servant of all humanity. It was said he rode a mule while his servants went on horses. To emphasize his piousness, he used the title of priest and was simply called the "Presbyter".'

'Are these the actual descriptions of PJ's kingdom?'

Volodya swayed, then turned to Jason:

'Yes, but from this point on his legend moves from the real into the realm of the fantastic, into a world of magical beasts and strange imagery—including the Phoenix, of which there was but one in the world at any time.'

Volodya told how the Presbyter's table, cut from a single emerald, could feed a thousand guests—the mighty and the low. Like those at Solomon's table, none went hungry. Everyone had work and found rest. It was also said that a magic mirror stood before his court, through which he could see into every corner of his realm—

'—like the mirror at Hogwarts,' Sonja said, momentarily entranced by the image. 'Sorry, besides the fiction, what evidence is there?'

The first official report, Volodya resumed, came from a conference between Pope Eugenius and Bishop Hugh of Jabala, held near Rome at the end of 1145—.

'—so what happened?'

'The Second Crusade, eventually, but it was such a fiasco that the Christians were left worse off than before.'

'Sorry, Volodya, I meant what happened to Prester John?'

'*Pardon.* The Pope was told how a priest-king, a Christian soldier called John, made war on the Muslim city of Ecbatana... Although defended by Persians and Assyrians, the three-day siege saw Prester John's army emerge victorious. He then moved his army toward Jerusalem to assist the stranded Christians. Unfortunately, his men couldn't swim across the Tigris and so were forced to return.'

'Return?'

'They went back home—'

'—and where was that?'

'I don't know, probably China-Mongolia. It appears Bishop Hugh wanted to demonstrate that relations with distant allies would be bedevilled by environmental factors, as much as by differences in culture. As you know, historians have identified this as the defeat of a Turkish-Persian ruler and, for a brief moment in history, the Mongol Khans were mistaken as allies against Islam. As we said, the Chinese-Mongolian Empire followed a blend of Buddhism and Christianity, one closely related to Manichaeism, so it's easy to see how physical events and spiritual beliefs blurred into each other.'

The idea was enthralling: was Almeida's murder also such a case? Had the real and symbolic events spilled into each other? His murder certainly was iconic.

The Bear lumbered on:

'We next hear about Prester John in the late twelfth century when a letter, written in Latin to Emperor Maximilian, circulated the Holy Roman Empire. With the invention of the printing press it became Europe's first best-seller; and in the centuries to follow, more versions were found with ever more embellishments.'

'That seems to be the case with all good stories,' teased Sonja.

'For whatever reason, be it fantasy or escapism, the story inspired adventurers, explorers and scholars. They all hoped to find the realm of Prester John and so, between the twelfth and thirteenth centuries, theses stories were fervently recorded all over Europe.'

'Hence the sudden appearance of the Grail legend?'

She glanced at Jason, nudging him under the table to keep quiet.

Volodya continued:

'Wolfram von Eschenbach drew on pre-Islamic ideas from Arabia, where the phoenix was reborn every few hundred years or so, making Prester John the grandson of an Arabian queen from Zazamanc. Remember, the biblical Land of Kush was spread across present-day Saudi Arabia, Yemen, Eritrea, Ethiopia and Somalia—including the Red Sea and Horn of Africa. Like the Celts of Gaul and Britain, they occupied both sides of the sea. By the late fourteenth century the Presbyter's kingdom was identified with Ethiopia, rather than with Arabia or India.'

Volodya waved for the bill.

'Marco Polo never found him,' tossed in Jason again, 'so Genoese cartographers were the first to say he lived in Africa.'

'Hey,' inserted Sonja, 'that's an alluring prospect for any explorer, especially those looking for reasons to venture beyond the Sahara.'

She watched Volodya fiddle with his ring. He was about to leave, that much was clear:

'Portugal was at the helm of Europe's expansion and led this quest into the fifteenth century. Mlle Sonja, I'm afraid that's all I have time for today... *au revoir.*'

After promising to call, followed by a grizzly hug, they parted at the Jardim's grand fountain. The setting sun cast long shadows across the botanical gardens as they strolled back to their pensão—a plastered house with decorative wrought-iron balconies and narrow shuttered windows. It stood in the crook of a cobbled lane, drenched in light, and provided a secluded spot to enjoy Volodya's gift. His vinho verde proved a good choice for the meal they ordered—a traditional fatty, salted fish. To Sonja's palette, however, the wine was no match for her favourite *Life from Stone.*

∃8

The true and proper home of the Grail is Paradise, the
perfect realm of the spirit where the Priest King, John,
its last guardian, reigns benignly from his castle within
the Garden of Earthly Delights.

John Matthews, *The Grail: Quest for the eternal* (1981)

'Aha, like most mythical realms, Sonja, the kingdom of Prester John symbolises the spiritual centre of our world.'

With this Mendle ended their call. She'd skyped him while drying her hair with a towel, wearing little else but a white cotton T-shirt. Phoning him was always easy, as he never used his webcam. Why, he would ask, why should he comb his beard for every caller?

Then tell me why, why mow the lawn when your neighbours are on holiday?

She had been discussing notions of Paradise in Judaic folklore when Jason came up to google the old Ethiopian caravan route—the same one taken by Pêro da Covilhã.

Where was this fabled court, he wondered, and what linked the Ark to Britain's Grail legend? More importantly, how was Prester John linked to the Grail? Was the hallowed Grail temple in Africa too?

If the evidence existed, he wanted it.

Jason had been to Aksum a few years before, on an archaeological field trip, when the embattled frontier between Ethiopia and Eritrea was still accessible. He'd gone to examine excavations at an Iron Age site on the old road down to the Red Sea. Here, at Yeha, he found a carved limestone ibex which, experts agreed, could be linked to the ceremonial stone birds of Arabia *and* Zimbabwe. As yet they had no proof, only an hypothesis: northern winters drive the birds south.

Is King Arthur to Britain what Prester John was for Africa?

So what now, Britain or Africa? He still had a BA travel magazine stuffed inside his satchel and, rummaging through its crumpled pages, found a flight map: England or Ethiopia? Easy, it would be London, as he was going there anyway.

He presented his plan as soon as she hung up. Sitting on the bed in only a T-shirt, she reached for her pants.

'First, let me get dressed, then you can talk…'

She fingered her way around the bed, inelegantly, trying to retrieve her clothes. Dias was right, size and distance were relative.

She had good legs, long and slender, with smooth shoulders. Jason seemed not to notice. He had a plan to work out:

'Why not come with to London,' he suggested, 'we can both go via Paris and see the Ethiopian manuscripts at the Bibliothèque nationale —if that's feasible?'

It was a ridiculous plan, of course, as he already had a return ticket from Lisbon. But she could see the idea really excited him. *Tsjonge*, he could be so casual, so overtly confident, and so frustratingly vague! Yet he was taking responsibility for their travel arrangements.

Let him continue, I'll dress once he's gone.

'We can stay with my brother, Anton. I'll attend the conference while you visit the British Library.'

Oh, so he'd thought it through that far?

'Leave, when?'

'Tomorrow.'

Why not, Paris is on my way?

'I'll go with you as far as Charles de Gaulle, *nota bene*, after that you can do what you want, but I'm going home.'

'Sure.'

'And there's one condition, Jason, you have to plan our route or I'll be lost before we reach the border. After Mossel Bay, it can happen anywhere. Now go buy a map while I get dressed and pack my bags. *Boas noites!*'

'Hold on, first read this,' he said excitedly, handing her a copy of John Matthew's *Grail*. 'I bought it at the second-hand bookstall by the park, yesterday, thinking you'd like to read about the legend yourself. Look what's scribbled inside.'

He pressed the book into her hands. Inside the back cover were several lines, just legible, written in smudged pencil:

> German poet Wolfram von Eschenbach (1170–1220) wrote finest romance of the Grail legend, completed in c.1207. Parzival (Parsifal) half-brother = Feirefiz = son of Belacane an Arabian (or Black) Queen from Abyssinia (or Ethiopia) and identified as the southern Terrestrial Paradise of Africa

MOTHER		FATHER		MOTHER
Herzolyde	←	Gamureth	→	Belacane
↓				↓
"clear as the light of the sun"				"black as night"
↓				↓
SON				SON
Parsifal				Feirefiz

> Marrying Herzolyde (European) and Belacane (African) Gamureth reconciles Light+Dark, Old+New, West+East uniting both Christian and Arabian (pre-Islamic) traditions. Parsifal's black and white speckled half-brother = Feirefiz. Feirefiz (French *vrai fils*) the true son, or two-coloured son, is part-European and part-African. Feirefiz is the father of Prester John = Last Guardian of the Grail.

Lost in thought, she handed back the book, her movements slow and deliberate. She stayed seated, her T-shirt tucked around her thighs.

'Can I get dressed now?'

'Wolfram,' he added, as if he hadn't heard, 'claims the Grail's final resting place is in the East and makes Prester John its last guardian.'

'Yes, but what were they guarding, and from whom?'

'Right. As children, Uncle Noor told us that Gibril Tarik did not stop at Cordoba as planned, but went on to Toledo in search of an Emerald Table that once stood in Solomon's Temple. It had a solid top and—after Tarik's many adventures—was taken to Damascus, then the capital of a caliphate that extended from Spain to India.'

'So they guarded this emerald slab, *really, that's it?*'

'No, not according to Wolfram, who says Pazival's father is buried beneath it, somewhere near Baghdad. It's not Gamureth's tomb they protected, but the Grail itself.'

'Like the Ark of the Covenant?'

'Yes, that's why I think there's a parallel between Solomon's Table and Menelik's Ark. Both were transferred from Jerusalem to a centre of religious learning—where they'd be safe—as if they contained a sacred teaching or hidden power. And, incredibly, it's said that both originated in Atlantis...'

All is possible if the impossible is true.

Bewildered, she exclaimed: 'Wait, wait, wait! For someone usually so sceptical, why rush off to Paris?'

'Why? Because Joseph of Arimathea brought the cup to the West and became the first guardian of the Grail. Don't you see, *Parzival* is written in a metaphoric language: West and East do not necessarily represent Christian and Muslim—but past and future, old and new, just as the sun sets to the West and rises in the East. Which is why Japan is called the Land of the Rising Sun. Likewise, the stars move across the sky from east to west. Don't you see, symbolically, the future is in the East and—'

'—and the future is not what it was,' quipped Sonja, still confused. She eased off the bed, smiling, and sent him on his way.

Once gone, she hurriedly slipped on her pants. She now knew that Almeida was like a righteous potentate, a sort of Prester John, who governed an independent state with isolated religious communities. And, like the Presbyter, he also preserved one of the oldest blends of Christianity in the world.

From the window she watched Jason walk over to the corner shop. Two mopeds hurtled passed, like racing demons, almost knocking him off his feet. The afternoon light bleached the plastered walls, accentuating his smooth dark skin.

30

The Cape was discovered on the way to Prester John.
Ralph Shepherd, *Invisible Africa* (1996)

Later that night, before falling into bed, Sonja checked her emails. There was only one she stopped to open.

From: mendle@sam.org.za
Sent: Sunday, July 18, 21:08
To: awayfromhome@gmail.com
Subject: Prester John
Laurence asked that this be passed on to you:

Prester John

The Realm of Prester John was an esoteric legend or device designed to manage schismatic Christianity and the renewed drive toward a unified age of spirituality during the medieval Crusades—setting a precedent for the European Renaissance. At the epicentre was the Rosicrucian flame of Gnosis burning in the lamp of Nestorian Christianity in the Eastern world, a flame seeking to transmit itself westward again.

For several centuries the esoteric Orders used the legend of Prester John as a ploy to influence the turn of historic events— especially the political interplay between East and West—and to maintain a balance of power conducive for the cosmopolitan culture of the Renaissance with its hybrid philosophy, art and spirituality. Ultimately, Prester John represented the elusive Platonic ideal of the philosopher-king held by the Christian world as the representative of a kingdom to be sought within, firstly, before it could be realised outwardly.

Here, below Laurence's message, Mendle went on to explain that the legends of Prester John and King Solomon overlapped, significantly, as both sovereigns ate from an emerald table.

Had the tales spread via Jerusalem, she speculated, *along a north-south axis?* Possibly, as crusaders going to the Holy Land came from Britain, Iberia, India and Ethiopia. In fact, the legend of priest-king Lalibela, Emperor of Ethiopia c.1185–1225, tells of his sojourn to Jerusalem and suggests that he returned to Aksum with a small band of knights (the Knights of Solomon?) who wished to see the Ark for themselves. Today, pilgrims gather by the sacred shrine of the Ark to receive holy water from its Guardian—from the Pure One who lives permanently within its precinct. On his point, Mendle also explained:

> Graham Hancock argues that the presence of the Templar Cross demonstrates the Knight's involvement in the design and construction of the rock-hewn churches at Lalibela. A Templar connection was also confirmed by Padre Francisco Álvares who, on finding Pêro da Covilhã, recorded a legend about the white men that helped build these churches. They were master builders and their patron, St Bernard of Clairvaux, was behind the simultaneous and rapid appearance of Gothic architecture in France, most notably at Chartres.

A mere coincidence, Lalibela and Chartres?

Well no, Volodya claimed that the two were spiritually connected. The impulse in Europe manifested above the ground, soaring to new heights; whereas in Africa it delved into the rock, implanting itself anew, as it did a thousand years before in the catacombs of Rome.

A reincarnating spirit, he had added, *a regeneration of the earth itself.*

Tradition has it that in the fourth-century reign of King Ezana, Greek-speaking Syrians (Nestorians) brought Christianity to Ethiopia. Ezana's realm thus became part of the Hellenized world and, to show his conversion, he adopted the equilateral Greek cross as his emblem. At the time Ethiopia was comparable to Egypt, Persia, Babylonia and Byzantium—also sending emissaries to Jerusalem and Rome.

But in North Africa, weakened by internal conflicts, the Christians would be swept aside by waves of invading Muslims. Ethiopia alone stood intact, the last outpost of Christianity in Africa, its Golden Age soon forgotten in Europe—and so too its legend of the Ark.

TRAVEL

40

The use of travelling is to regulate imagination by reality, and instead of thinking how things may be, to see them as they are.
Samuel Johnson, private conversation (14 September 1777)

Ahead lay a long drive. The next few days would not be easy. On the road temperatures were bound to soar and driving a car without air-con would be testing. Spending so much time alone with Jason would be a test too, as he drove hard and (still unaccustomed to right-hand traffic) tended to veer across the road. He steered Bart's Volvo as if it were the Argo, and they on a perilous journey against time.

She took a sip of water and reminded herself that she was still on holiday, if only for a few more days, and that there was no need to rush off or accomplish anything.

Sonja liked him, yes, but she wasn't sure why he'd come to Lisbon, or why he now wanted to head for Paris? She would remain cautious: research was research and a colleague should stay a colleague.

She was not one to have an affair, certainly not a beach romance like she'd had at Luz all those years ago. That summer she became a teenager, slim and demure, turning heads in a floral dress from the Bijenkorf. As she recalled, Raul had a mop of unruly hair and clumsy hands—and she'd never heard from him again.

She leant her head against the window, using her bag as a cushion, while the little car rumbled on, vibrating against her skull. Her mind wondered back to the ash-grey skull in the SA Museum which, like an empty shell, still echoed the surf against the shore.

Her neck felt stiff and her shoulders ached. She needed more sleep. Restless and rueful, she shifted uncomfortably while internalising the loose ends they'd gathered. Almeida's murder seemed like a Turban, skilfully concealing the ends from which it was plaited.

Like most long-distance travellers—from Marco Polo to Neil Armstrong—she knew small experiences matured best over time. She also knew that these experiences could mellow into memorable moments; just as a green wine produces an unforgettable palate.

Her memories matured vividly: such as waiting for a dust-yellow MarcoPolo bus in the sweltering heat, seeing an impoverished farm on the sun-scorched coast, walking windward to the Holy Cape and, finally, standing on a stone-paved wind-rose. Like that giant Wild Fig on the banks of the Liesbeeck, the rose radiated in all directions.

Her memories of those white-sailed ships were as fresh today as the children's paintings at the Dias Museum. Past and present met in moments of reflection too, she realised. She recalled rushing through Lisbon's art museum with its low ceilings and dimly lit galleries, her hurried visit ending abruptly before the stoic and inscrutable portrait of Prince Henry. His sombre face, wine-brown like the Camissa.

She remembered climbing the cold spiral stairwell at Belém Tower; its narrow steps polished smooth by passing shoes. Then, from its terrace, seeing the fat Tagus flow toward the sea, forever forward, melon-green like the Atlantic. Built after Almeida's death, the Torre de Belém looked like a caravel with a bastion terrace for its foredeck and a tower as its poop. It was a masterpiece of architectural rhetoric, an unsinkable stone ship.

It was here that Sonja had first seen the elegant and emblematic Manueline knot, chiselled in stone, symbol of a world united by one king and one empire. The knot was used—as were heraldic shields and armillary spheres—to add legitimacy to Manuel's reign. He was keen to present himself as "The serene and all powerful ruler, on this side of the world and beyond the sea, and always visible". Always visible, like the northern Pole Star.

She'd seen traces of Portugal's Golden Age on every street corner; each and every building emblazoned with signs of the *Descobrimentos*. The equilateral Christ Cross appeared on rib-vaulted ceilings, tiled floors, castle gatehouses and church façades. Likewise, the Templar Cross appeared as keyhole plates, door latches and archer's windows.

She'd seen both used to striking effect at Tomar, uniting not only the past and the present, but the Knights Templar and the Order of Christ. Like the Southern Cross, the Templar Cross was to be seen in a new place every day.

She shifted again, slipping off her shoes and crossing her bare legs over Jason's satchel. There was not much room in their little Argo. Driving on the edge of night, the sun set to port.

She fixed her gaze on the long road ahead. Her mind full of fleeting impressions, some viewed in reverse, as if seen over a shoulder or in a rear-view mirror.

They were driving north, toward a land of shorter days and cooler nights. Behind them lay a windy coast with its broiling sun. Ahead, wet midlands with sporadic showers.

They meandered along narrow rivers and between undulating hills, passing scattered churches, temple ruins and megalithic dolmens.

She closed her eyes and drifted off.

Half asleep, she imagined a botanical garden with a fountain, a bridge beside a graveyard, a cave by a spring, a man in green foliage, a red-ochre ship and an ox-blood setting sun. Her memories blurred, mixing reality with fantasy.

She recalled an antiquarian book shop, but not its whereabouts. She remembered an art deco basement café, but not in which district they'd been. She could picture the ornate tiles of an underground metro, but not what line they were on. She saw floors paved with tombstones, cold and smooth, including the name DALMEIDA, but not what became of his brothers and sisters.

She saw a wooden mermaid, once a ship's figurehead, chained to a museum wall. She saw an eagle, wings spread wide like the phoenix, clawing a decapitated negroid head. She saw the moon, deep-yellow, like a cat's eye, peering over the mountain's ridge. She saw a crimson cloud, fire-red, like a winged dragon devouring a church spire.

She slumbered among images of St George's dragon, St Vincent's ravens and St James's scallop. She saw gargoyles, leafy green-men, and loaves of bread shaped like the Mountains of the Moon. Somewhere they passed a service station where an inflatable Michelin Man posed as Munster's *Monoculi*...

Why these experiences should make an impression and not, say, Camões's tomb, she didn't know. Stumbling upon the poet's resting place in Belém engendered no emotion, even though his epic poem presented her with an important insight into Almeida's death. Her instinctive distrust of Camões left her feeling indifferent. He valorised too much, praising Gama's cruelty toward the heathens.

Including Gama's flogging of Gaspar?

There were countless acts of brutality, as vivid as the impalement of Titus van Bengal, including a monkey on a pole beside a village café. Her journey was, after all, not a rational experience.

She sat up for a sip of water.

Smiling back at her, Jason assumed she'd been awake and asked: 'Then what about Almeida's family?'

'Well,' slowly adjusting her hair, 'there are overlapping facts, facts where the exoteric and esoteric intersect.'

'But what do we actually know about Almeida? As yet, we don't even know when he was born...'

She watched as he stared ahead, one hand on the Argo's helm, the other waving in the breeze. She raised four fingers in reply:

'We can be sure of at least four dates. First, 1484, when Almeida was implicated in the conspiracy against João II and fled abroad.'

'Returning in 1492?'

'Yes, which is also the year America was discovered.' She prodded him with her empty water bottle: 'A date, an accurate historical date, and from a scholar who's on holiday. Impressive!'

She continued her summation:

'The second date is 1493, after Columbus returned. Almeida was instructed to sail west and claim, officially, or before Spain could do so, the New World for Portugal. It was then thought to be Japan. However, the matter was settled diplomatically—'

'—until Portugal claimed Brazil for itself, in 1500.'

She pulled herself upright.

'Let me finish! Third, 1505, when he became viceroy after Cunha's illness. And then, finally, his assassination in 1510, while returning to Lisbon under escort.'

'So how do these dates fit together?'

'Well, based on our findings, there are several historical certainties which, like keystones, hold our overarching facts in place. We can use them to build a case, stone by stone, until we have enough to argue reasonable doubt in court.'

She spoke as if sharing a secret:

'First, like Camões, Almeida blended rationalism with superstition, doctrine and divination. Secondly, like Gaspar, contact with foreign cultures provided him insight into the arcane knowledge of the East. Thirdly, like Dias, he secured a sea route around Islam's stranglehold on trade in the Mediterranean. Fourth, like Prince Henry, he desired exchange with potential African allies below the cordon of Islam. And now, like Prester John, he'd founded an independent state with ties to one of the world's oldest blends of Christianity.'

'Sure, but this isn't enough to prove *why* Almeida was murdered?'

'I know, but for now, it's all we have to go on.'

They needed more facts, more details, that much was clear. And to do so meant delving deeper into recorded histories, official reports and personal testimonies...

They sped forward, toward the black Pyrenees, Jason steering the Argo into a sea of darkness while she slept, like a curled up cat, on the ship's prow.

41

*But our concern is not with what St James and his
disciples may or may not have done, but with what
later generations of Christians chose to believe.*

R A Fletcher, *Saint James's Catapult* (1984)

'Europe's road to the End-of-the-Earth, to beyond the black stump,
reopened when the Moors were driven back in 812—and since then
saints, sinners and peddlers have walked the camino de Santiago. It's
an awesome walkabout today.'

The sunburnt pilgrim spoke in spatters, eating his red-hot tortilla in
the crowded tavern. They listened to each mouthful, hoping another
table would soon be available.

They'd met him at a crossroad on the Camino. They were heading
in opposite directions, but took lodgings together. For one night only.

'The cult of St James united the petty kingdoms around one faith,'
he added, 'and for the first time Spain had a common hero.'

That was a lucky stroke, Sonja reflected, since the saint's grave had
only been discovered *after* the road reopened, one year after, in fact,
though the pilgrim wasn't sure if the Apostle had been there at all—
to preach or to be buried.

Not that it mattered to this pilgrim, as he had faith and a new pair
of walking shoes. He'd been to Santiago de Compostela several times
before, and was back for the Saint's Feast on 25 July. The rest of the
year he worked as a salesman-cum-lay preacher in Queensland.

Wiping his mouth, he explained: 'Yeah, that's a week away, right,
and without my Nikes.'

He slipped off his thong and lifted a hairy foot from under the
table, declaring with pride:

'Hey, check this out, three weeks on the road and I got the blisters to prove it!'

Three weeks? Three days in a car was enough for her. Anyway, why should anyone choose to suffer? As Mendle once said: *None suffer more than a tortured convert or a forgotten hostage.*

'Sant'Iago,' the sandy Aussie declared, 'is the old Spanish word for Saint James. His legend says Compostela comes from *campus stellae*, meaning "field of stars", and that this is an old megalithic star route. We reckon the son of Zebedee is buried here, below the cathedral, in a tomb beneath his shrine. He is the patron of Catholic Spain and Christian pilgrims, and our protector against the Muslims—along with St George and the Archangel Michael, of course.'

'A Moorslayer *and* a Dragonslayer!' muttered Jason.

The Pilgrim swallowed his potatoes, unperturbed:

'They say the Saint visited Charlemagne in a dream, telling him to liberate the tomb from the Moors.'

'Wait, you said the tomb was only discovered *afterwards?*'

'Look, it's a legend, so dates don't apply.'

'Why, are legends ahistorical?'

'Yeah, which is why schoolbooks leave them out. The soldiers saw St James in the sky before the battle, making their victory easy graft.'

Jason smirked: 'The mani-king of M'banza-Kongo had the same vision before his battle of succession. As a new convert, he fought for the largest city in sub-equatorial Africa.'

The point was lost on the Pilgrim. He merely leapt back:

'Charlemagne dreamt the stars would lead his army to the tomb, right, and so the star route became *El Camino de Santiago*, "The Way of Saint James", or simply today, the Milky Way. Early pilgrims said it was formed by the dust of their fellow travellers. Like them fellas in our Outback.'

Jason sniffed a weakness in his prey:

'So what came first; the dream or the dust?'

'First the stars,' said this Chaucerian Aussie, unaware of his foe's stealthy approach. Like a hyena, Jason closed in:

'Most Stone Age hunter-gatherers, from aboriginals to bushmen, see the night sky as the campfires of their Ancestors: the brighter stars belonging to those recently departed, the dimmest ones to those already long gone.'

As a layman, he didn't care much for anthropology. Kangaroo-like, he bounced from subject to subject:

'Unable to recapture Spain, Charlemagne's knights were ambushed in the Pyrenees, where his brave-hearted nephew Roland was killed. Serious pilgrims start up there.'

'So Charlemagne is connected to the knights of St James *and* to the pilgrims of Santiago?'

'Right. Santiago's intervention is shown in works of art around the country—always on a white charger, red sword in hand, trampling the enemy underfoot—and he's seen like that in Russia and Ethiopia too, or so I heard from a fella traveller.'

'A saint with a sword!' snarled Jason, smelling blood. 'Doesn't his motto say: "James's sword is red with the blood of Islam"?'

'Yeah, *Sant'Iago da Espada* or, if you want to call a spade a shovel, it's the "Military Order of Saint James of the Sword". King Fernando created the Order three centuries after the road reopened, knighting several nobles for offering their protection on his section of the road. Though Spanish, Fernando was a Latin Christian. Both Rome and the Moorslayer were invincible!'

'What proof—the fact that Islam was repelled?'

'Yeah, too right!'

So, can the impossible be true?

It seemed St James was to Spain what St Michael was to France—and the rest of Christendom too. The Pilgrim reckoned this was why St Michael had the same badge in Normandy:

'Le Mont Saint-Michel used to be called Mont-Tombe, but not because St Michael is buried there. No, his scallop was purloined by French pilgrims going home. But I reckon you don't believe in angels or the intervention of saints?'

'No, why,' scoffed Jason, 'why should I?'

'Sometimes, maybe once in a lifetime, someone does something for you which you don't have time to do yourself.'

'Which others do for us?' checked Sonja.

'Yeah.'

'Explain?'

He wolfed down the tortilla, smearing his chin with his sleeve.

One more week before the Feast, she reflected, amazed, *how ravenous would he be by then?*

'We don't have to do everything ourselves, others can do some of it for us—we live through our mates and rellies.'

'Wait, y'mean others do what we can't or won't do ourselves?'

'Unable. It's an ancient law of karma where the biblical "sins of the fathers will be visited upon their sons". Except, this is the reverse of that law, where all good shall be passed on to future generations.'

'How neat!'

'Floats my boat,' hollered Jason, also awed by the man's appetite. Their guest wiped his mouth again, washing down the tortilla with a warm tankard of beer. The tavern was a hole for thirsty souls.

All good shall be passed on to future generations?

Sonja excused herself, saying she needed to unpack. In truth, all that chilli was too much for her.

She wanted to undress and take a long shower, in private. Perhaps check her emails. At least some things had changed on the Camino. Today's lodgings had electricity, running water and wireless internet.

The Santiago Pilgrim talked while Jason mused over Feirefiz, the half-brother of Parsifal, who'd inherited the best of both worlds—he too had a white father and a dusky mother. It was an interesting formulation for a Gemini, though Jason only partly believed that stuff —his other half did not.

42

The strain of another sweltering day in the car showed on their faces. Having started early, they'd driven north via French tollgates and fuelling stations, from one roadside refrigerator to the next. Along the way a spotty cashier said it was the hottest day in living memory. Though only a teenager, she said it must be true as they'd announced it on the radio. After eight hours in the car, now south of Paris, Jason declared their Scandinavian coupé better suited for colder climes.

Seeing the volume of traffic ahead, they dismissed the City of Light as a destination and turned off for Chartres. Why not, he thought, having heard about the Gallo-Roman amphitheatre and aqueduct. Although both structures had long since disappeared, instinct steered him toward the crown of the old pagan hill.

In a crooked street below the Cathedral's spires, near the stream, they found an inconspicuous chambre d'hôtes for the night. Jason left the car on the curb and, grabbing their bags, followed Sonja into the hallway. She'd already rung the desk-bell.

A moment later the landlord appeared, bumping open the kitchen door with his boot, while balancing a dinner tray above the scuffed counter. Imitating a WWI flying ace, he aimed for the mahogany runway and landed his tray with perfect precision. The door swung back to reveal a hand-painted sign:

Propriété Privée

With his long Gaulish hair and hanging Vercingétorix moustache, he looked more like an old Gallic warrior than a French fighter pilot. And to their surprise he smoked his Gauloises publicly. He spoke to Sonja in rapid-fire French, acting as if she'd flown in alone.

She arranged for a twin-room as Jason appraised the vintage décor: the original wooden panels, mosaic tiles and glass bricks struck him as retro-chic. Behind a tower of postcards hung a huge 1969 poster of the Cathédrale Notre-Dame.

'It was the year of Our Miracles,' said the owner, offering Sonja a tired-looking armchair, 'one American guest was cured of arthritis, another with tuberculosis—and I won the lottery!'

A colourful housekeeper shuffled by, presumably to prepare their rooms, while the landlord regaled them with weary pilgrim tales:

'They came from all over, including Rosslyn, but we have fewer visitors today. Climatic change has been bad for business.'

Jason wondered what, if anything, had changed here in forty years?

Sonja smiled politely, saying they were happy to rest. But she was not to be spared so easily. Seeing the books under her arm, their host suggested she look for the sculpture of Aristotle above the front door. That is, on the west façade:

'According to early pilgrims, it depicts The Philosopher writing an esoteric work, regrettably, now lost. You should take a stroll—'

She sank into the armchair: 'That can wait, later perhaps.'

'How about a drink then?'

Her feet, neck and shoulders ached—a shower was all she really cared for, and some fresh clothes. Jason looked edgy and asked for a double-espresso. He needed the acidity.

Their host ducked behind the counter and set the coffee machine, his voice barely audible:

'Our Cathédrale is an encyclopaedia of esoteric wisdom,' he said, before his hairy face reappeared. 'Ours is a monument to the Gothic *intellectus spiritualis*, architecturally, and best seen in the West Portal—like the West Window of Tomar's Convento de Cristo.'

'You mean their spiralled Chapter window?'

'Yes,' he added, making an oily espresso. 'Tomar is as emblematic of Templar mysticism as Chartres is for proto-humanist mysticism, but I suspect you already know of the *Secretum secretorum?* If not, let me tell you what I heard from a passing pilgrim.'

They had no choice but to sit and listen, at least until the slippered housekeeper returned. So they waited, too tired to protest.

'I have a postcard of Aristotle—here, let me get it—showing him seated at a writing block with his styli and ink horn. Here, Aristoteles, look, that's him, The Philosopher himself.'

She held up the card for Jason to see. There was one just like it in the dossier, stuck inside a wire-ring notebook. The implications were obvious. She redirected:

'So Aristotle's science was assimilated here at Chartres?'

'Yes, his "rediscovery" came via crusaders and pilgrims returning from Palestine and Compostela. In Moorish Spain, of course, he'd already been savoured by scholars of Islam-lite—by the Caliphate's privileged few.'

'Privileged, why?'

'Because Aristotle's ideas weren't accepted by all Islamic scholars. His concept of divinity and immortality did not fit comfortably within Muslim orthodoxy. Nor among orthodox Catholics.'

'Neither did his idea of an eternal creation?' she added, recollecting her own Protestant upbringing.

'Yes, right again. Nevertheless, the twelfth-century Renaissance in France, and later in Italy, was one of extraordinary energy and innovation, with Chartres becoming the nursery for this intellectual development.'

As Ethiopia was for medieval Africa, murmured Jason to himself.

Their Gallic Warrior stubbed his cigarette, announcing:

'They say Chartres is where the Incarnation of the West took place. Our cathedral school set the course for studying Greek, Judaic and Islamic philosophy—including mathematics, engineering and cartography—all of which were later assimilated at Paris University.'

'Through which Aristotle's ideas entered mainstream thinking?'

'Professors of the first French Academy fought fiercely against it. It was a new intellectual front where Islam clashed with Christianity: rational philosophy versus dogmatic theology.'

They heard shuffling feet on the boards above. Their host returned to the cathedral's orientation:

'The West Portal refers to the future, to the Last Judgement and New Jerusalem. North represents the Old Testament, as usual, and South the New. It's a traditional orientation and found at sacred sites all over Europe. Tomar's Convento follows a similar symbolic order. I see you have their guidebook too.'

Sonja recalled the symbolic language of *Parsifal* wherein East and West were metaphors for the Past and Future, respectively.

Making of Istanbul or Jerusalem a crossroad for the Present?

'In 1969, when those miracles took place, Kenneth Clark described our West Portal as one of the most beautifully carved ensembles in the Western world,' the landlord glowed with pride, 'and yes, he said it on BBC too. Sculpted figures emerge from the architecture as self-conscious individuals, filled with passion and emotion...'

Their Gallic Warrior was indefatigable:

'Later, when you look for the figure of Aristotle, see him as The Philosopher of Hellenism, Judaism, Islam and, of course, Christianity. His natural science influenced the East; whereas his logic and meta-physics flowed into the West. And yes, coincidentally, scribes from ancient Egypt are depicted in the same pose; with pens, pigments and parchments. The Louvre has one from Saqqârah that once held a reed pen, now lost. Unlike Aristotle, conveniently, the Egyptian wears only a loin cloth.'

'Unlike the tablets of Moses,' teased Sonja, 'esoteric knowledge isn't carved in stone either. Anyway, besides some notes found in the first century, most of Aristotle's writings have been lost.'

Was this work the one described in the folios?

There was little chance of asking their host while he expounded on the importance of Aristotelian and Neoplatonic philosophy, from the practice of imitating nature to that of putting reason over faith. He rapidly extolled how generations—from al-Rashid and al-Farabi to Ibn Sina and Ibn Rushd—strove to reconcile Aristotelian concepts within the traditional teachings of the Qur'an:

'The works of the latter two scholars, Ibn Sina and Ibn Rushd, were taken to Italy, hence their Latin names: Avicenna and Averroës. Today both are better known in the West where, in fact, Averroës is regarded as the finest Aristotelian philosopher of the Muslim world. And yet he was esteemed, reviled, exiled and pardoned, all in one lifetime—a common scenario then, it seems. As an Andalusian-Arab physician he fell under the protection of the Almohads and wrote a medical encyclopaedia, while also serving as chief judge in religious and civil affairs. However, his uncompromising ideas clashed with the

Orthodoxy of the East and pre-empted his banishment until, at least, the Caliph had him rehabilitated. Averroës spent his last years in self-chosen seclusion, dedicating his time to philosophy until he died at Marrakech in 1198.'

The old lady flushed a toilet upstairs.

'It was Averroës who cut the knot of Islam, claiming philosophy and theology were equal, though separate, and that both led to the truth—eventually. His commentaries became the primary texts for Aristotelians, gaining him the prestigious title of The Commentator. The liberal professors at Paris University, such as Albertus Magnus and Thomas Aquinas, promoted his rationalist ideas while a student-cum-court translator took his work to Italy.'

The landlord lit another cigarette, scratched his jaw, and pointed out that Aristotle's work ranged from natural science to harmonizing prophecy with philosophy, faith with reason.

'At that time, however, the Catholic Church denounced Averroës's so-called "double truths". That is, saying something was true through reason while its opposite could still be true through faith. Rome's condemnation was aimed at Siger de Brabant who, as the main proponent of Latin Averroism in Paris, challenged the concept of an immortal human soul. Siger followed Aristotle and Averroës, arguing that creation was an ongoing process, without end, and that only the human spirit continues to exist after death.'

The Guerrier Gaulois spat out a shred of tobacco, offering a bizarre footnote:

'A Brabantine chronicler said Siger was stabbed to death; killed by a demented secretary wielding a quill. His Italian assassins claimed Siger deserved his death as he'd done enough damage with his pen. Like the Mafiosi, his murder had to be symbolic.'

Like the stone in a dead man's mouth.

The colourful housekeeper returned. Sonja leapt at the opportunity to *douche* while Jason stepped out to repark the car.

By some miracle it was still there, unticketed.

Perhaps there was a God, after all?

ЧӘ

The origins of Chartres are lost in the mists of time, where legend and history are interwoven, and have been further confused by the imagination of later centuries which mingled a Druidic tradition with a pre-Christian virgin-mother cult...

Malcolm Miller, *Chartres Cathedral* (1985)

After sitting all day, Sonja chose to stretch her legs before nightfall. She strode toward the cathedral, hauling a fatigued Jason behind her. Too tired to carry his own camera, she took it with in her backpack.

'Hurry up, while the light is still good.'

Long shadows clung to their shoes, reluctant to leave before the last rays of sunlight left too. The Ancestral Spirits watched their slow approach, two unwitting interlopers, as they reached the deepening north porch. The sculptured stone released the sun's warmth. Here stood Solomon and the Queen of Sheba—the patriarch and mother of Grail Christianity—anticipating a new moon in the East.

The Santiago Pilgrim had told them to look for the staff, pouch and scallops of St James in the southern portal. She led Jason around the church, her mind wandering elsewhere:

'It was Queen Isabella, more so than Ferdinand, who put an end to the al-Andalus Academy,' she explained, only half-heartedly looking for the Apostle with a staff instead of a sword. 'Before they sacked Granada, it had libraries and mosques, scribes and scholars, sacred scrolls and, yes, Jason, ancient Greek manuscripts too.'

The weathered sandstone glowed a warm hue as the sun set beyond the town. Jason sagged against the steps. Like a soft-fingered caress, fatigue pleaded for his surrender. He would submit, blissfully, as soon as Sonja stopped demanding so much attention. *No, she never stopped to breathe, not even now.*

'From what I recall—having been to Granada as a student—the Alhambra was a fortress-palace clustered around a terraced hill and, at its centre, had an ingenious network of baths, pools, fountains and canals. Water was used for regulating temperature, irrigating gardens and, of course, for washing rituals. It was supplied via a single source, the Darro, to emphasize the preciousness of water. The subtle effect of cascading water, colour-filtered water and fragrant-scented water all enhanced the notion of a discrete Granadan paradise.'

She found the portal of St James and waited for Jason. He slumped beside her, aware of how little he'd seen of the world and that, now too tired to take another step, he'd be going no further today.

'Napoleon's troops converted the Alhambra palaces into barracks, remember, as they did at Tomar and Abrantes.'

She pressed on, knowing Jason had no will to talk back:

'In Granada, Ferdinand's men plundered the libraries and seized the philosophical and scientific manuscripts. Most administrative and historical documents were burnt during the following weeks, as these were regarded as either irrelevant or superfluous. Rampant pillaging was common after a crusade. In fact, Alexander's soldiers did the same when they plundered Persepolis.'

Sonja tugged at his sleeve:

'Come, now to the front façade, then we'll go back home…'

While surviving texts were translated into Latin and Hebrew, or so the Gallic Warrior had said, Aristotle's praise for nature struck clerics as heretical: 'Church doctrine was based on the Neoplatonic dualism of a perfect but fallen world. It was no new dispute. Proponents of each had long debated the world's vices and virtues.'

She slowed down, waiting, Jason sinking with every step.

'As our host told us earlier, Averroës argued that there ought to be no conflict between religion and philosophy, belief and knowledge, as they were merely separate ways of arriving at the same truths.'

Reaching the front door, she halted.

'While Aristotle's work in logic and metaphysics was all but lost, his ideas were still being studied at Granada in 1492. Granada was the last centre of Islamic learning in Spain and so, yes, Jason, I guess a translation of his lost treatise was likely to be found there.'

She stared across the red-tiled roofs, the sun now gone, formulating her thoughts into a coherent statement: Like Averroës, Almeida was an exiled-returnee who reconciled faith and reason; promoting a coherence between religious rationalism and scientific endeavour.

Her formulation felt like a touchstone, a keystone of sorts, as she came to understand the nature of Almeida's commission...

Dragging Jason to his feet, she offered him an arm and sauntered off—the Ancestors watching them depart down the hill.

Walking past low timbered shops and cellar doors, neither saw the man waiting in the shadows, under the eaves, until he rushed out and confronted them.

'*Dossier, le dossier?*'

Sonja recognised him instantly, not by name, but by what he wore. He was dressed in coal black, again.

She stepped sideways, bumping against Jason as the man snatched at her backpack. Instinctively her hand tightened on the strap.

'*Le dossier!*' He demanded.

She squeezed her elbow, clamping the bag under her arm.

'*Give the dossier, merde!*'

She held tight: '*Verdomme, let it go!*'

Unable to pluck it free, he fled down a side alley.

Jason gave chase.

'Wait, Jason, stop,' she yelled. 'Come back!'

He slowed down, looking over his shoulder, then retraced his steps. Breathless.

The goliath had vanished as abruptly as he'd appeared.

'W-wh-who is he?'

Jason heaved: 'Dunno, never seen him.'

'Yes we have, twice, in Lisbon and Tomar.'

'Then he knows about us?'

'He knows about the dossier. He tried to steal it. Did you see that, he grabbed my bag! Please, let's go. I want to get off the street.'

'Sure, and I should move the Volvo too. It's easy to spot a vintage coupé on the road. That's probably how he followed us to Chartres.'

They agreed to leave for Paris at first light.

At its heart, the quest for the Holy Grail has always been a quest for the Magdalene.

Dan Brown, *The Da Vinci Code* (2003)

After their encounter with the Black Goliath, Sonja thought of little else but how she could lose herself in Paris. Napoleon's "New Rome" lay only an hour away: vast, grandiose and anonymous.

Driving there she asked herself who else knew of the dossier, besides Jason and Prof Mendle. Moreover, who knew of the treatise before the fall of Granada, assuming, of course, that there was a connection?

Already in the twelfth century, if not before, Aristotle's teachings had inspired the School of Chartres and the University of Paris. His portrait above the cathedral's front door demonstrated this.

She knew Western civilisation was indebted to Greek, Hebraic and Islamic philosophy and, in turn, that these had been influenced by the Egyptians, Phoenicians and Arabians. After all, fair Europa was the daughter of Phoenix...

A car sped by. Sonja had to pull her mind back to the road.

They headed for Paris's inner quarters and found two quiet rooms near Ste Marie Madeleine, from where they could walk to the library. Finding a place for the Argo proved less easy.

The Bibliothèque nationale was housed in a grand neo-classical building that outshone Mitterrand's inglorious riverside monument. The old library was more comfortable too. Its manuscript room was crammed with antique cabinets, elegant reading tables and a spiral staircase from which all higher shelves could be reached. Throughout their visit, no one dared use the tall wheel-ladder.

They saw fine examples of the fabled Phoenix, the exquisite Queen of Sheba and, as Jason had promised, the paradise of Prester John. Here too, they found the Aethiops and fabled creatures of Africa, as in the print he'd given her in Cape Town. The imaginary geography of the Middle Ages put these creatures in Ethiopia—a land where pagan miracles abounded and where precious stones could still be found in the bellies of serpents.

But Sonja was too tired for all this. She needed to rest. Jason too, she noticed. So they returned, seeking relief from the July heat, and since his air-con malfunctioned, she let him share her room.

So far he'd been an easy travel companion: confident, intelligent, humorous and (despite his odd body tan) even attractive. But while willing to chase ogres, he was still too yellow for her.

From her bed she flipped through the TV channels until she over-heard a Catholic Freemason talk about religious conspiracies; from the Secret Archives of the Vatican to the Library of Congress, from the Inquisition to the Holy Grail. Inevitably, to things Dan Brownish.

She recalled *The Da Vinci Code* hype and how it spawned a series of commentaries, guides and games. Duty-free stores, talk-show hosts, and new-age groupies all propagated it. But most of all, it became a marketing phenomenon. It had made fictional history fashionable.

The pseudo-histories of *The Code* belonged to an age-old esoteric tradition in the West. While Brown's bestseller did well to popularize this *histoire*, much of what it incorporated was mere speculation and conjecture. However, it was the marriage to Mary Magdalene that had irritated her most. Not because the outcry was insincere—as she explained to Jason afterwards—but because the liaison between Jesus and the Magdalene had been so sensationalized.

Well, no matter how tantalising the prospect, especially of deceit or betrayal in historical writing, she would not be lured into believing Almeida's murder was a conspiracy—or even a ritual murder.

If he had been assassinated, even sacrificed, then she wanted to find the truth. If that was still possible.

A half-hour later, while Jason washed his shirt, she sat puzzling over the historiography of the Grail. Brown's narrative drew upon an obscure legend claiming that the Magdalene had provided the Grail family with a sacred bloodline—a legend with a lineage? To be fair, Sonja had not read Brown's books or seen any of the movies. The fervour around him had crushed her interest completely.

But as everyone now knew, Brown had borrowed his story from an earlier book suggesting the Cathars were the curators of the Grail and the Templars the protectors of the Legend. The authors of *Holy Blood, Holy Grail* had set out, already in 1982, to add certainty to an unstable history. And they'd succeeded ingeniously.

She knew, moreover, that no history could be recorded with such certainty; no events written without leaving gaps, no action without some inscribed meaning. And like Christ's death, Almeida's murder was also real, ritualized and iconic.

The heat made her lazy, so she doodled in Jason's notepad until, leaning across and taking his pencil, he scrawled two words:

S o n j a = J a s o n

'All five letters recur in both names and,' he said shifting closer, 'such anagrams were used to seal alchemical secrets.'

Sonja felt a sudden flush of apprehension. It was the first suggestive move he'd made. She didn't want to jeopardise their friendship, not now, no, not when they still had a few days together. No matter how sultry it was, she'd sleep in a large T-shirt and he'd better do the same—and keep his shorts on.

They lay on separate beds for an hour or so, dozing on-and-off as the oppressive heat passed. Lying by the window her mind drifted back to the languid Tagus, the forgotten Camissa, and the enigmatic Rivier of Stef Bos.

Like a Troubadour, Bos was an interloper in his own country and his ballads had been the inspiration for her trip to Cape Town. She felt he sang for her, wrote for her, even summoned her to forsake her Northern Lights for a Southern Cross; her dark Waterland for a dry Wasteland. And like a river, his songs were forever changing.

45

Here begins the Book of thy Descent
Here begins the Book of the Sangreal
Here begin the terrors
Here begin the miracles

Anonymous, *Perlesvaus* (c.1210)

Sonja had never been able to live with an unsolved mystery. Even as a child she could hardly sleep until every riddle had been solved. Thirty-something years later, each question required an answer and every problem its own solution. For her it was an emotional necessity, not an intellectual requirement.

'Was it an assassination?'

She leant back on the divan and tipped off her shoes. They sat in the atrium of the pension, enveloped by purple cushions and scented lavender, the sun now well passed its apex.

'And if so, was it motivated by politics or religion?'

'What evidence is there, either way?' he asked, finishing his cheese sandwich.

Jason had slung his satchel over the back of the chair, his bare legs hanging nonchalantly over the armrest. She waved the unnumbered folios in the air:

'The folios say he was killed for disloyalty; whereas the messages say it was for his secret liaison. Perhaps, perhaps he—'

'—perhaps he was jealous?' said Jason, stripping the lavender in the pot next to him. 'Then why imprison Albuquerque?'

Rubbing a sprig between his hands, he rose to tip the young waiter, a dusky student from Marseille, then came to sit beside her, his bare leg resting against her arm. She did not respond.

'Right, read it again,' he suggested casually.

She held up the message, pointing to the first paragraph:

'We know that Almeida had a commission, possibly to reconcile the Abrahamic and Dharmic, the rational and the mystic, but what we don't yet know is *who* issued this instruction?'

'Do *you* know?' he asked, askance.

'No, but we can eliminate those who wished to destroy him, such as those antagonistic cabalists. They'd already ousted him from India.'

'If not the inner circle, then who? Did the Knights of Santiago have a secret bond with Rome, and if so, what do we know about it?'

'Nothing, at least not yet,' she said standing up. 'All I know is that a year after Granada, *nota bene*, only one year, the Order of Santiago lost its independence. Isabella had asked if Ferdinand could join, a request no one could refuse, and so he became its new Administrator. Perhaps Almeida overheard their plans during the siege of Granada? Y'know, I think Volodya knows but isn't telling, for whatever reason. I'll call him later, after my shower. But first, let me use our bathroom before the other guests return.'

She reached for her bottled water.

'Sure, I'll finish my espresso, then see you upstairs.'

Their bathroom was on the third floor, at the end of the passage, and so she first went up to fetch her toiletries. Once alone, she stood under the shower, motionless, letting the cool water stream over her face and body. She thought about those who knew of Almeida's commission, such as Gaspar, Jorge de Mello, Lourenço de Brito and Martim Coelho. Even Albuquerque? But what about the women?

True, what of all the mothers, daughters, wives and mistresses? Where were the women in this story, like Henry's natural daughter? *Perhaps I should re-read that Tabula?*

Sonja hurriedly dried herself and returned to their room, anxious to call Volodya. This time, wrapped in a bathrobe, she sat on the corner of her bed and dialled his Skype number. His contact details were the last thing he'd given her—along with the vinho verde.

Busy connecting…

Waiting, she heard Jason come upstairs to use the bathroom.

Did Volodya know of any esoteric link between Portugal and India? Had he heard of a secret commission, perhaps?

He was suddenly there, on her screen, wearing his sailor's shirt and anchor-like watch. From his neck hung a chunky chain. Despite the blurred background, she could see a row of nautical knots and model yachts behind him.

At home, she guessed, *in his study?*

Her questions about a "principal design", however, soon made him restless. His Slavic features flashed across her screen, as if deflecting attention. Instead, he told her about his grandfather, a protégé of the Imperial Russian Navy, who'd known Moscow as the self-proclaimed "Third Rome" of Tsarist Christendom:

'Once, as a child, I crept under our dining room table to eavesdrop on the after-dinner talk. We were at my grandparents' apartment on Leningradskiy Prospekt, and they began discussing a naval officer who'd defied both king and country to follow his conscience. I heard one of the guests argue that no military corps could tolerate mutiny within its ranks, even at the highest level, to which my grandfather, Dedushka Mikha, replied: "Our first loyalty should be to ourselves, not the State." Hushed table-talk was common in the Soviet Union, especially among friends and family, but seldom repeated outside.'

Volodya explained how, as a boy of only eleven, he'd fallen asleep between their satin slippers and polished boots. He also recalled (but didn't say so now) how his young aunt wore stockings from Paris and that her veiled thighs had aroused his first boyhood fantasies.

He'd relished that same sensation on meeting Sonja, but suppressed his desire as it was bound to cause him trouble again. His attraction to Roxalena had been erotic too, and look where that had left him.

Sonja's question drew him back.

'Oké, Volodya, and *so?*'

'That's where my interest in western values and a universal rule of law began,' he declared. 'Yours was a society so different and yet so similar to ours. No doubt my grandfather heard the story from other seamen, as there was a long-standing friendship between our navies. Peter the Great built the Russian fleet after studying in Holland. He not only imported Dutch technology, but took your best artisans and sailors back home with him.'

'And this officer?'

'*Khorosho!* He was Admiral Francisco d'Almeida, and his conscience dictated that men should not yield to a corrupt authority. Though bound by a strict code of honour, he kept a secret treatise for himself, an ancient manuscript from Arabia...'

O Providência!

Was it mere coincidence, she wondered, to hear the same tale from a man she'd met by chance, twice. And having seen him for the last time, what harm could there be in talking about it? As long as she left out their skeleton, *El Portu*, the one whose skull belonged to Almeida.

Instead, she suggested the possibility of a ritual sacrifice and waited for a reaction, but he registered no surprise. He merely remarked that rumours had a way of returning whenever the truth was involved.

She refocused: 'So is it true, I mean, about this manuscript?'

He shrugged heavily, the staggered transmission blurring his face. Choosing his words carefully, he added:

'Dom Francisco had been a confidant of kings, a decorated knight in the Ordem de Sant'Iago and a scholar of the arcane. He'd sworn to give alms to the poor, to aid the sick, and to honour his wife. As a knight of the sword, he joined the *Reconquista* in Spain.'

'Why Spain?' she stared back, trying not to show her excitement.

'Because the Order chose to demonstrate its loyalty to the Spanish monarchs. Portugal had been split by several struggles for succession and, after years of strife, the Castilian and Aragonese chapters were without a Grand Master to represent them jointly. Plus the Order had been reduced by faction fighting, assassinations and resignations —both in Portugal and in Spain.'

'Oké, but then—'

'—for eight years, from 1484 to 1492, Dom Francisco and his son took part in the final campaign against sultan Boabdil, whose brief reign was benchmarked by shifting alliances, civil strife and lingering jealousies within his harem.'

Women?

She sat up, unable to contain her excitement.

'Boabdil fought with his father, his uncle and with King Ferdinand. Like his shrewish mother, he fought with everyone, and to secure the throne, she competed against the other wives in the harem.'

'Hey, so there *are* women in this story?'

Sensing her enthusiasm, he took a hurried detour:

'According to custom, all sons of the Sultan enjoyed equal rights. So their mothers competed for support, as can be expected, especially when it concerned potential successors. Granada was therefore split between the supporters of Fátima, Boabdil's mother, and a beautiful young Christian slave called Isabella de Solís, renamed Zoraya. The crisis erupted when Boabdil's father chose Zoraya over his mother. By deceit and connivance, his father lost Granada's support and was forced to flee, seeking protection from an uncle at coastal Malaga. Boabdil thus became the last Nasrid ruler of Granada. However, he would live up to his unfortunate name and die in exile.'

'Poignant story. And this, this Almeida?'

'The Dom was wounded in the siege and held captive within the Alhambra's enclosure, along with hundreds of other Christians and Jews. He may have died, were it not for the custody provided by a certain Nasrid family. As a result, he developed a close bond with a particular nobleman—I heard he was an *amir* or prince—whose wife took care of him during his convalescence.'

She smiled. *Jason called the Moor Majid, for "Noble Glory"*.

'We really do reinvent stories about Moorish Princes, don't we?'

'*C'est la vie!* Yet through a heart-felt friendship with this prince, the Dom obtained an alchemical stone—a rare and sacred pearl—which he later hid in a cross made by a Jewish goldsmith.'

Volodya raised his own chain and pendant, a golden ram, emblem of the Golden Fleece. She'd seen the same design in the Ridderzaal.

'Didn't Henry's navigators wear similar medallions?'

'*Da da*, but remember, the men who served the Avis belonged to the Order of Christ. The Dom had to change Orders before sailing to India. Anyway, first things first, back in Granada he acquired this Aristotelian treatise—previously referred to as the *Sierra Nevada*.'

'Previously?'

'Yes, it's lost again.'

'Of course, the best evidence is either lost or stolen—'

'—or sold,' he added smoothly.

'Either way, it always costs more than an academic can afford.'

'What matters is that it was first taken by Alexander to India, and then "rediscovered" after the fall of Granada.'

'Wait, what happened to Almeida after Granada?'

'He went back to Portugal, awaiting favour from João II—'

'—and then?'

'Well, it was a turning point in Portuguese history.'

Sonja fidgeted with the volume control.

'Sorry, Volodya, what happened to Almeida?'

'*Pardon*, it was a turning point for him too. As a knight, he'd taken a vow to pass on all that came his way. Instead, he kept the pearl and treatise, probably because his masters, many of whom were Spanish, had been corrupted by their own vanity. Then, one generation later, the Spanish Jesuits reorganized Portugal, limiting the leadership of the king and taking responsibility for the princes' education. So when the Inquisition arrived, many Jews fled to Holland, but you know this already. I think Almeida knew the tide would change too.'

'Wait, so he obtained this stone and book. What exactly does that mean? Were these given to him or not?' She repeated indelicately: 'Did he steal the manuscript, or was it a gift?'

'Alas, that isn't clear. The two enjoyed a unique bond—so I guess it was given—either way, this knowledge was carried North.'

'Wait, wait, is there any evidence for this?' she asked incredulously. 'Your story lacks no dramatic characters—'

'—evidence? Yes, Basil Valentine has described how he travelled to Compostela, in peril of his life, and that whosoever benefited from this knowledge should thank God he completed his journey.'

'So this occult knowledge—for which one may be murdered—was exchanged across national borders?'

'And between Orders. Remember, Dom Henrique's parents came from Portugal *and* England, which not only strengthened political ties between the two countries, but also secured support for the Knights of the Garter and the Knights of Christ. Chivalry was still common in Dom Francisco's lifetime and armed knights saw themselves as Grail heroes. Like their Templar and Teutonic brothers, they formed a vast cosmopolitan network—'

'—and this Basil Valentine?'

'Basilius Valentinus, also known as Stefan Rauter, was more than a fictitious character, although references to him tend to be evasive... He is usually associated with the School of Hermetic Philosophy, of which the oldest fragments are Arabian in origin. Contact with the *Corpus hermeticum* in Europe was only made during the second half of the fifteenth century.'

'Hermetic?'

'*Da*, after the young Greek messenger, mediator and interpreter.'

'So the *Corpus* was the talk of courts and universities?'

'*Précisément*, and not only among French scholastics, but your Dutch humanists too. It was the source of Rosicrucian mysticism whereby the arts and sciences of Western Europe were given a new impetus. Mlle Sonja, the occidental renaissance is indebted to such founts of knowledge.'

'Like the commentaries of Averroës?'

'Valentine's study of Aristotle helped bring about the intellectual transformation of Western society, yes, as had other Middle Eastern sources—'

'—and Almeida?' she asked restlessly, toying with her empty bottle, 'What about his voyage to India?'

'The trip cost a fortune. There were twenty-two ships and fifteen hundred soldiers, including Spanish, Italian and Flemish merchants, as well as a private banker from Germany—rather like the wealthy tourists on one of Richard Branson's spaceflights today. Anyway, their trading vessels sailed with the Portuguese fleet around the Cape, running up the East coast to Kilwa, Mombasa and Melinde, before crossing over to Calicut—'

'—pillaging along the way? Hopefully that's not the space tourism Virgin Galactic has in mind?'

'*Non*. No, the German trader, Balthasar Springer, recorded their passage and, with illustrations by Hans Burgkmair, had it published in 1506. His voyage is rather exaggerated, but then these books were written for the vivid imagination of armchair-travellers—'

'—what about Aristotle's treatise?'

'Sometime between the fall of Granada and his appointment as Viceroy, Almeida returned to the Catedral de Santiago where, in secret, he showed it to scholars—including one acting under the aegis of Thomas Malory. It was the latter who informed Basil Valentine of the work's existence. This was the last work of Aristotle to enter Western society and those who came to hear about it expressed great interest. Dom Francisco must have recognised its importance as he made covert arrangements to have it couriered to Basil Valentine. And so, to divert suspicion and to avoid inquisitors, a woman acted as his courier. I don't know her name, unfortunately, except that she took the work to France.'

Sonja adjusted the controls again.

'There's only one woman in this entire story and you can't recall her name? Volodya, really, you must know who she is?'

'No, her name was never mentioned.'

A woman without a name. Like the Queen of Sheba, unnamed in the Qur'an yet known throughout Arabia? Sonja could no longer contain herself, blurting carelessly:

'Like the Grail keeper, she must have a name! Volodya, please...'

His voice faltered: '*Pardon*, Mlle Sonja, I know nothing about her. Or where she came from.'

'Nothing—you never heard *who* this woman was?'

A long pause.

'I heard she passed on Aristotle's treatise in Andlau.'

'Andlau?'

'*Da*, a small Romanesque town in Alsace, at the foot of the Vosges mountains. She was killed in the church above—'

'—killed. Why?'

'Because she was Dom Francisco's accomplice.'

'Accomplice?'

'*Tochno!* Almeida had betrayed the Order.'

'So who?'

'Mlle Sonja, I tell you all I know.'

'Then tell me!'

'Her assassins were sent by the Ordem de Sant'Iago.'

'The knights of Santiago de Compostela?'

'*Da*, the same.'

46

The realm of the fabulous Prester John,
like certain other mythic "lands", is, in fact,
a symbol of the supreme, spiritual centre.
Juan Cirlot, A Dictionary of Symbols (1962)

'Who are you searching for, Sonja? Is it that woman Almeida shared his secret with?'

Jason spoke using his hands, making vain gestures in the air as the Argo veered off course without its helmsman. Making matters worse, he drove too fast. Sonja wiped the spilt water off her lap.

Oblivious, he continued:

'Your Moscow Maverick gave no name and no address. You don't even know if she really existed, do you?'

'No,' she began, opening a map across the dashboard, 'no I don't, but we're looking at the results of her life—real or not.'

Sonja had no evidence, no authentic artefact and no tangible proof —nor any substantive lead to go by. And yet, despite all her doubts, she believed there was something behind these coincidences—linking the dossier to the folios—and so wanted to pursue it while they were still in France.

Had the dossier-owner and folio-author ever met?

It was Aristotle, she recalled, who said history explains what we are but not what we may yet become, to which Prof Mendle had gently added: 'That's why you need more poetry.'

I certainly need more to solve this riddle.

'Oké, we're so close, let's go to Andlau and see what we can find. We need concrete facts about Almeida's associates.'

'Fine, as long as I'm back by Sunday,' he said, driving eastbound out of Paris.

Studying the map, she plotted their course toward Alsace.

'Hey, Andlau, there it is, in the north-eastern corner of France, up against the German border,' she said, struggling to keep the Z-folds under control. He glanced over and saw a tangled mess of red-and-yellow lines.

'Looks like a knot of roads to me.'

'On the hill above Andlau is a church, look, Le Mont Sainte-Odile. It's a long shot, Jason, but that could be it!'

'It's a long way to drive for an unknown woman,' he grinned.

'But well worth it. Let's head for Strasbourg and stay the night; it's only a few hours away. Perhaps we'll be in time to watch highlights of *Le Tour*. How's that for motivation?'

'Original. Today's stage is from Marseille to Montpellier.'

'I thought you needed an incentive,' she said, smiling generously, the smile she knew he always enjoyed. She also knew his tan-stripes came from cycling.

The car sped forward as he checked the rear mirror. He wanted to be sure the Black Goliath wasn't following them. They had both felt his presence in Paris.

'Just drive there safely, the chance to lose ourselves will do us good. We'll go on to Andlau in the morning.'

'Sure. So how far are we from the border?'

'Let's see,' she said, battling with the map again, 'Alsace runs along the Swiss-German border, so we're close. Relatively speaking, we're very close. Why?'

'Because I read somewhere that Parsifal visited a hermit living in the Hollenberg caves above Arlesheim, just across the Swiss border, now called the Ermitage. And so I thought—'

'—right, you just thought?'

'Well, I also hoped.'

'You're so full of hope, Jason Tomas!'

'Actually, you mean full of bullshit, don't you?'

'Yes, and that too.'

47

The Grail takes its place in the "hermetic tradition" ...embracing the Druids, the Gnostics, the Cathars, Atlantis and the nineteenth-century occult societies.

Richard Barber, *The Holy Grail: The History of a Legend* (2004)

The Ermitage lay in a mountain cleft where, over millions of years, seeping water had formed a series of limestone caves and lakes, hence its association with names like "hollow rock" and "hollow mountain". The Ermitage itself had been named after the hermits living in these caves. Once a sacred pagan site, the caves were now accessible via a labyrinth of gravel footpaths and hand-cut stairs. A chiselled cross and crumbling wayside shrine marked the sanctuary's conversion from primal wood to romantic park.

Sonja rested below the summit, out of breath, peering back the way they'd climbed. She saw day-trippers stroll by with walking-rods and summer hats, their voices echoing between the trees. A soft breeze whispered through the foliage as the world below retreated—as it had that stormy weekend in Cape Town. That was now one month ago.

She stood with Jason on the gravel apron before the Parsifal Cave, accompanied by two young students, Frankl and Andrea, natives of this Celtic Christian portal to the Otherworld.

'Legend says this is where Parsifal visited the Hermit Trevrizent,' began the fair-freckled Frankl. 'Look how the lip of this cave was cut to support a lean-to at the entrance.'

Frankl led them inside to show another detail; above their heads was the fossilized imprint of a marine shell.

'The sign of the pilgrim,' jeered Jason, 'so where are all the gonzo travellers now?'

'It's the symbol of St James, the cousin of Jesus,' called Andrea, standing by the entrance. She'd walked to Compostela the summer before. Six weeks. Alone.

Frankl scrambled up above the cave, taking Jason with him:

'This specific site is supposed to be a natural energy node, a sort of geopathogenic zone, and up on the ridge the paranormal activity is at its strongest.' He directed Jason's gaze toward a cluster of elm-trees. 'That's where the mistletoe flourishes.'

Jason replied with a jaundiced grin: 'So the Druids were here too?'

'Yes. The Celts used mistletoe to invoke the earth spirits—as the Greeks did with the laurel and the oak.'

Jason felt uncomfortable. Without a rational scientific methodology or a reasonable explanation, he could but venture sceptically into the world of necromancy:

'As a Gemini, Frankl, I half-doubt and half-believe this nonsense. One part accepts, the other not.'

Jason turned to leave, having seen enough.

'I'm a Gemini too,' said Frankl cockily, overtaking on the descent, 'so part of me thinks you speak in half-truths. As Twins, we're meant to reconcile dualities—'

Despite his humour, Jason was shocked by the boy's honest reply. How could this Frankl have such insight—or was it just a platitude with perfect timing? His own world of empirical certainties was far removed from this boy's psychic reality.

'Shall we go?' asked Sonja, as Andrea and Frankl scampered off. Taking Jason by his arm, she pursued them down the hill.

'They want, they want to show us a spring,' she said breathlessly.

The four of them followed a stream that skirted a sage-green lake, until they reached its source. Nestled between the trees was a dark, stone-hewn trough from which water gently spilled.

'It's the Odilia Spring where, once upon a time, a blind girl bathed her eyes and regained her sight. She also hid in these caves—'

'—according to legend,' added Frankl, 'she fled to these parts when told to marry a man she didn't love.'

Andrea took Frankl by the hand: 'People walk here before sunrise, in silence, especially at Easter. They say the water has special healing properties. I keep some of it bottled in my room—'

'—and you use it?'

'Only to wash my face.'

Sonja lent forward to taste the water. It was cold and sweet.

'There's no substantive difference in the water,' noted Jason flatly, 'water is water, whether collected before or after sunrise. The only difference comes from what you choose to believe.'

'I believe the water heals you,' repeated Andrea sincerely.

'Sure, in all rituals action focuses attention and concentrates our efforts. We empower ourselves and become well. Or, at least, we feel young, strong and motivated again.'

Andrea didn't reply, but walked ahead, leaving Jason a step behind. He followed like a scowled-out mongrel, knowing he'd rationalized too much. Yet again. *Eish!*

☩ ☩ ☩

On Andrea's advice, Sonja and Jason checked into a guesthouse on the upper slopes of the Hollenberg, set above neighbouring Dornach. Like its environment, Haus Friedwart appeared not to have changed in decades. It was clean, comfortable and immaculately designed— though unlike any auberge they'd ever seen.

Well, except in fantasy comics or children's fiction.

Dornach seemed to belong to another world, a world as quaint as Hogwarts or Hobbiton, where JK Rowling and JR Tolkien would be at home. Taking a stroll before dinner they saw more curved roofs, skew walls, arched windows and carved doors. Dominating the grassy knoll was a bald concrete colossus which Jason assumed was a WWII bunker—until he learnt it was the Goetheanum of Rudolf Steiner. It was built in the 1920s, after the original wooden structure had burnt down, allegedly torched by right-wing arsonists.

Sonja and Jason had stepped into a world inhabited by the Other, a world whose centre gravitated around the School of Anthroposophy. It was an esoteric academy. One that stood quietly apart.

'It is to this world that those insular youngsters belong,' he joked, 'and they aren't the only odd ones we've met.'

He began to count the others on his hand:

'First, there's a maverick Muscovite, a footloose Brisbane pilgrim, and a hairy landlord in Chartres. Next, the black goliath from Belém. And lastly, an unorthodox museum undertaker in Cape Town.'

She nodded happily, taking his arm. The raking light fingered its way across the knoll as they fell into step, following their shadows back to Haus Friedwart. Once inside they clambered up the stairs, ever so quietly, before Gollum discovered who they really were.

Two witless interlopers.

Sonja settled down to watch the sunset while Jason took her laptop next door. He'd been preoccupied all afternoon, almost to the point of distraction, ever since walking with the youngsters.

'I want to check out the Celts,' was all he said.

According to the archaeological record, the perennial headwaters of the Rhine, Rhône and Danube had sustained the Helvetii Celts and given rise to the first Transalpine civilisation—as the Camissa had done for the San below Hoerikwaggo.

While Switzerland retained its Celtic place-names, little remained of its religious sanctuaries or beliefs after Julius Caesar's campaign in this neck of the woods. Although his victories over Vercingétorix and Arioviste were crucial for the creation of the Roman Empire, the two battles did consolidate the Gaulish and Germanic tribes. The most important Celtic cities were thus in France and Germany. Not here.

✝ ✝ ✝

Sonja sat by the window as the orange sky sank away, wondering what had upset Jason. He seemed to have no time for pagan rituals, miraculous healing or the paranormal forces of nature. Neither did he appear to have any time for "soft" science while on holiday.

His frustration stemmed from the youngsters' convenient lack of historical detail and their youthful innuendo about sacred rocks and holy wells. It had clearly irritated him when they claimed all things were connected, mythically and miraculously, and that archaeologists had lost touch with the spirits of springs and forests. Excavators need to respect the oracular and therapeutic function of nature, they had glibly added, as if he didn't know that himself.

Jason needed to be with those who shared his sense of rigour and academic discourse, or he'd go stark raving mad. Moreover, Sonja reckoned, he probably needed an extra stiff brandy-coke too.

48

The road to Le Mont Sainte-Odile was closed for repairs and came to a standstill when workmen took to having their lunch in the shade. Even under the broadest elms the temperatures soared to 40°C. The sky became cerulean-blue, flecked only by an odd speck of cloud.

Temporary deviation signs led their Argo along the picturesque Alsace Wine Route, between rolling hills and rising vineyards, until they reached Andlau at the base of the Vosges mountains.

'We'd better stop to get directions. There, at Tourist Information,' she pointed ahead, 'and ask for a map.'

He thought another stop unnecessary. They'd refuelled, refreshed and replenished an hour ago—while coming up from the south—and so a map wasn't going to help. Especially not when ad-hoc signs gave ample advice. He prided himself on a keen sense of direction and a reputation for never getting lost. At least not when he was driving.

He halted before the ever-familiar 'i' sign. Sonja lent over to peer in the shop's poster-plastered window. No one stirred within, nor were there any tourists about. The staff were on a midday break, according to a notice hanging by the front door, and would be back at only 14h. It was an annoying half-hour away. So now what?

Déviation PL

Ste ODILE

Jason decided to drive on and follow the deviation signs. Having seen them ahead, he knew he couldn't get lost. Even if he tried.

The detour took them via timber-framed houses and flower-decked balconies, past a square with a dancing bronze bear, and then around and about, slowly, to a towering Romanesque church.

'This isn't right, though it's as good a place as any for an overnight stop,' she observed, examining the map. 'It's supposed to be above the town. I'm sure Volodya said the church was *above* Andlau.'

Jason followed the detour as it returned to the stream. Crossing a little bridge, the road meandered out of town and led up to a dense deciduous wood. The leafy trees reminded him of the vast indigenous forest on the Garden Route. The opposite was true for Sonja:

'Your Tsitsikama is like the Vosges, your Winelands like this Wine Route. Comparisons, literally, have a physical point of view.'

Jason drove on without seeing the next sign, and soon began to wonder if there would be another, after all? He fell silent, anxious he'd taken a wrong turn at the bottom of the hill. Much to his relief, Sonja seemed unaware of his dilemma.

Reaching the high-set village of Hohwald, he suggested they stop at the local tourist office. It was 14h anyway.

Minutes later, without a word of French spoken, he returned with a fist-full of brochures, boasting with characteristic confidence:

'As I thought, it's the next turn to the right, just ahead.'

She found his attitude as disarming as it was irritating. He could be so sanguine and nonchalant. Anyway, from the car she'd seen the next deviation sign herself. It was her turn to keep silent.

'Getting lost makes it harder for the Black Goliath to find us,' he said, as if that had been his intention all along.

He slipped the clutch, dropped a gear, and steered the Argo deeper into the forest. After the turn, the road kept going up.

'The boy at Tourist Information explained, in broken English, that Saint Odilia was born blind but regained her sight when baptized at the age of twelve. Her parents came from this side of the mountain, and after an enforced confinement in a convent somewhere on the other side of the forest, beyond a bend in the Rhine, she returned to establish this cloister.'

Sonja had no idea where this fabled "other-side-of-the-forest" was. As her father said, it was always somewhere farther away.

'We heard yesterday, remember, that Odilia gained her sight after bathing her eyes in the spring—not during her baptism. A good story obviously mutates and multiplies.'

'Anyway,' said Sonja carefully, 'I don't think Saint Odilia is the one we're looking for. Her name is supposed to be unknown—'

'—or merely suppressed?'

'Perhaps, or just a well-kept secret.'

'Either way, she needs a name,' he said, rounding the bend on the broadside of the road, 'so let's call her Elza or Elzas.'

'As the Dutch do for Alsace, Jason, not bad!'

Reaching the summit, the trees parted to reveal the bulky edifice of Le Mont Sainte-Odile. One glance at Jason's brochures showed it to have several enclosed spaces: a tree-lined courtyard, a garden terrace, the church, of course, as well as a museum, hotel and library. After twelve centuries it also had flushing toilets, home-made delicatessen, and wireless internet.

Jason drove up to the entrance, looking for free parking, but found none between the rows of tour buses.

'Where do they all come from?' he exclaimed, stopping to watch the spectacle. 'I thought this was a remote mountain sanctuary?'

'Summer holidays,' explained Sonja, amused. 'Nothing is remote in Europe anymore, and most of the camper-vans we passed are Dutch. Anyway, we're safer here than in Paris.'

They were surrounded by day-visitors, hikers, mountain bikers and, of course, a perennial prey of nuns. Families picnicked on the lawn as their children clambered around the garden. Couples photographed themselves beside the rose beds while, behind the Argo, angry tourists remonstrated with a flag-toting guide. Jason sat in awe as a convoy of wheel-chairs trundled passed, its tyres crunching the gravel, leaving a trail back to the Roman Gate.

'Jesus, and I thought we came here on some solitary quest!'

'So we did, with questions of our own, so don't worry about these pilgrims. Let's just pretend we're accidental tourists.'

'Talking of tourists,' he quipped, 'just look around you, there must be a good restaurant up here too. Why not go in while I park the car. We can meet on the church steps in ten minutes.'

✢ ✢ ✢

Jason drove back to where the camper-vans lined the perimeter of a field, as on a mountain stage of *Le Tour*, and found all manner of cars herded together into a laager—but without the Red Devil or Black Goliath.

Leaving the Argo, he drifted back towards the monastery, following visitors on a meditative footpath called the Way of the Cross. It was a root-entangled path encircling the sandstone outcrop upon which the monastery itself was built. Here he met a pair of sunburnt pilgrims resting in the shade.

The first had a ruddy complexion and wore the shell of St James over a striped cotton caftan. Amazingly, she looked like Jojo in his technicoloured Dreamcoat. Her companion had a hennaed beard, a plaited ponytail, and a wide brimmed sun hat slung around his neck. He held the obligatory pilgrim's staff with its dangling calabash, and carried a familiar-looking Lonely Planet under his arm.

Caiaphas with the Book of Books.

Jason halted, pointing to the book:

'Hi, anything about a murdered woman in the church?'

'No, friend, only the story about how Odilia healed a blind man at the spring below those trees, at a place called the Miraculous Source,' said the bearded pilgrim with a heavy American drawl. 'They say she struck a rock and water gushed out. It's where we filled our calabash.'

'Thanks. I thought the guidebook may have said something—'

'—no, there's no murder here. Except for Odilia's father, Eticho, the Duke of Alsace, who rejected her for being born blind. She was a feeble child and he feared others would think God had punished him for his own past wrongs—'

'—all the same,' added the red faced woman, while shaking sand from her sandals, 'the Duke wanted a son for his first child, so his wife asked a wet nurse to hide the babe in a convent at Baume-les-Dames, safe from her father's wrath. Odilia remained in foster care until her brother, whom she'd never seen before, came to find her—'

'—after receiving her sight,' said the bearded one, 'when she turned twelve, miraculously.'

'Oh yes, during her baptism,' recalled the ruddy-faced one.

'Then, after their return to Alsace, Odilia's father had her brother killed for this betrayal—so I guess you're right, there *is* a murder.'

'Sure, but it isn't her and it wasn't in the church up here?'

'Nope, it seems not, my friend.'

Jason knew Sonja was waiting but couldn't resist one last question. He had to know who it was they should be trailing:

'So what happened to Odilia?'

'What happens to all girls of legend, they get married to a prince,' said Ruddy Face. 'Odilia too, or so it was promised. But she refused and fled to the mountains until her father's henchmen caught up with her. Trying to seize Odilia, however, a cleft in the rock opened and miraculously concealed her. She had access to the Otherworld—'

'—sure, and where's this magic cave today?'

The pilgrim raised his stick and pointed beyond the trees:

'Duke Eticho was so enthralled by her miracle that he converted Hohenbourg Castle into a convent. After his death it became a refuge from Rome and, as its first prioress, Odilia lived here until her death in the early eighth century. So, go find her tomb, my friend, and travel well...'

Jason now realised the two women lived eight hundred years apart. Le Mont Sainte-Odile seemed like a dead-end trail.

49

I took my trouble down a dead-end trail
Reachin' out a hand for a holier grail
Emmylou Harris, *Deeper Well* (1995)

It was a flawless afternoon with only a breath of air to stir the trees. Scattered clouds obscured the sun, now high above, as Jason scurried through the Roman Gate.

He crossed the courtyard, passing under a row of ancient limes, and reached the church in a sweat. Sonja sat waiting in the shade, restless, her water-bottle empty.

'Jason, where have you been, I thought you were lost?'

His heart sank, not for having kept her waiting, but because she thought he could get lost parking a car:

'Jesus, I'm sorry. I'll stop for any map you want tomorrow.'

'Well, never mind,' she said, feeling sorry for him, 'I had time to read the monastery's early history. The road up here was made by Roman soldiers who occupied the outcrop, calling it *Altitona*, hence Hohenbourg. It's a natural fortress, and at its far end they built a watch-tower. Come, from out there you can see the French-German Rhine Valley—'

'—and the church? What about going inside?'

'I already have, but it's not the one we want. The original burnt down in 1546, fifty years after our Elza was killed. Only the twelfth-century buttresses are still visible. Here, look at the base of this one.'

'That's it? Now we have no name *and* no church,' he exclaimed, 'Jesus, this is a dead-end trail.'

'Wait, Jason, first the rock on which the tower was built. I want you to take a photo for me. Come, this way.'

He followed her around the church to a narrow stepped terrace where a magnificent view greeted them. It was a panorama of serried vineyards, wooded hills and, as far as their eyes could see, the green plains of Alsace. To the right lay the Vosges and, opposite, eastward, the Black Forest. It was an impenetrable post, a strategic location for any occupant: friend or foe, Celtic or Roman, French or German.

Even Nazi officers.

Jason wondered if Altitona—or whatever it was once called—had also been a palaeolithic paradise. *A paradise for those who came, for those who stayed, and for those who never left?*

At their feet lay several empty graves, chiselled into the red bed-rock, long since polished smooth by wind and ice.

'A medieval cemetery,' she said, 'and down those steps is what we came for—'

'—what?' He spun around: 'The two chapels?'

'Yes, first, in front, the Chapel of Tears, then the Chapel of Angels,' she announced, sensing a new clue was at hand. She repeated what was in the brochure:

'This one here, beside the cemetery, is where Odilia prayed for the soul of her father.'

Sonja led the way, stooping as she entered the first sanctuary. The tiny chapel was empty, save for its marble altar and stone floor. The door closed gently behind them.

'That's where she knelt to pray,' whispered Sonja, pointing to the stone in the middle of the floor. 'Odilia came here every day.'

They leant together for a breathless minute, shoulder-to-shoulder, as their eyes accustomed to the dark.

'Nothing else seems as old,' he observed, 'at least not since Elza was murdered. Even the decorative stone-mosaics appear to belong to a revivalist period. Pity, it must once have been very beautiful—'

'—small and beautiful, yes, but it doesn't do anything for me.'

'No?' His disappointment was audible.

'It's not the place.'

'Not?'

'All I'm saying, is that it doesn't feel right.'

'Sure. I feel neutral too.'

'Hey, I'm not neutral, I just don't feel this is the r-ri-right place.'
Jesus, why so edgy?

Sonja had put herself under pressure to find an unknown church, an unnamed woman and, now, an uncertain group of assassins. Plus, Jason had begun to expect too much from her. She stumbled, unsure and unable to recall what Volodya had said about the murder.

'Look, this is not Tomb R-r-raider or Relic Hunter where X marks the spot,' she spluttered, 'we don't need to know *where* she was killed but, rather, *why* she was murdered?'

They were alone, unaware of those waiting outside. For a moment their bodies touched, self-consciously, until a prick of light pierced the door jamb. They turned, distracted by the sound of a shoe scraping the paving, as someone tried the door, then left it ajar, allowing light to flood in. Jason stepped out, expecting an irate tourist or, worse still, the Black Goliath. Seeing no danger, he beckoned her to follow.

Moving to the door, she saw a mosaic with a triangulated eye above the lintel. Gold light radiated down from the eye, blessing a church of some sort. She'd seen that symbol before. Had the monastery been used as a Masonic Lodge?

Even so, Odilia's attribute was a pair of eyes. Two open eyes, not one.

'Sonja, are you coming?' hollered Jason. She followed, still adjusting her eyes to the sunlight as he ducked into the second sanctuary—a square chapel perched on the furthermost corner of the outcrop.

Erected in the eleventh century, the mosaics were redone after WWII, in 1948, to be exact, or so Jason gleaned from the brochure. He sought comfort in cold facts. All that speculation at the Ermitage had unsettled him.

Romanesque church architecture, characteristically, provided plain exteriors and decorative interiors—and this chapel was no exception. The ceiling was covered with lavish mosaics showing the Mysteries of the Archangels and, against the far wall, a modest stone altar.

Against the opposite wall was a dazzling apparition of a horseback rider and a serpent-tongued dragon. St Michael held a shield in his left arm and his lance with the right—thrusting the latter through the beast's throat.

O Providência!

'That's how Almeida was slain!'

'Jesus, dramatic stuff...'

A pregnant woman trudged in with her young daughter, dropping a coin into the slot-machine by the door. There was a blaze of light, accompanied by a loud electric boom, as the mosaics lit up to reveal details not seen before.

'Look, behind the dragon, it's Odilia and her mountain sanctuary. And there, beyond the Archangel, a flat-topped mountain crowned by a walled castle—with a temple-or-something inside.'

'It's Le Mont Saint-Michel of Normandy,' exclaimed Jason, 'the abbey-fortress our Santiago Pilgrim told us about. D'you know there is a St Michael's Mount in Cornwall too? Together they protect the English Channel, like the Pillars of Hercules do at the entrance to the Mediterranean.'

'That may be an inspiration, but this one isn't built on the beach or seen at high-tide—it rises from a mountain out at sea. Look, look at the distance between the mainland and the island.'

True, the sea surrounded the castle.

'There's also a caravel between it and the shore,' she added eagerly. He felt her quick breath against his arm.

Thinking it wishful projection, he stepped up for a closer look. Sure enough, it did resemble a caravel.

'A caravel?'

'You realise what this means, don't you?'

'Sure, the Portuguese were here too—'

'—be serious, Jason, please. According to the book from Coimbra, the earthly realm of Paradiso is on the summit of a flat mountain, surrounded by sea.'

She led him outside to explain:

'It seems that behind every medieval Grail legend is a quest for the eternal Paradise—for the New Jerusalem, as Volodya calls it—and that this Paradise is where nature's secrets will be revealed and all man's suffering washed away.'

'Like blindness and spring water,' he taunted, 'the recurrent motif of our last two days. As at Arlesheim, so too above Andlau?'

'—wait, Jason, that's it! That's why Elza came here, to this convent, far from the affairs of the world—Charlemagne had granted Le Mont Sainte-Odile immunity in the early ninth century, and so it became a school for the daughters of the empire. Remember, each convent had its own library. Not only was it a safe place to hide from adversaries, but the convent also stimulated the idea of a terrestrial paradise. The image of St Michael and the dragon testify to this. Like the mountain monasteries of Montserrat and Montségur, this place must be linked to Europe's earliest Grail legends—'

'—and to the pagan sun cults?'

Jason was a step behind.

'As I see it, solar mysticism was the bedrock of Grail Christianity and practiced at Sagres, Montségur, Arlesheim, Chartres, Le Mont Saint-Michel and, right here, on the Odilienberg. People came since prehistoric times to see, at least once in their lifetime, a place where divinity dwelt. It appears that they also went on a Great Pilgrimage, via Le Mont Sainte-Odile, to Chartres. These places are all shrouded in mystery, not because pre-Christian mysteries were kept secret, but because it was dangerous to deviate from official Church doctrine— from the Latin rite on the other-side-of-the-forest. And of course, as we said, that depends on where you stand. If you ask me, I think it was on this side of the Alps.'

She had gained a new insight: Like Odilia of Hohenbourg, Almeida came from a noble family whose role aided Christianity's esoteric flow into Western Europe. This allowed for a new humanism, for one literally on the other side of Rome.

'As the Santiago Pilgrim said, others do what we don't have time to do ourselves, so I'll ask a museum friend to take a closer look at the codex. Shall we go?'

Following the exit signs, she led Jason toward the courtyard until they reached the Gift Shop. Here she stopped to buy two postcards— one to send Andrea, the other for Frankl—while Jason went ahead to photograph the Roman Gate. She watched him through the window, scouting around with his camera under the lime trees, unaware that he was, in fact, looking for signs of the Black Goliath. To Jason's mind, the ogre was a disproportionate Knight of Ni.

50

*Here, in the days of yore, Holy Prioress Odile was living
and for ever and ever she reigns over Alsace like a mother.*
Inscription over the Roman Gate, Le Mont Sainte-Odile (undated)

Rüttiweg 36
Dornach
CH4143
Switzerland

Saturday 24 July

Dear Andrea

We found an 8thC cloister in the Vosges, above the town of Andlau, where the legend of Odilia may have originated. It goes as follows:
A blind girl is bundled off to a convent before her rich father can have her killed, or disowned, for being an ill and feeble child. At the age of twelve, during her baptism, she gains her sight and is renamed *Odilia*. When found by her younger brother, Hugo of Hohenbourg, she returns with him to join her family. Enraged by Hugo's betrayal, her father has him killed and—being now without an heir—arranges for her to marry a prince. In defiance, she flees to the other side of the forest, to the mountains where, once discovered, she cannot be captured as a cleft in the rock hides her from her father's men. Awed by this miracle of nature, he provides a convent for her use—now Le Mont Sainte-Odile. She died in 720 and her tomb remains intact.
Best regards
Sonja

51

'Where have you just come from?' asked Parsifal.
'From over there, sir, from a worthy man, a holy hermit who lives in this forest.'
Chrétien de Troyes, *The Story of the Grail* (c.1190)

Juraweg 21
Dornach
CH4143
Switzerland

Saturday 24 July

Dear Frankl

Warmest thanks for showing us Parsifal's cave and the Odilia spring.
I appreciate the time you spent with us, including your explanations.
I found a few lines in *The Story of the Grail*, Chrétien de Troyes's 12thC
romanz, describing how the naive Parsifal met the Hermit:
"He rode on, weeping through the wood until he came to the hermi-
tage. Here he dismounted, disarmed, and tethered his horse to an
elm tree, then entered the hermit's cell. In a little chapel he found the
hermit, a priest and a clerk—this is the truth—who began the highest
and sweetest service that can be held in a holy place. Parsifal went on
his knees…" Chrétien fails to mention where, but as he lived in what
is today north-eastern France, the Ermitage may have been his
intended setting. Let me know what you hear, as I want to establish if
or when such events ever took place.

Best regards
Sonja

Home

52

All life is but a wandering to find home.
William Rowley et al, *The Witch of Edmonton* (1658)

'*Bonjour!* I'm glad you called, as there's so much more to tell,' began Volodya smoothly. 'I always wanted to pursue that manuscript and the things Dedushka said about it, but I'm no historian, so perhaps you could do some research for me?'

Research?

'Well, I'm not sure that fits my plans,' answered Sonja cautiously, already uncomfortable about the way she'd spent her sabbatical.

'*Malheureusement.* Anyway, I'm happy you phoned, if only—'

'—if only to ask about Almeida's anonymous accomplice, the one killed in the church?'

She stopped, startled by her own impatience, but she had questions about Le Mont Sainte-Odile, questions only Volodya could answer: Where was the church? Who were the assassins? And what happened to the treatise? *Moreover, why was it all so damn important!*

Yes, her impatience was uncalled for, yet she'd driven all the way to Alsace and returned with nothing tangible—merely an insight. And now her time had run out. Plus Jason had gone on to London for his archaeology conference.

'You *do* recall us talking about that mysterious woman, right?'

Her voice sounded shrill, unfamiliar, not like her own. But Volodya seemed not to notice. While his face was too blurred for her to read, he breathed steadily as he spoke, saying something-or-other about

Almeida's accomplice and Parsifal's sister—both of whom seemed to have undertaken a perilous journey.

Sonja couldn't conceal her haste: 'D'you remember which church?'

'As you know, Sonja, it can be dangerous exposing yourself to the Grail mystery as it requires a purified ego. Look at Parsifal and how long it took him to figure that out.'

I don't need an initiation, only an explanation. Instead, borrowing a well-travelled phrase from her father, she replied:

'I value the warning, Volodya, but doubt if my journey will be as rewarding as Parsifal's.'

Drawing his breath, he began to explain:

'The church is better known as the Abbaye d'Andlau and stands at the top end of town.'

Andlau! Tsjonge, if we'd only known that then.

'So, not up at the convent? Then what else is below?'

'According to legend, Odile had a vision in which John the Baptist led her down to a sheltered little valley where she founded a second abbey, incorporating a hospital, known as the *Niedermünster*. It burnt down in 1542, four years before Le Mont Sainte-Odile itself, yet the nearby well still cures eye disease.'

'The Miraculous Source below the monastery, where water comes out a rock, where Odilia healed the blind man?'

A little miracle in her Alsatian paradise.

'*Da*, the Odilienberg was Odilia's paradise of ruddy stone.'

'We heard her remains rest intact, in the crypt. D'you still believe in relics and miracles, Volodya?'

'Me, no, not anymore. But in Russia, as elsewhere, it is commonly believed that relics enable miraculous physical healing to occur. This is why the devout still go on pilgrimages. Orthodox Christians—like your Latin Catholics—believe the saints will return to collect their hair, teeth, nails, fingers, arms, legs and, of course, their heads. That's why the devout preserve these remains.'

As Isis did with the dismembered Osiris. Or why men like Napoleon, Stalin and Michael Jackson are embalmed?

Sonja checked: 'Is that why the devout still collect relics?'

'*Da*. Poor Elizabeth of Hungary was dismembered after death as it was rumoured she'd be declared a saint, and so everyone wanted a piece of her. That's why the faithful still visit the shrines of the saints, in case one of them reappears. According to a local oral tradition, the Knights of Santiago brought a Holy Blood relic to the Odilienberg in the early ninth century. However, the "speaking" relic most closely linked to Andlau is the skull of Saint-Lazare.'

'Who?'

'*Saint-Lazare*,' he repeated. 'Lazarus of Bethany.'

'The one Christ brought back from the dead?'

'*Da*, it was an initiation. According to Eastern orthodox traditions, the young Lazarus fled to Cyprus where he became bishop and lived until he was sixty. When his sarcophagus was rediscovered in the late ninth century, Emperor Leo VI had it translated to Constantinople to protect it from plundering pirates.'

'So what happened to his relics?'

'Around 890 Leo presented Lazarus's skull to Empress Richardis —who, by the way, also came from Alsace—as a gesture of goodwill between Eastern and Western Christians.'

'Wasn't she married to Charlemagne's great-grandson, Charles the Fat, the one who stormed Rome and had himself crowned Emperor?'

'The same, *da*. He later repudiated Richardis for adultery. Anyway, returning from her pilgrimage in Palestine, she visited Constantinople to greet, as Empress of the West, the Emperor of the East. In tribute, Leo gave her the skull of Lazarus, keeping the rest of the skeleton for himself. However, the skeleton was stolen by French crusaders when the Doge of Venice passed through. Don't forget, the Fourth Crusade sacked Constantinople and wrested power from the East.'

She knew about the violation of the city's holy sanctuaries, but not that Lazarus had risen and then disappeared, twice.

'Here in France he's better known as Saint-Lazare de Marseille.'

'Because his bones are in Marseille?' she jested, trying to lighten the mood—but she still could not gauge Volodya's humour.

'The Western esoteric tradition, on the other hand, and particularly Gypsy folklore, claims that Lazarus came to Marseille with his sister, Mary Magdalene, after being expelled from Palestine by hostile Jews.'

'Gypsy? You mean Roma?'

'No no, *Gyp'sy* derives from *Egypt* and formerly referred to migrant labourers displaced by war. They followed the crusaders and pilgrims into Europe, joining nomadic nations wandering in from the East.'

'Travelling via Hungary, too?'

'Yes, along the old Carolingian silver route. But Lazarus and Mary sailed without a rudder, oar or mast, and came ashore near Marseille. They brought the Sangreal to France—'

'—the Grail? I thought it came with Joseph of Arimathea?'

She was having difficulty keeping up.

'*Da,* and several years later, after converting the local Celtic tribes, Mary retired to La Sainte-Baume—*baumo* means "holy cave"—where she died after thirty years' penance.'

'A lifetime of penance?'

'*C'est la vie.* From here on tradition splits between the Benedictines and the Dominicans. Following fears of further Muslim invasions in the eighth century, the Benedicts believed Mary's relics were translated from Aix-en-Provence to a new abbey in Burgundy and, ever since, pilgrims have visited Vézelay to pay homage to a casket of her relics. The Dominicans, on the other hand, believe her skull never left Provence and that her remains were only discovered, officially, in the late thirteenth century.'

'Wait, what is it with all these skulls?'

'As Shakespeare shows, a skull proposes a relationship between the living and the dead, between our present and their past. That's why Adam's skull is such a powerful symbol in the Abrahamic religions. According to Judaic legend, Shem and Melchizedek buried his body —or, at least, his skull—on Mount Golgotha, which is why we call it the "place of the Skull".'

But why this emphasis on skulls?

In fact, only the day before, driving back from Alsace, Jason had related a Yoruba folktale wherein a man finds a skull mounted on a pole outside a neighbouring village. To the man's astonishment, the skull speaks, so he asks why it's there: "Because I talked too much." Appalled, the man enters the village and asks to speak with the chief. Taken to the royal enclosure, the man describes the abomination he has seen—a talking skull—until the chief replies: "Then show me this marvel, or regret your lies!" The man is escorted back to the pole but now, of course, the skull remains silent. So the chief has the poor interloper beheaded and mounts his head in the place of the skull. 'That's what happens,' was Jason's jaundiced conclusion, 'when you interfere in the affairs of others.'

Sonja couldn't stop thinking of Titus van Bengal's head on that dusty road outside Cape Town. Or, for that matter, king Badu Bonsu II's head which Leiden University had once kept in a bottle. His head had been taken by Dutch soldiers after Bonsu killed two emissaries from Holland. According to one cynical colleague, king Bonsu had strung his victims' heads from his throne—making his in a bottle worth two in the bush.

War trophies, she understood, displayed brute force. The extreme case being twenty thousand amputated noses after Japan's invasion of Korea in 1597. These trophies were recently returned in a symbolic gesture of reconciliation.

Volodya was an enigmatic discussant who constantly veered off at a tangent. While following his leads, she seldom managed to tie all his loose ends together. She was not as agile as he in pursuing separate legends simultaneously. Moreover, she wanted to ask if the skulls of Lazarus and Adam were connected in any way. But she could only unravel one thread at a time. Her question would have to wait.

'As with religion and science, there's a notable difference between relics and specimens,' she heard him say on his end of the line, 'relics focus belief; specimens promote scientific knowledge.'

'Oké, so what about the skull of Lazarus?'

'Well, some say it belongs to Western Christendom, others to the East Roman Empire. Given the schism between Latin and Orthodox beliefs over papal authority, this is not surprising.'

'Volodya, the skull?'

'*Pardon*. Some say the Saint's relic was brought to Andlau and put in the crypt, where it can still be seen today.'

'And what do *you* believe?'

'That it *is* the Lazarus Skull. I think serious scholars—including a descendant of Sainte-Richarde, Count Christian d'Andlau—would agree that the skull could only belong to The Friend of Christ, to the one called Lazarus or John. Under Andlau's crypt is a well—an ancient *exitus* and *reditus*—which once symbolised the epicentre of the pilgrim's labyrinth. And long, long before that, the well provided a passage to the pagan underworld, to the Celtic "Otherworld".'

'A talking spring, *incredible*, since the Greeks too knew that a cave or well led to the Otherworld. Ironic then, isn't it, that the Celts went and sacked Delphi and silenced its ancient source forever?'

'The magic of the Other is always more powerful than one's own. Ironic, *da*, as descent precedes paradise.'

'Da *what?* Do you think it's another miraculous source?'

'Yes, Andlau is a source with healing powers for infertile woman. According to legend, a mother bear revealed the source to Richardis. Richardis saw it scratch the ground and uncovered a spring beneath the rocks. The church was built upon that site.'

Sonja had seen the bronze bear at Andlau's public fountain.

'Wait, you remember the chapel with the brilliant mosaics?'

'The Chapel of Angels?'

'Yes. Jason and I went inside and saw Saint Michael with the Grail Castle.'

'*Da*, like Sagres, Le Mont Saint-Michel came under the influence of the Benedicts. Why not visit the church in Andlau tomorrow?'

'I can't. I'm back in Leiden.'

There was a moment's silence.

'*Bon*, then let me give you the address of a friend from Driebergen. Her name is Clara Berga, also Dutch, and she'll tell you more than I about the Portuguese in South Africa. She also taught in Alexandra township, outside Johannesburg. I'll send you her details—'

'—wait, I have a query about Basil Valentine. You said he helped introduce this arcane knowledge into Northern Europe?'

'*Arcana Arcanissima, précisément.* Eastern esotericism had flowed West until, redirected by men like Almeida, it went North into Western Europe and South into East Africa.'

'Well, Camões says the Cape preserves Almeida's memory with his bones. Cape Town was not only at earth's extremest end but, at the time, the furthest south of all Holland's colonies. In other words, Almeida's skull rests at the base of this North-South axis.'

Volodya nodded, adding:

'A close friend of Clara's, Zeylmans van Emmichoven, described Table Mountain as an altar upon which rests the base of the World Cross—with its intersection at Jerusalem.'

59

*...and Hottentots stove in Francisco de Almeida's head on
some obscure South African beach.*

Ronald H Fritze, *New Worlds: The Great Voyages of Discovery* (2002)

S: no, the authenticity of a relic is not dependent on scientific proof

J: then what makes the Lazarus Skull authentic?

S: if legend says it's genuine, then proof is unnecessary

J: even if traditional belief denies what is known empirically? —sounds like another double truth to me

S: ways of knowing are relative, anyway, who says scientific knowledge is superior to belief?

J: no academic bullshit, please, what if a cautious historian and a cynical archaeologist know it's not genuine?

S: if the relic is functional, then it must be genuine

J: so historical truths don't matter?

S: apparently not, what matters is how we imagine our lives changing because of it, or what we choose to do for it

J: so you believe reality is our truth, our interior truth?

S: yes, as Prof M says, truth lies in what we believe

J: that's far too slick for me, relics are used as gifts, ransom, debt-repayments and war-trophies

S: or for restitution, as with Asantehene Badu Bonsu's head,
    which the Dutch recently returned to Ghana for burial...
    Bonsu was doomed to remain a restless interloper, unable
    to communicate with his family in the afterlife, although I
    honestly doubt anyone knew he was missing

J: ever heard about the skull of Hintsa kaPhalo?

S: who?

J: Hintsa the Great, 1835, paramount chief of the amaXhosa,
    and killed in British custody during the Cape Frontier Wars

S: no, sounds spectacular, explain?

J: he was deceived, captured and shot by the British... then
    decapitated

S: a trophy skull?

J: yes, until a traditional healer, Tilana Gcaleka—so-called
    after the original Xhosa clan—claimed the Ancestral Spirits
    had instructed him to find the head of Chief Hintsa. He
    was told peace would not be restored to SA before the skull
    returned and was reunited with Hinta's remains in the
    Transkei. It all happened just after Mandela came to power

S: and so?

J: after a sacred quest, filmed by SkyTV, Gcaleka found the
    skull in Scotland

S: where?

J: in a forest near Inverness

S: why there?

J: because that's where the Ancestral Spirits led him :)

S: don't joke about it, who's this Gcaleka?

J: he called himself Nicholas Tilana Gcaleka—a sangoma,
    lay-preacher and liquor salesman

S: so what happened next?

J: Gcaleka brought the skull back to SA and with lots of pub-
    licity, demanded an apology from the UK royal family

S: and the Xhosa royal family?

J: King Xolilizwe, a direct descendant of Hintsa's successor,
    called Gcaleka an impostor and had the skull confiscated by
    local police

S: what then?

J: the law in SA prohibits the private possession of skeletons, or human body parts, so UCT's Dept of Forensic Medicine was given the skull for safekeeping until—or rather, amid all the legal wrangling—someone did a little research

S: and?

J: the skull was analyzed by palaeo-anthropologists at three separate universities, including UCT, and subsequently found to belong to a mature female from the Hebrides

S: a woman?

J: yes, it didn't fit the African spectrum at all, proper DNA results don't lie about human origins... so the skull went back to Scotland, I'm not sure when

S: and Gcaleka?

J: last I heard he was living in Cape Town-Nyanga East and better known as Rev Mzwandile Nzulwana... he still believes the skull belongs to Chief Hintsa

S: but what do *you* believe?

J: I would never trust a lay-preacher or a liquor salesman... I had one for a father

S: so even a hardened empiricist can be superstitious?

J: yes, blame it on my upbringing

S: a true Gemini should be able to reconcile different systems —why not treat science and faith as a pair of twins?

J: no, because one is always more equal than the other... there always needs to be a hierarchy of knowledge

S: now you really are joking, hey?

Sonja waited. A slow minute passed. Her chat-box remained empty. She assumed Jason had logged off...

So his father was a preacher?

She let Skype run and went to make a cheese sandwich, her mind drifting back to the dirty divination bowls in the SA museum. As for the physical evidence they'd collected, they still had no proof.

If the evidentiary procedure has to stand alone, then what of the skull we found? Either way, she speculated, *our physical evidence will neither prove nor disprove any assassination plot...*

Jason was back on line.

J: I found a link to an Italian veteran soldier and travel-writer, Ludovico di Varthema, who was among the first to enter Mecca and Medina disguised as a pilgrim

S: like Pêro da Covilhã, a Christian or a Jew?

J: don't know, but like Gaspar, he travelled from Alexandria as a convert under the adopted name of Yunas, or Jonah, and escorted the annual pilgrim caravan to the holy places of Dar al-Islam where he saw the sacred Black Stone

S: Arabia's holy of holies?

J: yes, brought there by Angel Gabriel when Abraham built the Kaaba

S: don't pilgrims touch the stone because it absorbs sin?

J: it isn't holy, it's a solid red-black meteorite

S: now don't get academic with me, do you have a date?

J: two hundred and fifty million years ago

S: be serious—a date for Ludovico, not the stone!

J: 1503

S: and the link to Almeida?

J: Ludovico joined the Portuguese in 1506 and served under Tristão da Cunha...
Almeida knighted Ludovico himself, for helping to fight the Egyptians, Arabs and Turks...
he stayed at Cochin for a year-and-a-half, until 1507, when he sailed to Lisbon via the Cape of Good Hope

S: wait, the dates are important, since he would have been in Cochin when Almeida was Viceroy

J: yes, having arrived with two Chinese Christians

S: Nestorians?

J: probably, as he'd just come from South-East Asia— Sumatra, Borneo and Java, returning via Cape Comorin

S: sounds like the end-of-the-earth to me

J: yes, see Ludovico's *Itinerario*, published in Rome, 1510

S: the same year Almeida and Gaspar died

J: whatever, you know dates best

*To guarantee the church, the house of God,
I founded the noble Order named the Fleece.*
Jean Molinet, *Epitaph of Philip the Good* (c.1467)

'The legend of the Golden Fleece is based on voyages made around 1500BCE, when seaborne gold-prospectors crossed the Black Sea,' said Volodya, 'although the story's origins date back far further.'

Sonja adjusted the webcam, surprised to hear from him so soon.

'Dating back to a distant pre-Christian Georgia?'

'*Da*, where they washed alluvial sediments through a sheep's skin, trapping the grit in its fatty curls. So, *voilà*, the legend is partly true... at least one part is history, the other allegory.'

'Allegory? Why, because the argonauts were like astronauts?'

'*Précisément, bon.* Both possessed courage, undertook voyages into the unknown and went beyond their respective horizons—'

'—as had Dias,' she said, testingly, 'going to the Back o' Beyond?'

'Yes, that's why they nicknamed him the "Captain of the End".'

'Who, Dias?'

'*Da*, because he brought his men back from the End-of-the-Earth, from *Ultima Thule*, whose limit was yet unguessed.'

'Well, I can't leave home without a TomTom.' He seemed not to share her humour. 'Sorry Volodya, please continue.'

'*Merci.* There are some obvious parallels between the founding of an ancient Greek state and the emergence of the Portuguese nation: Jason and Henrique were both princes who sent seafarers to the ends of the world and did what others thought impossible: they made the promise of return a reality—'

'—but Prince Henry never sailed far himself.'

'No, but that made him no less adventurous. Since Antiquity the southern hemisphere was believed to lead to the Underworld—the World's End—where the natural order was reversed.'

Sonja nodded, recalling what Jason had said about crossing the equator at sea. It felt as if she'd crossed a line herself.

Was Toynbee's panoramic history really so idiosyncratic? Was his view still too transgressive for a social historian?

Pulling herself back, she heard Volodya explaining how the voyage of the Argo symbolised a descent into the Underworld—a world of initiation:

'Reaching the southern hemisphere, the Portuguese saw the fixed star of Canopus—so named for Jason's pilot—in the sign of the Argo. It was seen below Orion and Sirius, which occult etymologists linked to Osiris and Isis, and their return from the Underworld. Osiris and Isis symbolise resurrection and renewal.'

'I thought we were talking about Prince Henry?'

'*Da*. His navigators had to face terrible sea monsters and, like the dragonslayers of yore, had to vanquish the unknown.'

'Hence the popularity of St George?'

'*Khorosho*, but there's something else. Dom Francisco visited France in the late 1470s, remember? Well, some say he also went to Bruges to see the Holy Blood relic, the one Thierry d'Alsace brought back from the Second Crusade. And as you know, Thierry was the father of Philip of Flanders.'

'The same Philip for whom Chrétien wrote his *Parsifal?*'

'*Da*, some say the relic's acquisition was invented to add credibility to the House of Flanders, as the procession of the Holy Blood only dates to 1350, two hundred years later. As you know, it was a time of war, famine and the pest—'

'—and miracles?'

'*Da*. Today residents follow the procession, acting out scenes from Flemish history and the bible, followed by bouts of heavy drinking.'

'Yes, but where's the link to Almeida?'

Sonja felt their discussion had lost focus.

'*Bon*. Two centuries later, in 1430, Philippe le Bon of Burgundy founded the Order of the Golden Fleece, *la Toison d'Or*, to safeguard his church and its sacred relic. The grand founding occasion also marked his marriage to Isabel of Portugal, daughter of João I.'

'And sister of Prince Henry?'

Volodya nodded: 'Isabel came with a handsome dowry, a cultured entourage and some of the best merchants and artisans from Lisbon.

She played an influential role in Burgundy's affairs where, for a brief period, Catholics and Protestants were able to worship side by side. The Order's insignia was a golden lamb and the parade opened with a procession of costumed Argonauts—representing the Knights of the Golden Fleece.'

'Wait, this link is too slender for me. Almeida wasn't even born in 1430. Volodya, please, it's all a bit vague...'

She knew the broad historical lines, but not the Burgundian detail. Her study of Europe's political history covered the *exoteric* succession of kings and their bloodlines—but not the *esoteric* events behind the rise-and-fall of royal houses. So, in that case, what more did she know about the alliance between Philip the Good and Isabel of Portugal? Philip was not only the Duke of Burgundy and among the wealthiest princes of his day, but had the most splendid court outside Rome and co-controlled the economic centres of Europe. Flanders and Brabant were part of his inheritance and, to strengthen his position, he aligned himself with England and Portugal. Isabel was his third wife.

But for Sonja, it still didn't add up.

'I suspect Isabel's marriage was prompted by Portugal's expansion into foreign markets,' she reflected, 'as her brother Henry had been making remarkable progress in West Africa, bringing back increasing measures of coveted slaves and gold.'

Volodya smiled, judiciously, flashing his own gold:

'Before 1385, when Isabel's father seized the throne, the kings of Portugal belonged to the House of Burgundy. It was a relationship that went back two-and-a-half centuries.'

'But,' she replied, 'but Burgundy was a territorial cluster formed by inheritance, treaty, capture and purchase. Anyway, there are too few women in this story. What else about Isabel?'

'Jan van Eyck painted her portrait while visiting Lisbon, two years before her marriage to Philip. Then, with the help of experienced Portuguese ship builders, she established a shipyard in Bruges. Like most new towns in Western Europe, Bruges was a centre of economic and artistic freedoms and the birthplace of the free personality. As a patron of the arts, she surrounded herself with painters, musicians and poets. She was good at politics and had a profound influence at court, often representing Philip on diplomatic missions.'

'And Almeida—you said he visited Bruges?'

'Da, in 1468, to see the Holy Blood relic.'

What is it with these damn relics?

'Via Mary Magdalene, Nicodemus and Joseph of Arimathea, dried traces of Christ's blood found their way to the Odile Hill in Alsace, the island of Reichenau on Lake Constance, and to Rosslyn Chapel near Aberdeen. And to Bruges, of course.'

'Almeida would have been ten, perhaps fifteen, and accompanied by his father. But I've never read about his trip. Sorry, Volodya, I'm struggling with all this meaningless detail.'

Embarrassed by her own imprudence, she added quickly:

'After accompanying Afonso to France, Almeida isn't heard of from 1478 to 1484—that's six years—after which he reappears in Lisbon. According to his biographer, Joaquim Candeias Silva, he passed his time at court, waiting on the Perfect Prince upon whom he now depended. And during this transition, the young Almeida had neither title nor property to speak of.'

'Then there's a gap in the historical record?'

'Yes, that's why I think this is when he started a family. Lourenço was born around 1480.'

Volodya drifted on:

'The ageing Afonso left Tours humiliated by the lack of support after his defeat at Toro. It had been a costly journey and so, not wanting to return empty-handed, he fled toward Palestine disguised as a pilgrim repenting his sins. He died a few years later, in 1481, and I assume Dom Lopo and his family attended the grand state funeral in Lisbon. So why not assume Dom Francisco visited Bruges too? Or, perhaps, that he was born several years earlier.'

'I can't, Volodya, I'm supposed to be a historian. Would you like to assume that all Russians are descended from a maternal African?'

It was time to say good-bye. Volodya had an unexpected visitor, so he hurriedly finished: 'Sir Isaac Newton says classical astrology was fixed between the time of the Argonauts and the Trojan wars.'

'Why's that?'

'Because the Argonauts are placed in our night sky, not the heroes of the Trojan wars...'

55

These effects include... soil from his grave, several hairs from
his beard, his footprint and some of his extracted teeth.
Murat Belge & Ara Guler, *Guide to Topkapi Palace, Istanbul* (1994)

Where are the remains of Muhammad or Abraham? Or the skulls of Adam and Lazarus? What about the body of Mary or the head of the Baptist? What of the dismembered bodies of the saints and prophets; all their hair, teeth, nails, fingers, arms and legs? And what of those "holy foreskins" in Rome, Chartres or Santiago de Compostela? How do these differ from the fangs, claws, shells, seeds and stones stuffed into divination baskets at the SA Museum?

Sonja raised the issue of Almeida's skull on the phone, telling the startled Mendle that he had some bones to take care of himself—and before the year ended.

He'd offered to do something about Almeida's memory too, though he wasn't sure of the timing. In the meantime, he promised to ask the museum's marine biologist, Soraya, about the nature of a pearl.

And so, with largesse and a semiotic sense of humour, he invited Soraya for dinner at La Perla, a popular restaurant at the foot of Table Mountain. Each linen-bedecked table had a silver perlemoen menu holder, echoing an era when mailships still called at the Tavern of the Seas. For her *hors d'oeuvre* Soraya ordered a portion of oysters, Mendle the creamy white mussel soup.

'A pearl,' began Soraya with professional detachment, 'a pearl is a nacreous concretion made of filmy layers covering a foreign body trapped in a bivalve mollusc.'

Mendle wondered if her oysters were an *hors d'oeuvre* or simply a *bivalve?* Soraya was a typical lab scientist—a candid observer of the miniscule—with an interest in tidal rock pools, patio-gardens and, after Mendle's own heart, the crossword puzzle. She continued:

'It is formed through the union of substance and material, such as between an animal membrane and a sand granule. The process takes several years, although artificial pearls are manufactured in less time. A genuine pearl is usually whitish and hue-shifting, hard, and with an unmistakable tear-drop or smooth oval finish.'

'Soraya, excuse me, but what are the symbolic associations?'

'A pearl can be a small fragment of molten metal, a piece of clean coal or a lump of boiled sugar. You get pearl eyes, pearl buttons and, of course, pearl lace. Also, a woollen jersey is said to pearl when—'

Redirect, Morse!

'—I mean, does a pearl have any symbolic value?'

'Yes, it was the world's most prized jewel before the discovery of South Africa's diamond fields.'

'Aha, but besides its value then, does Vermeer's pearl earring *mean* anything?'

She looked perplexed: 'I'm sorry to disappoint you, Mendle, but Vermeer's spectacular pearl was an artificial French invention, then fashionable in Holland. Unlike cultured pearls from Venice, these were made of very thin glass spheres filled with *l'essence d'orient*, a preparation of white wax and the silvery scales of fresh-water fish. Vermeer painted the same earring nine times, while similar pearls are found in contemporary works by Metsu, Ter Borch and La Tour.'

'But what does the pearl *symbolise?*' he stressed again.

'Oh well, of course, there's a medieval Ethiopian legend about the Pearl of Adam. I found it while looking for a bible-story to read the children last Christmas—'

'—I thought you were Hindu?'

'Yes, but we also give presents.'

'Aha, as did we. I guess our Indo-European roots go beyond the sacred rivers and divine waters we have in common—including a belief in karma and ketchup on fries?'

Soraya nodded, savouring her last morsel, and then continued:

'Hindus and Coptic Christians are not so different. Both share a belief in rebirth and the afterlife. Anyway, in this story God creates the earth, the heavens and the Garden of Life. During creation He secretly places a white pearl inside Adam's body. The pearl is passed from generation to generation; through the bodies of Noah, Enoch, Abraham, Isaac and Jacob, then to David, Solomon and Joachim, until Joachim passes it on to his wife, Hannah, in whom it begins to stir. The pearl grows and grows until a child is born, a beautiful girl, who becomes the Virgin Mary.'

He looked at her in surprise: 'You know the Old Testament too!'

She took it as a compliment.

'The idea isn't new, y'know, not since Plato said "we're imprisoned in our bodies like an oyster in its shell". Anyway, the workings of pagan spirits and deities were represented as episodes in the legends of Christian saints.'

His eyes filled with appreciation, as if seeing her for the first time. He'd not regarded Soraya as anything but a staff-scientist. But, then, he hadn't enjoyed the company of a mature woman for a long time—especially not one so attractive as Soraya. Not sure how to express himself, he clumsily resumed their discussion:

'This Judeo-Christian narrative confirms the Solomonic line of Ethiopia's Royal House and—I think it's from the *Kebra Nagast*—also accounts for the presence of the Falashas and their influence on Coptic Christianity.'

'Aren't they the group who went into exile?' she asked, lowering her voice to a whisper, 'aren't they the "Black Jews" of Africa?'

'Yes. *Falasha* means "exile" or "stranger".'

'Oh, and there's the story of how Zoroaster was preserved in an iridescent pearl. Legend claims that the prophet's physical body was transformed by, or perhaps into, a pearl. This pearl came from Persia and was born out of fire and water.

Aha, an alchemical process? Mendle felt rejuvenated:

'A foreign body born out of opposites and transformed by heat and liquid, coated in ash and salt—'

'—actually carbon, it's carbonate of lime and potassium.'

Pearls of wisdom, he thought, as she cleaned her plate, *the philosopher's stone is carbon transformed!*

Mendle drew a deep breath.

He also drew on the Kabbalah, including all he could recall from the Judaic mystical tradition in medieval France and Spain:

'The philosopher's stone represents a conjunction of opposites, the reintegration of spirit and matter, like the stone that fell from heaven —the *Lapis exilis*—of which the meteorite in Mecca is a sacred touch-stone. Cosmic intelligence comes from stones that "fall to earth to fill the heads of men", though not as it does in Hollywood.'

Zoroastrian dualism, he reflected, strove to reconcile the forces of light and dark, goodness and evil. According to various legends, the three Magi were Zoroastrian priests who anticipated the rebirth of their patriarch in a far-off West. So much he knew and had discussed with Sonja. But that Zoroaster and Jesus were one and the same entity, *oi-vey*, this he'd not actually contemplated before.

Ah, it's an esoteric mystery? His mind leapt with renewed excitement. *Perhaps the Pearl of Zoroaster is connected to the Grail of Christ—since both symbolise the inner transformation necessary for the renewal of the spirit in man.*

Is this possible? Well, perhaps.

Zoroastrianism had been the state religion in Persia before the Muslim conquest. It was tolerated by Islam, as both faiths were based on an ethical monotheism with a transcendent creator. Furthermore, after a final judgement, the creator would divide all beings into an afterlife of heaven and hell.

In Iran, however, Zoroastrians were persistently persecuted and fled to India where they established a religious-refugee community. That was around the tenth century, he seemed to recall. Today they outnumbered their co-religionists back in Persia. Soraya's former husband was from Tehran, though she never spoke of him...

'Hello, Mendle, are you listening? I said the *Nag Hamadi* scriptures of St Thomas tell of a young boy who leaves home, or goes into exile, and then slays a dragon and seizes its priceless pearl.'

'Ah, dragon-pearls from China. I thought we were talking about sacred pearls in Persia?'

'Really, so you missed all I said about pearled horses in India?'

'I'm afraid so,' he shrugged, apologetically.

Like Morse, Mendle could look hapless when it suited him.

'So, once again then, right? There's this Hindu rite where a horse is adorned with pearls before being killed. It's a ritual sacrifice known as the *asvamedha* and only performed for kings; and then only rarely as it was such a costly affair.'

She paused to see if Mendle was listening.

He reacted positively, so she continued: 'A wild stallion was chosen, consecrated by the priests, and then allowed to roam free under the protection of a royal guard. If the horse crossed a neighbouring territory, that ruler would have to adapt-or-die according to the expanding kingdom's dictates. Finally, before its death, the horse was anointed with oil and adorned with pearls. The king's first wife then enacted the climax of this rite: she would mimic copulation with the sacrificed beast, symbolically uniting the virility of the king with the fertility of his land. Y'know, I find the idea of ritual sex strangely thrilling.'

Mendle blushed, sidestepping the topic:

'Horse sacrifice and ritual mating appear in many Indo-European cultures, as with the Celtic-Roman horse-goddess, Epona. No wonder you chose another bed-time story for the kids.'

She laughed. 'Actually, this *is* their favourite story. They always ask me to tell it again.'

'Well, rather tell me more about the Pearl of Zoroaster.'

'Oh, the pearl was stolen by Arabs and taken to Jerusalem, where it hung in the al-Aqsa Mosque, until it disappeared again.'

'You mean stolen, again?'

'Probably. In Muslim tradition the pearl represents Paradise, which is why the Blessed live in pearls. So if you're looking for symbolism, Mendle, pearls are known as the Pearls of Paradise.'

'Aha, the pearl contained Zoroaster's body as the cup contained Christ's blood,' mused Mendle, finishing his soup. *And, perhaps, it was the same pearl Almeida found in Granada?*

56

Tell to me truly: in Paradise
What meaneth the Pearl unblemished?
Anonymous English Bard, *The Pearl* (c.1350)

Sonja typed in *basil valentine*, followed by *pearl*, and then hit the search button. Google located one quarter of a million references in under a quarter-second. The first caught her attention:

Basil Valentine, by Religious Vows am bound according to the Order of... Do thou Reader attend, if you find the Pearl of great price...

She clicked again and found herself looking at an annotated copy of Valentine's *Triumphal Chariot of Antimony*.

She scrolled down, down. It seemed as endless as it was confusing. Worse yet, the text was written in a prosaic style in which each and every word was loaded with special meaning; where all its "pointes" and "prickes" bristled with significance.

Nearing the end of the text she caught sight of an unusual insert—added centuries later by an editor—marking a new section:

[Author's Pilgrimage]

When I, according to my vow, undertook a Pilgrimage to St James, to visit that Holy Place as a Stranger, I prayed to GOD, and bound myself with a Vow, that if he granted me a happy Return to my Monastery, I would render him due Praise. He granted my Request, and I daily return Thanks to him. But I thought many more would have rejoiced with me, and may have given thanks to the same GOD for the famous Reliques which I brought with me to our Monastery (for the Consolation of the Poor, and many Others), that it might procure to itself a Name, in this perishing Valley of Tears, that could not be wiped out by any Oblivion. Yet few were rendered either better, or more grateful to GOD, for so great a benefit; but persevered in Derision and Contempt of that which GOD will vindicate in the Last Day.

She scrutinized the page to see if it revealed anything of Valentine's meeting with someone else, someone acting as or under the protection of Thomas Malory. That is, assuming they were contemporaries.

However, cross-checking Wikipedia for Valentine's biography, she learnt that scholars weren't able to agree on his identity, let alone on the century in which he lived.

He was a Benedictine from the Rhineland, once part of Alsace and, like Münster and Gutenberg, also born in Mainz. Despite a dearth of evidence on Valentine's life—even his name is uncertain—public records indicate that he had been at St Peterkloster, Erfurt, in 1413, and became Canon of the Priory of St Peter's near Strassburg.

Strasbourg, the "Town of the Roads", lay south-west of Erfurt and on the French side of the border today, hence the different spelling. Erfurt and Strassburg then shared the same trade and pilgrim routes, the same ecclesiastical district and the same bishop. In short, they were bound by wheat and wine, faith and economics—and both to Rome and Compostela.

Valentine's pilgrimage to the Holy Place of St James, to the shrine of James the Greater, suggests he went to Santiago de Compostela. Compostela was the most popular destination for Christian pilgrims, after Jerusalem and Rome. Such a journey would have been possible, as he was away for long periods at a time and, by his own account, travelled in disguise or, at least, entered Compostela incognito.

This raised a curious issue: why, as a renowned scholar, should he fear being recognised by fellow Benedictines—or, was he more afraid of the Knights of Santiago? Volodya had hinted that Valentine was protecting someone, someone he went there to meet.

Furthermore, Valentine prayed for his safe return, making a vow with God and not, no, *not* with the patron saint of travellers, St James. He clearly feared meeting more than the usual dangers on the road.

Sonja scrolled back to where it described how Johan Tholde had collected, edited and published Valentine's work at the end of the seventeenth century. Tholde included a note by Valentine himself, allegedly handwritten, describing how he journeyed in peril of his life and that those who benefit should thank God he returned safely.

She'd read it too, but at the time failed to realise that Tholde was Secretary of the Rosicrucians and thereby obtained manuscripts from Valentine's pupils in the Rosy-Cross Academy.

Well, she speculated, if Valentine went for a secret rendezvous then we should be asking for *whom* or for *what* did he risk his reputation, his safety, and even his priesthood?

Moreover, if Valentine wanted to attend the Saint's Feast in July, he'd have been away in mid-summer. As with most events in his life, his pilgrimage was still unconfirmed. On the other hand, she guessed, he may have travelled to Compostela more than once in his life.

While scholars disagree on Valentine's dates, most sources put him between c.1394–c.1522, making him a hundred years old when, or if, he ever met Almeida.

According to Volodya, Almeida obtained Aristotle's treatise during the fall of Granada. Although the siege lasted several years, she'd found no reference to him being injured, captured or even released. There were only accounts of refugees and deserters fleeing the city, including an estimated two hundred Christian captives released when the city was handed over. Could Almeida have been among them?

If so, why was Volodya being so vague? Was there something he didn't want her to know—or did this story have no historical detail, like a legend? In the end, Sonja knew, any clandestine operation revolved around one critical question: *Had their lives even overlapped?*

57

'Are you staying home to avoid going out?' asked Mendle, pleased to be using his webcam again. Sonja looked vulnerable. Nervous.

'My life slowed down after the last scare. Really. I saw that ogrish man again, here in Leiden, when I went to Albert Heijn. I think he followed me back from the shops, although I didn't dare turn round. I'm simply being paranoid, of course.'

'But are you safe on your own? Shouldn't you call the police?'

'And tell them what—that I'm being followed by a man in black? Prof, they'll think I'm paranoid too. No, Bart is coming to stay.'

'Aha. Perhaps your time will be spent mixing preparations, testing effects and observing new properties?' beamed Mendle, brimming with expectation after their last email. 'Did you see my attachments on Nicolas Flamel and Basil Valentine?'

'I did, and read both with interest. Thank you. But to be honest, the parallel trips to Compostela are too coincidental—'

'—you mean too similar in structure and content?'

'Yes, as if it's the same story. Both men went to Santiago in disguise seeking the protection of a pilgrimage and both returned in peril of their lives because of what or whom they'd seen. More specifically, both received arcane knowledge of a rare and precious book which, I understand, explained the transmutations of minerals and metals. Yes, these seem to belong to the same story, a mutation of sorts, like the legends of Solomon and Prester John—'

'—but there *is* one crucial difference,' he tested.

'How so?'

'Flamel undertook his journey *before* Almeida was born.'

'That doesn't exclude it being the same story. I think one legend has been attributed to two independent historical-mythical figures. Who is this Flamel, anyway?'

'Aha, Nicolas Flamel! He is the unseen alchemist in *Harry Potter*, the Grand Master of Sion in *The Da Vinci Code* and *Holy Blood, Holy Grail*, and before that, in the *Hunchback of Notre-Dame*, Victor Hugo says—'

'—no, enough!' she pleaded, 'just give the historical facts.'

Even his bushy brows couldn't hide his disappointment.

'Flamel's brother was in charge of the Duke of Berry's library and the friend of printers, book dealers and collectors. Flamel himself was a scrivener and, by his own account, acquired this book in Paris when he was about twenty-one, around 1361, after which he completed his apprenticeship and was then old enough to be regarded an adept. Semiotically, of course, we still hand over the Keys of Life at twenty-one. Anyway, the manuscript Flamel acquired is exhaustively known as *The Sacred Book of Abraham the Jew, Prince, Priest, Levite, Astrologer and Philosopher to the Tribe of Jews who by the Wrath of God were dispersed amongst the Gauls*. It is also called *Aesch Mezareph*, although they preferred longer titles back then. And curiously, Sonja, Wolfram von Eschenbach claimed the original account of the Grail had descended from Solomon and the Queen of Sheba.'

Unsure of the connection, she let him continue.

'Then in 1382, having studied the book without success for another twenty-one years, he travelled to Spain where a converted Jew elucidated it for him. On his return, Flamel claims to have performed alchemical transmutations, though never claimed to be an alchemist himself. The book uses a secret word for Morning Star, *Maranatha*, which is an old alchemical allusion to Mercury.'

'The Twin?'

'Aha. The pre-Islamic Arabians recognised a trinity of heavenly bodies: the Moon, the Sun and the Morning Star—also known as *Athtar*. Like Mercury and Venus, Athtar passed "through the sun" every few hundred years and was thus linked to the death and rebirth of the Phoenix. As a messenger of the gods, Athtar is the forerunner of the One who Returns for Eternity and so, eventually, Christ says: "Behold, I am the bright Morning Star." When Christianity first reached Ethiopia, the name used for Christ was *Ashtar*, after the Arabian divinity, of course. Ah, the twins indeed!'

'Prof, what of Flamel's facts?'

'Right. He led a modest life and died in 1418. However, toward the end, he purchased land and several properties. By then he'd founded and endowed fourteen hospitals, seven churches and three chapels in Paris alone. His altruism spread when he provided funds for similar projects in the country.'

'—wait, Prof, finish Flamel first,' she pleaded in vain.

'Sir Isaac Newton annotated Flamel's works with painstaking care and attention to detail, even copying one entire manuscript by hand. Today the *Book of Abraham* is housed at the Bibliothèque de l'Arsenal and Flamel's in the Bibliothèque nationale.'

'*Oh nee!* Had we known, we could have seen these last week!'

'Never mind, they'll always be there. Anyway, about the parallels between Abraham and Aristotle: the book of Abraham was bound and covered; whereas Aristotle's was no more than a set of notes. Both refer to an ancient treatise on the secrets of nature and each could have been original, though written in translation. Flamel's book was full of Greek and Hebrew texts, while Aristotle's was in Aramaic. Averroës, remember, came from the Andalusian Academy where Flamel sought erudition.'

'Flamel? I thought he went to Compostela?'

'Apparently not, it seems he went to Cordoba or Granada. These were the last schools of Islamic studies in al-Andalus and a translation of Aristotle's treatise would have been there. In Almeida's narrative a Moor plays a prominent role—the man you call Majid—whereas in Flamel's story he's a Jewish adept, the so-called Master Canches.'

She thought of Balthasar, the Moor of Christmas pageants past:

'Perhaps Jew and Muslim are synonymous—representing the best potential converts to Christianity?'

Mendle leant toward the webcam: 'Curious you should say this, as Abraham and Muhammad are successive incarnations of the same entity—formerly known as Ar-Brahm of Atlantis.'

He paused for her response.

'*Oi-vey*, I see you have difficulty with that one. Anyway, it's what Laurence once said over lunch, adding an interesting afterthought: "I find it difficult too, of course, but have to believe what I hear".'

She was still staring in disbelief when he concluded:

'Queen Isabella disrupted this age-old esoteric tradition when she separated the Jews and Muslims from the Christians. An irony, don't you think, if Abraham and Muhammad *really* were the same!'

She was speechless.

'Anyway, Flamel found his pearl of wisdom and travelled to the ends of the earth to decipher its meaning. First to Spain, and then on to India, where some say he still lives today.'

✝   ✝   ✝

Mendle was an associative thinker who found meaning in diversity. Sonja, on the other hand, sought hers in depth rather than breadth. She liked his interrogative style, while he, in turn, knew her ordered questions kept his mind from imploding.

'Take another look at Valentine's *Triumphal Chariot* and you'll detect correspondences with Aristotle's *Sierra Nevada*. First, both claim that water is the first Matter from which all things are and have been made: "Water, by the Dryness of Fire and Air, forms the Earth…" Water is a universal solvent without which life couldn't exist, a point on which modern science agrees. Secondly, Valentine's *antimony* and Aristotle's *quintessence* are conceptually similar in that all matter, and thus all life, originated from the stars—both say physical matter began with the ethereal essence out of which the celestial spheres were made. Their respective cosmogonies support contemporary postulations about the origins of our universe… No doubt other links exist between them and, should you find these, may reveal more about the content of the *Sierra Nevada*.'

Mendle paused to wet his lips. Until now she'd not seen the half-jack behind his desk lamp.

So, that's why he prefers no webcam.

'Anyway,' he resumed, 'despite the uncertainties of Valentine's life, it is acknowledged that the *Currus Triumphalis Antimonii* is his most significant contribution to chemistry and dates from 1500—around the time Almeida passed on the *Sierra Nevada*. This is only guesswork, as Valentine's treatise may have appeared fifty years earlier. For your interest, the most popular edition of the *Triumphal Chariot* was published in Amsterdam with a commentary by Theodorus Kerckringius —which is the version I sent you. Dutch publishers were a lot more tolerant than their Catholic counterparts.'

'Well, I trawled through it and found his propositions about the mysteries of nature to be as perplexing, inspiring and illuminating as those of Rudolf Steiner—not that I've read much by the latter, only commentaries by independent writers. And while your suggestion of a transpersonal link between Aristotle and Valentine is engaging, it's beyond my bounds of credibility at the moment. Please, let's rather discuss their karmic connection another day, I'm still struggling with what Laurence said about Paracelsus returning as Carl Jung!'

Paracelsus was born in 1493 and, like Jung, was Swiss. He travelled to Germany, France, Italy, Hungary, Russia, Sweden, Denmark and the Netherlands... Furthermore, assassins in the pay of the orthodox medical faculty allegedly aided his unexpected death.

Another assassination?

Farther back in time, or so Mendle also mentioned, Jung had been St Paul. According to Laurence, Saul-Paul had been an intemperate wanderer who'd struggled with his ego. Despite his initiation, he was a victim of vainglory in that the ego identified too strongly with the ideal. Jung's task was to spiritualize the racism of the Aryan psyche— a psyche so glorified by Richard Wagner—and thereby complete Paul's mission as the Apostle to the Gentiles...

Wait, wait, wait!

For now, she had only one question:

'Why, why the *Sierra Nevada*?'

The Professor looked up, his bushy brows obscuring his face. Sonja continued before he could begin:

'—but why does Volodya want it so badly? It's as if he expects *me* to know something about it—'

'—or he wants *you* to find it. You say he collects maps and icons?'

'Yes, manuscripts too.'

'Aha, your collector may be after the mother-of-all-manuscripts, the pseudo-Aristotelian *Secretum secretorum*.'

'The Secret of Secrets?'

'Exactly, the *Arcana Arcanissima* of Antiquity. I thought it was a phantom work,' admitted Mendle, 'a fantasy of wishful secrets.'

'The Gallic Warrior,' she recalled with humour, 'told us it was a work of neo-Templar mysticism and the fount of Western humanism. You're so full of secrets yourself, Prof.'

'Ha, and I thought you'd say I was full of Glenfiddich! The oldest source is the Arabic *Kitab sirr al-asrar*, a compendium for rulers which purports to be from Aristotle to Alexander. It was written as a missive and probably delivered while Alexander wintered at Gordium, after the Oracle of Siwa proclaimed he would rule all Asia. It offers advice on the ethics of good governance, wise statecraft, astrology, alchemy, and, of course, the magical or medical properties of plants, gems and numbers. All in all, the letter offers a unified science which only a moral leader with intellectual integrity was capable of understanding.'

'In short, the Grail of Grail-sciences?'

'Aha! Yes, the *Secretum secretorum* included a copy of the Emerald Tablet, or *Tabula smaragdina*, which dealt specifically with a cosmology for wise rulers. The *Tabula* usually appeared at the back of the book, being a later addition, and its text attributed to Hermes Trismegistus, the Thrice-great Hermes...'

Mendle expounded while she listed the emeralds found thus far. There was Ptolemy's emerald sea, Muhammad's emerald mountain, the emerald table from Solomon's Temple and—possibly the same— the emerald table of Prester John. There was also the emerald cup of San Juan de la Peña, the sacred emerald of Venus, the alchemical emerald of Mercury and the emerald that fell to earth from Lucifer's forehead. And now, to top it all, there seemed to be an Emerald Tablet of Hermes-something-or-other?

58

*A proper set of human ethics is only possible with
a proper acceptance of karma and reincarnation.*
Joseph Mendle, private conversation (24 July 2010)

Sonja's life came to a literal standstill in July. With little else to do at home, she filled her time reading as much as she could, though none of it proved useful to her VOC research. She'd reached an impasse out of fear for the future, she suspected, but couldn't admit to herself which came first: her fear of postponing the Tropenmuseum or that of bumping into the Black Goliath.

Like a stamp collector who forgets countries still exist, she fell into a realm of obscure factual minutiae; of details that required such close examination that her world outside lost focus. And so her nights were crammed with the *Secretum secretorum* and the myopia of its appended *Tabula smaragdina*…

She learnt that the *Tabula* was among the most esteemed texts in the canon of Western occultism, with Hermes as the revered father figure behind the Hermetica and the Renaissance Hermeticists. Like the stone tablets of Moses, Hermes Trismegistus inscribed the entire wisdom of Egypt on this *Tabula*. It is said he "carried an emerald, upon which was recorded the philosophy of the Ancients, including the caduceus, the medieval symbol of mystical illumination".

According to tradition, the *Tabula* was discovered in a tomblike cave, still clutched in Hermes's hand. Legends differ on who found it:

some claim it was Sarah, the wife of Abraham, while others say it was Apollonius of Tyana in 100CE, a remarkable two millennia later. From the seventh century, copies appear in various Arabic treatises under such titles as the *Secret of Creation and the Art of Nature*, the *Secrets of Nature* and the *Secret of Secrets*.

Hermes's stone was inscribed in Phoenician and, allegedly, revealed the evolutionary processes of nature: nature as a living record of our universe's history. The first Latin copy appeared around 1200 and, despite the usual losses in translation, the *Tabula's* most profound passage remains its opening paragraph:

That which is above is like that which is below and that which is below is like that which is above, to achieve the wonders of the one thing. This is the foundation of astrology and alchemy: that the microcosm of mankind and the earth is a reflection of the macrocosm of God and the heavens.

The folios also referred to Hermes as the founder of alchemy and to Maria Hebracia, sister of Moses, as the guardian of this knowledge. Sonja knew that Jewish, Persian and Arabian tutors, particularly Avicenna and Averroës, had advanced it as a canon on medicine within an Aristotelian context. By the thirteenth century the concepts were Christianized by Albertus Magnus and Thomas Aquinas until, once again, it was transformed as a new spiritual science under Paracelsus and Basil Valentine...

Just as the Phoenicians introduced an alphabet based on signs for different sounds (helping to inaugurate the transition from pictorial ideas to abstract thought in Western society), so too the *Tabula* led the transition from abstract spiritualism to a more down-to-earth spiritual science—a process that prepared the way for Aristotelian thinking.

So then, what is my preparation for?

59

In the Hermetica, a Graeco-Egyptian series of writings on cosmology and spirituality attributed to Hermes Trismegistus/Thoth, the doctrine of reincarnation is central.

Wikipedia Foundation, *Reincarnation* (2010)

From: jmendle@sam.org.za
Sent: Wednesday, July 28, 10:08
To: awayfromhome@gmail.com
Subject: Rosicrucian Enlightenment

Dear Sonja

I hear Bart was discharged and is now staying with you. I hope you take extra care of each other—notwithstanding his withdrawal and your paranoia. Don't be alarmed, but my house was ransacked last night while Laurence and I were attending a performance of Beethoven's *Eroica*. Whoever they are, they left no stone unturned, and left my study behind in a mess.

Laurence says you should know that Hermes Trismegistus is an entity who appeared as Thoth and, later still, as Pythagoras. Even Wikipedia seems to have stumbled onto his origin and identity. You must be onto something important yourself, as the Ancestral Spirits have spoken again:

Rosicrucianism

The Rose-Croix is a symbol of the mysterious Rosicrucians. The Rosicrucian Order came to light in the early seventeenth century with the publication of the "Rosicrucian manifestos", abruptly announcing an ancient brotherhood of secret adepts. Christian Rosenkreuz, the reputed founder of the Order in the fifteenth century, was said to have discovered a long-lost body of oriental knowledge and wisdom. The manifestos were first published in Germany and intimated the commencement of a new cycle of activity under the then universal Grand Master, Sir Francis Bacon, who had himself composed them.

Since then and to this day, there have been many Rosicrucian organisations, most with spurious links to the one true order. Rosicrucianism is itself very ancient and was the fountainhead from which sprung the mystical schools and secret traditions of Antiquity. It was the underground stream of the Hermetics.

The earliest traceable source comes from the Atlantean legacy of ancient Egypt, where it gave rise to the mystery schools of *Ros-Tau*, the Solar Cross. The symbol of the crucified sun was later represented as a crucified red rose. Ros-Tau was also an ancient name for the Giza complex of pyramids and temples. The site of Rosetta, where the famous stone inscriptions were discovered, was once called *Ros-Tau*. The Arabs referred to it as *Rashid*, being the nearest equivalent in their language. By this odd coincidence the Rosetta Stone—which was to unlock the secrets of Egyptian hieroglyphics—could be called the Ros-Tau Stone, or the Rosicrucian Stone.

Rosicrucianism spread in waves through the religious cultures of all the high civilisations in the Old World, inspiring the revolution of Akhnaton in Egypt's eighteenth dynasty and the religion Moses bequeathed to the Hebrews. Among the Israelites it became the Kabala, the Hidden Teaching, held in trust by the Essenes of Palestine and the Therapeuts of Alexandria.

It was the inner teaching of the Greek philosophers and, later, of the Neoplatonists and Gnostics. In Christianity it informed the heretical doctrines of the Arians, Manichaeans, Nestorians and Cathars. In Islam it was the mysticism of the Sufis, the wine that existed before the grape and the vine—that is, the timeless wisdom older than any school or tradition.

The Templar were the medieval custodians of this esoteric lore of the ages and, in turn, transmitted it through the Renaissance Hermeticists to the Rosicrucian Enlightenment of Europe—and, still later, into America. The "hermetic tradition" underwent three phases: Grail, Templar and Rosicrucian.

JM

6{}

The world is emblematic... the world of nature a metaphor of the mind.
Ralph Waldo Emerson, *Nature* (1836)

Sonja awoke with a sudden start, conscious of a slow and monotonous banging downstairs. The sound seemed to come from the back of the house, from her kitchen or garden shed. She held her breath, afraid to stir in the dark, and tried to identify the noise.

She could hear Bart breathing heavily, fast asleep, in the room next door. Should she call, or was someone else in the house? If so, would an intruder not have stopped that noise?

She crept down the carpeted stairs, barefoot, empty handed, and without a plan. Several options ran riot through her head:

What if I need to run across the street, in my T-shirt? No, first a kitchen knife!

She checked the hallway, the passage and, forcing herself forward in the dark, pried open the kitchen door. The banging grew louder. She peered in and found a window swinging free in the breeze.

Nothing seemed to be disturbed or out of place, until she saw the folded note lying on her table. She froze, someone *had* been inside! She snatched it up and read the scrawled message:

Whosoever believes in their eternal recurrence will return to
die the same death, until we have silenced you forever.

She'd seen that quotation, or one much like it, and instantly knew the dossier-owner had been pursued too. *Lieve help!* After checking doors and windows, she went up to bed, leaving Bart to his sedated dreams. There wasn't much else she could do at 4 in the morning.

Unable to sleep, she settled down with *The Grail: Quest for the eternal*. The book belonged to a paperback series on the spiritual sciences—from Alchemy to Zen—and was one of many John Matthews had written on the subject. She soon found herself turning pages fervently:

268

The symbol of the Grail has occupied a place in our imagination since awareness of it first dawned in the European Middle Ages; and it continues to exert a fascination upon all who come within its sphere of influence. Yet there is no single, clearly defined image of the Grail, or indeed evidence that it ever existed; opinions differ widely about the origins of the stories that have circulated in written form since the beginning of the twelfth century. Its outward shape is debated—it may be a cup, a shallow dish, a stone or a jewel—yet most agree it is a profound and mysterious thing, perhaps worth giving up one's whole life to find, even in the knowledge that the search may be fruitless.

Sonja stopped to listen, but heard only the rustling leaves outside. So, curling under her crisp damask duvet, she continued to read about the origins and development of the medieval Grail legend: No matter what form the quest took, the hero's goal was always the same—it was a life-transforming experience. *An initiation?*

Although the Grail could be represented by a physical object—such as the onyx vial found at Glastonbury, the emerald cup of Valencia, or the meteorite bowl from Montségur—the quest itself was not for a literal object. *But if not for something real, then what?*

An expression of mankind's unity with the divinity? Or was it, as Dan Brown had suggested, a sacred symbol for the Divine Feminine —manifesting through the bloodline of Mary Magdalene?

Sonja halted, listening to the leaves for a signal. Then read on.

Matthews explained how the legend was set in a Lost Kingdom where the Grail was accessible to only a chosen few. It was said to be kept in a temple, hidden by a dense mountain forest... its guardian being both a priest and a king, at once alive and dead... and the hero's reward being good fortune and, with some luck, the hand of the king's daughter.

Despite her growing anxiety, Sonja felt awed by the coherence between the Grail legend and that of the Presbyter's legend. From what she already knew, such similarities were more than coincidental.

Despite its local character, the Grail saga drew upon myths from around the world. In origin, these stories were neither Christian nor European, but combined attributes from Celtic, Persian, Phoenician and Arabian sources. Although the Grail was entrenched in the Western esoteric tradition as a symbol of Christ's teaching, much of the imagery had been borrowed from Eastern cultures—such as the sun in the cup of the crescent moon, heaven's falling stones, and the solitary rising phoenix. *All symbols of the eternal recurrence?*

Matthews continued. The story generally begins with Joseph of Arimathea, a wealthy Jew, to whose care Christ's body is given for burial. While washing the body, some blood flows from the wounds which he receives in a cup or dish. This vessel belonged to Joseph and was used by Christ at the Last Supper. Then, after Christ's body disappears, Joseph is accused of theft and thrown into prison... Here he is deprived of food until Christ appears in a halo of light and entrusts the cup to his care, instructing him in the Mystery of the Mass and its related secrets. Christ vanishes, appearing later among his disciples.

Miraculously, Joseph is kept alive by a dove that enters his cell and deposits a wafer in the cup, day after day, for almost thirty years—*an initiation in itself?* He is released in 70CE and goes into exile, joined by his sister, her husband Bron, and some followers. They travel west, by sea, to where the Mediterranean civilisation ended.

To Marseille, again?

The first Table of the Grail is constructed to represent the Table of the Last Supper, at which twelve may be seated and a fish laid in Christ's place. According to some, Joseph then sails to Celtic Britain —along the ancient Phoenician trade route—where he sets up the first Christian church at Glastonbury, dedicating it to the Mother of Christ. Here the cup serves for the celebration of the Mass in which all present participate—from priest to worshipper—after which the rite is known as the Mass of the Grail. Unlike the old rites of sacrifice, the new Mass was a life-affirming and inclusive experience. Finally, a temple is built and an Order of Grail Knights established.

The split between Roman Christians and Grail Christians stemmed from a difference of opinion between their means and desired goals: *are Christians saved by grace or by individual karma, are we to seek Heaven or the Grail?* To Sonja's mind, the world was emblematic and represented everything we want it to signify. Dropping the book and dimming the light, she fell asleep and dreamt of far-off shores and foreign lands.

And the isle of the Crimson Bird.

6'1

*Then Jesus spoke other words to Joseph which
I dare not tell you—nor could I, even if I wanted to.*

Robert de Boron, *Joseph d'Arimathie* (c.1210)

From: jmendle@sam.org.za
Sent: Saturday, July 31, 09:10
To: sonja@homenet.nl
Subject: Joseph of Arimathea

I hear from Jason between conference sessions that you are pursuing relics, legends and the Lost Kingdom of the Grail. Such quests can easily lead to bouts of madness, so please take care. The Ancestors have spoken to Laure again:

Joseph of Arimathea

He was the uncle of Mary, Jesus' mother, and an influential Pharisee of the Sanhedrin. He claimed Jesus' bloodied body for entombment and, later, carried the blood-relic to Britain. The Grail is a mythical Christian vessel in which, ultimately, the sacrament of Holy Communion was to be invested. It is an ancient symbol of the Eucharistic Mysteries of Atlantis.

The karmic link between Francisco d'Almeida and Joseph of Arimathea, as well as their ties to Britain, will be of interest to Sonja in due course. About these lives we have more to say.

JM

His deeds were rehearsed by historians, dramatized by poets,
and then passed on as folk legend in numerous oral traditions.
Robert Silverberg, *The Realm of Prester John* (1972)

The Eucharistic Mysteries of Atlantis? How could the Mass of the Grail pre-date Christianity? Or were the origins of the Grail derived from earlier sun mysteries, from the rituals of rebirth and renewal?

Bart's mental condition slowly improved. He began to help around the house and took more interest in the affairs of the world. However, still afraid of strangers, he spent most of his time indoors. So did she, and behind locked doors too, especially after her kitchen break-in.

To get them both outside, Sonja prepared a Sunday brunch in her back garden. While he tidied up afterwards, she delved into another book on the historiography of the Grail—bought this time at Selexyz. By late morning she'd covered the salient points in an email.

From: sonja@homenet.nl
Sent: Sunday, August 1, 12:49
To: jmendle@sam.org.za
Subject: RE: Joseph of Arimathea

Dear Prof Mendle

I checked several references to Joseph of Arimathea and found the following in Richard Barber's historiography of the Grail:

1. An early source is the *Gospel of Nicodemus* (c. late 4thC) which, initially included in the Bible, describes the crucifixion in more detail than the other Gospels. Nicodemus and Joseph appear in the Deposition, the scene wherein the Holy Blood is most often depicted. After Joseph reproaches the orthodox Jews for condemning Jesus to death, he is himself imprisoned. Joseph

vanishes until, much later, he reappears to tell the disciples of Christ's resurrection. Both Barber and Laurence describe the Grail as a mythical object. Thus not real. French illuminations predate the early romance writings and suggest that these were part of an oral tradition before they were recorded—first in north-eastern France, and then all over Europe. The sudden flowering of the tale took a mere fifty years (1190–1240).

2. *The Story of the Grail* or *Parsifal* (1180–90) is the earliest *romanz* on the subject and written by Chrétien de Troyes. The drama unfolds within Parsifal's own lifetime and is set against the background of Arthur's court. While Parsifal breaks his sword beating on the gates of Paradise, the history of the San Graal is not given, nor is Joseph mentioned.

3. Robert de Boron's *History of the Grail* (1200–10) is a trilogy in which Part I is called 'Joseph of Arimathea'. It is an ambitious work and combines the main Grail themes with stories about King Arthur for the first time (earlier poems, if any, are lost). The author—himself a Burgundian knight—associates Joseph with Glastonbury but never states that Joseph went to Britain. Boron borrowed his ideas from the Apocrypha, particularly the *Gospel of Nicodemus*, and also links the Grail with the biblical Gospels for the first time. I think Boron is the first to describe the Grail as a vessel. While subsequent versions of the legend differ in their description of the vessel—from dish to chalice—all agree that the Holy Blood relic was brought west by Joseph of Arimathea. It seems the blood-relic was divided and redispersed as time went by. Joseph is also introduced as a soldier and—in accordance with the New Testament—presented as a *decurio*, a military title which came to mean "councillor" after translation. He is thus an appealing role-model for the knights these romances were intended for.

4. The next romance is the anonymous *Perlesvaus*, known also as *The High Book of the Grail* (c.1210), in which the historical guardianship of the Grail is outlined—from Joseph to Arthur. Arthurian Christianity is portrayed as fierce and elemental, a warrior-religion that was, I guess, meant to subdue and convert pagan Britain. *Perlesvaus* proclaims the new law of Jesus Christ against the Old Law of the Jews and Celts.

5. Next is *The History of the Holy Grail* (1230–40), also a trilogy, in which Joseph's wanderings with the Grail are compared to the wanderings of the Israelites and the Ark. The anonymous author relates the history of Britain—from the birth of Merlin to the death of Arthur. It recalls what you said about Camões's *Lusíads* as an inspired allegory about the Portuguese people. Again, such elaborations were probably designed to substitute Christian symbols in Judaic or Celtic folklore. The Arthurian legend may have been pagan in origin as it contains (retains?) tales of wonder and magic in a lost era.

6. Wolfram von Eschenbach, also a knight, wrote his *Parzival* (1209–15) during the civil wars that tore the Germanic people apart. Comparatively speaking, Wolfram creates an ideal and ordered society around the Grail Castle on the *Munsalvaesche* or *Monsalvat* (Savage Mountain or Mountain of Salvation). In the old Welsh tradition it was known as *Ynys yr Afalon* or *Affallach*. The Celtic Christian monks called it *insula Avallonia*, the isle of Avalon, out of reverence for the springs and lakes that gave access to the Underworld (recalling the marshy *isola Tiberina* of Rome). Joseph's name is added to Glastonbury around 1250. Around this time the Arthurian legend-cycle is first translated into Portuguese—including Boron's story of the Arimathean.

Given your bias for parallel stories, I thought I should point out the similarities between Almeida and Joseph of Arimathea. Both were senior political councillors and risked their careers and reputations; both were custodians of a sacred relic and, through their travels, linked Eastern mysticism to the emerging humanism of the Occident. In fact, Joseph acted as a sort of minister of mines for the Roman government and travelled to Britain. However, as far as I know, Almeida never went there. Perhaps Laurence will hear more…

Fondest, Sonja

PS: I'm sorry to hear that your study was ransacked last week. I had a kitchen break-in here a day later, while Bart and I were asleep upstairs, which left us feeling even more withdrawn and paranoid. I'll call this evening, to tell you more.

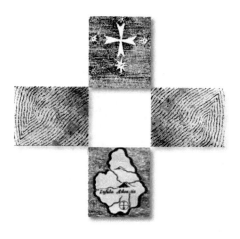

6ᴲ

Is it true that Britain is itself a fragmented survival of
the fabled continent of Atlantis, which sank beneath
the waves of the Atlantic thousands of years ago?
Knud Mariboe, *Encyclopaedia of the Celts* (1994)

Before leaving England, Anton drove Jason down to Cornwall to see the old parish church of St James in Kilkhampton.

'It's an encyclopaedia of Arthurian symbolism and built on the old pilgrim route to Santiago de Compostela,' said Anton, trying to sell the idea, adding that it had been restored by the great architect of the Victorian Gothic Revival, Sir George Gilbert Scott.

'Not much from before Almeida's life remains, except for an ornate doorframe dating to 1130, carved half-a-century before the Arthurian Grail legend itself was recorded.'

Anton insisted on making it a day trip, including a pub-lunch, as he wanted to hear about Sonja's quest for the ever-illusive *Sierra Nevada*. Despite the summer traffic, it proved to be a sensible plan for Jason's last Sunday abroad, since he needed to be distracted from the doping scandal threatening the finale of *Le Tour*.

'Some say Kilkhampton has the most impressive image of Joseph of Arimathea in all Britain. Admittedly, this is part of a restored stained glass window from the late nineteenth century.'

'So why bring me here, if nothing is authentic?'

'That's if you think revivalism lacks authenticity?' laughed Anton, steering his Prius hybrid up to the church. 'Anyway, Joseph holds a flowering staff in one hand and the chalice in his other. Some legends say he buried the cup at the foot of Glastonbury Tor, which is where Celtic and Christian beliefs fused. According to Herodotus, a Greek trader in 6BC first mentioned the "hidden people", the *Keltoi* or Celts. King Arthur was probably a converted Celt, a Hidden One from the forest. They even say he descended from Joseph, giving the legend a bloodline. Here he's romantically depicted as a medieval knight.'

'Then Arthur predates the Age of Chivalry,' blared Jason, bundling out the car with his camera. 'Do you have the century?'

'Perhaps the ninth?'

'Well, what does the evidence suggest—earlier?'

'Probably,' he replied, following Jason into the church.

'Anton, you don't really know, d'you?'

'No, but does it make a difference? More than any other church in England, Kilkhampton seems to attract the most secret of symbols or, at least, symbols have found a home for themselves here. I'm always awed by the concentration of mythological-esoteric symbols that find their way into one single church. These places seem to attract the mysteries of different ages and different sources, like Rosslyn Chapel. By the way, Kilkhampton and Rosslyn were built around the same time, sometime in the mid-fifteenth century. Isn't that awesome?'

'Most people just want to make a living, Anton, simple. That's why they end up going to marketplaces. I bet Kilkhampton was built on an old Roman road until a prosperous family chose to build a church here. With that came more craftsmen, shops and traders.'

Anton could not be flicked off so lightly.

'You're right, fine, but perhaps there is something in the earth itself, some geopathogenic energy that attracts both ancient and modern people to Britain? Perhaps we *are* a fragment of the fabled Atlantis? Plato had heard that the lost realm of Atlantis lay beyond the Pillars of Hercules, somewhere in the Great Outer Sea.'

'Jesus, Anton, this island has made you stark raving mad!'

'I'm a tax lawyer, Boet, so I need to be a bit crazy.'

Crazy? For an archaeologist nothing could be crazier than the idea of an Atlantean "lost city" beneath the Giza plateau of Egypt which (Mendle's clairaudient also claimed) would soon be rediscovered and become the new Jerusalem for a new state of Israel.

64

There is no one 'truth' about the Grail. All we can do is suggest how it may have arisen, and what it may mean, because, I would argue, the force that shaped it is not history, but imagination…

Richard Barber, *The Holy Grail: The History of a Legend* (2004)

A new email popped up on Sonja's screen. She had been searching for traces of Joseph and the Grail in Britain (at Jason's insistence) and stopped in her tracks:

From: jmendle@sam.org.za
Sent: Sunday, August 1, 19:51
To: sonja@homenet.nl
Subject: King Arthur and King Jesus, from El Aurenx

King Arthur and King Jesus
The Arthurian legends are based on historical facts from the Druidic culture of Britain during the fifth-to-sixth centuries. Romance-writers transposed them to a medieval context and included contemporary events from the 12–13thC, after which Thomas Malory compiled an anthology of Arthurian legends (c.1470) that has informed perceptions of the myth ever since.
The character names are neither historical nor fictitious but variant initiatic designations. Sometimes the same character appears under several guises and is given diverse names to emphasize different aspects of an adept's role.
King Arthur's legendary capital, Camelot, the Druidic seat of the Essenes in Britain, and named after Mount Carmel, had been founded long before the time of King Arthur. The Druids

were of the same order as the Essenes and Nazarenes in Israel, the Therapeuts of Egypt and the Chaldees of Mesopotamia. They were connected to the Order of Melchizedek and the Great White Brotherhood, as well as the former Kingdom of Righteousness in India.

Jesus' reincarnation as King Arthur recapitulated the ancient Atlantean Grail saga and invoked the Arabian morning star, *Athtar*. Arthur's death reopened the long-sealed mystery cult of spiritual regeneration—the so-called Way of the Grail.

Jesus and the twelve disciples were reincarnations of Joseph and the twelve patriarchs of the tribes of Israel. Later, they returned as King Arthur and the twelve princes of the Knights of the Round Table. They, too, had many names.

After the crucifixion, Joseph of Arimathea entombed the body and carried the blood-relic to Britain where, in his next life as Bedivere, he would return the blood-sword Excalibur to the lake and bear King Arthur's body to the barge for burial.

Some apocryphal traditions portray Jesus as a heroic religio-political figure—the dynastic heir to the messiahship of King David—who perpetuated the royal bloodline via his marriage to Mary Magdalene, by whom he had a child.

Messiahship in its original Judaic context was a dynastic king-ship rather than a divine incarnation (like an avatar). Jesus was a claimant to this messianic kingship, but it was a claim thrust upon him by the zealot Essenes because of his blood descent.

The Grail mystery was hidden in the blood-cult of dynastic kingship and part of Jesus' mission was to restore the Grail as a symbol of spiritual power by defeating claims of the blood-cult. Jesus sought to fulfil the role of the dynastic messiah and, through his ritual execution, to replace it with the spiritual messiahship of the Christ, the incarnate Logos. His marriage to the Magdalene was part of this dynastic role.

Mary Magdalene had indeed borne the son of Jesus after his crucifixion and resurrection, a son named Jeshua Justus, for his father. Jeshua Justus was the symbolic avenger of his father's murder as the ritual slayer of Set, or Satan. In the Gnostic cult of the Black Madonna, the Magdalene was revered as Isis—the virgin mother of Horus by the slain Osiris.

Mary Magdalene later reincarnated as King Arthur's sister, Morgan le Fay, by whom Arthur is said to have begotten the traitor, Mordred, via an incestuous liaison. But this is not to be taken literally. It signifies the incestuousness of the blood-cult and that Arthur's and Mordred's deaths were a ritual expiation when each slew the other.

Jeshua Justus would ordinarily have inherited the messiahship but, recognising the intention of his father's mission, held the role to have been superseded by a new spiritual dispensation. Jesus Justus's status as the abdicated messiah was thus hailed in the revolutionary mission of Paul; but the orthodox Nazarene tradition endeavoured to preserve itself through the leadership of James Justus, the younger brother of Jesus, and his dynasty. The struggle between these factions continued until 70CE when the Romans destroyed the Temple of Jerusalem. With this the orthodox messianic tradition of the Nazarenes ceased to exist.

Some modern trends of thought have tended to present the dynastic succession of the messiahship as having continued through the descendants of Jesus and the Magdalene, into the royal bloodlines of Christendom. However, they appear not to recognise that Jesus' true mission makes such claims pointless.

Dan Brown muddled the matter by saying their offspring was a daughter, Sarah. Others claim a son called Judah. Laurence says it was Jeshua, which I am inclined to believe. Remember, El Aurenx is the source, Laurence only a messenger.

Regards from us to you both.

JM

PS: Thanks for your call earlier. I'm glad we could talk and hope you feel better, knowing you're not alone. As Laure says, the Ancestors would not continue to speak if the messages put you in any physical danger. I believe you have their protection. One of us should speak to Jason too.

6⁵

To deny the historicity of a legend doesn't deny its value.
What cannot have happened was nonetheless thought.

Frankl Weis, private conversation (22 July 2010)

'Jesus!' exclaimed Jason across Heathrow's bustling departure lounge. Intermittent flight announcements echoed in the background.

'Can't you use another expletive?' Sonja complained, scrolling back to re-read Mendle's email. She was calling from Leiden.

'Jason, just listen and take care! Laurence says the Arthurian legend is based on actual events from the fifth-to-sixth centuries—'

'—that early? Then it is back to the Druids?'

'Apparently. I guess they had an academy—like Plato's Academy— to which many went and from which much influence spread. They worshipped a sun-god after the Egyptians or Chaldeans, I think, but left little of their acts and rites behind. Anyway, place-names show how pervasive they were in Britain, especially in the west country. You probably saw these around Kilkhampton.'

'Yes, but do you trust your necromancer?'

'He's a registered psychiatrist, Jason, a qualified practitioner, not a quack—so give it a break, please. Most of his clients don't even know he's clairaudient, or psychic, and that his spirit name is El Aurenx. Prof M will explain it all at International Arrivals tomorrow.'

Jason's endless scepticism was irritating her.

'Fine, so what else?'

'Well, the Romans arrived in the first century BC, but I don't know what happened five-or-so centuries later. True or not, the message itself is well written. Remember, Jason, no text or document is utterly authorative.'

'But you don't really believe his stuff about Atlantis, do you?'

'Atlantis as a Lost World? Maybe, in fact, I think that is what lies behind the Grail mystery. On a psychic level, the quest for the Grail seems to reflect the search for a Lost World. The symbolism is all too similar: loss and recovery being the lessons of death and eternal life. The Holy Grail in Arthurian mythology and the Lost World in the Masonic legend seem identical in object and design. Medieval poets composed the romances of the Round Table and, while they were about it, made Joseph of Arimathea the head of a military-religious Freemasonry. But, but do I believe Britain is a fragment of a sunken continent? No, not yet—'

'—but you believe the Jesus-Arthur link?'

'What, that they *are* the same soul? Well, Prof Mendle told me that Jesus-Arthur had been Ar-Thur in Atlantis; and then Melchizedek at the time of Abraham. Moreover, the Beloved John, son of Zebedee, returned as Parsifal; whereas John's brother, James, the pilgrim saint, came back as Galahad. Then—and this is where I have to stretch myself—they returned as Percy Bysshe Shelley and Lord Byron! Prof Mendle also said Wolfram von Eschenbach was Richard Wagner and so rewrote his *Parzival* as *Parsifal*. Yes, it seems all too i-in-incredible,' she waited as announcements blared above the noise, 'but as yet, I've found no reason why *not* to believe in reincarnation.'

'But what evidence do we have?'

'Evidence?'

'Y'know, proof, substantive proof?'

'Jason, how do we prove God exists? Or whether Paradise is real? Or if Prester John and the Grail really are—'

'—are the stuff of myths and legends?' he cut her off, checking the flight board as destinations and times rotated in an endless sequence. Having never seen these places for himself, how could he be sure they really existed. *Eish!* But then, he had no reason to doubt them either.

'As Prof M says,' continued Sonja impatiently, 'nothing is mere myth or legend when fact and fiction co-exist.'

'Then there's no objective reality?'

'No, it's all relative, at least to our human mind. Instead, we should be asking what truths can be found in the myths, legends and stories

we tell, or in the historical records handed down to us. More importantly, what truths do they contain for us?'

'But that doesn't make your truths objective?'

'No, Jason Tomas, it doesn't, but the point is that as human beings
we should remain inquisitive, compassionate and consequential in life
—that's what makes us human.'

'I thought you were a pragmatist—that you believed truth had to
be functional, that it needed to perform some common good?'

'Yes, but we could at least enjoy our lives *as if certain truths exist*. In
the end, it depends on what we are able to comprehend, on what we
can internalise. The rest is just chaos; unimaginable chaos...'

✢ ✢ ✢

Jason was one part European, the other African. His grandfather had
been a German missionary and his ouma "Bep" a Malay Kaapenaar.
She'd converted to Catholicism as a child and believed devoutly in
the mercy of God. Ironically, she married a man who later preached
God's wrath. Their son, Jason's father, followed in the same footsteps
and became a Lutheran minister.

Jason had since gone his own way—the Way of a Gemini.

On his mother's side came several uncles who, for as long as Jason
could recall, debated scriptures with his father: "Who was greater,
Abraham or Muhammad?" Except for Uncle Noor, who'd tell them
all adventure stories. Jason was thus half-Lutheran and half-Catholic,
and for good measure, part-Muslim and part-Coloured.

A Muggel and a mongrel?

His thoughts went back to Feirefiz, "parti-coloured like a magpie",
who inherited the attributes of both parents and became the father of
Prester John, the Last Guardian of the Grail. Feirefiz was depicted as
the Prince of Two-Colours which, for a bi-sexual Cape Coloured,
was an important formulation in shaping an identity.

Digression

Digressions are the soul of reading.
Laurence Sterne, *Tristram Shandy* (1759)

Sonja re-read the folios with incredulity. She'd been so focussed that she entirely skipped the section on Alexander the Great. Now, taking in more detail, she saw not only that Aléxandros straddled epochs, but that Almeida had previously been his admiral, Nearchus.

Almeida, a former life?

She googled for biographical back-up.

True, a certain Nearchus of Crete was admiral of Alexander's fleet and had sailed from the Indus back to the Tigris, opening a passage between the Arabian Sea and Persian Gulf... He commanded fifteen hundred ships and, using the monsoon, transported those too weak to march home to Babylon—the former winter capital of Persian kings. He reconnoitred the deltas, estuaries, islets and bays, as well as all the fertile and inhabited land they passed. From the geography taught by Aristotle, Nearchus believed they'd reached the Great Outer Sea.

Nearchus and Almeida, an Admiral and a Viceroy, and twice a commander of the endless Emerald Sea?

Was this more parallelism? She read on.

Nearchus was born on Crete and raised in Macedonia. As an heir of the new aristocracy, he was schooled alongside Alexander, son of Philip II... As Crown Prince, Alexander acted on Nearchus's advice by intervening in the proposed marriage between his epileptic half-brother and the daughter of a neighbouring Satrap. Nearchus went to Halicarnassus, then still a Persian port, to offer Alexander's hand (something he'd do again, in a later life, for Afonso V). Unnerved by

Alexander's rivalry against his brother, the Satrap withdrew his offer of an alliance. Enraged, Philip had the conspirators banished, including Nearchus (as would happen again to Almeida and the Duke of Bragança). However, they were all recalled when Alexander took the throne that same year, 336BCE. Nearchus was then twenty-four, Alexander only twenty. Was she seeing parallel stories everywhere, like the ever-familiar face of a lost lover?

Nearchus was one of Alexander's Companions and commanded the ports seized along the south-western coast of Asia Minor. From their initial foothold in the Achaemenid Empire, Alexander planned to move his army south, via Phoenicia, and then down into Egypt. The vast Persian navy, however, threatened to cut the Macedonian supply lines across the Aegean straits.

Since warships required constant repairs and supplies, command at sea ensured control of strategic ports and shipping lanes. While oared galleys were swift and manoeuvrable (due to their narrow tapering hulls), they were not seaworthy in poor conditions. With Nearchus patrolling the coast, Persian ships were driven out to sea. Moreover, their galleys were manned by Greek mercenaries and could not sail far without replenishing rations: fresh water was required every five days, food every ten.

Having secured his grain supply via the Hellespont, Alexander set off to conquer the eastern and southern limits of the inhabited world. For the next seven years, 330–323BCE, he was driven to reclaim his inheritance (and, some say, to flee his snake-worshiping mother).

Once back in Babylon, he planned another grand-scale campaign: the circumnavigation of the world via the Great Outer Sea. It would be a grand military, mercantile and scientific expedition.

Alexander was intrigued by the information Nearchus had gathered and instructed his Phoenician shipwrights (captured after the fall of Tyre) to build him new ships. Tree cutters, sawyers and carpenters were set to work—so that the first fleet could sail north, the other to the western limits of the world. The plan was two-fold: north to find where the Caspian ended and west, along the Arabian coast, to see if he could enter the Red Sea—the Sea of the Crimson Bird.

If so, he'd conquer Arabia Felix with its frankincense, myrrh, cassia and cinnamon, thus allowing mariners to sail on to Egypt—which he already controlled. Here, unmolested, his soldiers would dig a canal linking the Red Sea with the Nile—as Pharaoh Necho and Darius the Great had tried—and so open up the Mediterranean.

From Egypt he would conquer Europe and Africa—colonising the Scythians, Greeks, Etruscans, Romans, Libyans, Carthaginians and, of course, those hirsute Celts. As the Great Outer Sea bound all the world's land, so his empire would unite all its people.

The world would become a commonwealth of nations.

This continuous, ever-circulating body of water, known by modern oceanographers as the World Ocean, was a crucial factor in controlling climatic change. Reducing the effects of global warming was not only an economic and environmental imperative, she understood, but also an important step in uniting the nations of the world today.

It was something Alexander would have liked. She scrolled down.

To this end, Alexander had the marshes around Babylon dredged. The new harbour was designed to supply and maintain one thousand ships. His days were filled with site inspections and the affairs of state; his nights with his Companions discussing unknown islands and far-off lands. He followed the course of the Euphrates to improve canals and locks needed for passing ships—and even had Nearchus cut a creek near the mouth. Alexander also founded a coastal city and populated it with Greek mercenaries and retirees. From this point on and to the end, Alexander ignored predictions that his success would end in Babylon. Two incidents stood out in Sonja's mind:

First, on his return from India, an envoy of Chaldean Magi came out to meet him on the Silk Road. They prophesied his demise if he should enter Babylon by its eastern gate. Wikipedia, she noted, said it was Nearchus himself who delivered the message. Alexander altered their approach but found the swamps so impassable that, despite his own better judgement, he marched his exhausted entourage through the ill-omened entrance. Like Almeida, he observed such injunctions and premonitions to the very end.

Secondly, weakened by fever, Alexander lost his ability to speak— so a deathbed speech was improbable. Similarly, Almeida could not have given that heroic oration before his collapse—at least not with a spear stuck through his throat.

The author of the folios claimed that Almeida was conscious of his own karmic link to Nearchus and compared his *tempo longo* (long term strategy) with that of Alexander's intention to Hellenise Arabia. And, furthermore, Alexander's grand scheme of following the Great Outer Sea, east to west, would ultimately have taken him around the Cape.

But fate took another turn. Alexander died as Nearchus came to tell him that his ships lay waiting at the Tigris-Euphrates estuary. And so the campaign was never launched. As for Nearchus, it seems he died at Gaza around 312BCE, a decade after Alexander. Thus Nearchus and Almeida were killed at opposite ends of the continent: the former in the extreme north-east, the latter in the far-off south-west.

Two thousand years later, the cryptic folios concluded, Almeida navigated the same route but in the opposite direction, from west to east, as if consciously fulfilling Alexander's dying dream.

In his correspondence with king Manuel, Almeida not only justifies having secured frontier posts, but also compares himself to Nearchus of Crete, adding:

> In the days of Alexander the country's interior had to be occu-
> pied. We, however, must be content with fortifying certain
> points along the coast and so secure the ocean path to India.
> To succeed, we must wrest trade from the hands of the Arabs
> and take their place.

Aristotle's treatise gave access to the secret processes of nature and its creation, as understood in ancient Greece. This knowledge had been handed down to Plato who, in turn, passed it on to Aristotle. It was then taken by Alexander across South-Central Asia and, eventually, made its way back through Arabia and North Africa, before entering the European environment via the Iberian peninsula. And so the Platonic and Aristotelian streams were reunited in the Occident.

Significantly, Alexander not only used his soldiers and scientists to collect information, but also endowed his first library to Aristotle. He sought, as Pericles had done a century before, to combine power and enlightenment and thus unite people beyond the individual city-state. Alexander was a Neoplatonic philosopher-king with an Aristotelian desire to know the world: to understand it as much as to control it. Alexander was a true Seeker of the World.

According to Volodya, Alexander died before he could fulfil this great dream. He not only wished to reach the end-of-the-world, and thus unite East and West, but also wanted to visit Arabia Felix and to sacrifice at its altars. As the Phoenix once preceded the Grail, she understood, so too the lamb would precede Christ. But the Arabians were never Hellenized—unlike the Persians, Syrians and Ethiopians —and therefore never assimilated by Western civilisation.

Islam, like Christianity, regrettably, erased most traces of the pagan mysteries. Sonja surmised that they were linked to Aristotle's idea of creation emanating from a divine source or—as Mendle seemed to be telling her—to that continuous process of life, death and rebirth.

According to the folios, Almeida knew about the mysteries of the Hierarchies, about man's relationship to an ineffable Divinity, about the secrets of the Grail and of the world's own spiritual regeneration. The folios reasoned that Almeida's campaign against the Muslims was to combat their denial of the celestial hierarchies. In short, Islam erased the wisdom of Arabia, while Almeida strove to keep it intact.

She now knew that the religio-cultural exchange between East and West was, like that between South and North, the Principal Design behind the aspirations of Prince Henry, Dias and Almeida.

Perhaps the concealment of Aristotle's treatise was done to further this cause? Almeida was a commander-in-arms who expanded a neo-Hellenic empire eastward, as Nearchus had done, and so prepared cosmopolitan societies for the advent of universal values.

However, it remained an abstract concept. Sonja would have to return to Africa's most revered Cape, to the southernmost threshold between the Orient and the Occident, to discover that for herself.

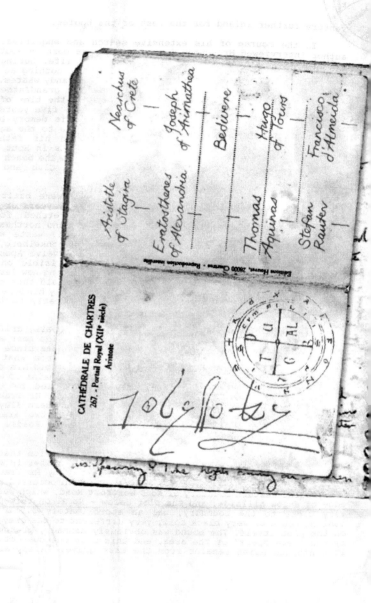

Nearchus of Crete — Joseph of Arimathea — Beduine — Hugo of Tours — Francisco d'Almeida

Aristotle of Stagira — Eratosthenes of Alexandria — Thomas Aquinas — Stefan Rauter

CATHÉDRALE DE CHARTRES
267. - Portail Royal (XIIe siècle)
Aristote

Éditions Houvet, 28000 Chartres - Reproduction interdite

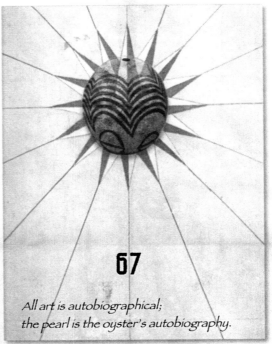

67

All art is autobiographical;
the pearl is the oyster's autobiography.

Federico Fellini, interview, *The Atlantic* (December 1965)

Volodya stood by her door with a bunch of red roses, unannounced, having driven up from Bruges to see a local antiquarian. He claimed to have an hour-or-two to spare and so, to avoid inviting him in, she suggested lunch at the Hortus. They now strolled along Leiden's most beautiful canal, Sonja leading the way to the botanical gardens.

She explained how the Rapenburg first served as a defensive moat, flowing east-to-west through town, following the historical course of the Rhine. While the Oude Rijn marked the once far-flung northern frontier of the Roman Empire, Leiden itself began as a marshy outpost which Renaissance city fathers had renamed *Lugdunum Batavorum*, hoping to reinvent a Roman pedigree. Others say *Leiden* came from the Celtic god Ludun or, like *London*, also meant New Troy. But more likely, the name simply came from an old word for "watercourse".

Today the oily canal glistened like a trough of pearls. The water was sage-green, the sky a promising blue, and Bart had chosen to go out boating. An encouraging turn for one who still felt so estranged.

Crossing the bridge, she stopped to sidestep two students chatting on their bicycles. Volodya failed to hear their bells and scuffed his Gucci's on the curb. Taking him by the sleeve, she added:

'Along this canal, in a shop adjacent to the Academie, Pieter van der Aa sold copies of the only known illustration of Almeida's death —though I don't know the name of his engraver.'

'No doubt Van der Aa reused the plates to print loose illustrations. He was a roguish collector, like me, and enjoyed buying and selling what others found valuable.'

'So what do *you* find valuable, Volodya?'

He slipped his arm through hers as they crossed the street.

'I have another print by him, the *Palais des Rois Mores de Granada*, which I bought on auction for forty dollars. It's no masterpiece, nor especially rare, but it is something I value.'

Why? Sonja was surprised, and said as much.

'Why? Because his print reminds me that some things in life are precious. Depicted in the distance are the peaks of the Sierra Nevada, and the *Sierra Nevada* is the one manuscript I most desire.'

They arrived at the Academiegebouw port and passed through the secluded stone-paved courtyard. Once used by nuns, it now belonged to Holland's oldest university, founded in 1575 in defiance of Spanish rule. Its adjoining Hortus botanicus was one of the earliest botanical-medicinal gardens of Europe. It was here that the first tulips were cultivated, imported from Persia, and where the Cape proteas were first recorded. Here the Swede Carl Linnaeus reorganized the garden according to his new classification system. Regrettably, he declined an offer to spend two years at the Cape, all expenses paid, collecting plants for the university. He felt the VOC was insufficiently interested in botany. And he would not have withstood the heat.

The Hortus was now a secret garden within a bustling city. Here botanical science and aesthetic pleasure mixed with the fragrance of summer flowers. Volodya and Sonja wandered amid colourful beds and shaded paths, with no particular destination in mind.

'Is it true that Alexander had no idea where he was going?'

'Da, Gordium lay on the busy East-West trade route across Persia which, according to Herodotus, was known as the Royal Highway. When Alexander marched east the Achaemenid Empire stretched from the Black and Caspian seas to the Egyptian and Libyan deserts; and from the Mediterranean to the Indus. It was the largest empire of classical Antiquity and, yes, he probably had no idea what lay beyond the empire's south-eastern borders. '

Sonja tugged his sleeve, interjecting:

'And from the empire's centre, near today's border between Russia and China, came the first tulips. They originated in the mountains above Islamabad, conquered by Alexander and Tamerlane, until the Dutch found an alternative route via the high seas.'

'Da, Gordium was a strategic citadel. It served the Macedonians as a temperate highland camp during the bitter winter of 334BCE. Here Alexander cut the Gordian Knot to fulfil the oracle that "who ever loosens the knot will rule all Asia". Known to sailors as a Turk's Head, this type of knot was intricately woven from strips of cornel bark and had no visible loose ends—like a turban. Since then the Gordian Knot has symbolised a stubborn problem solved by a stroke of ingenuity—or, more literally, by swift force.'

'Y'know *tulip* comes from "tuliban" and means turban?'

'*Merci*, Mademoiselle,' he said politely, not wanting to be waylaid. 'The knot demonstrated the inherent unity of Europe's crusading Christians, whether they belonged to the same Catholic obedience or not, including the pro-papal Teutonic Order. On a far deeper level, of course, the knot unites the esotericism of Greeks, Jews, Muslims and Christians—for whom the common fountainhead was Aristotle. We're indebted to Alexander for this exchange.'

Why am I not surprised? She sprang in:

'Aristotle was born a half-century before Alexander's campaign— or more precisely, fifty years before the Gordian Knot was cut—and his biographical facts are sparse and uncertain. What we know fills little more than one paragraph in an encyclopaedia. Most of it is based on facts recorded a century later, after he became famous, and tends to be speculative and full of repetition.'

Volodya reached for her hand. She began summarising briskly:

'In short, we know next to n-no-nothing about his life—'

'—what we *do* know,' he said, letting go, 'is that Aristotle was born in the summer of 384 and had at least one sibling—an older sister, Arimneste. Aristotle probably grew up in Stagira, a Greek colony, which his mother's ancestors co-founded. She was of elite lineage, from the isle of Euboea—'

'—to which Aristotle returned at the end of his life?'

'*Da da!*'

Leaping ahead again, Sonja resumed:

'His father worked at the harbour-capital of Pella which—like the name *Pierre* or *Pieter* suggests—literally means "stone". Today the inlet has silted up to form a wetland around the site. Dutch archaeologists are involved in excavating the tombs of Alexander's heirs and, as I'm sure you know, Leiden has a fine collection of classical antiquities too. Anyway, sorry Volodya, what else?'

'Aristotle learnt anatomy and dissection from his ageing father, a personal physician who served the Macedonian warlords. From his mother's side, Aristotle was considered part of Thrace's aristocracy. Though orphaned, his father's profession and mother's status gave him access to the court of Alexander's grandparents. But Aristotle was not impressed by courtly life and so, by the age of seventeen, his guardian Proxenus, the husband of his sister, sent him to study with older men at Plato's Academy.'

'In the public gardens near Athens?'

'Da, in a sacred olive grove watered by the Cephisus. Athens was the intellectual centre of Greece and, unlike Rome, not bound by city walls. Aristotle stayed for twenty years, studying logic and teaching rhetoric. Raphael's *School of Athens* represents men like Plato, Aristotle, Ptolemy, Zoroaster and Averroës, including an Alexander-like figure. The philosophers are there for influencing the school; Alexander for spreading its ideas.'

Sonja beckoned toward a bench, allowing Volodya to continue:

'After Plato died, Aristotle was not appointed head of the Academy, contrary to expectation. No doubt the council's decision was linked to his rivalry with fellow orators and rhetoricians—'

'—or because his ideas departed too much from Plato's?'

'Perhaps. But once he left Athens, Aristotle could not go home as Thrace had been annexed by Alexander's father the year before. Aristotle was then in his late thirties; Alexander not yet a teenager. Aristotle's home town had been destroyed and for this, two decades later, Alexander rebuilt Stagira to honour his mentor—'

'—wait, so where did Aristotle go?'

'Asia Minor. To his friend Hermeas, a Greek soldier-of-fortune and ruler of a coastal city then subjugated by a Persian overlord. Hermeas invited Aristotle to attend his court and act as advisor. Here Aristotle met Pythias, Hermeas's adopted daughter, whom he later married.'

'Out of love or loyalty?'

'Aristotle was thirty-seven, Pythias around eighteen. She bore him a daughter which he named for her. Although Pythias died early, their relationship must have been tender as she wished to have their bones interred together—a request Aristotle would remember in his will.'

'So it was for love *and* loyalty?'

'Yes, both, why not? Then three years on, after Hermeas was killed, Aristotle returned to Pella and at the behest of Philip II, was assigned a temple near Mieza, today Náousa. Here he was to teach the young Alexander, then about thirteen, and the sons of the new aristocracy—including Nearchus. The school was founded on a site sacred to the water-spirits, a connection sustained in Almeida's life. Then, in 334, Philip subdued the Greeks and Aristotle returned to Athens and founded his own school, at a place called the Lyceum. It was the first university—a model for Europe's modern universities—and the place where Aristotle devoted himself to teaching and writing for the next thirteen years. Today only thirty of his treatises survive, most as mere lecture notes.'

'Thirty-one, if you include the *Sierra Nevada*.'

'*Khorosho.* And after Alexander's sudden death in 323BCE, Athens rebelled against their Macedonian rulers and charged Aristotle for impiety. He fled, fearing the same fate as Socrates, and returned to Euboea where he died, soon after, aged sixty-three, complaining of stomach cramps. *Da*, he was probably poisoned too…'

More murders, more bones? She leant forward, lost in thought, as he explained how Plato saw reality as a set of ideas, knowable through reflection; whereas Aristotle believed reality existed in experience.

She was too distracted to take in more.

'Let's go for lunch, where you can continue over a pint of beer.'

Volodya nodded, glancing at his bulky Breitling. He still had an hour before his appointment with the collector. She led the way, again, past the weathered bust of Carl Linnaeus to the glass-covered Winter Garden. The erect, transparent greenhouse was a masterpiece of structural engineering (equivalent to the Louvre's glass pyramid) and contained plants from warmer climates; including several potted specimens originally from the Cape.

Set above the ticket office and gift shop, the café offered a splendid overview of the gardens and canal. It was exactly time for lunch.

Volodya ate his hodgepodge with relish while she explained how Leiden's *hutspot*—a stew of potatoes, onions and carrots, served with slow-cooked beef—was not a true Dutch recipe. The Spanish army had left behind a cauldron of stew when they abandoned the starving city in 1574. Like the tulip, it was an import. At best, the Dutch were a nation of traders—not culinaires or botanists.

'It was probably horse stew,' he said with a curled lip. 'Alexander's starving men ate horse meat and drank horse blood during their trek across the dessert. Only some made it back to Babylon.'

'Not the ingredients for a traditional dish.'

'*Nyet*, nor food for the king who would be God. According to the Sîwa Oracle, Alexander was the son of the god Ammon. After death, his body was transferred to Egypt, reportedly Alexandria, where he received divine honours. Like the ancient pharaohs, he was regarded as an incarnation of their greatest god.'

'I thought Alexander's tomb has been "rediscovered" at Sîwa?'

'The evidence is convincing, but the claim itself still unconfirmed. Symbolically, Alexander's tomb was long thought to be in the Latin Quarter of Alexandria; although his alleged gold sarcophagus was destroyed and his alabaster one stolen. Despite this, the last imperial visit was by the psychotic Berber-Arab Roman emperor, Caracalla, in the third century. What a confused soul, Caracalla believed himself to be the reincarnation of Alexander. Rome has had many misguided and egoistical rulers. Like today's Berlusconi.'

Sonja couldn't conceal her incredulity:

'Medieval romance-writers took Alexander to be one of Arthur's celebrated ancestors and, similarly, made Caracalla an early king of pagan Britain. Like the city fathers of Leiden, Anglo-Saxon historians tried to re-invent a Roman ancestry, but without the reincarnation.'

It started to rain lightly, a passing shower. The glass roof turned a tint darker. Setting aside his knife and fork, Volodya lent forward:

'*Incroyable?* Yes, in 1991, a controversial book on Alexander and his subsequent incarnations appeared in Denmark. It dropped out of nowhere, like a stone. The author, Margrethe Clara Grace, says it was channelled via Aron—Alexander's name in the spiritual world—and claims that his last life was none other than that of Elvis Presley! The book may be ahead of its time as only a few copies have been sold and, so far as I know, it still hasn't been translated.'

Sonja hailed the waiter before responding:

'So Raphael's *School of Athens* should include the King of Rock?'

'*Da*, it's incredible, I know, but you don't have to believe it—even though Alexander and Elvis both suffered from poor health and died prematurely. However, despite Clara's sincerity, I heard Alexander's last turn was not as the King of Rock but as Thomas Jefferson, the founding father of America.'

'Sorry, Volodya, but this really is incredible, even for a King that would be President! Where d'you get this sort of information?'

'The same as you: libraries, archives, private letters, biographies—and whatever karmic records I can find. But there will always be different accounts of peoples' lives, that's inevitable, until we learn to agree on their deaths. Take Almeida for example, or Alexander. And then, like you, I come across sources that are unreliable too—'

'—so Aristotle's most famous and notorious student was the young Alexander, who later became one of America's greatest statesmen?'

'*Da*, that's what I believe. It's also believed that Aristotle came back as Stefan Rauter (under the aegis of Basil Valentine) and then, more recently, as Rudolf Steiner himself.'

Aristotle and Steiner, both philosophers, first as a philosopher of physical science, then a philosopher of spiritual science. And twice as a literary critic?

'*Tsjonge*, with respect Volodya, but I find that beyond belief.'

'Then, believe what's true for you, Mlle Sonja.'

After lunch, taking her arm, he led her out to the street.

They parted in front of the Academiegebouw where, looking back across the canal, she saw him hail a car with a uniformed chauffeur. He climbed onto the back seat, unaware that she'd stopped to watch, and drove off toward Kaiserstraat. Sonja recognised his tinted Lexus and suspected, now somewhat aghast, that the driver was none other than the Black Goliath.

Lieve help, was she succumbing to her own paranoia, or did Volodya know this ogre? She hurried back to meet Bart and went home. Even with her doors locked, she no longer felt safe.

Damn him if it was a setup!

68

'A twenty-four year old Chinese man recently offered to sell his soul on the internet and attracted 59 bids. However, the value of his lot was semiotically ambiguous.'

Like Inspector Morse, Mendle was a master at trivial pursuit and the cryptic crossword: 'As for who reached the Cape first, I'd say it was *not* the Chinese—'

'—if not the Chinese, then who, the Phoenicians?' jested Jason.

'Ha, no, the Atlanteans!'

'Jesus, not you too?'

'Say, hold still with that lamp…'

Jason shifted hands, bright light flooding the sand-packed bones. Mendle wiped his bushy brows, his forehead wet with perspiration.

'Miraculous? See what's stuck inside here!'

He peered down, his hands shaking as he re-examined the skull. Wedged behind the jawbone was a bundle of dry leather—colourless, compact, wire-bound and brittle—inserted intentionally, indeed, like the stone in the mouth of a murdered Sicilian. He prized it free, leaving it intact for later examination. The grubby pigskin needed to be treated separately.

That would have to wait.

'So who came to East Africa first? Well, one of the earliest recorded explorers was a man called Harkhuf, an Egyptian caravan leader who travelled the Elephant Road south to Nubia and, some say, reached the land of Kush, today the Sudan.'

The Professor picked at the bone with a scalpel while his Doppelgänger kept the lamp steady. Jason found listening much easier when both his hands were busy. Despite his tan, he was ghostly pale.

'It's usually assumed that the earliest expeditions were made merely to enrich rulers and their dominions. Those we know about were launched from the Mediterranean, around 1500BCE, such as the voyage of the Argo. I say,' pondered Mendle under the glaring lamp, 'Homer's *Odyssey* may be the counterpart for Camões's *Lusíads*?'

Jason didn't dare blink.

'Good, hold it there. You know Perseus, the Greek dragonslayer, went on an expedition to Africa before saving Andromeda? She was a princess of mixed Phoenician-Ethiopian descent. And then there was that Roman governor—whose name I can't recall now—who sent a legion south to find the source of the Nile.'

He paused to wipe his brow again. Their lab felt like a tomb.

'Queen Hatshepsut, the only female pharaoh of Egyptian descent, sent an expedition to the land of Punt, in Somaliland, to find incense and gold. It was probably the first long-distance trade route in Africa. Punt was known as the Cape of Incense and served—like the Cape of Good Hope—as an *entrepôt* for Africa's vast inland riches.'

'Prof, hold on, I must change my grip again.'

'Yes-well-then-fine,' he paused for a moment. 'And then there was Pharaoh Necho who sent the Phoenician-Carthaginians beyond the Red Sea to see how far the land lay to the south, circumnavigating the entire continent in three years. I think it was around 600BCE or so. Herodotus never believed the sailors as they reported seeing the sun on the wrong side of their boats, that is, to the north of them, sailing east-to-west around the Cape. It's a fact we easily understand today, but was then seen as an evil omen.'

'A fact that eventually proved the world was round?'

Mendle beamed: 'It was an unimaginable experience; a moment of profound geo-physical truth—'

'—truth through experience and imagination?'

'Ah, exactly. The Phoenicians also sailed west around the bulge of Africa, reaching Cape Non and the Canaries, where they established a colony—a place sailors called the "impassable limit".'

He glanced up to see if his alter ego was listening. Jason waited, adjusting the light's arc.

'Hold it, there... now where was I? Ah, the perennial Phoenicians. Some even believe they made it to America.'

'The Phoenicians, the Chinese and the Irish? Why are all the epic expeditions always to-and-from America—St Brendan, Leif Eriksson, Columbus, Lindbergh, the Titanic and QE2, even Virgin Atlantic?'

'To find Paradise? For fame and fortune? Or just because countries around the Atlantic have controlled the transit of goods for the last five hundred years. Given that ninety percent of all world trade is still seaborne and supplies most of our energy needs, it doesn't take a rocket scientist to predict a new maritime era in the Indian Ocean. Look at Japan, China, India, and their surrounding states—including Arabia, Africa and Australia—they're all economically dependent on the free flow of goods across the sea. Safeguarding this flow through the Indonesian archipelago and the straits of Malacca or Ormuz will, no doubt, be a problem for our coming century—'

'—as we've already seen with pirates off Somalia?'

'Exactly. Whoever controls these traffic lanes and, indeed, access to the Pacific and Atlantic, will determine the world's future economy. I'd say China is the biggest threat today. The US fleets that protected the flow of trade for the past fifty years, making globalisation possible, can no longer fulfil this task alone. And as for Western Europe, ah, its position is once again peripheral.'

'Well, I wouldn't visit America, even if I was lost.'

The fluorescent light swung to-and-fro, flooding the floor as Jason readjusted his grip. He felt faint with fatigue.

'Please, hang the lamp,' said Mendle patiently. 'I'll soon need both your hands.'

Gingerly, Jason hung the tube on its stand.

'Anyway, the earliest southern explorers were probably Arabian seafarers, thrown off the East African trade route.'

Mendle peered behind the dry skull, checking for fractures.

Passing the tiny tweezers, Jason asked: 'What period, Prof?'

'From the tenth or ninth century BCE, when the Queen of Sheba sent her ships down Africa's East coast. Or when Arabian merchants sailed further south, adding to the evolution of the Swahili language. You should know, Jason, they traded silk, cotton, beads and china.

In return for ivory, rhino-horn and tortoise-shell, plus all your gold and slaves, of course.'

'Whatever. Muslims didn't introduce slavery to Africa, Prof, they just institutionalised it.'

Mendle looked askance at his colleague, then pursued his point:

'By the eighth century, says Soraya, Muslim-Hindu traders settled at Chibuene in south-central Mozambique. On occasion they came as far south as the ivory-rich Wild Coast, but then only when blown off course—'

'—or aided by the swift Agulhas current.'

'Ah, so early castaways could also have been Indian or Chinese, as they too traded with East Africa. Why, Jason, you found that opaque bowl at a Quena burial-site yourself!'

Jason was not to be provoked:

'Fra Mauro confirms their presence,' he added flatly, recalling the Chinese map in Cape Town's Library of Parliament.

'I thought the evidence was in dispute?'

Jason shrugged: 'It still doesn't disprove their presence.'

'Aha, a Double Truth, now you're talking like a true Gemini!'

They both grinned.

'I was hoping the first traveller was an Aristotelian scholar from Alexandria,' taunted Jason, florescent light exaggerating the cavities of the skull, 'but then thinkers don't travel as far as traders, do they?'

'Apparently not, unless by accident. But these travellers did change the maritime knowledge of the Indies.'

'According to Uncle Noor it was the master-geographer, al-Biruni, who first proposed that the Indian and Atlantic met below Africa. Arab navigators called the Indian Ocean the *Kumārī Duāb*.'

'Ah, great al-Biruni, the Father of Anthropology! Before Alexander, Darius the Great wanted to send a Persian fleet around Africa; but monsoon winds petered out below Mozambique, making it difficult to sail further south—'

'—I thought the problem was the square-rig,' cut in Jason, 'with a lateen-sail you can tack against the wind and return home, without waiting for a change of season.'

'Exactly, but our southern coast was too rough for junks or dhows. They weren't built for the open sea, but for off-shore reconnaissance and trade. Circumnavigation was then only a technical possibility.'

'Sure, but what if you couldn't see land?'

Mendle smiled.

'Ah, without the chronometer you were lost.' Mendle was amused to know that younger men could lose their way too. 'How strange to think it was only invented in 1750, and that for several millennia sailors had to use the stars to calculate their position at sea.'

But Jason wasn't listening. He'd been thinking about Faria e Sousa:

'An equestrian statue found in the Azores could prove the Chinese first discovered the archipelago—before the Portuguese.'

'True, the Catalan Atlas does show that they knew of it in the late fourteenth century, before Henry's navigators discovered the islands. But then Plato had heard about the remnants of Atlantis from the Egyptians, and someone may have identified it as the Azores? As for that Chinese statue, well, Jason, it's missing now. It's rather like the one they found in the mid-Sixties, or there-abouts, while building a railway bridge to the iron mines of Swaziland. Alas, both artefacts prove no more than a continuing trade network with China.'

'But didn't Admiral Zheng He command seven expeditions across the ocean in the 1420s?'

'Yes, introducing gunpowder and porcelain to India, Arabia and East Africa,' nodded Mendle, reaching for his Glenfiddich. 'I see you've been chatting to Gavin Menzies and Graham Hancock?'

'Yes, via Facebook. Menzies says the great junks were bigger than any Portuguese ship, the largest being 600 feet long.'

'The length of Solomon's Temple,' calculated Mendle. 'Say, if they were so big, why haven't we found any wrecks?'

'Because political intrigue in Peking stopped further expeditions? Had they continued, Zheng He's voyages of discovery may well have established a Chinese sea route into the Atlantic.'

So then, did they reach the Cape?

'One old Chinese astronomer of the mid-1400s said his ship drove passed the Cape. As you say, they probably rounded it by accident, Prof, and not by design.'

Mendle stopped and smiled broadly:

'So old men make mistakes too?'

'Yes, and by default, they also make history.'

'Ah, then I would've sold my soul to have been on that ship!'

69

That night, returning from the Concertgebouw, Sonja listened to her voicemails. The last message came like a bolt from the blue.

Volodya was dead. His body had been found by his housekeeper, a retired Ukrainian woman, and authorities said he'd been killed in a bizarre kitchen scuffle, following a break-in at his weekend datcha.

No arrests had been made. Nor were any suspects questioned. Not yet, at least. Since nothing had been stolen (except for the clothes he had been wearing), local police were assuming the killer was a passing vagrant. A funeral service would be held on the following Sunday.

It was now Monday night.

She stumbled into the moonless garden where all was still, except for the flickering television seen through her neighbour's hedge.

Who was this Volodya?

He came from a distinguished line of naval officers, some of whom had served in the Tsar's Navy, others in the Black Sea Fleet. His father was born in post-revolutionary Russia and, as a young sea cadet, had joined the naval command at Sevastopol. Volodya himself was no sailor or mariner, that much was clear, but he had understood Portugal's expansion and obsession with Africa.

If murdered—then why?

She came in to fetch her laptop, treading hypnotically up the stairs. Still numb, she booked a weekend flight to Moscow, without thinking of practicalities such as check-in times, taxi hire or hotel reservations. She would attend the funeral service—perhaps someone there could explain what happened?

Why had Volodya taken an interest in her? He'd seemed genuinely concerned during their last conversation, saying: 'It will not surprise me if you spend several years working and reworking this story, because there are always more and more insights to this enigmatic chapter in Europe's history—to which the Cape of Good Hope is connected through the death of Francisco d'Almeida, and the people of the South to events in the North.'

He'd made her aware of a personal connection, too, as if her own history was somehow bound to all this. Like a rumour, he added, history always had a way of repeating itself.

Well, history did repeat itself, at times regrettably, she thought, as if it had no designated course to follow. To her mind, Jared Diamond had shown that historical progress was circumstantial—the raw result of environmental and biological resources—rather than one of faith, fate or face colour. But what of historical direction, what or who gave that momentum?

By now she'd lost interest in masculine histories of the world where only the bold, the brave and the brutal made things happen. It began with a waning interest in the VOC; around the time Mendle passed on the first messages and new feelings began influencing her overview of history. Ever since, her imagination had been captured by small acts of greatness, like those of Odilia and Richardis, and by individuals playing discrete and often undetected roles in shaping a school, a society, a nation or, say, the entire outcome of a war.

That was not to say she believed in histories where women played an equal or central role, as had Isis-Sophia or Mary Magdalene. No, in her opinion, Dan Brown had over-emphasised the transmission of cosmic knowledge via a sacred bloodline and secret society.

Nevertheless, it was clear that mysticism was transmitted via many hands: from Hermes to Maria Hebracia, from Aristotle to Averroës, from Aquinas to Valentine, from one country to another and from one century to the next until, finally, it passed from Volodya to her.

Oh my God, I am living Sophie Neveu's story! No, not me, mine is more than circumstantial? She felt real empathy and, strangely, had never been so emotionally involved in a historical event before.

In that case, who else was involved, who else felt this way about Almeida's murder and, if there were any, would she recognise them? More importantly, would they be at the funeral on Sunday?

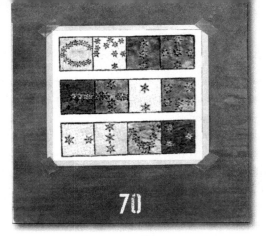

*True, I'm still young,
but nonetheless this something here has flung
the memory of a thousand lives upon me.*

Rainer Maria Rilke, *On the Prodigal Son* (1909)

Bart slept all day. An invisible hush smothered the house and for the first time Sonja felt alone—and disorientated. By midday she'd called Mendle to discuss Volodya's murder. She wasn't sure if she needed emotional support or rational advice. She certainly needed to hear his voice of reason again. Mendle was the one person with whom she could safely discuss the issue of karma.

Nodding, he explained that karma was an esoteric term for the law of higher causality wherein each individual was responsible for itself, for its course, and for its own fate in life. The law of karma was two-fold: cause and effect, confirmation and correction:

'As with the laws of physics,' he added, 'every action produces an equivalent reaction or consequence. And here every individual reaps the consequence of what he or she sows—as reward or penalty. Life is a learning experience, where right confirms and wrong corrects. Karma thus requires reincarnation to provide the opportunities for its operations beyond one lifetime.'

She was pleased to hear Mendle speak—his steady voice had a sobering effect on her. He spoke softly, explaining how the concept of past lives had been either trivialized or sensationalized in the West. Furthermore, while orthodox Jews and Christians saw reincarnation as heretical, fundamentalists condemned it as blasphemous and evil.

'Reincarnation,' she heard him say, 'should not be some obscure subject of horror films or music videos, but the focus of serious scientific research. Alexander's karmic profile, for example, is not that of a self-indulgent rock-and-roll star; but of a political thinker and revolutionary leader. He belongs to a singular group whose task has always been that of cosmopolitan leadership.'

'Then you also know about Thomas Jefferson?'

He nodded, again, stroking his beard all the way down to his chest: 'Yes, via Laurence, who recently received a message on the lives of Alexander and his fellow Archons.'

'Archons?'

'Ah, like the Argonauts, a select group of Companions travelling together since the beginning of time and to the ends of the world. They play epoch-making roles as family members, friends and rivals. Though remarkable, their conflicts are by no means extraordinary.'

'*Really?*'

'Yes, it's common for members of the same soul-group to work out conflictual relationships between themselves during incarnations. We ordinarily come as members of the same family, but this singular group is of such world-historic significance that its members are reborn as allies and opponents in the politics of their times. Laurence recorded their lives from the beginning of Egypt's eighteenth dynasty to the end of the twentieth century. Let me find his notes for you.'

Mendle dug among his papers, noting that Alexander's reputation was as complex as the Gordian Knot itself—ranging from a vilified mountain vagabond to one of history's greatest military leaders.

She recollected Johann Gustav Droysen's statement: "The name of Alexander stands at the end of an epoch in world history and the beginning of a new era." But had Droysen ever stopped to wonder if his hero would return to make world history over and over again?

Having found the notes, Mendle held them up to the webcam. She saw four columns, each with a dozen-or-so names.

'Wait, are the first Thothmes, Cyrus and Alexander?'

'Ah, exactly, then Ptolemy…'

'All those names are listed in the dossier. I couldn't understand why they were there, or what they meant until now.'

She could sense Mendle's excitement as he elucidated the names:

'The four columns record the successive lives of the four Archons and the transmission of their political leadership through the ages. There's no sacred bloodline or secret society, only a knot of karma. Let me forward their karmic histories to you.'

1.i Thothmes III	1.ii Amenhotep II
2.i Cyrus the Great	2.ii Cambyses II
3.i Alexander the Great	3.ii Ptolemy I Soter
4.i Ptolemy III Evergetes	4.ii Hamilcar Barca
5.i Setorius	5.ii Hirtuleius
6.i Trajan	6.ii Hadrian
7.i Aurelian	7.ii Probus
8.i Belisarius	8.ii Heraclius
9.i Leo III the Isaurian	9.ii Leo IV the Khazar
10.i Richard the Lionhart	10.ii Henry the Lion
11.i Walter Raleigh	11.ii Humphrey Gilbert
12.i Thomas Jefferson	12.ii George Washington

1.iii	Thothmes IV	1.iv	Amenhotep III
2.iii	Darius the Great	2.iv	Xexes I
3.iii	Antigonus I Cyclops	3.iv	Seleucus I Nicator
4.iii	Antigonus III Doson	4.iv	Antichus III the Great
5.iii	Julius Caesar	5.iv	Augustus Caesar
6.iii	Antonius Pious	6.iv	Marcus Aurelius
7.iii	Constance Chlorus	7.iv	Constantine the Great
8.iii	Constans Pogonatus	8.iv	Constantine IV
9.iii	Charles Martel	9.iv	Charlemagne
10.iii	Frederick I Barbarossa	10.iv	Frederick the Great
11.iii	Richelieu	11.iv	Gustavus Adolphus
12.iii	Charles de Gaulle	12.iv	Dag Hammarsköjld

Karmic histories

1. **THOTHMES III** **c.1504–1450BCE**	After the death of Queen Hatshepsut, Pharaoh Thothmes accomplished his unparalleled conquest of Palestine, Phoenicia, Syria, Mesopotamia and, finally, Nubia. Nicknamed the Napoleon of Ancient Egypt, he was in fact an early incarnation of Alexander the Great. Thothmes III and his successors—the four Archons—returned as the four founders of the Achaemenid Empire, starting with Cyrus II.
2. **CYRUS** **the GREAT** **c.576–529BCE**	Cyrus II expanded the Achaemenid Empire from Babylonia to Asia Minor. As a tolerant ruler, he liberated the exiled Jews from Babylon and allowed them to return and rebuild the Temple of Solomon. His three successors were Cambyses II, Darius the Great and Xerxes I —his fellow Archons again—who succeeded him and extended the empire to Egypt, the Indus and the Caucasus. They returned as the three generals of Alexander who would inherit his empire.
3. **ALEXANDER** **the GREAT** **356–323BCE**	Alexander conquered the Persian Empire which, as one of history's great ironies, he had founded as Cyrus the Great a century-and-a-half earlier. And, once again, he dreamt of sending a fleet around Africa. He founded the city of Alexandria—where he was to be entombed— which became the cultural capital of the civilised world and a centre of higher learning. His tutor, Aristotle, would be with him again during his next life in Egypt. He bequeathed his empire ambiguously "to the strongest" and upon his premature death the three generals—Ptolemy, Antigonus and Seleucus —contested the succession. Amidst their ongoing rivalry, each secured control over vast divisions of his empire. Although Alexander's vision of a world commonwealth was never fulfilled, the empire he created sowed the seeds for cosmopolitanism in the ancient world.
4. **PTOLEMY** **the BENEFACTOR** **282–221BCE**	Alexander's next life was as Ptolemy III, the beneficent Emperor of Egypt at the height of the Ptolemaic dynasty. As a patron of the arts, he added to the wealth of works in the great library of Alexandria, headed by Eratosthenes, a reincarnation of Aristotle, now a Greek geographer, mathematician and astronomer. Alexander's three generals returned as Hamilcar Barca (the father of Hannibal, who would lead the conquest of Hispania), Antigonus III of Macedon and Antiochus III of Syria. The Archons coursed through history like an ocean wave toward some as yet unknown shore. Their next lives were paired.

5. QUINTUS SERTORIUS c.123–72BCE	Quintus Sertorius was a Roman general and statesman during the civil wars of the late republic. He led a revolt in Lusitania and established a stable government with schools for military training—tilling the soil for modern Portugal and Spain. With his chief lieutenant, Lucius Hirtuleius (his twin Archon), he defied the power of Rome and conquered the Iberian peninsula. The other two Archons were reborn as Julius Caesar, the greatest general in Roman history and his heir, Augustus Caesar, who became the first Emperor of Rome. Mark Antony also joined this group, having been Alexander's general Lysimachus. In turn, the foursome next succeeded each other as the adoptive emperors of Rome.
6. TRAJAN c.53–117CE	Trajan was yet another outstanding campaign general in Spain, Germany, Eastern Europe, Syria and Mesopotamia. Age halted his imperial ambitions before reaching India, where he wistfully sighed: "If only I were Alexander!" Ironically, he did not know then who he had been. He was succeeded by the three adopted sons of Rome—Hadrian, who ended the empire's expansion and erected his eponymous wall in Britain, Antoninus Pius and Marcus Aurelius. From here on the empire began its slow and inevitable decline. Trajan and his fellow archons would appear again in two pairs.
7. LUCIUS DOMITIUS AURELIAN 212–275CE	Lucius Aurelian, Restorer of the Empire, consolidated the military recovery of the empire and built the Aurelian Wall around Rome. He was succeeded by his most able general, Marcus Aurelius Probus, who completed the wall and continued to combine the Roman forces against barbarian invasions. Hitherto the task of the Archon-group had been that of empire building and the protection of civilisation against barbarism in the Egyptian, Persian, Greek and imperial Roman ages—precedent to the Christian era. Under the Roman Empire, Christianity was tried and tested by persecutions and thereby succeeded as the new world religion and imperial order. Its final ordeal was under the tetrarchy of Diocletian and his co-rulers—Maximian, Galerius and Constantius Chlorus. As Emperor of the West, Constantius Chlorus, the "Pale", governed in Gaul and Britain. First married to a Christian woman, Helena, he was the more moderate of the tetrarchs and died having named his son, Constantine, as his successor. Against embittered rivals, Constantine the Great succeeded to become the sole ruler of the Empire. Initially a sun worshipper, Constantine was inspired by his mother and claimed to have had a vision in which Christ assured him victory in battle. He extended state recognition to the Christians and abolished their persecution. Thus was Christendom officially founded.

While baptized just before his death, Constantine tolerated paganism and founded Constantinople as the capital of the Byzantine Empire. Henceforth, the Archons' task was to defend Christendom against barbarism and fundamentalism and, later, to inaugurate the Protestant reformation against the hegemony of the Holy Roman Empire.

8. BELISARIUS 505–565	Belisarius was a general of Emperor Justinian and one of the greatest military leaders of all time. As the defender of Byzantium, he defeated the Persians, quelled an insurrection at Constantinople, then vanquished the Vandals and Ostrogoths, and repulsed a Bulgarian invasion. His military prowess was such that Justinian constantly feared a *coup*; but Belisarius remained loyal despite being briefly imprisoned on suspicion of treason. Justinian had him later restored to the honours he deserved. A similar drama would recur in their later reincarnations as King James I and Sir Walter Raleigh. After Justinian, Heraclius of Carthage was the next great Byzantine Emperor. He deposed the unworthy Phocus and defended the empire against Persian aggression. He recovered the revered Christian relic of the "True Cross", first identified by Constantine's mother, Helena. He involved himself in important theological debates and offered a controversial compromise on religious dogma. His reign was the turning point in Christian hegemony although, already before his death, the empire's possessions in Syria, Palestine and Egypt had fallen to the conquering Muslims. Constans Pogonatus, the "Bearded", grandson of Heraclius, was the Byzantine Emperor who halted the Muslim advance in North Africa. After Constans's assassination, his son Constantine succeeded him, repelling repeated assaults upon Constantinople by the Muslims.
9. LEO the ISAURIAN 680–741	Leo III was the Byzantine Emperor who brought the empire back from anarchy and successfully defended Constantinople against renewed Muslim assaults. While introducing notable reforms, civil and moral, he initiated a period of iconoclasm that led to his excommunication. He also issued a legal code that would serve the empire for the next two centuries, founding the so-called Isaurian dynasty. His grandson, Leo the Khazar, carried on the Isaurian policy of iconoclasm but died prematurely. His widow, Irene, acted as regent for her young son and reinstated the practice of icon worship. Charles Martel, the "Hammer", was a Frankish ruler who halted the advance of marauding Muslims at Poitiers, thus ending their progress across France. Although only a skirmish, the victory unified Christian warlords and prepared their subjects for a new Empire. His grandson, Charlemagne, became Holy Roman Emperor of the Franks. As the most celebrated ruler of medieval Europe, Charlemagne patronized learning and the rule of law.

10. RICHARD LIONHEART 1157–1199	Richard I was the son of King Henry II and Eleanor of Aquitaine (queen consort and the patron of Chrétien de Troyes), and spent his early years waging war against his father. On his succession, he restored the sovereignty of William the Lion over Scotland, annulling the treaty of vassalage imposed by his father. Richard spent most of his reign in the Holy Land, leading the Third Crusade against Saladin, for which he became a romantic figure of legend. Henry the Lion, a powerful German prince, was an ally of his brother-in-law, Richard Lionheart, and that of Frederick Barbarossa—but took no part in their crusades. As Holy Roman Emperor, Frederick the "Red Beard" strove to restore the glory of the empire while consolidating power in Germany and Italy. He initiated the Third Crusade and, after gaining two victories over the Muslims, drowned crossing a river in Turkey. In turn, Frederick the Great, the "Wonder of the World" and a grandson of Barbarossa, became the new Holy Roman Emperor and defied both the papacy and the Lombard League, for which he was repeatedly excommunicated (like his father before him). He led the Sixth Crusade and concluded a ten-year truce with the Sultan of Egypt, Al-Kamil, the nephew of Saladin, who ceded Jerusalem to the Christians. Frederick had himself crowned King of Jerusalem to consolidate the alliance between East and West. Curiously, he aspired to be a philosopher-king like Marcus Aurelius.
11. Sir WALTER RALEIGH 1554–1618	Walter Raleigh and his half-brother, Sir Humphrey Gilbert, were the celebrated adventurer-explorers of Elizabethan England, promoting the colonisation of the New World by the English. Gilbert, an able military commander and member of parliament, succeeded in founding the first English colony at Newfoundland, America, but was shipwrecked and perished on his return. Raleigh's life went far beyond this and constitutes a rich legend of adventure. As the reincarnation of Belisarius, Raleigh was karmically linked to Queen Elizabeth's successor, James I, who had once been Emperor Justinian. Jealous of Raleigh, James kept him imprisoned in the Tower of London under an unjust death sentence for treason, which he had commuted to life. Raleigh persuaded the king to release him in order to search for gold in America—including the famed city of El Dorado. But when this expedition failed against the Spanish, James reinvoked the death sentence and had Raleigh beheaded. Sir Francis Bacon, his contemporary, alone understood the karmic nature of Raleigh's life and that of his downfall. Raleigh's own intellectual achievements include his scientific discoveries, several diverse poems, and his *History of the World*. Raleigh and Gilbert would return to wage a war of liberation against the English. Their association through many past lives would bring them to a fitting finale as Thomas Jefferson and George Washington, perhaps the two most important figures of the American Revolution.

Raleigh and Gilbert were counterpoised by Cardinal de Richelieu and the brilliant Swedish king, Gustavus Adolphus, also paired again. As Louis XIII's chief minister, Richelieu became the virtual ruler of France. He opposed the Habsburg hegemony of the Holy Roman Empire and subsidized the pro-Reformation, anti-Catholic invasion of Germany by Gustavus, the "Lion of the North". As an irony of history, Richelieu and Gustavus opposed the empire they had once founded as Charles Martel and Charlemagne; and which they inherited again as Frederick Barbarossa and his gifted grandson, Frederick the Great. By allying the French with the German Protestants, Richelieu and Gustavus effectively redirected the outcome of the Thirty Year's War —ending the embittered Counter-Reformation—and so reset Europe's political-religious balance of power. Richelieu not only established France as the first military power of Europe, but laid the foundation for its grandeur in the seventeenth-century. He also patronized literature and founded the French Academy.

12. THOMAS JEFFERSON 1743–1826

Thomas Jefferson was a revolutionary leader, a political philosopher, and the main author of the Declaration of Independence. He was also President of the United States and a brilliant American exponent of the Enlightenment. This was a most fitting life for one formerly known as the "Defender of Men".

The founders of Egypt's Ptolemaic dynasty—the Greek royal family of Hellenistic Egypt—ultimately reappeared as the founding fathers of America: Ptolemy I returned as George Washington, Ptolemy II as Benjamin Franklin, and Ptolemy III as Thomas Jefferson.

The Archon-group not only returned to found the Union of America but, in their next occurrence, strove to free the world from Nazism and to keep the peace in the precarious post-war era.

Overseeing this group was an entity—the group's prime minister, if you will—who last appeared as Winston Churchill. Long before that, as the founder-pharaoh of Egypt's eighteenth dynasty, Ahmes I, he accomplished the military liberation of Egypt. The Semetic Hyksôs— the Asiatic invaders who subjugated Egypt since the time of Abraham, also called the Shepherd Kings of the north—were now driven out to Jerusalem and the remaining Hebrew population enslaved. Ahmes's antisemitic karma recurred in a later life as Pompey the Great, the Roman who seized Jerusalem and desecrated the Temple, beginning the Roman occupation of Judea. He expiated this error by opposing the antisemitic Nazi regime in the twentieth century.

71

Karma makes history possible.
Graffiti outside the Truth and Reconciliation Commission venue, Cape Town (1998)

Sonja was a historian's historian. Her first love had been historiography. Growing up in a multicultural society prepared her for the interdisciplinary studies she came to choose at university. She'd been a top student and graduated *cum laude* after presenting her thesis on the semiology of history. Her argument was simple: the past is always open to new interpretations and, therefore, open to re-interpretations in the future.

She'd argued against a canonical view of history, claiming that no one group of people or set of events could define who the Dutch were —as traders, sailors, builders, migrants or refugees—nor was there a single unifying heritage for the Netherlands. As a nation, the Dutch had to negotiate a new identity that encompassed their VOC past, their role in WWII, and their future within the EU.

That was then. But what about now?

Instead of decrying idiosyncratic constructions of world histories (which she'd done as a student), she now found herself re-reading the works of Herodotus and Toynbee. She was haunted by what Volodya had said: 'Panoramic histories, as Toynbee discovered on the train between Istanbul and Calais, are best viewed through a passing coach window. Reincarnationalists tend to view history in the same way.'

Toynbee or not Toynbee, that was her question. Her interest no longer revolved around grand world histories but in the karmic history of select individuals or groups. However, to accept the role of karma, critically, she would have to transgress a respected academic line—

and "crossing the line" was a professional taboo. *Lieve help*, what if her colleagues saw her now: *She leaves on a research trip, steals a dossier from an overseas museum, and then returns believing in karma!*

Intellectually marooned, she fell between a rock and a hard place: would she be willing to argue that our past, as much as our future, is karmically linked? Or that karma makes history possible?

Well, yes, perhaps, look at Alexander.

According to Laurence, Alexander's successive lives were bound to kings and statesmen who'd advanced a cosmopolitan culture and a universal code of law. If that were so, did civilisation fulfil a purpose? Was there a trend in historical direction? If so, did the achievements of ancient empires, of medieval Christendom, of Western humanism or modern democracies fulfil some sort of karma?

That's what the Archon message seemed to be about, or not?

Mendle also told her about the bundle of dirty pigskin, intractably bound with wire, which he'd found lodged deep inside the victim's mouth. It had been inserted deliberately, most probably after death, to conceal a message in Old Portuguese. He elaborated:

'I had it translated yesterday, and it says: "Do you desire this once more and innumerable times more?" It's an odd question, originally posed by Nietzsche's daemon, for which I think the answer should be: "Yes, and I live so that I may desire life again".'

She stalled, his next statement pulling her upright:

'Far more importantly, this echoes the quotation you found in the dossier, remember, about believing in your own eternal recurrence? Both questions prove the presence of a cabal so evil that its members will kill those who believe in reincarnation. More so, the cabal is still intent on silencing people who persist with the belief today—until the concept of recurrent lives disappears forever.'

She was ready to admit that her evidence—historical, esoteric and mythological—concurred on one central issue: life did confirm right. But did it also correct wrong? What once seemed so unfathomable was now self-evident: life was a tedious learning experience.

Well, in that case, what have I learnt?

Simply that, as first Viceroy of the Indies, Almeida led Europe's entry into the Asian environment, re-establishing direct links between the East and West after the fall of Constantinople.

And what else?

At this stage she'd formulated eight keystones regarding Almeida's exoteric and esoteric background:

As a man of higher belief, Almeida blended folk superstition with religious rationalism, divination with doctrine, fusing notions of grace and karma. As a diplomat he had contact with soldiers, envoys and monarchs from the Middle East, acquiring arcane knowledge from Greek, Hebraic and Moslem cultures. As an admiral he secured the carreira da Índia with his Blue Sea policy, severing Muslim control of traditional trade routes to-and-from the Mediterranean. As a knight in the Ordem de Cristo he promoted exchange beyond the cordon of Islam, forging ties with potential allies in East Africa and West India —from Melinde to Malabar. As a viceroy he governed the Estado da Índia with the world's oldest blend of Christianity in East Africa and South Asia, preserving elements of Hinduism, Buddhism, Judaism and Islam. As an exile he returned with a translation that reconciled faith and reason, promoting coherence between Christian humanism and Aristotle's natural science. As a noble he aided the flow of Grail Christianity—a solar mysticism independent of Rome—allowing the waning sun wisdom of Arabia to enter an emergent Western society. As a councillor (or so Prof Mendle proposed), he assumed custodianship of Zoroaster's pearl, linking vanishing Oriental mysticism with the emerging humanism in the Occident. And most recently, she'd learnt, Almeida expanded Portugal's influence around the Indian Ocean Rim, helping cosmopolitan societies prepare for the advent of universal values.

She also understood that Almeida's death linked Southern Africa with Northern Europe and, as a direct consequence, Dutch, French and British settlers had colonised the Cape—and *not* the Portuguese.

Now Volodya's death gave cause for further questioning. Was he, by whatever other name, on the beach that Friday morning in 1510? And, if so, what of her *own* involvement in Almeida's murder?

Realignment

72.

Osiris, you went away, yet you have remained,
You were asleep, yet you have awakened,
You died, yet you live again.
Pyramid Texts 1004, necropolis of Memphis (c.2300BCE)

The Cape of Storms lay far to the south and had become a vague and distant memory. Like Ponta de Sagres, the Cape was now a fantasy more than a reality. Since then so much had happened.

And now Volodya was dead.

She felt estranged, unable to recall his face, as if he'd never existed. If so, had he startled a thief or was he the victim of a premeditated murder? If nothing had been stolen, was he killed because of something in his obscure past or something he'd recently uncovered?

Although he'd given no details, Volodya had asked her to look for something in Holland, something he himself could not do. He had alluded to it at the Hortus, offering to discuss it on his next visit to Leiden. What if it had been the *Sierra Nevada*? Had Volodya found out where it was?

The Sunday she returned to Holland was also the day that he first mentioned it, asking her to do some research at a house-museum, a royal residence of some sort. He implied that it was something she could easily do, given her position, something only she'd have access to as a curator. *My God, he played me? I was set up...*

Exhausted by recent events, including Bart's convalescence, her imagination seemed to blend seamlessly with her new experiences. In her mind, fact and fiction fused. The notion of transpersonal lives now blurred with older conspiracy theories. Was it irrational, she feared, to think that all things were connected after all?

What of Almeida and I?

Her life no longer seemed the same, it had found another rhythm, a new direction. The seasons rotated in reverse, the sun crossed the sky backwards and traffic rushed off the way she'd come. She had not only crossed a continent, but the equator too. She was an interloper in her hometown and a stranger on once familiar streets. It seemed Bart was not the only one with adjustment problems.

Her world had been turned upside-down, starting with Laurence's messages, and her journey had become more than a mere pilgrimage. Her life was now an initiation into a world of relics, resurrections and recurrent lives.

Only one month remained of her sabbatical. That is, one month in which to complete her VOC research for the Tropenmuseum. She'd gone nowhere with it since leaving Cape Town, and would have to work night and day to finish it in time.

Curiously, it was the disparity between official records and informal testimonies that had first drawn her attention to Almeida. But that had all changed. Now she was struck by the gap between historical scholarship and karmic investigation, between exoteric evidence and esoteric insight.

So, where to now?

Her current interests were of little consequence in Amsterdam—the "Dutch Jerusalem" of sixteenth-century Holland—since Almeida's murder was an Afro-Portuguese drama with Spanish, English, French and German actors. Yet, even if Spinoza played no part, there had to be a Dutch connection somewhere. And she was going to find it...

It was an irrational, even irresponsible decision, but she trusted her instincts. She would contact Clara Berga as soon as possible. It was what Volodya had suggested, and the timing felt right.

✠   ✠   ✠

Using the *Telefoongids* to trace the number, she soon had Clara on the line. From the outset they struck a good note and were quickly talking about Volodya. Having told her how they met, and of their mutual interest in Almeida, she asked what more was known of his death.

'It happened at his summer datcha, outside Moscow, where he'd gone fishing for the weekend...'

Clara had been told it was a gruesome affair: his body was found despoiled, flat on the floor, with his tongue cut and his teeth smashed. His throat had been severed by a sharp bladed weapon, like Almeida, execution style. And all his clothes were gone.

Clara knew no more, having lost touch with Volodya in recent years. They'd been close for a long time, before the early Eighties, when she left to teach in South Africa. After that he moved to Kiev where he'd made lots of money, or so she'd heard from his family.

'Yes, I loved his father, back then. But I'm too frail to attend the funeral now. It's simply too far away for me.'

Endeared by the gentle voice, Sonja suggested: 'What if we travel together?'

She offered this as much for herself, and for her own sense of safety, as she did for Clara's well-being.

'Oh, how very kind, but I'd only burden you. His father and I were engaged during the Cold War. It was a short courtship, though very romantic, and I would have married him had he not met my friend Margo. We were both studying in Moscow and ended up drawing lots for him, before my silly jealousy ruined our friendship. She won. Margo was from London and very posh. Her father was a famous spy, a sort of double-agent, though we didn't know that at the time.'

Clara coughed hoarsely.

'Don't worry, it's not my health, but my vocal cords. I lost them after a failed throat operation in Johannesburg and haven't been able to speak with my own voice since. Please excuse the sound you hear.'

Sonja was having difficulty understanding all Clara said. Her voice had become dry and brittle, like the bones at the SA Museum. She imagined a frail and delicate woman.

'Well, I hear you well enough.'

Clara cleared her throat:

'At least I wasn't silenced forever. You and I can still speak for ourselves, unlike Almeida. Unfortunately—'

'—oké, but it's not been forever. Volodya spoke for Almeida.'

'True, but Volodya only spoke about it privately. Perhaps you will speak out publicly? Through an exhibition, or perhaps a publication, so the world will know what happened.'

'*Really*, is it that important?'

'Oh yes, it is, *very*.' Clara swallowed with difficulty, her throat tight. 'It's important, yes, because several royal-houses in Europe—and the emergence of our modern nations—would have followed a different course had it not been for Almeida's murder.'

Now his murder changed European history too?

'Why? Because the Dutch rather than the Portuguese established a colony at the Cape?'

Almeida's life seemed like a shuttle, she thought, weaving diverse strands of destiny and history into a single tapestry.

'Yes, and through various alliances with the House of Orange, the French and British were to follow. Germans and Russians too. This would not have been possible if the Cape was a Portuguese colony. In the end it doesn't matter if Almeida was ambushed or assassinated; it's the net historical result that counts.'

'Well, I heard via an independent source that it was both: Almeida was first ambushed by the natives and then ritually executed by his own men. His assassins seized the opportunity to fulfil an order of execution.'

'Call it what you want—opportunity, destiny, coincidence, even providence, whatever—it sealed his fate and ours.'

'Aren't they two sides to the same coin: chance and fortune?'

'Yes,' said Clara weakly, 'and by chance or fortune we also know where he's buried.'

'You know?'

'Yes, my friend Max Stibbe identified the site fifty years ago.'

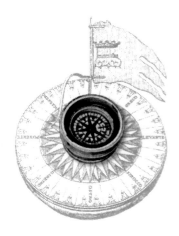

73

I am
this tiny wooden boat
afloat
on an endless sea.
My compass-heart
locked
on Table Mountain.
Bernard Levinson, *I See You* (2001)

Jason left Wits campus after his final seminar. It was a grim, muggy afternoon and the sky over downtown Jo'burg turned a pallid yellow. Driving out on Jan Smuts Avenue, he skirted around the aggressive urban sprawl and headed towards the dappled streets of Parkwood. Sonja had asked him to examine the mural of *T'kama-Adamastor* at the university's library. He was now on his way to meet the artist.

Cyril Coetzee's studio wasn't easy to find. Jason had fancied an old farmhouse, not an apartment in a leafy suburb. On the door hung a medallion, an emblematic Rosy-Cross, like a small pocket compass.

A Rosicrucian compass-heart?

Jason knocked twice and waited, then repeated with more vigour. It seemed no one was at home…

With his hands cupped around his eyes and his nose pressed against the window, he peered in for a sign of the artist. The interior was crammed with canvas rolls, stretcher frames, easels and packing boxes. He suddenly heard his name called behind him.

'Hello, you must be Jason?'

'Yes, hi, I wasn't sure...'

'That's because we live next door. I use that side only as my studio. Here, come this way.'

Cyril Coetzee led him into an open-plan living room filled with books, paintings and rare collectables. The dining table had been set for three. Large pots simmered on a freestanding stove.

Jason hesitated.

'My wife Astrid will join us for lunch. She's just gone down to the shops, so let me show you around. See here, we broke through the wall to combine our two apartments.'

Jason slung his satchel over a chair and, via an interleading study, followed Cyril into a well-lit studio full of canvases, drawing boards and rough sketches. It was a world of filtered light, mixed colours and the pungent smell of genuine turpentine.

'I teach at the university but give classes here in the evening,' he said, as if apologising for the mess. 'Let's have a drink, shall we?'

Ambling back they passed an original pencil sketch.

'Is this your drawing for T'kama-Adamastor?'

'Yes, that's how it first came to me. The entire composition was set down from the start. As you know, Adamastor protected the Cape of Storms from those who dared discover it. I chose to personify him as a Khoisan man, though in myth he is the Cape mountain chain, like Pyrene of Spain.'

'Pyrene?'

'Yes, Pyrene had been turned to stone too, hence the *Pyrenees*. She protected the pre-Christian sun-mysteries of Iberia.'

'That's probably where Camões found his inspiration. Adamastor, likewise, protected the moon cult of our Khoisan?'

'Perhaps,' he said, opening a wine bottle, 'the goddess Pyrene was introduced via the Phoenicians on the coast. She protected the heroic light-bringers, like Melkarth-Herakles, who defended Iberia against successive waves of invaders: the Romans, Visi-Goths and, of course, the mighty army of Hannibal.'

Cyril went on to explain how, like the ancient Titans, Adamastor had fallen in love with a nymph and was banished to the farthest corner of the world. Adamastor was seen as a tormented figure filled with anger and anguish:

'Adamastor was a grotesque giant, a deformed and vindictive ogre who personified the character of the Stormy Cape. This was his forbidden portal, a threshold between East and West, from which he guarded the continent's secrets.'

'Sure, turning the Gama-vs-Adamastor clash into a metaphor for that between modern man and the classical gods?'

It sounded like something Mendle would say.

'Yes, well, at least for Camões,' agreed Cyril, offering Jason a glass. 'Mankind's inevitable triumph over the gods symbolised the triumph of the Renaissance over the Medieval, humanism over dogmatism.'

'Speaking as a Capetonian,' Jason reflected, 'Adamastor epitomizes all that was Other in the European mind. For the sixteenth-century Christian, including men like Camões, Adamastor symbolised that which remained irrational, pagan and non-Aristotelian... Adamastor represented everything still novel in a continent they wished to save from itself.'

'True, Adamastor sits at the root of all white semiology invented to cope with the African experience,' added Cyril, still talking while he checked the stove, 'which is why modern poets present him as the embodiment of a continent resentful of any attempt to disturb its ignorance and gloom. Historically speaking, Gama's confrontation with Adamastor symbolises the conflict between Europe and Africa, between Empire and Colony, civilisation and barbarism—'

'—becoming the foundation myth for a White Africa?'

Cyril nodded, removing the pot from the stove.

'Yes, liberal nineteenth-century writers maintained the notion of an immutable, enigmatic and barbarous "Dark Continent". Jan Smuts, son of General JC Smuts, repeated the sentiment in his preface to *This Africa of Ours*. Here, read it, while I drain the pasta. I hope you like pesto and gorgonzola?'

Jason opened the book to the marked page:

> Africa surrenders her treasures slowly and almost reluctantly, as though it grieves her to be disturbed. That is why her history is so effectively obscured... And in the background the mythical stories of gold and diamonds, of Prester John and the rulers of Monomotapa and the mines of the Queen of Sheba...

Astrid was a gregarious woman with a round face and flawless skin. She fed their daughter while Cyril served dinner, describing the Grail stories of southern Africa.

Astrid listened until the child was sated, then passed her on so she too could eat. Turning to Jason, she asked pointedly:

'Have you read Eco's *Baudolino*?'

'No,' he admitted, 'but I did finish *The Name of the Rose*.'

He did not care for religious intrigues, he carefully explained, even less conspiracies of the Latin rite.

'That's no failure, it's the point Umberto wants to make. To pursue something intangible is an act of devotion—or an act of madness.'

Jason grinned, relieved. Astrid continued:

'Well *Baudolino* is the same ingenious and erudite combination as *The Rose*. As usual, Umberto combines arcane medieval knowledge and modern critical theory. Both books are playful and profound.'

'Sounds like another heady mixture.'

'Oh, but it is! Baudolino is a self-confessed liar who goes in search of the Grail—or *Grasal* as he calls it—and travels east seeking the lost world of Prester John.'

'I heard they acquire a wooden bowl and take it to be the Grail. Then squabble among themselves as to who should keep it?'

'Right, and their silly confrontation is fatal. It isn't the real Grail, of course, but what counts is that the search is kept alive, even if it can't be found.'

'I guess no one should ever find it,' said Jason with his mouth full, 'otherwise we'll just stay home and watch DSTV?'

'Yes, and Baudolino concludes that his readers should not be told about the Grail either, because belief in its existence makes men wander like lunatics under a full moon.'

Jason recalled Prof Mendle's warning about bouts of madness while searching for the Grail—and how obsessive he'd felt in Alsace.

It had happened to Monty Python too, he recalled, when audiences for the Broadway musical kept going back, night after night, hoping to find by some sleight of hand a grail hidden beneath their seat.

'Seeking the truth,' said Cyril seriously, 'means we believe it exists, no matter how hard it is to find. And if we ever find this Truth, then it must be preserved like the Grail, for centuries to come.'

'Then it's better not to believe in anything?'

'Well, there's a big difference between *examining* and *believing*. As Aristotle said, "the unexamined life is not worth living".'

Astrid rose to take their baby to bed. Turning in the doorway, she concluded over her shoulder: 'Only a good night's sleep makes life worth living!'

Jason suddenly felt tired.

Clearing the table, Cyril mentioned how a young history teacher, after much self-examination, came to believe he had been Francisco d'Almeida in a previous life.

'*Who?*'

'Walter Johannes Stein, an Austrian Jew in pre-war Germany. He dreamt that an ageing sea captain was murdered by his crew while their ship lay at anchor in a bay. Aided by an esotericist, he identified the event as the historical death of Francisco d'Almeida at Table Bay. Stein's retrospective vision would have remained a mere footnote after his death in 1957, shared only among his confidants, had it not been for his diaries. His vision is all the more remarkable since he describes the murder-weapon as a *flamberge*, a flame-bladed spear; the kind used by sixteenth-century European mercenaries. Thus not an assegai. Stein's dream has been well documented by his biographer, Johannes Tautz. If you read German, take my copy...'

Jason wavered, knowing Sonja was more interested in past lives and may prefer a Dutch version herself. No doubt she would also know where to find an esoteric bookshop in Amsterdam.

74

From the deck to the desert,
from the mountain to the sea,
Cape Town has become part of me.
Lueen Conning-Ndlovu, District Six Museum, Cape Town (1999)

To her surprise, Sonja found Stein's biography tucked away upstairs at Athenaeum Books, and read the relevant pages going home on the train. She could barely wait to tell Mendle.

From: sonja@homenet.nl
Sent: Friday, August 13, 21:17
To: jmendle@sam.org.za
Subject: Almeida and Stein
Dear Prof Mendle

As you no doubt heard from Jason, Francisco d'Almeida was reincarnate as the medieval historian and modern economist, Walter Johannes Stein (1891–1957). His biographer, a fellow German, made this connection public in 1989. A half-century earlier, Stein himself had a "retrospective vision" in which he witnessed his own murder aboard a sailing ship. He knew this to be a past life experience, noting: "My last death on 1 March 1510, about 60 years old. I remember it Friday 27 June 1924." This was no isolated experience. Stein had similar insights into his other past lives and documented each with meticulous care. Two months later, Stein identified his vision as the murder of Francisco d'Almeida. Rudolf Steiner, a colleague from Vienna, confirmed it by saying: "That's how it will have been."

The documentation was found among Stein's private papers. Of Almeida's murder, Stein himself wrote:

One gains an insight into former lives through grace, and an experience of this sort holds many surprises. One might think it a terrifying experience to relive your own death (by this I mean the last death before your present life). But that is not so. It is a joyous experience. I experienced the murder of an old man, a ship's captain, who met his death emerging from a hatchway onto the upper deck. There, beside the ship's cables and the mast, he was struck down by the spear of his enemy. It was a strangely shaped ritual spear, the blade of which had a wavy outline. This spear struck him above the teeth of his upper jaw, killing him instantly. I experience this in all detail. The landscape—it was sunset—the captain's uniform with its ornamental metal buttons, the heavy tread of the old man as he climbed the companionway. My interest centred more on the wonderful ease with which I streamed out of my body than on the person who had thrown the spear. Nevertheless, my love went out to him in gratitude. One would not expect to be so grateful to the person who kills you. And yet it is so...

Comparing the main sources, a few anomalies seem to emerge: The Portuguese had failed to entice natives back to the boats and, as far as I know, there were none aboard the *Garça*. It is thus unlikely that Almeida was murdered by an angry herder. Furthermore, Stein's vision describes how a spear killed him; whereas the folios imply a ritual piercing on the beach when Almeida was already dead.

While conceived and recorded independently, both sources say that he was ambushed and concur on one unmistakable point: *Almeida was ritually executed by his compatriots.*

It is of less interest to me who drew the first weapon or wielded the final blow. As we already know from the initial messages, Almeida's executioners simply wanted to stop him reopening esoteric intercourse between the Orient and Occident.

Boas noites!

Sonja

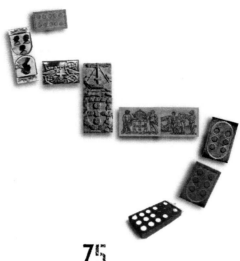

75

Any fact becomes important when it's connected to another.
The connection changes the perspective; it leads you to think
that every detail of the world, every voice, every word written
or spoken has more than its literal meaning, that it tells us of
a secret. The rule is simple: suspect, only suspect...

Umberto Eco, *Foucault's Pendulum* (1989)

The next morning, between packing a suitcase and eating a hurried breakfast, Sonja logged on to find Mendle's reply.

From: jmendle@sam.org.za
Sent: Saturday, August 14, 10:25
To: sonja@homenet.nl
Subject: Almeida and Stein, to clarify

Dear Sonja

I forwarded your email to Laure and received a reply early this morning, saying the first lines came to him on Table Mountain and that he had to rush home to finish it. He thinks you have precipitated what else needs to be known, but should take care of those who actively suppress karma and reincarnation.

Among these is a man, apparently a friend or associate, who opposed Almeida under Isabella and Ferdinand. Even earlier, serving Theodora and Justinian, he tried to suppress this knowledge. As a clue, it seems, his name translates as "Friend".

I hope the following message clarifies:

Francisco d'Almeida

Francisco d'Almeida was the same soul as Walter Johannes Stein, an associate of Rudolf Steiner. He had previously been Count Hugo of Tours at the court of Charlemagne and, much earlier, the same soul as Joseph of Arimathea. Francisco was ambushed and assassinated on the beach at Table Bay, not aboard his ship. The ritual piercing with the lance was done afterwards. It was thrust through his throat, from under the chin and upward, emerging above the upper teeth.

The vision, as sometimes happens, was of several different time frames superimposed into one continuous set of events. Stein saw himself, as Francisco d'Almeida, coming out his cabin and simultaneously witnessing his fated end, so that it appeared as if the murder occurred on the ship's deck. About Almeida we may yet have more to say.

Waiting at Schiphol, en route to the funeral service, she checked her inbox again. There was more from Mendle:

Hugo, Count of Tours, is described by Trevor Ravenscroft as "one of the leading initiates of the Holy Grail in the Dark Ages". Ravenscroft had been Stein's student in London and used Stein's research for his book *The Spear of Destiny* (1973). His publisher bullied him into a non-fiction title and, being an alcoholic, he agreed for the extra money. *The Spear* turned out to be a sensation which, like *The Rose* and *The Code*, popularized esoteric knowledge while blurring fact with fiction.

Laurence says Ravenscroft was karmically linked to Thomas Malory (d.1471) and thereby obtained esoteric knowledge from the same man twice. Malory's *Le Morte d'Arthur* (1485) appeared in several revised editions among which, it seems, are traces of the *Sierra Nevada*. While Malory's identity remains enigmatic, like that of Basil Valentine, I'm intrigued to know more.

For now, we can only suspect.

JM

PS: This morning I realised that 'd' equates closely with 'th' (old pronunciations were variable and somewhat adjustable).

A ri math ea

A l meid a

76

Volodya's funeral service was held at St Mikhail's church where he'd been christened forty years before, in the spring of 1970, when the Cold War thawed and religious services were done as blat-favours for well-connected families.

Sonja found the dusky candle-lit interior too decorative for such a solemn occasion and, to her dismay, realised that the hallowed icons evoked no emotion in her (most were cheap reproductions anyway). But then neither had the ornate mosaic at Le Mont Sainte-Odile, the one dedicated to the same Archangel.

Was her preference for simplicity too Protestant?

The square church brimmed with women in black shawls and men in bulky leather jackets. Wearing her vintage sunglasses, Volodya's ex-wife looked like she'd walked off a Fellini film set. His four older brothers stood before the open casket, their backs to the tall gilded iconostasis, never once looking at Roxalena.

Volodya lay with his hands crossed, clasping the emblem of the Golden Fleece. His family bade farewell amid chanting, weeping and kissing. Oblivious to their parents' grief, several grandchildren played outside on the steps, enjoying the brief Indian Summer sunshine.

The Black Goliath wasn't among the guests, of that Sonja was sure. Such a hulk was hard to hide. This in itself was strange, as he was the only other person she'd ever seen talking to Volodya.

She felt disappointed, somehow let down, as she had prepared herself for the encounter, rehearsing their conversation over and over in her head: *Who are you? And what did Volodya want with the Sierra Nevada?* Streetwise, she also packed a Taser stun gun in her bag. Admittedly, her bottle of water was easier to handle in self-defence.

In front of her stood a man who looked as much out of place as she. He wore a tailored suit, unlike the other men, and had a self-assured

329

presence about him. He appeared constitutively Other, and yet so familiar, that she took him to be from Western Europe too. He also spoke English, not Russian. And when he offered his condolences, the family seemed not to recognise him, including Volodya's mother.

Having paid her own respects, with a sealed letter from Clara, she sought him among the guests lingering outside, but he'd already left. A pity, as he was her one and only lead, potentially. With him gone, she trundled out to Sheremetyevo International, hoping to bump into him at Terminal 2.

This Other Man wasn't there, of course, although the thought itself appealed to her. She found the idea so irrational, so ridiculous, that she wondered if the spontaneity of her actions made her feel this pleasure? Perhaps she needed more poetry, after all? But not now, please, not when her feet ached from standing so long in that church. Three hours later, with delayed queues at check-in, she scrambled onto the plane and took her seat. She'd have preferred a window, but that didn't matter now, she simply wanted to read Stein's biography.

She soon learnt of a trip made to Spain and Portugal in 1932, seven years after his retrospective vision, hoping to find traces of himself as Francisco d'Almeida. It was around Easter and he began at Santiago de Compostela. According to his biographer, Johannes Tautz:

> On Maundy Thursday Stein sat in the Cathedral, in front of the Saint's grave, in order to reflect on the history of the place. Pictures formed themselves in his mind relating to the time of the battles against the Moors in which Almeida had taken part as a knight of Santiago. He saw in his mind "the knights riding through the south gate of the city. They were youthful knights who knelt down to receive Communion two at a time, sharing the Host between them. In this way they each sealed their comradeship-of-arms." In the procession of the pilgrims, Stein espied the figure of the alchemist Basil Valentine whom he (as Almeida) had encountered there.

Enthralled by the account, she could hardly wait to read more, but the name Basilius Valentinus brought everything to a halt. According to Volodya, the meeting of Almeida and Valentine had been on an astral plane, as in a dream-state, such as between a sangoma and the Ancestors. She read on, loose words swimming before her eyes.

She no longer browsed, she obsessed.

Stein arrived in Portugal on Good Friday and, entering Lisbon by Easter Sunday, felt as if he was "at home with every step".

This feeling accompanied him throughout his stay.

At the Torre do Tombo he found the first tangible trace of himself, the official *cartas* signed by Viceroy D'Almeida. He copied the "bold, self-willed pen strokes", noting how easy it was to imitate his former signature. According to Tautz, he also discovered an inscribed stone:

Here lies Dom Francisco Almeyda,

1st Viceroy of India, who never lied nor ran away.

She halted. *Discovered?* Had it vanished or was the original meaning lost in translation? Perhaps the "discovery" was part of his retrospective vision? The folios transcribed a slightly simpler inscription:

Here rests Francisco d'Almeida

who never lied or feared.

Oddly, it echoed what the Grand Master of Alcantara, Granada, had for his own epitaph:

Here lies one whose heart never knew fear.

Tautz's biography gave no further facts, other than to say it was a tombstone with Almeida's epitaph... If so, where was it now?

Had it been erected at the Cape, or taken to Portugal? Was it in Lisbon, or in Evora where king Manuel also held court? Had it been desecrated by his enemies, or lost among the tombstones of Abrantes? Compared to Albuquerque and Gama, it was a modest tribute to a national hero.

Tautz's lack of historical detail was frustrating. Irritated, she looked around for refreshments, she desperately needed a drink. There was a trolley coming up the aisle.

Returning to the biography, she learnt that Stein had remained in Lisbon, stirred by memories of past events. Here again, Tautz offered no details, saying only that Stein was aware that he and his associates had been connected in the fifteenth century.

Sonja ordered a sauvignon blanc from the leggy stewardess with a laddered stocking, and proceeded to read diagonally.

She'd given up on the facts, for now.

What followed was a visit to the Torre de Belém where Stein drew the following conclusion: "This is the point from whence the spirit of the new age set forth in the fifteenth century."

It was the so-called African Century, an era ruled by the principles of war and justice, which then characterized Almeida's career. Stein recognised this universal karmic phenomenon and knew that his ego had matured with the passage of time. Past lives, Sonja understood, brought about soul-changes in us.

Stein's encounter with his own past self—as a forceful diplomat and fearless soldier—came as a shattering experience. He was shocked by his past and the brutality of that age. In bold contrast, Albuquerque had been proclaimed the "Portuguese Mars" and was then popularly hailed as the "Caesar of the East".

It was no easy book to read. The translation was problematic and the biographer made assumptions about the reader's familiarity with esoteric concepts. There was no introduction, no glossary.

Sonja looked for the stewardess as the flight deck announced their descent into Schiphol. It had stopped raining and passengers could expect fair weather. Arrival time would be ten minutes earlier. Sonja continued frantically. She wanted to finish the chapter.

She scanned the next paragraph. Here Tautz claimed that 1492—the high point of Spain's inglorious expulsion and expansion—also marked the beginning of a new age; an era in which the Knights of Santiago played their part.

The captain prepared the plane for landing. She felt relieved that someone else, albeit arbitrarily, had decided she should stop reading. Shutting the book, her eye caught the words:

Mount St Odilia

She fumbled, almost dropping the book in the aisle, as she searched the page. She soon learnt that Stein had found an obscure legend about the Grail at Le Mont Sainte-Odile:

A second equally ancient legend he discovered himself in the convent on Mount St Odilia. It was through these discoveries that the first historic connections came to light... The main characters were portrayed as recipients of a blood-relic and as advisors to Charlemagne. These characters were connected to Mount St Odilia and the monastery of Reichenau in the far-flung East-West relationship. They were representatives of an esoteric, anti-Catholic Christianity. Thus it was confirmed that the story of the Grail began in the eighth or ninth centuries.

Then Odilia is a historical character in Wolfram's Grail story? Sonja drew a deep breath. *Oké, what does that mean for us today?*

Stein presented his Odilia research in Berlin, around 1927, and via an Eliza von Moltke was shown Steiner's private notes on Odilia and her historical connection to the Grail.

Sonja checked the references and found Stein had written a book: *The Ninth Century and the Holy Grail.* She flipped back to find her place, pages falling open to reveal a photograph of Eliza von Moltke herself. The adjoining text was a revelation:

> Referring to his lecture she told him of the walk to which she had been invited by Dr Rudolf Steiner in the cave-embedded precincts of the Ermitage when she visited Dornach for the first time in August 1917. Rudolf Steiner described this as the place in which Odilia sought refuge from the persecution of her father, Duke Eticho. *S Odile*, as she was called—the *Sol Dei* or "Divine Sun" in Latin—then founded a convent at Le Mont Sainte-Odile in Alsace, which rayed forth an esoteric Grail Christianity independent of Rome.

Likewise, Godfrey of Bouillon and Hugo of Tours strove to engender independent centres of Christianity, also on the other side of Rome, between Jerusalem and Alsace. It was in Alsace itself that Hugo held several possessions. Curiously, both Hugo and Almeida ended their careers in disgrace after each delayed in the execution of their orders. Both men served their own conscience first.

From her window she saw the rectangular parcels of land around Schiphol. While each plot was separately owned, they combined to form a functioning and productive entity. The pilot tipped the wings and banked the plane to the right. It seemed the world was a single, living economic organism.

She also read that Stein promoted a single, world-wide economy: "Such an economy," he'd said, "if free from political or governmental interference, could restore old relationships between East and West." In short, he wanted to reopen channels of economic exchange; just as Almeida had tried to do spiritually.

Stein's concept of economic solidarity was part of three interrelated functions for a post-war society; the other two were equal rights and cultural freedoms. Whoever compiled the dossier knew that too.

77

*It's not true that life is one damn thing after another;
it is one damn thing over and over.*

Edna St Vincent Millay, private correspondence (24 October 1930)

'Sonja, beware the ogre,' said Mendle, sitting in his study, 'his name is Ben Mordechai. He was a special marine in Afghanistan and, until recently, served as a mercenary for some private military company, like Blackwater Worldwide. From what I managed to piece together, Volodya recruited him to follow you—for the dossier or manuscript, I'm not sure—but was himself assassinated when his interest in you became too personal. It seems Volodya became too fond of you.'

'R-really, but why?' her incredulity was self-evident.

Mendle had called to hear about the funeral and to share his latest news. He sat with the same pharaonic blanket over his shoulders and a fresh drink in his hand. The cat lay asleep on his briefcase.

Some things do change, she observed, noting that the curtains were open and that his sash-window had been repaired.

'It's an ironic twist of history, as Laurence told me over lunch, since Mordechai had been a palace guard under Volodya and acted as his informant and assassin. Mordechai served as a volunteer-soldier in the Order of Santiago and, it seems, periodically spied on Almeida. He was a reputed marksman and involved in that tragic crossbow incident at Mossel Bay. But more important, at least for you, is this: Ben Mordechai still believes your dossier should be destroyed.'

She stared at Mendle in disbelief; more was unbearable. But he was too excited to hold himself back. The cat leapt off his desk.

'Yesterday Laure suggested that Volodya's ex-wife, Roxalena, had been none other than Leila ez Zagal, cousin of sultan Boabdil and one of the fifty hostages kept as ransom during the capitulation of Granada. She not only converted (what choice did a slave-girl have?) but also acted as Isabella's informant and as Alonso's private whore. However, he rejected her in a fit of jealousy, fearing she had betrayed him with Ben Mordechai. Further back in time, before Gibril Tarik landed at Gibraltar, Leila had been a chamber girl of Count Julian of Ceuta, the legendary Christian who betrayed the Hispanic Visigoths. She was called Elana (an echo of *Rox-alena*, perhaps) and went with Julian's daughter to the court of Roderic in Toledo which—and for me this really is the best part—which is where Solomon's Emerald Table had been kept. In the end, Leila-Elana lived in Spain, twice.'

'Sorry, Prof, but why tell me all this?'

'It's about the eternal return, once more. Just like the Pythagoreans, Nietzsche believed in the transmigration of souls and that similar events occur over and over to the same people. Virgil also describes how history repeats itself and that "the great line of centuries begins anew as a second Argo carries its chosen heroes to another war, to another shore". Ah, even recent historians describe the siege of Granada as a repetition of the Trojan wars. Alas, it's not history that repeats itself but we who do, as General Patton once said: "I die to be born a fighter, only to die again, once more." Anyway, my favourite lines on this matter are by Dante Gabriel Rossetti.'

Mendle stepped back from the webcam to recite:

I have been here before
But when or how I cannot tell;
I know the grass beyond my door,
The sweet keen smell,
The sight, the sound, the lights around the shore.

78

We praise the Great Director, and say with one another,
Augustus's dominion, nor conquering Alexander,
Nor Caesar's mighty genius, has ever had the glory
To lay a cornerstone at earth's extremest end.
VOC foundation stone address, Castle of Good Hope, Cape Town (1666)

'Who was Max Stibbe?' asked Sonja, when she reached Driebergen.

She'd caught the intercity train and was still puzzling over Clara's friend, the one who had identified the murder site fifty years ago.

'Stibbe joined a group of Dutch teachers and went to South Africa during the Apartheid era, hoping to make a difference in education,' explained Clara, setting the coffee percolator. 'At the time you could only teach blacks and whites together in private schools. So that's what they did. It was a social experiment. Yes, they were inspired by Dr Zeylmans van Emmichoven who visited Cape Town in 1961 but, sadly, passed away in his sleep the night before his return. Ten years later, after much struggle, Stibbe died there too. The ashes of both are scattered on Table Mountain.'

'So you all knew each other?'

'Oh yes, though we weren't all there at the same time. Some went for only a year. I stayed for fifteen, until 1999, when Mandela retired. His task was done and so was mine,' she paused, adding modestly, 'of course I had a far smaller role to play.'

Clara stooped under the pot's weight as she poured the Douwe Egberts, her left hand shaking as the cup rattled in its saucer.

'Thank you, no milk, please. So, Max Stibbe knew where Almeida was buried?'

'It seems so, he pointed it out to a colleague, alas, now also passed on. It was at the mouth of the Liesbeeck River.'

'You know historians have speculated on the location for decades, some even claiming it was on the beach at Saldanha or Hout Bay. So how did Stibbe know, was it intuition, or had he read about it?'

'Oh dear, that I don't recall, it was far too long ago. But Stibbe had an uncanny gift for finding things in nature. For instance, he'd say "let's go to Namibia and find rocks" and not "let's go look for rocks". He knew exactly where they were, as if they were waiting for him—'

'—an uncanny gift?' said Sonja, hesitating when there could be a plausible explanation. 'Perhaps he had prior knowledge of particular geological formations in that specific area? If you know what you're looking for—and have the right permit—you can still find diamonds scattered along the Skeleton Coast.'

'Perhaps,' said Clara, unperturbed.

They sat by her living room window. The apartment was crammed with original Sixties G-Plan furniture: upholstered chairs, standing lamps, fabric shades and a low sideboard with matching coffee tables. Her teak bookcase strained under the weight of traditional esoterica, contemporary literature and African history.

Sonja noticed a pile of books, neatly set aside, including pictures of Albuquerque and Almeida. She recognised the latter's portrait from the British Library: MS Sloane. There was also a copy of Almeida's signature, probably the one Stein hand-copied in Lisbon. Frail as she was, Clara had taken care to make Sonja's trip worthwhile.

'Tell me about your Zeevaarders Groep,' asked Sonja, 'about the friends you referred to on the phone?'

'Oh, yes. We were an informal group that met in Utrecht or Den Haag, otherwise Amsterdam, to discuss the Portuguese mission in Africa. We kept it going for years.'

'When was that, Clara?'

'During the early Eighties, before I went to teach in South Africa. *Een speculaasje?*' She rose to fetch the biscuit tin from the kitchen.

Sonja looked around the room. There were family snap-shots, a few portrait photographs, religious postcards, watercolour paintings and an array of precious stones.

Shuffling back, Clara said: 'I took the liberty of inviting a colleague to talk about the Odilian Grail saga. He's made a detailed study of

Stein's *Ninth Century* and our historical links to Charlemagne's court. So we can talk about Almeida in the meantime.'

Clara settled down in her beige leather armchair, a Gomme classic, while Sonja asked the question most vexing her that morning:

'I understand the link to Almeida, that is, as a previous incarnation of Stein; but you express a rather unusual empathy for Albuquerque. Personally, I sense no goodness in him. None. You obviously do?'

'Yes, because they made history together.'

'But unlike Almeida,' Sonja added, 'Albuquerque was ambitious, brutal and cruel. As a governor, he was both wilful and wily—'

'—and impulsive and temperamental, like Stibbe, so much so that Stibbe's own friends regarded him as Albuquerque reborn.'

Sonja was taken aback. Stibbe's name had come up twice in two days, and on both occasions he'd been linked to dramatic revelations. Could he be Albuquerque, returned? Or did this perpetuate a sense of continuity among his associates, a sort of self-fulfilling prophecy?

The downstairs-bell rang. Clara rose again:

'—that must be Frans Luthring. Let me open the door for him.'

Frans greeted Clara in the hallway, his soft sonorous voice carrying through to the living room. It was only when he walked in that Sonja saw how young he was: thirty-something, sturdy, and with flowing dark hair. *The Other Man from Volodya's funeral.*

'Hello, I'm Frans Luthring. I see we have some mutual friends. Why haven't we met before?'

'Sonja Haas, hello, I only met Clara today.'

'But, weren't you at—'

'—yes, I met Volodya on holiday in Portugal, last month. He came to see me in Leiden before his—'

'—he was here, in Holland?'

'Yes, unexpectedly, to see an antiquarian. We became acquainted through a mutual interest in Francisco d'Almeida.'

Settling her guests, Clara quietly announced:

'We were just talking about Almeida and Albuquerque—'

'—and their possible connection to Stein and Stibbe,' said Sonja, self-consciously fingering her hair into place.

'The Albuquerque-Stibbe connection has never been confirmed,' noted Clara. 'It's only speculation—'

'—well, I can ask a clairaudient to confirm the connection. There may be more to this…'

'Please do,' said Frans, 'it's always better to know more—not less.'

'I'll simply ask who Albuquerque was in the twentieth century. All we need is his name and where he lived.'

'Is that all?' Clara asked, her throat hoarse and dry.

'Yes, only *who* and *where*—'

'—where we die,' added Clara, shifting forward to save her voice, 'where we die is also where we plant a seed for our future.'

'For whose future, those passing on or those left behind?'

'Those coming back,' volunteered Frans, 'it has to do with how we choose to live again. For a better world, hopefully.'

Sonja fell silent, thinking about the bones in the SA Museum and what should be done to set the record straight and… and how much more pleasant this Frans was compared to Jason. Jason couldn't share what lay outside him, or what was of concern to others; nor had he the will to change himself or the world in which he lived. A frightful prospect for one so young, and likely to stay a bachelor.

Frans picked up the conversation, saying:

'How we die is significant—murder, suicide, old age, accident—as is how we suffer in life, not only in death, but through injury, infection or illness.'

'As with Tristão da Cunha,' tested Sonja, 'Manuel's first choice for Viceroy, until a temporary blindness made him step down?'

'Oh dear,' said Clara, concerned, 'then his sight was restored?'

'Yes,' answered Frans, passing Clara the biscuit tin, 'he sailed with Albuquerque's fleet a year later.'

'Furthermore, Albuquerque was sent to assume control after three years, in 1509, and to ensure that Almeida returned to Lisbon,' noted Sonja, 'but it seems the timing was in dispute.'

'Most commentators say Almeida refused to hand over his power to Albuquerque, but I suspect something else was at stake as they were always jousting with each other.'

He leant forward, offering Sonja the *speculaas*.

'That's a gallant way to put it, Frans. They were b-bl-bloody rivals who couldn't be left in the same room together—'

'—and yet fought side-by-side against Castile?'

'Yes, which is why I suspect a crisis in their relationship.'

'Why, because Albuquerque's family came from Spain? That's true, yes,' he acknowledged gently, 'but there were plenty of Portuguese men who crossed the line when offered something better elsewhere, as did Columbus and Magellan. The Spanish monarchs favoured those willing to sail West, rather than around Africa. Anyway, after taking Ormuz, Albuquerque's men deserted him—'

'—and fled to Cochin, where Almeida offered them protection and the promise of pardon?'

Frans smiled lightly:

'Yes, that seems to have been Almeida's only error of judgement. He accepted their testimony *ex parte*.'

Sonja began carefully. 'If—and I'm only speculating—if it was an error, then Almeida would have had good reason to pardon them. Ormuz was not part of Manuel's expansionist plans.'

'Agreed, Albuquerque wasn't told to seize Ormuz. He did so out "of his own free will".'

'Wait, can we return to what you said about injury and death?' redirected Sonja, 'I may not share your feelings about Albuquerque, but I am fascinated that he went lame and died bedridden.'

'He was sixty-two years old, wounded and sick, and a great Caesar.'

'Yes, perhaps unequalled among his contemporaries, but I believe he played a hand in Almeida's assassination. So it interests me, after what you said about injuries, that he lost the use of his one arm?'

79

Birth is not a beginning; death is not an end.
Chuang-tzŭ, *Keng Sang Ch'u* (c.300BCE)

It was Sale Night in Leiden and Sonja went into town to buy herself a
new Nespresso machine. After which, browsing at Selexyz, she found
Miriam Estensen's modest *Discovery: The Quest for the Great South Land.*
Paging through a chapter on Portuguese India, the last paragraph
grabbed her attention:

> Albuquerque died in 1515, as he returned ill to Goa after his
> second conquest of Ormuz, at the mouth of the Persian Gulf.
> He dictated a last letter to his king, had himself dressed in the
> velvet garb of a commander of the Order of Santiago, put on
> spurs and sword, and with a final effort stood to watch as his
> ship approached the stronghold he had created. He died
> shortly before dawn as the ship came to anchor.

Later, as she cycled home with her bags, a large black Lexus bolted
over Rapenburg bridge and raced towards her, forcing her to swerve
into the gutter. Her front wheel twisted against the curbstone as she
fell on the cobbles. The car disappeared across the river, leaving her
with a buckled Gazelle and a sprained ankle. It was Volodya's Lexus.
*So now Ben Mordechai drives a stolen car? Perhaps the police won't think I'm
paranoid after all...*

80

The essential teaching of this message is that the experience of life is itself a teaching, and that there is a transcendent and liberating truth to be realised beyond formulation: the truth of our identity, origin and destiny.

Laurence Oliver, *Out of Eden: The Book of El Aurenx* (2001)

From: jmendle@sam.org.za
Sent: Saturday, August 21, 11:06
To: sonja@homenet.nl
Subject: Past Lives, from El Aurenx

Dear Sonja

A brief reply to your request. Albuquerque was reincarnate as Lord Horatio Kitchener. Laurence says the similarities in their lives are apparent, if you care to look for them.

Kitchener (1850–1916) was a prominent British field marshal, diplomat and statesman. Pro-French in sentiment, he joined the Franco-Prussian War of 1870–71 whereby Alsace-Lorraine (including Le Mont Sainte-Odile) were ceded to Germany.

Significantly, the outcome united the new German Reich and set the stage for Kaiser Wilhelm II's expansionist programme of the early 1900s. Kitchener himself served in Sudan, South Africa, India, Egypt and, back in Britain, as Secretary of State for War at the onset of World War I.

So far, I've found several parallels:

First, Albuquerque and Kitchener were notoriously cruel and severely censured for their treatment of convicts and prisoners of war. They both served in India, reorganizing the naval and armed forces at their disposal and, above all, desired to be made Viceroy—a title that would elude them both in the end.

Second, they both censured the Jews and opposed the spread of Islam, becoming obsessed with their campaigns against the Ottoman Turks. Albuquerque wanted to raid Muhammad's tomb and present the sacred remains as ransom for the Holy Sepulchre in Jerusalem; whereas Kitchener had the remains of Muhammad Ahmad disinterred and scattered to terrorise the Dervish army around Khartoum. Bizarrely, Kitchener kept the Mahdi's skull as a war trophy.

Both died alone and at sea. Kitchener's body was never found. Churchill reported on both the Anglo-Dervish and Anglo-Boer wars and, curiously, found himself implicated in a conspiracy to kill Kitchener. Nothing was ever proven.

You'll find more in any Encyclopaedia.

Personally, I'd like to know who this Albuquerque-Kitchener was in a much earlier life. Was he perhaps one of Alexander's Companions; or with Nearchus when they set out to conquer India? No doubt Kitchener's name Horatio (aka Timekeeper) is some sort of clue?

Finally, I asked Laure what he knew or had heard about the historical figures in your research, and received the following karmic biographies from him. While some of it may be repetitive, I hope it adds to what you already know.

I attach the four pages below:

Karmic biographies

1. FRANCISCO d'ALMEIDA

Let it be known to Sonja that Francisco d'Almeida had been incarnate as Potiphera, an Egyptian priest from On (today Heliopolis), who gave his daughter in marriage to the patriarch Joseph. Other lives include Joseph of Arimathea, who brought Christ's blood-relic to Britain; then Bedivere, who carried the dying Arthur to the barge that transported his body to the isle of Avalon; and as Count Hugo of Tours from the great court of Charlemagne. As the lives of Joseph-Jesus-Arthur are linked to one and the same entity, so too is the soul of Francisco d'Almeida through his cycle of lives as Potiphera-Joseph-Bedivere. His karma is still connected to the karma of Jeshua Christos, the Logos incarnate.

2. CHARLES MARTEL

In his life as the Byzantine Emperor Constans II Pogonatus, he curbed the spread of Islam across North Africa. Similarly, as the Frankish ruler Charles Martel, he halted the advance of Abdul Rahman al Ghafiqi and ended Islam's progress over France. As an aside, for Sonja, Martel's success was largely due to the introduction of schooled horses and an armoured cavalry. While only a skirmish, his victory unified Christian warlords and prepared the ground for the Carolingian Empire—with his grandson Charlemagne becoming Holy Roman Emperor of the Franks. Martel would return to France as Cardinal de Richelieu and Charles de Gaul. As President, one of his great achievements was to unite France, and later, again, the French, by ceding independence to Algeria. From a karmic perspective, De Gaul's unexpected decision can be viewed as reparation for what he did as emperor Pogonatus in North Africa.

3. CHARLEMAGNE

Back in the distant past, during the first exodus of Israelites from Egypt, Charlemagne ruled as Amenhotep III. At this time Moses (then known as Osiraes) confiscated the Ark of Amen and bequeathed it to the Hebrews as the Ark of the Covenant. Charlemagne's other auspicious lives include Augustus Caesar, Marcus Aurelius, Constantine the Great, Frederick the Great and Gustavus Adolphus. It is worth noting here that Augustus Caesar founded the Roman Empire; and Charlemagne the Western European Empire, for which he is known as the "Father of Europe." The Cross of Lothair at Aachen Cathedral reveals this karmic link. He returned as Dag Hammarskjöld, the UN secretary general who intervened in several East-West crises and strove for the stabilisation of modern Africa. Through his past lives and up to the last, he pursued the Platonist ideal of a wise and just philosopher-king. Hammarskjöld was neither a king nor a ruler, but essentially a leader and a philosopher.

4. HENRY the NAVIGATOR	Prince Henry was the same soul as the biblical Simeon; the prophet Jonah; and the disciple Simon Peter, also called the "Big Fisherman". Jonah and Peter are associated with large fish and, to acknowledge his former incarnation, Jesus referred to Peter as "Bar-Jonah". Other lives include Bors and Hugues de Payen, both of whom were Grail Knights.
5. FERDINAND and ISABELLA	While King Ferdinand and Queen Isabella consolidated Spain into a single centralised power, much of their success may be attributed to Pope Alexander VI, the degenerate father of Cesare Borgia, about whom Sonja may want to know more. Their intolerance of both Jews and Muslims, which can be traced back in many past lives, suggests that they knew Abraham had reincarnated as the prophet Muhammad.
6. SOLOMON and the QUEEN OF SHEBA	Solomon and the Queen of Sheba were twin-souls who came together in several lives, notably as Thothmes and Hatshepsut, Simon Zelotes and Mary Salome, Lancelot and Elaine of Carbonek; Colonel Olcott and Madame Blavatsky. The son of King Solomon and the Queen of Sheba, Menelik, was the legendary first Emperor of Ethiopia who brought the Ark of the Covenant back to Egypt, and then on to Ethiopia, where it remains to this day. Menelik returned as Abraham Lincoln to campaign for America's Union and the abolition of slavery. Barack Obama is not therefore the first "black" president of America, nor will he be the last to claim the succession denied him in ancient Rome. It is an irony of history that Obama had been Britannicus, son of Emperor Claudius by his scandalous wife, Messalina, later killed for plotting a *coup d'état*. Claudius (Bill Clinton) remarried, seduced by his ambitious niece Julia Agrippina (Hillary Clinton), who persuaded him to disinherit his son in favour of her own, Nero. After usurping power, Nero had Britannicus killed on the eve of his fourteenth birthday, before he could reach traditional manhood. While Britannicus was a true heir who never came of age, the Clintons demonstrate how wrong corrects.
7. ANTONY and CLEOPATRA	Mark Antony had been General Lysimachus in Alexander's army and his love affair with Cleopatra—heir to the Ptolemaic dynasty and the last pharaoh of Egypt—was a re-enactment of their lives as the legendary lovers Aeneas and Dido, a Trojan Prince and the Queen of Carthage. Cleopatra herself claimed to be the reincarnation of Isis. They would ultimately reincarnate as Franklin and Eleanor Roosevelt. Franklin was elected to an unprecedented four terms as President of the United States. He died before the conclusion of World War II, during which he had been part of the Big Three triumvirate with Churchill and Stalin.

8. Sir WINSTON CHURCHILL	Churchill is celebrated for his leadership as Prime Minister during World War II and as Britain's greatest statesman of the twentieth century. He consciously evoked the Treaty of Windsor to ensure Portugal stayed with the Allies and did not join Hitler and Mussolini (unlike Spain which, unofficially, aligned itself with the Axis powers). As a scholar of history, he received the Nobel Prize for literature in 1953. Of interest here is that he wrote a study of John Churchill, First Duke of Marlborough, an ancestor and his previous incarnation. Lord Marlborough became commander-in-chief of the combined English and Dutch armies and is considered one of the great military leaders of modern history. Before this he was William the Lion, King of Scotland; and Alfred the Great, a descendant of Charlemagne, the first King of the English. He is thus, correctly, called "the Greatest Briton". As Clovis I of the Franks, he was the first important Merovingian ruler and the one who made Paris his capital. He married the Burgundian Princess, Clotilda (later St Clotilda) who converted him, and thereby the Franks, to Christianity. He thus laid the foundation stone for the Holy Roman Empire under Charlemagne. Sonja may want to note that Churchill fought in British India and served as a war-correspondent during Kitchener's campaigns in Sudan and South Africa.
9. ADOLF HITLER	Known as Belzebul of Atlantis, he was reborn as Nimrod the biblical tyrant-king of Mesopotamia; then as Nebuchadnezzar the Babylonian warlord who seized Jerusalem and banished the Jews to Babylon; and, again, as the vainglorious Herod the Great, King of Judea, who rebuilt the Temple of Jerusalem. He later returned as Landulf II of Capua, a sorcerer of great evil; and later still, as Philip II of Spain, who used the Inquisition as a regime for ruthless oppression.
10. BENITO MUSSOLINI	Emperor Nero (the son of Julia Agrippina), was reborn as Benito Mussolini and became, again, a tyrant and megalomaniacal urban planner. After abusing the citizens and victims of Rome, both Nero and Mussolini were briefly imprisoned on Ponza Island. Nero was despised for his cruelty and the persecution of Christians, committing suicide after the Senate declared him an enemy of the State. He died fearing he would be torn to pieces. In turn, Mussolini was hated for his denial of human freedoms and, trying to escape, was shot and killed—his mutilated body given no rest for the following ten years. Infamously, both despots left their mark on the Eternal City.

11. JOSEF STALIN	Stalin had been Ivan the Terrible, first Tsar of All Russia, who created a new state but is remembered instead for his cruelty. In an earlier life he invaded the Land of Rus as the tyrant Tamerlane, or Timur, a former descendant of Mongol conquerors who married into the family of the late Genghis Khan.
12. NAPOLEON BONAPARTE	Napoleon Bonaparte, "Man of Destiny", rose to become Emperor of the French and went on to conquer almost all Europe. As one of history's greatest military leaders he inaugurated, following the French Revolution, a new world order of constitutional law—the *Code Napoléon*—enacting the liberty and equality of its citizens, including the freedom of religion. Napoleon was nevertheless an autocratic tyrant acting under a cloak of democratic government. This was not his first incarnation on French soil, however, as he had previously been King Philip IV of France, infamous for his suppression of the Knights Templar. In turn, Philip IV had been Genghis Khan and also, as another irony of history, the notorious Attila the Hun. Notably, both Genghis and Attila are remembered for being short in stature, broad-chested, and having a large head. Moreover, what Attila overran, Napoleon would try to overrule. Sensing his karmic kinship to other great conquerors, Napoleon exhorted others to "Read over and over again the campaigns of Alexander, Hannibal, Caesar, Gustavus, Turenne, Eugene and Frederic... This is the only way to become a great general and master the secrets of the art of war." At the time, he claimed to be the reincarnation of Julius Caesar and Charlemagne, and was not far wrong, having been Cesare (Caesar) Borgia, son of Pope Alexander VI, commander of the papal armies and an eminent statesman; as well as the High Priest of Israel, Caiaphas, who betrayed Jesus to the Romans. Further back in time he was hailed as *Neapollyon*—the new Apollyon, the "Destroyer" of Atlantis.

PS: Contrary to conventional wisdom, size is no indicator of evil or ambition. Laurence is a mere 5'1" and the humblest man I've ever met. But seriously, having once poisoned Britannicus, Nero may try it again with Barack Obama. The poisoner was a woman from Gaul, a Celtic Druid called Locusta... Anyway, enough for now.

If you want more, let me know.

JM

81

*The history of the Grail is the history of the world. And
the history of the world is the history of East and West.*
Walter Johannes Stein, *The Ninth Century and the Holy Grail* (1928)

Sonja and Frans met in the glass-covered café overlooking the Winter
Garden of the Hortus. Her swollen ankle felt the cold. It seemed a
fitting place to recall their mutual acquaintance, Volodya Vasilevsky,
and his ogrish assassin.

'The last time I was here, two weeks ago, Volodya spoke about the
other lives of Aristotle and Alexander. I regret not asking what he
knew about his own past—but then I probably lacked conviction.'

Frans paused, choosing his words carefully:

'Volodya once told me he was karmically connected to Malik Áyáz,
a Jew or Russian slave, possibly from Crimea, who became Governor
of the port at Diu.'

Again, one who never went to sea?

'Well, he never mentioned it, though I know of Malik's intervention
and that it caused Lourenço's death. Perhaps this explains Volodya's
obsession with Almeida's commission and how he tried to put things
right between them. Perhaps he intended to do some good with the
treatise after all?'

'Yes, and from what I knew of him, he had the potential to do so.'

'Wait, what about Malik's enslavement?'

'Well, the Ottoman sultanate imported Russian and African slaves,
twenty thousand annually, to supplement his army and navy.'

'So Volodya's problems stem from a time before the Tsar's Fleet?'

'As did his problems with women,' said Frans, his voice deepening, 'he was also involved with Empress Theodora.'

Mendle had warned her of this Byzantine tryst with Theodora.

'I guess that's why they keep coming back as men... Anyway, what about the women in Stein's life? Didn't he have two wives and a daughter—like Almeida?'

'Yes, while in Portugal Stein wrote to his first wife, Nora, every day. It was like a diary. One of these letters was about their daughter, Clarissa Johanna. Stein felt that she had been Juâna la Beltraneja, the one sent to the Convento de Santa Clara at Santarém.'

'Wait, wait, wasn't she "retired" for refusing to marry Ferdinand and Isabella's son?'

'Yes, well, that's what Stein felt. He also believed that his brother Friedrich, to whom Nora was deeply attached, had been Almeida's son Lourenço. Friedrich was killed on the Russian front when, in the face of certain death, he let his men retreat while holding the line, blowing himself up to save them. It's the same design in his two lives.'

'Did Volodya say anything about Portugal's Principal Design?'

'You mean the East-West Grail quest?' asked Frans, rhetorically. 'Yes, he believed the division between East and West dated back to Atlantis, to a time when the centre of civilisation collapsed and only the far-flung colonies survived. Historically, this geo-political design originated when explorers set forth to re-unite the dispersed world. They became the precursors of Alexander the Great, Prince Henry and Dag Hammarskjöld—to name but three Seekers of the World.'

'Volodya and I never discussed Atlantis or the mass migrations, but I did hear him say that the Grail quest began as a longing for the Lost Paradise?'

'Yes, and since then the world has been separated by moon cults and sun worshippers—of which Christianity is a recent consequence of the latter—the Grail quest became the search for the Light,' he halted, 'I'm sorry, this is not supposed to be a sermon.'

She laughed. 'No, no but I think you missed your vocation.'

Frans seemed amused.

'I always wanted to be a minister, so I studied theology at Utrecht. However, I soon realised my real interest lay in esoteric Christianity. That's when I met Volodya.'

'And then?'

'Volodya introduced me to the esoteric writings of Stein, especially his work in education, and so I became a school teacher instead.'

'Do you have any children?'

'None of my own—perhaps because I'm unmarried—but teaching is what I do best. Children bring out the best in me.'

'Do they?' she smiled, clumsily. 'Perhaps I should try some day.'

His sturdy expression softened into a smile:

'Children really do change the world—like Romulus and Remus, Moses, Joan of Arc and Kaspar Hauser—or young Odilia, of course. They all left their mark on history.'

'Actually, I wanted to discuss the Odilian Grail saga.'

'That's what I guessed when you suggested coffee. Well then, as we know, both Stein and Volodya shared a mutual interest in Odilia and visited the Abbaye d'Andlau—'

'—with the spring under its crypt?'

'Yes. There's an old carved stone, like the navel-stone or *omphâlos* at Delphi, which plugs the sacred source. The sculptured she-bear could be antique too. The Delphic Oracle lost its power when European Christianity advanced and astrology became the more popular form of prophecy. Likewise, Odilia's well is stilled today; its voice muted by the sound of passing tour busses—'

'—and caravan campers from Holland. I see you have Stein's book. May I look?'

Frans handed her a cloth-bound edition of *The Ninth Century and the Holy Grail*. It was a heavy German tome with stiff, rough-edged pages that turned slowly. Inside she found the anagram:

$$s \; o \, d \, i \, l \, e = s \, o \, l \quad d \, e \, i$$

A Girl of the Light? Sonja took it personally, having spent many of her childhood holidays at Luz, near Lagos, a place itself named for the light. A similar anagram, encircling a pentagram, stood in the dossier. She showed Frans the two related pages, with the pictures of Odilia.

He was keen to see more and, while browsing through the dossier, explained how Odilia had helped introduce Grail Christianity to the West. This esoteric wisdom laid the foundation for a hybrid spirituality and philosophy in the Renaissance.

'So who was Odilia, exactly?'

'Literally? The daughter of Duke Eticho.' Frans tilted his head, not sure if that's what she had asked.

'Yes, but besides her Carolinian connections?'

'But this *is* what makes Odilia so important. The royal houses of Europe still include her as an early relative—especially in the Dutch, French and German bloodlines. Next time you visit Driebergen, I'll show you the imperial family tree. I live behind the Kaiser's former estate, in a woodcutter's cottage, once used by the ageing emperor.'

'The exiled Wilhelm?'

'Yes. He was a relative of Queen Wilhelmina.'

'Really?'

'Wilhelm and Wilhelmina trace a common ancestry back to the House of Orange-Nassau and, against her better judgement—and Wilhelmina was a sober judge of character—she granted him exile in Holland after WWI. He lived at Huis Doorn for twenty-one years, until his death in 1941, having never returned to Germany. He is entombed on the estate, above ground, in a modest mausoleum, after saying he'd only return when his country needed its Kaiser back.'

'But what's the connection to Grail Christianity? If the royal houses of Europe believed they shared a common ancestor going back to Charlemagne, how does that make Odilia special?'

Frans paused, a light smile on his lips:

'You may think it absurd, but Kaiser Wilhelm had been her father, Duke Eticho, hence his predilection for the German federal states and his idealization of Frederick the Great, the "Soldier-King". The federal states incorporated Alsace-Lorraine and, to reinforce these bonds, Wilhelm recreated a castle to immortalize German culture in medieval Alsace. Chateau Haut-Koenigsbourg and the convent of Sainte-Odile sit on neighbouring hills. Uncanny, don't you think, that Eticho-Wilhelm converted two castles, one around 700, the other in 1900, thinking each time this would improve his image? He was a vainglorious soul. Anyway, he dedicated Huis Doorn to his Prussian ancestor, Frederick. Please, Wilhelm is not my type of hero, nor do I favour his taste for bloodhounds, hunting or wood-chopping. Despite its beautiful roses, Huis Doorn remains a thorn in Dutch society. However, as a residence-cum-museum of the last German Emperor, it marks an interesting intersection in modern history.'

Sonja spilt her coffee: a royal residence and house-museum. It was exactly what Volodya had alluded to!

82

Huis Doorn marks a crossroads in the history of twentieth century Europe... No other spot is so symbolic for relations between the Netherlands and neighbouring Germany.

Dick Verroen, *Huis Doorn: Residence-in-exile* (2005)

Later that week, after the cold front had passed, Sonja returned to Driebergen to see Huis Doorn. Frans was waiting at the station with a friendly smile, a supportive arm, and a well-warmed car. He'd also pushed her seat back, attentively she thought, as Doorn was a mere ten minutes away. Even when driven there slowly.

'How's your ankle?' he asked, easing the car into gear.

'Oké, thanks, as long as I watch my balance and travel light.'

She adjusted her seat-belt.

'Well, Kaiser Wilhelm never travelled light. A hundred years ago five train-loads arrived to fill Huis Doorn: fifty-nine wagons in all. His private possessions came from his former palaces in Potsdam and Berlin—including his books, paintings, miniatures and jewels—not to mention the gifts he'd collected over three decades as Emperor.'

'And his wardrobe; I heard he dressed for every occasion, including morning prayers.'

'Yes, and for the camera too. They say he was the first media star and loved to be filmed. Cinema was still very new and, coincidently, the property was purchased from a grand-aunt of Audrey Hepburn.'

'Wait, first explain why Volodya wanted me to come here.'

Turning right, toward Doorn, Frans gathered his thoughts:

'It was rebuilt in 1350 as a turreted castle—after fire destroyed the original—and then as a neo-classicist country house until, in 1919, it was redone as the residence-in-exile for Kaiser Wilhelm's family. The royal household required electricity, hot water, flushing toilets and private bathrooms. His servants were given a separate staircase with new quarters in the converted attic.'

'*Natuurlijk*, an essential arrangement for a happy household.'

'Following Wilhelm's death and the family's departure, his estate remained virtually intact during the German Occupation. However, after WWII the property and its inventory were confiscated by the Dutch. With a few exceptions, little has changed, as you'll see for yourself. But first, let's see how well you can walk?'

He parked at the so-called Renaissance Gatehouse with its brick-gabled façade and flag-shuttered windows. Here, under the port, she halted before a pair of hirsute figures bearing the royal badge. The Wild Ones again. *So pagans protected this perimeter too.*

Taking Sonja by the arm, he led her along a meandering footpath. The estate graced a nineteenth-century English landscaped garden with tree-lined lawns and flowing flower-beds.

'To keep himself fit, the Kaiser cut down thousands of trees and split millions of logs, building vast stacks of firewood while denuding an entire forest in the process.' Frans raised his hand to point. 'See those trees over there? It's taken two generations for them to recover.'

Leading her gently on, he compared Wilhelm's castle to Odilia's convent, hinting that both were linked to Aristotle's manuscript.

'I thought the convent was famous for its long-lost *Hortus deliciarum*, another work altogether—and of course, for the tomb of Odilia.'

'Yes, plus the Holy Blood relic from Charlemagne's court—'

'—which five Santiago knights brought there in secret.'

'On the back of a camel, like the one shown in the dossier. There's still a path up to the Odilienberg called the Way of the Camel.'

'Volodya had mentioned it too, adding that an anonymous woman was murdered in the church at Andlau.'

Her foot hurt. Frans slowed down so she could lean on him.

'Yes, killed in the Abbaye d'Andlau for her part in the East-West saga. She was a secret courier. Unnamed.'

'Well, Jason and I called her Elza.'

'After Alsace, yes, a good pseudonym. Then you know about Eliza von Moltke, the friend of Walter Johannes Stein and Rudolf Steiner?'

'No, why?'

'Rudolf Steiner told Eliza von Moltke that she'd been Odilia in an earlier life and had, as the "Girl of the Light", sought refuge from her father at the Ermitage. Eticho's dukedom lay between the Vosges and the Rhine, today Alsace proper, though may not have reached as far south as Arlesheim. Or, at least, he'd lost all favour in the region after oppressing its people and devastating their valley. He was notoriously wicked. I think that's why Odilia felt safe there and, in turn, why the farms around Arlesheim became the property of Mont Sainte-Odile. As a private land holder, the convent could offer them her protection. Odilia also left her traces at the St-Odilienberg Klooster, Roermond, up against the German border, where I first went to school.'

She was enchanted by her sturdy, erudite and attentive companion; and the youthful air that surrounded him.

'Frans, you said Duke Eticho returned as Kaiser Wilhelm?'

'According to Steiner, yes, and I suspect the Kaiser's obsession with wood-chopping was a revenge on the oracular tree spirits from his past. Odilia fled to the forest, remember, to escape his wrath. Steiner also told Eliza that her husband, Helmuth Count von Moltke, had been Odilia's brother Hugo—'

'—the one who had betrayed their father? How did Count Moltke and the Kaiser deal with their karma in the twentieth century?'

'Good question. Eticho and Hugo's karma was not resolved, only repeated during WWI. After a difference of opinion, the Kaiser asked Count Moltke to resign as his Chief of General Staff. Hugo-Helmuth thus followed his conscience, twice, only to be rejected by the same man each time. What's more, Odilia was healed by a Celtic bishop. Did you know that Charlemagne's maternal grandfather was a Celtic Christian and that Irish monks not only attended his court in Aachen, but first brought Christianity to Alsace? Charlemagne's grandfather, Count Charibert, founded twelve Irish-Celtic monasteries and was already aware of Odilia's significance in the eighth century.'

'Charibert?'

'Charibert was an initiate, better known in his next life as Christian Rosenkreuz. Count Hugo of Tours, a son in the House of Etichonen, was related to Odilia and shared this connection. Charibert was the first to travel to Baghdad, in 768, followed by Hugo in 811. Abbasid Baghdad had become a centre of learning with its hospital, library and observatory. There was a brief period of peace, prosperity and unity—a period in which caliph Haroun al-Rashid and Charlemagne promoted technological and economic exchange, including a hostel for Christian pilgrims going to Jerusalem. The Academy of al-Rashid became a brilliant conduit for Aristotelianism in the Arab-Muslim world. Al-Rashid came back as Francis Bacon, the fountainhead of modern scientific empiricism, and was directed by the spirit that worked through the man we know as Shakespeare today.'

Overwhelmed, Sonja deflected:

'If Abraham really did return as Muhammad, then the Middle East conflict must be one of the greatest ironies of all time—what a pity the wrongs in life can't be corrected sooner.'

'Like Sagres, the monumental efforts of Baghdad have been revised by historians. They say the Bayt al-Hikmah, or the House of Science, was no more than a grand depot or bureau for copyists.'

She stopped by the front steps to rest again. He continued:

'Remember, from an acorn the mighty oak will grow; or, to use a modern metaphor, from the flapping butterfly a mighty storm shall blow. So, gently forward, Sonja. It was here, in Baghdad, that Greek and Persian manuscripts were assembled and translated into Arabic, and where the Arab world intersected with Grail Christianity. Odilia was born around 660—or, at least, before the advent of 666—as an impulse against the dark forces of the Apocalyptic Beast who worked through the Academy of Gondishapur, Iran, to permeate the empire in the East. It's in this Odilian-light that Almeida's actions should be judged. His brutal attacks on Muslims in Granada, Kilwa, Mombasa, and also in India, were directed against this evil force—not against the people themselves. This ever-recurrent force usually manifests in the guise of a new religion, sect or cult. I believe Almeida made contact with an esoteric stream from Arabia in the same way that he gained access to it in Granada—that is, through friendship. It was also he who, in his former life as Hugo of Tours, brought the Holy Blood relic to the Odilienberg on the back of that camel. There are clues to be found in the surrounding village chapels.'

They entered the house via the basement steps, in time to join the final tour for the afternoon. Trailing behind a German group, Frans explained how Aristotle's manuscript was mislaid, or rather forgotten, inside Huis Doorn:

'I heard that it was in the attic, hidden among his antiquities, which were never unpacked. He had no space in his study, so they remained upstairs, untouched. I think that is why Volodya sent you here.'

Reaching the first room, opposite the Kaiser's study, Frans pointed out the imperial family tree—and true to his word—the genealogist had put Odilia on a short low branch, and Eticho at its stem.

The history of the world is but the biography of great men.
Thomas Carlyle, *On Heroes, Hero-Worship and the Heroic in History* (1840)

Frans and Sonja visited Huis Doorn the following Friday (carrying two inconspicuous torches in their pockets), and slipped in before the doors closed. Intent on finding the Kaiser's antiquities, they mingled with the last visitors until they alone were left upstairs. They then headed for the Silver Room, as planned, to hide behind the display cabinet containing the imperial dinner service. The towering cabinet stood across a corner, with enough space for them both to wedge behind, against the wall. No one walking by would be any the wiser.

Their plan was reckless yet modest, as they only wanted to search the attic. Overnight. More so, their crime was set in motion with alarming ease, as happens all too frequently in law-abiding societies.

What would my colleagues say now?

Sonja was too far gone to worry about it any more. She'd deal with the fall out at the university afterwards. Anyway, Frans had agreed to submit whatever they found, so that the authorities could dispose of the "loot" appropriately. It was a lesson they'd learnt from Almeida.

The building was secured from outside, around the perimeter, and not within—where the lonely ghost of Empress Dona still lingered. They were safe, as long as they kept quiet and remained out of sight.

Once the guards had completed their rounds, Frans whispered:

'Given the strict rules of separation between local staff and the royal family, each with their own staircase, the converted attic provided a

perfect place for the Kaiser to store his archaeological antiquities—
including a cache for his priceless manuscript.'

'*Really?* Surely it was no place for an ex-Emperor to visit alone, in
secret, without arousing suspicion? Even if he was having an affair,
which I doubt, the attic was not the place for a hurried escape.'

He assured her: 'It's here, in the attic, that's what Clara told me.'

'Oké, but I imagine the Kaiser would want to take the manuscript
out from time to time, to feel its vellum or smell the leather. A more
suitable place would have been his vestibule, surely? It was accessible,
yet private and—as last week's museum guide told us—a place where
he led his staff and family in worship every morning. It was also
where he could survey his secret with a vigilant eye while others had
theirs closed in prayer.'

Frans put a finger to her lips.

'Softly now. They seem to have left downstairs. Shall we start?'

'Fine, I'm right behind you.'

Holding on to his belt, she crept out and followed him to the stairs.
Here he took her hand and, without a word, tiptoed up the last steps.
The Ancestral Spirits remained silent. The Kaiserin too. Reaching
the top, Frans found the little service door unlocked (a fire precau-
tion, he'd observed beforehand). It led to an unfurnished, airless attic.

They searched for an hour-or-more, but there was nothing to find:
no hidden box, no concealed trapdoor, no hollow wall—only pallets
stacked with ageing catalogues and drying flower bulbs.

But no lost manuscript. No lecture notes. No secret.

So, left without alternatives, they returned to the stairs and waited
for morning to arrive. To pass the time, Frans told her about the real-
life figures behind the Grail story, such as the historic Parsifal and his
relationship to Landulf II of Capua—also known as Clinschor—the
villain from Sicily. Sonja vaguely recalled that he had come back as
Adolf Hitler, or so she'd garnered from the dossier's *Karmic biographies*.

She heard Frans saying that under the influence of Count Landulf,
Pope Nicholas I had been drawn to the dark circle of bishops from
Capua and, simultaneously, to the light emanating from the Odilien-
berg—itself an old Celtic solar mystery centre:

'In the end, Pope Nicholas split Europe by separating the mystical
liturgy of the Eastern Orthodox church, which could still induce deep
spiritual experiences, from the sacred kinship and aristocratic Grail

traditions of the West, thus positioning Rome-Italy-Central Europe as the new axis for Christendom…'

The hours passed as in a dream, while her head swirled with all this detail. According to Frans, the Fourth Councils of Constantinople in 869 signalled the final break between East and West. It was the year in which Pope Nicholas condemned the mystic three-fold man and proclaimed, instead, that humans had only a body and a soul—with no separate spirit. In short, there was *no reincarnating spirit*.

'I think that's why the Templar seal shows two knights on one horse —the first is our living soul, the second the spirit that inspires us.'

Such historical-esoteric matters had not meant much to her before. Now it drew things into place like the invisible ends of a knot.

According to Clara, Frans later continued, the Kaiser wanted to use Aristotle's treatise in secret negotiations with the British. It would be his trump card at the negotiating table, as he needed Churchill's support for his restoration of the Prussian monarchy. And like the Kaiser's father, Churchill was an alleged Masonic Grand Master.

'Allegedly?'

'No, he was a mere office bearer of the Lodge, and then only for a short period in his early career, having resigned before WWI. So any conspiracy theory is unlikely. Of far greater importance to the Kaiser were Churchill's political allies in Britain and America.'

'But where's the connection to Almeida?'

She'd lost the Anglophile thread.

'Well, Stein had a secret meeting with Churchill, around 1939, in which he discussed the ominous forces behind Hitler's rise to power. Churchill, it seems, was interested in "manipulating" Nazi occultism. After their meeting, Stein put his notes in a trunk and shipped them off for safekeeping—at least until the war ended—but the trunk was washed overboard during the Channel crossing. Just before his death, Stein said he would return by the new millennium and, of course, continue his research. For this he would need those notes again and so, I suspect, the dossier is an attempt to reconstruct what was in that trunk. Look at his initials on the cover flap: WJS.'

True, how obvious—Walter Johannes Stein—yet she'd failed to see it herself. She sat silently, questioning her own *histoire* and the people she had contact with since finding the skull: Prof Mendle and Jason, Volodya, and now this handsome Frans Luthring. Bart too, as their relationship had recently been re-established. She wondered what sort of past they all shared; or what future they may have together?

O Providentia!

It was a long wait, and the stairs became ever harder as the minutes turned to hours. She leant her head on his shoulder and drifted off. Intermittently.

He woke her at first light and led the way back to the silver cabinet. Squeezing side-ways against the wall, he pressed in close beside her. *Next time, remember a toothbrush!*

At 10:15, fifteen minutes after the first visitors arrived, they slipped out via the basement—the same way they'd entered the day before.

As they stepped into the sunlight, momentarily blinded, the Black Goliath leapt down from where he'd been hiding.

He had waited for them all night.

Unobserved, he'd concealed himself on the forecourt stairs (now no longer in use), and had watched everyone coming and going.

Leaping over the balustrade, he grabbed Sonja's backpack by its strap. She screamed, thinking he was after the treatise:

'Let go, *verdomme!* We don't have it!'

'*Le dossier, nyet?*'

'No, let go!'

The strap tore loose as she ripped her backpack free. He stumbled, off balance, falling forward as he turned. His head struck the bottom step, face first, as he hit the stone.

A startled guard rushed forward, yelling as he came. Frans grabbed Sonja's arm and swung her round, pulling her close to him. She peered over his shoulder as the uniform passed in a blur of blue.

They, at least, were safe. Frans turned her away as a second guard scrambled up to the body. Ben Mordechai lay face-down, motionless, a dark inky pool spreading across the pitted stonework.

Sonja buried her head in Frans's shoulder, not wanting to see the ogre's face as the guards rolled him over. She already knew that his jaw had been smashed wide open.

In the commotion that followed, caused by a bus-load of frightened schoolchildren, Frans led her behind the row of trees and back to the Renaissance Gatehouse. The Forest Ones had protected her, again.

*It seemed like the hand of God suddenly appeared
to set matters right where we had gone wrong.*

Field Marshal Lord Alanbrooke, *War Diaries 1939–1945* (2003)

From: jmendle@sam.org.za
Sent: Saturday, September 4, 12:38
To: sonja@homenet.nl
Subject: Almeida and El Alamein
Dear Sonja

While Almeida's murder has drawn your attention to a long-lost manuscript which, dare I say it, may never be found, the messages from Laurence demonstrate how European history—and Africa's future—have been directed at certain junctures, as if a helping hand reset critical events at crucial times. One striking example, for which Laure has also provided the karmic background, was the miraculous intervention that changed the outcome of World War II. You may want to compare this to Almeida's death afterwards—but first, the historical facts:

In the early afternoon of 7 August 1942, only hours after his appointment as the new British commander in North Africa, William Gott was killed on a "safe" flight path over Egypt. Shot by a stray German pilot, Gott's unescorted plane crash-landed in the western desert. Unable to free himself from the burning wreck, Gott was consumed in the blaze.

With much difficulty, deliberations resumed in Cairo until the inexorable Churchill listened to his senior military advisors— especially Chief of the Imperial General Staff, Sir Alan Brooke (who would afterwards describe Churchill as "a genius mixed with an astonishing lack of vision"). Be that as it may, Field Marshal Montgomery was chosen to command the 8th Army with immediate effect and, only three months later, defeated Rommel at the second battle of El Alamein. By the way, Sonja, more Germans were captured at Tunisia than those taken after Stalingrad, and that excluded all the Italians! The victory was a turning point for the Allies as it prevented the Axis powers from taking the Middle East. Had Rommel seized the Suez Canal and the Iraqi oilfields, who knows, the world would be a very different place today.

In his war-time diaries, written secretly at night, Alan Brooke singled out the momentousness of this event:

"Looking back at what occurred at Alamein, and after it, I am convinced that the whole course of the war might well have been altered if Gott had been in command of the 8th Army. In his tired condition, I do not think he had the energy or vitality to stage and fight this battle as Monty did."

Now then, here's what Laurence says about the joint lives of Montgomery and Rommel.

El Alamein and D'Almeida

Montgomery of Alamein (1887–1976) was previously incarnate as Scipio Africanus of Rome; and Erwin Rommel (1891–1944) as the famous Carthaginian, Hannibal, the "father of strategy". As already shown, ancient Rome bequeathed several notable leaders to our era. Though not often the case, there are some astonishing parallels between their lives, as if much the same drama needed to be re-enacted. As with Almeida's death, a helping hand redirects our actions and achievements during historical junctures. This ensures that grand scale imbalances between political powers, or between the forces of evil and our will for freedom, can be corrected from time to time.

Scipio Africanus the Elder (234–183BCE) was the greatest Roman general before Julius Caesar. He lived in the time of Cato the Elder, who was his public enemy. During the Second Punic War, Scipio triumphed over Hannibal the Carthaginian (247–182BCE). Hannibal, of course, was the celebrated son of Hamilcar Barca, and championed his father's cause against Rome by crossing the Alps with an army of mighty elephants. He inflicted crushing defeats on the generals sent against him, including Scipio, but was eventually beaten back. Scipio raised a volunteer army and set about preparing a counter-invasion from Sicily. He wanted to take the war to the desert while Hannibal, with an exhausted and depleted army, was confined to the south-western toe of Italy. However, it took two years before Scipio could attack Carthage, by which time Hannibal had returned to take charge of the city's preparations and its defences. With Hannibal back, negotiations were terminated.

By late October 202, Scipio had routed the Carthaginians but unexpectedly spared the city. He dictated moderate terms of submission and allowed Hannibal to remain as its civic leader.

Once again Carthage prospered as the commercial capital of the western Mediterranean, so much so that at Cato's behest, the aristocracy of Rome demanded its destruction. Hannibal fled Carthage and sought refuge with Syrian king Antiochus III, at Ephesus. Decades later, when the Romans demanded his extradition, Hannibal committed suicide by poisoning.

As Laure says, Scipio returned as Montgomery and confronted his old nemesis again in North Africa. Hannibal, now as Field Marshal Erwin Rommel, was renowned for his desert warfare. The battle of El Alamein began in 1942, once more October, and Montgomery triumphed, forcing Rommel's Afrika Korps to surrender early the next year. In 1945 Rommel was accused of complicity in a plot to assassinate Hitler and, rather than go on trial, chose to commit suicide by taking cyanide. Hannibal-Rommel thus took his own life, twice, by swallowing poison.

Hannibal's brother Hasdrubal Barca, says Laurence, returned as General George S Patton (1885–1945) who commanded the US forces in North Africa, though he never engaged Rommel in direct combat. He was eccentric and outspoken in his beliefs on reincarnation; amusing his men with tales of ancient desert battles. Ironically, his egotism let him see himself in the role of Hannibal, rather than as the younger brother Hasdrubal. As you know, their father Hamilcar was one of the four Archons.

Laurence also reminded me that General JC Smuts had been Cato the Elder, Scipio's vociferous opponent during his North African campaign. Smuts attended the Allies' deliberations in Cairo and, while his actual role is not clear, it seems he backed Brooke's nomination for Monty. Thus, by supporting Monty, Smuts made good for what he did as Cato, when he actively opposed Scipio in Rome. By the way, if Churchill had been killed, Smuts may have become Prime Minister of Britain.

Gott's gruesome death—trapped inside the burning fuselage—was vividly retold in *Fire in the Night* by Colin Smith: "Out of these ashes would arise 1st Viscount Montgomery of Alamein, Britain's best known and, for a while, most popular soldier since Wellington and always Brooke's first choice for the job."

Lastly, you remember Trevor Ravenscroft? His *Spear of Destiny* describes how, after seeing Wagner's *Parsifal*, Hitler became obsessed with the Grail quest, its relics and its sites—including the cult of a sacred spear and secret society. The Führer tried to turn the Bayreuth Master into a party hero by using his last operas to fuel the gospel of National Socialism. Ravenscroft claims that Hitler committed suicide on hearing how Patton's men had seized the spear in Nuremberg. Well, true or not, he does tell the story of a chain of men who possessed the Spear, from Herod to Hitler, and how each sought to change history by wielding its occult power. Furthermore, he seems to hint at the same karmic Herod-Hitler connection.

Ravenscroft says many things, some of which are blatant lies, but what is less known, and for you perhaps important, is that he was sent to assassinate Rommel in Tunisia. The raid failed when his commando unit was captured. As a POW (1941–45), he escaped thrice but was recaptured each time. After the war he sought treatment in London from Stein, with whom he went on to study for twelve years. His alcoholism, Ravenscroft alleged, was the result of his wartime torture in Germany.

'It's important for us,' Mendle told her later, 'to see these past lives in their proper context. As Churchill himself said: "He must indeed have a blind soul who cannot see that some great purpose and design is being worked out here below, of which we have the honour to be the faithful servants." This is reflected in Churchill's own past lives. So too with Alexander, whose nature as a military leader and empire builder is embedded in the testimonies of his biographers—including those who wrote about Sertorius (the "New Hannibal"), Trajan and Belisarius. The chronicles of Alexander's diverse incarnations, though written independently, record his role in establishing a cosmopolitan culture and common heritage. Whatever contemporary historians say about him as a mere vagabond from the mountains, his collective lives do prove otherwise.'

Like Almeida and Stein? She could see from Stein's life, set against the rising tide of National Socialism, that he strove for an independent world-economic organisation—a commonwealth of economies that would unite East and West. To his mind, such an organisation would lend assistance to the distribution of raw materials and their means of exchange; foster the international distribution of labour; and create an equilibrium between agricultural and industrial nations.

Stein's plan for economic unity received attention from the Belgian and Dutch royal families and, with support from King Leopold III and Queen Wilhelmina, eventually contributed to the formation of a Benelux alliance. Indirectly, Stein's pragmatic proposals laid one of the foundation stones for the European Union—and behind this lay the idea of Rudolf Steiner's three-fold social order.

While willing to accept Stein's "historical conscience" and the idea that karma *does* make history—that, yes, we *do* make things happen—Sonja remained undecided on the issue of reincarnation and the eternal return. As yet, she'd not spoken to Mendle about Almeida's priesthood in ancient Egypt, or about the adjacent karma of Europe's political leadership. Such matters would have to wait.

However, what struck her now as significant was Alan Brooke's remark that an external hand can set matters right, at least from time to time. Spoken by a veteran soldier and a sober military advisor—one who was also Chief of the Imperial General Staff—this was the independent confirmation she had needed.

What could be next?

85

So as through a glass, and darkly
The age long strife I see
Where I fought in many guises,
Many names, but always me.
General George S Patton, *Through a Glass, Darkly* (1922)

From: jmendle@sam.org.za
Sent: Sunday, September 5, 11:03
To: sonja@homenet.nl
Subject: Lost Atlantis, from El Aurenx
Dear Sonja
Greetings again from Cape Town, where a late winter lingers.
Laurence asked me to pass this on to you, saying you'd know
what to do with it when the time is right.

Lost Atlantis
I am El Aurenx from the sacred land of Atlantis, one of the
Sons of God who entered this world through the wombs of the
daughters of men. I was reborn twenty-three times, and shall
return once more.
My child, I wish to draw your attention to Atlantis, to the time
when our continent broke up into clusters of small islands.
Seismic disturbances threatened to submerge what was left of
dry land and seafarers set forth from the Atlantides to seek new
lands to inhabit—westward to the Americas and eastward to
the Mediterranean.

I was a navigator at that time and undertook expeditions to the East and West, bringing home news of settlements established by earlier emigrants and of other lands to be colonized. I also explored the Atlantic as far south as Antarctica, the forgotten outpost of Atlantis before it receded toward the polar region. I eventually lost my life in a shipwreck off the southernmost coast of Africa—near the Cape of Good Hope—where I was to be twice reborn many ages later, first as Laurence Oliphant and again, today, as Laurence Oliver.

Atlantis was a continent of two large islands in the Atlantic Ocean, of which the Azores and West Indies are still remnants. It was the seat of an advanced culture and civilisation from 24000 to 15000BCE. Atlantis was the original home of the mythical gods of antiquity until it collapsed in a cataclysmic destruction between 15000 and 12000BCE, giving rise to the universal Flood legend. Although the remaining archipelagos were still occupied by surviving Atlanteans until 9500BCE, massive emigrations had already established colonies which became the epicentres of our greatest postdiluvian civilisations: Egypt, Mesopotamia, China and Mesoamerica. Of interest to you, my child, is that the coast of southeast Africa was settled by shipwrecked seafarers from Atlantis. Bare in mind, here, that the shoreline has shifted dramatically since then.

El Aurenx blesses you.

Laurence says the name El Aurenx is not a real name, but only used to identify him. In the spiritual spheres, words for names are unnecessary since identification is expressed as an idea.

JM

We shall not cease from exploration
And the end of all our exploring
Will be to arrive where we started
And know the place for the first time.

T S Eliot, *Four Quartets* (1942)

'The wisdom of Atlantis was introduced into Egypt, Persia and India by Hermes, Zoroaster and Buddha respectively,' began Mendle, 'and since you know of the first one, I want to pass on what Laure heard about the latter two. Zoroaster returned periodically within a dynasty of Persian prophets (8000BCE–1000CE), while Buddha ranged from the founder of Buddhism, Gautama Siddhartha in the 6thC BCE, to the silent sage of India in the twentieth century, Ramana Maharshi. It was a gradual reformation whereby Buddhism rejected Hinduism's metaphysical esotericism in favour of non-dogmatic rational inquiry.'

'As did Aristotle and Averroës in the West,' said Sonja, picking up the discussion, 'advocating rationalism over metaphysics?'

'Exactly.'

She heard him chuckle as he fumbled with his webcam. He was clearly pleased to hear from her again. It had been a hectic week of email correspondence. He babbled on, like the Camissa:

'Mahayana Buddhism transformed the esotericism of the East and Almeida may have seen a parallel in Aristotle's reworking of western philosophy...'

She had called about Almeida and El Alamein. But Mendle clearly had other matters on his mind, directing her attention back in time:

'The centuries-old Silk Road was a conduit for trade, technology, language and belief. The Manichaeans not only upheld that the same truths were found in the teachings of Zoroaster, Jesus and Buddha; but they believed each master reintroduced the wisdom of Atlantis.'

'So the Manichaeans really did want to reconcile Hindu polytheism with the monotheism of Judaism, Christianity and Islam? Well, all I know is that the latter three are linked to Melchizedek.'

'Ah! Melchizedek, the Canaanite priest-king of Salem, or *Jeru-salem*, who came down from the mountain to give Abraham bread and wine —a sacrament from the Most High God, one higher than *Yahweh*.' Mendle rubbed his nose, accentuating his pharaonic appearance. 'After centuries of animal sacrifices the incarnate Christos reinstated this ancient Canaanite offering, using his body as a sign for the bread and wine. In my opinion, the Grail mystery is linked to the old pagan Canaanite-Hamite traditions that connect Solomon with the priest-queen of Sheba.'

He was an anthropologist through and through, yet all she wanted was that he stay on safe and familiar ground.

'Your Judaic tradition says Sheba came from the South,' she began, 'yet the Arabians and Ethiopians both claim her as their own?'

'According to the Ethiopian legend, the Sunburnt Queen returned from Jerusalem, pregnant, and gave birth to a son Menelik. She ruled from her ancient capital at Aksum until her death, and was entombed in a royal chamber, underground, presumably behind the local police station.'

'Prof, please, be serious—'

'—ah, but I am. The palace's foundations were destroyed by road builders during the Italian occupation. Mussolini favoured engineers, not archaeologists,' added Mendle woefully, 'look what he did to the Forum in Rome.'

'I know, it's under a road too.'

Mendle beamed back:

'The Italians looted Aksum's royal tombs and pillaged the ancient monasteries, including many magnificent stone stelas. In a twist of fate, the Italians were captured and taken as POWs to South Africa where they helped build our most beautiful Cape mountain passes. Alas, many died.'

She'd driven over these passes on her research trip.

'Perhaps it's a fitting retribution, like Almeida's punishment for plundering Kilwa and Mombasa?'

'Aha. Aksum's stelas lie scattered across the dry plains, surrounded by crumbling brown fields and scrubby gardens. Once a magnificent city, it now lies in ruins under ever-shifting dust and sand. I say, Jason took some great photos when he was there, so why not ask him?'

She'd not heard a word since Heathrow—and after all they'd been through—what an alter ego!

'However,' continued Mendle, 'archaeological evidence shows that Aksum is not contemporary with ancient Jerusalem. While Aksum dates back to the first century, it can't be linked to Solomon's Jerusalem eight centuries earlier. The gap is simply too big.'

'So Ethiopia's Queen of Sheba is mere fiction—or did her legend originate elsewhere?'

'Ah, the Arabian legend offers a clue,' explained Mendle patiently. 'A turn-of-the-century expedition from Germany found evidence of a Christian shrine in an ancient pagan temple. The site is linked to the Sabaeans, then the Iron Age kingdom of South Arabia; and recent archaeological and linguistic evidence suggests that the Arabs were the catalyst for the first urban civilisation in Ethiopia. They needed Africa's iron, of course.'

'And the Queen of Sheba, what's her connection to Christianity?'

'She's the Black Madonna of crypts and wells. Sheba is Our Lady of Under-the-Earth.'

'Well, I know she was revered as a mother-earth figure in Southern Europe. There's a small chapel dedicated to the Black Madonna at the place where Charlemagne found her image, following a dream, before setting off to reclaim Moorish Spain. He didn't succeed, oké, but that's not relevant here. There are over two hundred statues of Black Virgins in France alone, most of them from the twelfth century, including one copied at Chartres after a woman giving birth. She was worshipped by Celtic Christians as a pre-figuration of the Virgin but destroyed, I think, by soldiers during the Napoleonic Wars. Chartres is the site of a megalithic healing spring and the place where you find the first Marian sanctuary in France. But what's her link to Ethiopia?'

'According to legend, King Solomon dreamt that the sun shone more brightly over Ethiopia than Israel, and took this to mean that the Most High God had left the Temple of Jerusalem for a new abode in Africa. Whether it's historically true or not, belief in this story directed the Ethiopian Church and State for the next centuries.

The legend offered unity, stability and a common ground for Jews, Christians and Muslims.'

'Oké, so we have the three Abrahamic religions again.'

'Exactly. The foundation for Ethiopia's royal house is recorded in the *Kebra Nagast*, the Glory of the Kings, dating from the fourteenth century. The emergence of the biblical legend and the resumption of the Solomonic line coincides with this period, following the defeat of the Zagwe-Lalibela dynasty in 1270. As part of its official ideology, the new Solomonic dynasty introduced the idea that its rulers were descended from Menelik, the sole offspring of Solomon and Sheba—which, coincidently, is a claim Laurence has just confirmed.'

Sonja interrupted: 'Jason claims the Zimbabweans did it too when they rose in power during the same century. They also used foreign birth and a sacred lineage to legitimise their new dynasty.'

Mendle smiled:

'The Queen of Sheba links Arabia, Israel and Ethiopia through the legends of the Temple, the Ark *and* the Grail. These three mark the transition from a pre-Christian mysticism to the mysteries of Christ. Once again, remember, it was Gaspar who gave Almeida access to Judaic esotericism and, as an Alexandrian Jew, may also have given him access to the teachings of Hermes Trismegistus.'

'And the idea of reincarnation?'

'Ah yes. The Phoenicians were indebted to the mysteries of rebirth and resurrection from Egypt. After all, the Phoenix was linked to the Egyptian Benu bird—the One Who Returns, the Recurrent One.'

Following the events leading up to El Alamein and its parallel at Carthage, Sonja felt drawn to the Phoenix and the Sankofa bird. Back in South Africa a curator had shown her the latter (in the form of a Ghanaian goldweight) to demonstrate Egypt's lingering influence among the Akan of modern Ghana. Recalling this, Sonja felt it was time to fly south again—just like the Recurrent One.

To be honest, she'd also heard Ben Mordechai wasn't dead. He'd been hospitalised for surgery, detained for observation, and then released with a fine for unruly behaviour—or so Mendle had found out. But as the police had no victim, no assault charge had been laid, and now he'd disappeared without paying his fine or settling his bills.

Return

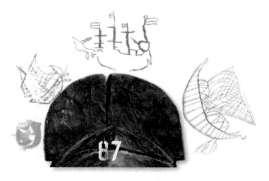

History and geography record acts and facts, but myth and belief explain why men act and which facts they choose to explore.

Malvern van Wyk Smith, *Shades of Adamastor* (1988)

With renewed state budget cuts, the Tropenmuseum had to downsize its exhibition programme. Sonja's component would be postponed.

As a result, she suddenly had two spare weeks and so returned to South Africa for a brief visit. Here she found the Mother City resting in its scalloped bowl, like a pearl, silent and still.

It was mid-September, just before South Africa's National Heritage Day, and not much had changed since her visit that June—except for little things like better airport parking, improved city access and arty boutique hotels.

The break would do them both good, she'd told Bart beforehand. And there'd be no Black Goliath.

She'd also raised the issue of Almeida's bones, again, telling Mendle to settle the matter once and for all, before the year-end, as it was exactly five centuries since the massacre.

The Professor had agreed on the timing, and suggested they look for a solution after her arrival, say at Café Paradiso, where they could discuss the options. Jason had sent a last-minute sms inviting her to stay with him. Bart too. Like Cape Town's upgraded infrastructure, Jason's timing also had room for plenty of improvement:

> Fetch u@airport
> for supper 2mrw
> nite with Mendle
> and Prof MvWS

⁜ ⁜ ⁜

'The next step is easy to guess,' began Prof Malvern van Wyk Smith before dinner. 'After Ptolemy said the source of the Nile lay in the Mountains of the Moon, the Terrestrial Paradise and Prester John were automatically linked to the same realm. The assumption that he was light-skinned had been an age-old canard of African exploration. In fact, rumours of a lost white kingdom, first recorded by Herodotus, fuelled African adventurers from classical mythology down to Rider Haggard, Wilbur Smith and Sol Kersner.'

Jason sprang in: 'These men had one thing in common, they all dreamt of finding the beautiful and ageless Ayesha, "She Who Must Be Obeyed", the reincarnation of a long-lost lover.'

Sonja was vexed by Jason's confidence and, more so, by how easily he amused her brother. She was jealous, of course, having cared for Bart without much success herself.

Tsjonge, and now this sudden improvement?

Mendle proposed they consider the buffet before ordering from the menu, promising the English Professor the first word.

'Well, *bon appétit*,' began Malvern, again, once they were all seated. 'Italian scholars were convinced that the realm of Prester John had survived in isolation and so, in turn, the Portuguese never doubted they'd found him in Abyssinia. Cristóvão da Gama, Vasco's son, led a campaign to succour support against the Muslims and saw himself as a conquistador forging links between two great Christian kings. Moreover, Cristóvão was fired by a vision of Saint James—'

'—as had the mani-king of Kongo,' interrupted Jason.

'Yes, but it was a brief moment of inspiration. Alas, the Portuguese were massacred fighting the imir of Ethiopia. After which, Cristóvão was decapitated and his head displayed on a pole—'

'—like Titus van Bengal,' cut in Jason again, but Sonja nudged so hard that he nearly bit his own tongue off.

'Let our guest continue,' she hissed.

'Thanks. Well, fatigue and disillusionment set in when Portuguese soldiers and Jesuit missionaries were banished from Abyssinia in the early seventeenth century. However, rumours of a fabulous empire continued migrating south and, for a while, these were linked to the kingdoms of Zimbabwe and Monomotapa, reaching Zululand in the late eighteenth century. Old legends die hard, as Rider Haggard knew all too well, penning *King Solomon's Mines* in 1885.'

Turning to Sonja, he added: 'Yes, the book *is* still worth a read.'

'I'll note that for my holidays,' she said smiling. 'I'd like to compare him to that "Adventurous Generation" who scrambled to the last few corners of the world: Shackleton to the South Pole, Bingham—the real Indiana Jones—to the Inca temples of Peru, and Otto Rahn to Montségur to explore the Grail Castle. As a travel-writer, Haggard was no exception, nor was his Southern Paradise an isolated case.'

Jason nodded, his mouth full of lasagne.

'Indeed. Dante invoked this tradition when he placed his island of Purgatory off to the South, with Titans to guard the watery transit to Paradiso. It was his imagery that inspired Camões and, over time, the Mountains of the Moon were displaced further and further south until they formed the barrier range around South Africa. The Italians identified the Mountains of the Moon with the Cape Fold Mountains and, inevitably, the Cape Peninsula with their Terrestrial Paradise—'

'—well then, here we are tonight, dining at Café Paradiso,' inserted Mendle jovially, 'at the Tavern below our Table.'

Jason and Bart exchanged grins. Sonja pressed on:

'Then Ptolemy's Mountains of the Moon and Dante's Mountains of the Sea were both identified with Table Mountain?'

'Yes, and as you know, Dante's *Divine Comedy* describes Paradiso as a mountain surrounded by forest from which two streams flowed. The undaunted Ulysses sailed for five months until, under the stars of the southern pole, he suddenly saw "a mountain obscured by distance and of a height never seen before".'

'So Table Mountain was imagined before it was discovered?'

Mendle refilled their glasses, nodding thoughtfully: 'It's the most startling mytho-poetic allusion I've ever heard of. Not only did Dante anticipate it rising out of the sea, but he predicted it would be found below the Southern Cross—at the southern antipode to Jerusalem.'

Malvern smiled: 'Indeed, Dante's description of Table Mountain pre-dates the first Portuguese sighting by one hundred and fifty years. Then, a century later, as reports filtered back, Venetian mapmakers took it to be Dante's visionary Mountain of the Sea—'

'—hence the vernacular *Hoerikwaggo*?' interjected Jason.

'Doubtful,' said Mendle, 'the similarity is a semiotic coincidence, not an obtuse historical connection.'

'Indeed,' said Malvern, savouring the sauvignon's flinty aftertaste.

'Table Mountain was identified with Paradise and Robben Island with the Isle of Purgatory. The island and mountain were separated by a treacherous water crossing and, over the centuries, the Cape itself typecast as a land of suffering and salvation; a place to purge the soul and attain enlightenment; a *Tormentoso* and an *Esperança*. There could be no Paradise without a Purgatory, no Cape of Storms without a Cape of Good Hope.'

'I heard the Templars practiced a threefold initiation,' added Prof Mendle. 'Faith out of Doubt, Hope out of Torment and Love out of Strife. The patron saints of Faith and Love were Peter and John. Hope, of course, was St James. Rounding the Cape thus symbolised a transition through the second phase: from Torment to Hope.'

For a moment no one spoke. A waiter cleared their plates and left them with the desert menu. Mendle resumed:

'A forgotten poet of Victorian Cape Town wrote that there could be no paradise without its serpents.'

He recited his favourite couplet:

Alas 'tis true,
This paradise has lurking serpents too.

'What a hoot, who penned that?' enquired the English Professor.

'Arthur Vine Hall, if memory serves me well, in a little poem about Table Mountain, from around 1900.'

'Memorable.'

'I learnt it at school,' continued Mendle, 'while reading about the adventures of Prester John. Buchan's narrative skill, local knowledge and biblical imagery appealed to adventurous schoolboys like me.'

Again he cited:

Whatever serpent might lurk in it,
it was a veritable Eden I had come to.

Mendle smiled, distracted, indicating to a nearby waiter that their bottle was empty. She nodded back. Malvern let Mendle resume:

'Ah, Buchan drew primarily upon Portuguese sources and describes Prester John as an Abyssinian king whose realm spread far south, all the way down to the Great Lakes. While he claims the Portuguese never got there, there's no doubt in his mind that Prester John was a great conqueror as well as a great Christian priest and king.'

Mendle paused, toying with his empty glass. The young waiter was still busy clearing a neighbouring table. He continued:

'Buchan claims the Bantu found it easy to mix pagan practices with Christian emotion. His "Africa" is barbaric and ghoulish—yet exotic, mysterious and magical. For him the continent remains populated by witches, sorcerers and devil worshippers.'

'What about Prester John?'

'Ah. Buchan tells us how the Portuguese sent out expedition after expedition hoping to find him. He also mentions how Albuquerque tried to make an alliance with Prester John so that by stealth and deception, the Portuguese could seize the Holy Sepulchre.'

'Wait, the Holy Sepulchre in Jerusalem?' checked Sonja.

'Yes, or so Buchan says—'

'—wasn't Prester John long dead by then?'

'Probably.'

'Well, I don't think the Prester actually lived *that* long,' qualified Sonja, 'as there was always an office bearer, like the Pope, to whom the title was awarded even after the legend itself had passed.'

'Fumo,' said Mendle, 'the title was *fumo*, meaning "priest", "king", "chief", or simply, "one of the royal family".'

'Seizing the Holy Sepulchre was only one of Albuquerque's mad schemes,' Sonja continued. 'By using horses to raid Medina—a city of pilgrims, *nota bene*, not soldiers—he planned to seize Muhammad's coffin as ransom for Jerusalem. He also planned to dig a canal and divert the Nile, hoping it would ruin the Mamluk Sultanate of Cairo.'

'But if the legend was already dead,' enquired Malvern, 'what was Albuquerque looking for?'

The waiter returned, smiling, bringing with her a new bottle.

'I guess Albuquerque was after something sacred—'

'—aha, the Grail Stones of Africa, the sacred Ndhlondhlo itself!'

'What?'

'The *Ndhlondhlo* or Great Snake of the amaZulu; and the sacred totem of the Nguni, Sotho and Shona people. Africa is not only full of serpents, but has its surprises too!'

'So I keep hearing,' smiled Sonja.

'Buchan says the Great Snake was the necklet that once belonged to Prester John and, as a fetish or talisman, ensured the supremacy of whoever possessed it—'

'—like the Lance of Longinus?'

'The same, both lance and necklet guaranteed political power.'

First Hitler, now Shaka Zulu? Sonja pressed on:

'SS leader Heinrich Himmler was obsessed with finding the Grail. He persuaded young Otto Rahn—who'd identified Montségur as the Grail Castle—to join his department of Ancestral Heritage. From then on Rahn blended the Grail legend with a National Socialist ideology, transfusing it with "the true northern bloodline".'

'Shaka was born out of wedlock too, giving you another ruptured bloodline,' said Mendle, redirecting their conversation, 'and Buchan describes him as a Black Napoleon, though I doubt if that's original. He claims Shaka slaughtered two million people trying to seize the necklet; although contemporary population estimates don't support this figure.'

'Who knows how many died?' said Malvern. 'Shaka's reign lasted a mere decade, during which a hundred chiefdoms were united into a formidable kingdom. Since then the Zulu Kingdom has survived assassination, military defeat, invasion and occupation. But who really knows what it precipitated regionally? The insurgence of white settlers in a denuded Natal—and the myth of the empty landscape—distorted whatever evidence still remained.'

'As with Canaan, so too in Zululand—first a Boer republic, then a British colony,' noted Mendle, with self-conscious satisfaction.

'The myth of the Promised Land, indeed! But Buchan did get one thing right,' noted Malvern, 'the centre of authority had been shifting south for centuries, taking with it the Paradise legend.'

'From what I recall, Buchan linked it to the southward movement of the warrior tribes fleeing the Congo, displaced by the baMaravi.'

'Well, to make a long story short, Buchan claims that the demise of Monomotapa left a gap as fresh tribes came down and pushed into Natal and the Cape. They regarded themselves as the heirs of a great prophet and law-giver, but forgot his religion. Today the amaZulu remember only that he was a great conqueror—'

'—an All-Great conqueror,' added Jason, 'the term *Monomotapa* was adapted from *Mwene Mutapa*, meaning "Lord Conqueror". It was a title used for the ruler of the vaKaranga, then living on the great central plateau.'

'Mashonaland. Northern Rhodesia?'

'Right. When the Portuguese arrived, the vaKaranga had moved to the plateau's northern edge, where it drops off to the Zambezi Valley.

Their empire was the successor of gold-bearing kingdoms to the south, built among the boulder-topped hills of the Limpopo, where they built in stone rather than with clay or grass. Tradition has it that the vaKaranga migrated north, from their capital at *maDzimbabwe*, under the leadership of the Monomotapa.'

'And the knock-on effect was the plunder of Kilwa?' checked Sonja.

'Yes, indirectly, both Zimbabwe and Monomotapa belonged to a social network where, interestingly, the snake was a recurrent motif. In the palace complex of Great Zimbabwe the snake represents the "one who guards the still waters in mountain caves". It is the sacred place where god is seen as the Stone of the Pool.'

'A watersnake sanctuary,' said Mendle, turning to Jason, 'like the cave-church you saw at Lalibela. Rahn and Buchan were obviously fascinated by the same sort of caves and their rituals.'

She recalled Jason's own boyhood craze for speleology, adding:

'The cave at Monségur was flanked by two monoliths, like the Phoenician temple of Herakles and, between the white limestone stalagmites and crystals, the path led down to the bowels of the earth. Furthermore, Rahn and Buchan describe how each sacred object—a grailstone and stone-necklet, respectively—fell into a deep recess, as if swallowed by a cleft in the rock, where they remain hidden today.'

Mendle signalled for the bill.

Turning to Jason, Sonja surmised: 'Like the legend of Saint Odilia, such caves seal their mysteries from the world. As archaeologists and historians we need to recover the debris lying beneath such legends. We need to look beyond the ash of our past.'

'The Imrahana cave is pre-Christian,' said Jason, 'and became a sanctuary of Prester John in the Zagwe-Lalibela period. It is also said that the Queen of Sheba descended from the snake-slayer, Arwe.'

'Ah, of course, her ancestors were snake-worshippers,' said Mendle, raising a bushy brow. Then, turning to face Sonja: 'Anyway, whether you believe this or not, Ethiopia is still a great holiday destination.'

'Well,' she side-stepped, 'Buchan's sense of history and geography may be suspect, even anachronistic, but it seems his book *is* worth a read—and the myths themselves worth reconsidering?'

'Indeed,' said Malvern, 'they explain why the British acted against the Zulu and which facts colonialists chose to accept about the origins of the Zimbabwe Ruins.'

'I say, why not come by my house tomorrow and collect the book. Perhaps we can do lunch together?'

Sonja agreed with a smile, relieved to know she could sleep in late. She was here on holiday. There was no returning to the archives. Not this time.

Mendle glinted with delight.

It was late, everyone was tired, particularly Sonja and Bart after their long flight. They could stay with Jason, which was going to be fortuitous, as Bart seemed to be enjoying his jaundiced company.

Still, she could hardly believe Bart's miraculous recovery.

It was Malvern who had the last word:

'I suppose our serpents made the fairest Cape a place of danger and exoticism, so much so Europeans felt both bitten and blessed living in the shadow of Table Mountain.'

88

"As the leader of my people, I will assume the
collar of Umkulunkulu in the name of our God
and the spirits of the great dead."

John Buchan, *Prester John* (1910)

Sonja sat in the shaded corner of Mendle's patio-garden, enjoying the
scent of freshly watered flowers. He'd hosed down the deck to cool it
off, much to the chagrin of his cat, who'd taken refuge on the wall.

The garden had been Ruth's little paradise during her long illness.
Luxuriant shrubs, now overgrown and unkempt, sprawled from the
raised beds. A *Ficus benjamini* stood pot-bound by the kitchen door.
His wife had passed on two years before.

'Cancer,' he said, joining her at a wrought-iron table still covered in
layers of thick enamel paint. He set a pair of books in front of her.

'I'm sorry to hear that. I can't imagine such a loss.'

'Life has its own purpose. It's for us to know what roles to play.'

He shifted uncomfortably, knowing he was too large for the garden
furniture. He'd also forgotten to put out the cushions.

'I guess so,' she said cautiously.

Mendle sensed her inexperience with death and dying, as he'd done
in June when talking about memory. He redirected:

'*Umkulunkulu* is an old Zulu term for the Ancestral Father Spirit who
watches over his people.' Mendle leant in to pick up his first book, the
promised pocket-edition of *Prester John*, adding:

'Buchan discusses it on two-or-so pages, from page seventy-eight to
eighty. As we discussed last night, the notion of a Terrestrial Paradise

shifted southward as populations migrated down the Rift Valley, past the great lakes, following the mountain chain that ran further and further south. People settled along the way—the Matabele and Shona in Zimbabwe, the baSotho and amaZulu in Natal, the amaXhosa at the Cape—and according to Buchan, they all looked back to a great warrior-king, one they called by a hundred different names.'

'Including *Fumo*?'

'Possibly, although Buchan doesn't use the term himself. The first Portuguese castaways called Zululand's coastal plains *Terra dos Fumos*. They trekked to Delagoa Bay, now Maputo, hoping to board a ship bound for Sofala—*maPuto* being the local word for *the Portu-guese*. They heard others say it was the land of the Komati, hence Terra dos Macomates or *Komati-land* today. Now here's my point, this region was ruled by a mysterious chief called Viragune, about whom more may have been said but nothing else recorded. Look, here, read this.'

He leant forward to find the paragraph:

> That is how the Zulus first appeared. They brought with them the story of Prester John but by this time it had ceased to be a historical memory, and had become a religious cult. The Zulus worshipped a great Power who had been their ancestor, and their favourite word for him was Umkulunkulu. The belief was perverted into fifty different forms, but this was the central creed: Umkulunkulu had been the father of the tribe, and was alive as a spirit to watch over them.

Since Sonja had no anthropological background, she couldn't assess the legitimacy of such an extraordinary claim. She could only trust her intuition and rational training; but as Africa wasn't Aristotelian, she knew that wasn't going to be easy.

'What about the necklet of Prester John?'

'Buchan goes on to say the fetish descended via the maZimba and vaKaranga, and that the wars of the sixteenth century weren't fought for new territories, but over possession of this necklet.'

He lowered the book so she could follow, paraphrasing:

'Here, look, wars were fought for the Great Snake to which Shaka owed his conquests and for which Mosilikatse fled to Matabeleland. That was after Mosilikatse tried to steal it. According to Buchan, it disappeared with Shaka and so, as a result, Dingane and Panda never inherited it. Nor could Cetshwayo ever find it, though he searched the length and breadth of Zululand for it. Without it, Buchan claims, the Zulus lost their chance of becoming an enduring empire.'

'And does Buchan describe the necklet?'

'Indeed,' replied Mendle, thumbing the pages. 'Aha, here it is, the sacred Snake of John: a string of rubies, the largest being the size of a pigeon's egg, oval-shaped and cut *en cabochon*. This technique was replaced by faceting in the fifteenth century, so it probably predates Almeida. Characters were engraved on each stone, like the emerald tablets of Hermes.'

'So the necklet looked like a snake, a burning snake?'

'A blood-red snake,' he said, passing her the book, 'for which great warriors slew each other. A perversion of this necklet, according to Credo Mutwa, was the township tyre-necklacings of the mid-1980s. As such, these killings inverted the symbol of the Great Snake.'

'Wait, I see here we have a Keeper of the Snake, like the legendary Grail keeper?'

'And rightly so. Sacred artefacts were kept by the tribe's respected elders—usually shamans and necromancers—who knew the tradition and symbolic value of each piece.'

'Like the Turin Shroud and the Lance of Longinus, or the bodies of Adam and Muhammad?'

'Ah, the same, indeed!'

'And the necklet of Prester John—if it really existed?'

'Plenty of objects entered pre-colonial societies by way of explorers, traders and castaways—I once made a list of items acquired when destitute survivors passed through Natal—but no string of rubies has ever been found, not so far as I know. This particular group came ashore after the *Santo Alberto* ran aground, near the Mtata River, and walked 1500kms north, reaching Delagoa three months later. I think it was the longest trek undertaken by castaways along our coast.'

'So how many shipwrecks were there?'

'*Oi-vey*, far too many. The Wild Coast is notorious for its storms, surging seas and swirling mists. It gets its name from the rugged terrain and dense sub-tropical forest.'

'So Nature, not the Native, was wild?'

'Right. The lush-green coastal plateau is still wild and inaccessible. Its deep-cut rivers, isolated tidal lagoons and sheltered white beaches are among the few unspoilt secrets of southern Africa. A secret still appreciated by locals farmers and fishermen—'

'—so I heard from Don Pinnock. His family spent their holidays somewhere up the coast.' She paused. 'Sorry Prof, you were talking about shipwrecked survivors?'

'Ah, let's have lunch first. Is a Woolworths ready-made okay?'

She accompanied him to the kitchen where an Eatwell lasagne and a Caesar salad had been set aside. Each on their own tray.

'Ah yes, the Portuguese lost several ships along the Wild Coast. In each case the survivors suffered dreadful privations and casualties. Among those from the *São João Baptista*—which struck a reef near the Mzimvubu River mouth—four hundred castaways came ashore, but only twenty survived the walk.'

'Is that where Port St Johns gets its name?'

'Indeed,' he said, opening a bottle of wine. 'At the time, the *São João* was the biggest ship afloat and its loss seen as Portugal's greatest sea disaster ever. Ever! Tragically, the castaways made one fundamental mistake: they followed the shore and starved on a diet of shell-fish.'

'They didn't eat fresh fish?'

'Oddly enough, no.'

He poured two glasses. 'Shall we go back outside?'

'Yes, thank you. That's odd, as fish is typically Portuguese. What about the Xhosa and Zulu, didn't they catch fish?'

She took the tray with the Caesar salad and followed him out, back to the table. He chose the iron bench this time.

'Apparently not. They ate no fish, had no boats, and couldn't swim. Their economy was based on cattle. The Quena, on the other hand, well, they built stone fish traps in the intertidal zone.'

'From what I saw at Mossel Bay, trapped fish were speared when the tide went out?'

'Yes, but the Portuguese neither hooked nor speared fish. In a land full of unfamiliar fruit and insects, they soon went hungry. Very hungry. To make matters worse, they didn't know that brackish rivers had fresh water upstream, so they suffered from unquenchable thirst—starving or dying of dehydration.'

'So, doubly cursed.'

'With the benefit of hindsight, the survivors of the *Santo Alberto* walked inland to find villages from which to obtain milk and meat.

They were fortunate enough to have two slaves who spoke fluent Portuguese and, I think, some isiXhosa. Ironically, more than half their slaves chose to stay with those they met along the way—about a hundred in all—while the rest went on to Delagoa Bay.'

'António do Campo, one of Almeida's captains, was among the first ashore at Delagoa, though I never realised so many others remained. According to the Tabula, António died with Almeida at the Cape.'

'Ah, most of our early information about South Africa comes from the Portuguese, many of whom walked to safety with their Malagasy and Indian slaves. Among the *Alberto* survivors was an Indian woman, unnamed, who could go no further. It isn't clear if she remained in a village or was left for locals to find.'

'I can only imagine—'

'—as far as I recall, two women *did* make it to safety. Here, please, let me show you.' Mendle took the second book wherein a folded postcard marked the spot. 'Ah yes, it was the widow Dona Isabella Pereira and her young daughter, Luiza, a beautiful girl of sixteen.'

'Of course she was beautiful,' said Sonja with a mischievous smile. 'Among hundreds of bellicose men she had to be young and fair—otherwise you'd have no narrative tension, no sense of anticipation. Anyway, I see this book has an interesting title: *Who Really Discovered South Africa?*'

'Ah, Burman again. I guess the adventurous boy dies hard too.'

'That's oké, as long as you don't make juvenile judgements about history,' she teased, as he shifted his weight on the bench. 'But what of all the trinkets exchanged for food or water?'

'Jose Burman says the *Alberto* survivors bartered copper and a basin-full of nails; whereas the Zulu traders wanted to exchange their cattle for a cauldron, which the Portuguese refused to part with, obviously. As for Dona Isabella, she'd been married to the Captain of Ceylon and carried all her jewellery with her.'

Sonja's heart skipped a beat, thrilled by the chance of finding something precious—like a ruby.

'So what did the survivors get in return?'

'Cows mostly, sometimes lamb, also milk, butter and millet cakes. Beans too. Or honeycomb. But nothing had a fixed value. And then the amaZulu wanted three times more for a cow than the amaXhosa, though both were reluctant to part with symbols of power—'

'—like the Quena from whom Almeida—'

'—exactly, cattle symbolised status, wealth and prosperity.'

'More so than their wives?' she interjected. 'I read that cattle were used as payment for a new wife and that a woman could only enter the cattle kraal on her wedding day. She was otherwise not allowed to milk cows?'

'No, young boys did the milking. Anyway, castaways were made to pay a customary tribute to the chief whose land they crossed. It was like a toll or levy. Interlopers were expected to reward the custodian clan for the rivers, animals and plants they intended to use.'

'As the Portuguese should have done at the spring in Mossel Bay?'

'Indeed, and what a colourful sight it was, imagine, two hundred oddly-clad men of different races, many with soft smooth beards, driving their bellowing cows through rolling grass and flooding rivers, transporting two white women in swaying hammocks—'

'—like pilgrims travelling to the Holy Land?'

'Aha, a devout troupe singing to the beat of drums and cymbals, though in this case it was probably a kettle and clanging pot lid.'

'And they were probably more desperate than devout?'

'Ha! Yes, by local standards they were a wealthy clan and so had to pay more. Compared to Goa or Ceylon, goods were expensive and had no fixed price here. They also had no mutual currency: one cow could cost the Portuguese several copper pieces, a pair of kettle handles or a broken astrolabe.'

'And people? Did they barter their slaves too?'

'Ah, that I don't know. Burman only tells us how some remained behind when the weather worsened. It rained on end, day and night, as winter approached. So the survivors abandoned their weak, in-cluding that Indian woman and several over-worked slaves, as well as two sailors suffering from dysentery (probably caused by drinking too much milk). There was also one Alvaro Gonçalvez, the boatswain's father, seventy-five years old and too frail to walk any further.'

'And so they stayed?'

'Ah, yes, according to Burman, there were plenty who did, as it was far safer to stay behind.' Mendle flipped back a few pages:

> ...the slaves elected to remain there. This was to happen again and again during the trip, for a Negro slave the easy life of the Transkei must have seemed like Paradise.

Like those other countless victims of piracy and shipwreck—including pilgrims going to the Holy Land—who ended up living among local tribesmen. It was often better than the poverty they'd left behind.

Sonja wondered what became of the remaining slaves and how, if at all, they adapted to a new life in southern Africa. Castaways posed no threat of invasion or displacement, and were thus allowed to settle. But how much they'd actually integrated, Mendle couldn't say.

Coincidently, Don Pinnock had told her about a community called the abeLungu, "the Whites", who descended from English survivors on the Wild Coast. She'd also heard of a seven year old girl who, cast ashore during the 1730s, became the Great Wife and Mother of a Mpondo royal house.

Mendle's cat leapt down and settled on his lap. He seemed to read Sonja's mind, adding: 'Barring a few exceptions, we don't know what happened to them, unfortunately—'

'—but what about their jewellery? Do their descendants still have any, or has any been traced? Such evidence must be invaluable!'

She sounded unduly impatient.

'Say, easy does it, Sonja,' he said, passing her Burman's book. 'Alas, little if any material evidence has come forward.'

She sat wondering why they'd found no evidence of Almeida's visit? According to the records, Almeida's men bartered with the Quena. Yet no single item appeared to have survived. No wooden rattles, no glass beads, no metal mirrors, no pewter rings or copper rods. Not even a button, a buckle or a clasp. Nothing?

That night her dream returned. Now the herdboys ran into the sea, splashing and shouting while Jason waded into the surf toward her: "Come home, or the sea will take you." Bart was there too.

This time she awoke without anxiety.

89

Everything had a story to tell, every feature of the landscape
seemed to conceal its own private tale of mystery and tragedy.
Hazel Crampton, *The Sunburnt Queen* (2004)

'As you know too, Sonja, the Wild Coast is a strange and mysterious place,' noted Hazel, 'nothing is what it seems at first glance.'

They sat at a long mahogany table in the Pinnocks' dinning-room. Hazel Crampton was a former political activist and an ex-cadre in *Umkhonto we Sizwe*, then the ANC's military wing, and had received her MK-training in East Germany.

Since then she'd written a book on the nineteenth-century castaway from England, Bessie, the Great Mother of an amaXhosa dynasty. Hazel knew more about Wild Coast castaways than anyone else:

'With an open sea route around Africa,' she began, 'more ships passed the Cape and, inevitably, more and more were shipwrecked. The Wild Coast became a veritable mariners' graveyard. Although most were Portuguese, there were also Indian, Malagasian, Javanese and Japanese slaves among them. Survivors first headed north, to trading stations on the Mozambican coast; whereas the English, French and Dutch went down to the Cape. Either way, it was a perilous trip. Most succumbed to the unfamiliar terrain—unable to cope with its extreme temperatures, flooded rivers, hostile natives, preying animals and poisonous snakes. They also died of dehydration, starvation and disease.'

'So I heard,' said Sonja, recalling her talk with Mendle. 'The thirsty drank their urine and the hungry ate their shoes.'

'Yes, ironically, as the natural resources were abundant. However, they didn't know where to obtain drinking water or edible food. One miserable group hungrily devoured a mariner's chart, probably made of pig skin, and died soon after from mercury poisoning.'

'Like the poisoned monk in *The Rose*?'

'Totally,' agreed Hazel, 'the records read like an Umberto Eco. It's hard to believe reality isn't fiction.'

'Incredible!'

'Yes, but first pass me the salad. Thanks. Well, there are also stories of survivors who lost all they had, including their sanity. Such was the fate of a nobleman, Sebastião Lobo da Silveira, who was too obese to walk and offered his precious jewels to anyone who would carry him. He was left, finally, without food, under a cloth-tent on the beach... Then came a French boy, Guillaume, who was attacked by pirates, shipwrecked, captured by the amaXhosa and, eventually, adopted by Chief Sotope. There are other stories of castaways who spent their lives with the natives—like the eccentric French cook found living in a village forty years later. A passing group of Dutch survivors tried to take him home, but he refused to leave. Almighty Moses, forty years!'

'Like those unfortunate crusaders seen by passing pilgrims, living as bearded woodcutters or hermits beside the Dead Sea?'

'Yes. It took a Malabar slave, known as Mieje to his Dutch masters, nine months to reach the Cape. He is thought to be a survivor of a VOC ship that ran aground off the Wild Coast. What happened to Mieje following his incredible journey is not known, officially, but one hopes his ordeal won him his freedom. What a tragedy if he struggled all that way, through a land of free blacks, only to be enslaved again on reaching civilisation? He simply disappears from history. There's no further record of him at the Cape. Castaways and slaves were seldom given a place in history...'

'Hazel, wait, these stories are *incredible!*'

Sonja shifted closer.

'Well, there are tales of abducted natives who never saw their home again; and Arab traders who stole off with the women they captured.

There's a pitiful story of Portuguese survivors who, for instance, stole cattle, cut crops, plundered villages and burnt homesteads. They not only beat and shot the startled natives, but when hunger took hold of their senses, even ate their victims.'

Cannibalism.

'No ways, that's extreme,' said someone else.

'But true. A group who came ashore near today's holiday resort at Kenton-on-Sea were particularly sinister. When their compatriots—both white and black alike—died of natural causes, their bodies were roasted and eaten. Since this failed to provide enough meat, survivors began sentencing their own companions to death for the most trivial of misdemeanours—including the children.'

'Extreme,' said the same voice.

'Totally. And they say everything in Africa is extreme. Well, news of the atrocities spread quickly, so that villagers were forewarned and prepared. One abject Portuguese survivor recorded that "the kaffirs had been told we ate men and so waited for us pre-armed".'

'I heard of the survivors,' said Sonja, 'but not about their atrocities. Portuguese brutality was prevalent along the entire eastern seaboard —from the Cape of Good Hope to the Horn of Africa—yet despite the conflicts, few castaways were persuaded to leave their new home. They'd found their terrestrial paradise.'

'Given their previous social status, their new life was far preferable,' added Hazel. 'Most had once been slaves, seamen or artisans. Even women found their situation here more favourable.'

'Certainly not the aristocratic Isabella Pereira and her daughter?'

'No, nor poor Eleonora de Sala who went stark raving mad before her ordeal ended. She was a *São João* survivor who landed on the beach near today's police campsite, and crawled ashore with her family. As a noblewoman, she asserted her right to certain privileges and was carried aloft by her surviving servants, as were her children. After three months, her litter-bearers had either died or absconded, so she was forced to walk the rest of the way beside her husband, the former Governor of Diu. They were robbed by locals on the beach, shortly after arriving in Delagoa. First their weapons, then their jewellery, and finally their clothes. Dona Eleonora is said to have fought back feistily, but was restrained by her husband who feared she would be killed. He tried to cover her in a shawl, but she threw herself down and buried her body to the waist in a pit of sand. She refused to move and eventually died there, in the sun, a few days later, next to her two dead children. Her husband—who'd already lost an illegitimate son on the journey—buried his family in silence. Then, without a word, he walked off into the forest and was never seen again. As Camões aptly says: "Despoiled by savages, those who escape are left to wander naked over the burning sands…".'

Having listened to their conversation, Don Pinnock passed the roast-vegetable platter, adding:

'The tragedy of Eleonora de Sala inspired more poetry than any other woman in Portuguese history—and from South Africa came as many stories of young, beautiful castaways. These belong to the oral tradition of the Eastern Cape and Natal South Coast where, still, you can see a black guy with blue eyes—but who otherwise looks like any other Xhosa or Zulu.'

Sonja took the platter. Hazel continued:

'While researching my book, I found the Wild Coast crawling with castaways that weren't of European origin. There's a Xhosa-speaking clan who are descended from Arab-Muslim castaways and, until a few decades ago, foreign origins were evident in their features. It's also visible in their early photos. Their hair was straight—atypical for the amaXhosa—and the women renowned for wearing theirs down to the waist.' She gestured the length with a scooping hand.

'So, where does the long hair come from?'

'They are descendants of one Bhayi, who'd been abducted by white traders and taken to sea. He and his wife were later ship-wrecked along our coast, but as she was barren, he married an amaMpondo girl with whom he had six children.'

'So he was—'

'—Indian, according to an isiXhosa historian, although we can't be sure. *Bhayi* means "brother" in Hindi. He was a skilled craftsman, evidently, who carved ivory earrings and armbands from elephant tusks. He produced beaten brass bangles and secretly smelted gold in the forest. Like Bessie, Bhayi is the parental figure of an amaMpondo clan who still remember their ancestors from the sea. You can read about Bessie in my book. She's better known as *Gquma*, the "roar of the Sea", to honour her strange arrival. Her name was given by a local sangoma after she was found at Lambasi, the Bay of Mussels, around 1737. My book is called *The Sunburnt Queen*—and it's not a novel.'

'That's oké, I'd still like to read it.'

'Then borrow my copy,' said Patricia walking by, 'as long as I get it back when you're finished.'

'*Bedankt*, but that's not necessary. I'd prefer to have my own to take back to Holland.'

'Oh, my God, from Holland!' exclaimed Hazel. 'Please don't be offended by what I said about the Cape Dutch?'

'Why should I? Slavery is no national issue. It's for all humanity to deal with, like freedom or equality. Anyway, I'm interested in the first Portuguese callers at the Cape and researching their contact with the natives. D'you know of any rare or sacred artefacts that survived? I'm not talking about the occasional coin or button, but something really precious—like a stone necklet.'

'No, not that I know of, but I recall Bessie had a brush and mirror. It was said that things salvaged from her wreck were first secured in a wooden chest and then stored in a hut, probably a granary. She wept when the contents were unpacked for the first time, and stole off with the brush and mirror... Thereafter, and for the rest of her life, she would brush out her hair each evening, no doubt the way she'd seen her mother do before. It was a ritual she observed until she died and one her adoptive family regarded with deep respect, especially the young children who came to watch. According to local legend, she'd weep softly while doing so.'

Later that night, sitting before her own mirror, Sonja imagined a lonely Englishwoman brushing out her long straight hair in silence, surrounded by incredulous black children.

90

Many will find it hard to believe what I have revealed in this book,
but I am not in the least concerned, because whether I am believed
or not, everything I write here is true.

Credo Mutwa, *Indaba, My Children* (1966)

After a brisk walk with Bart and Jason, now somewhat inseparable,
Sonja phoned Mendle to ask if the museum had any pre-settlement
artefacts of possible foreign origin:

'There must be evidence of cultural exchange with the Arabians or
Indians, even the Phoenicians?'

Mendle had taken the call in his office.

'Ah, alas, there are no clear traces of such encounters. Except for
an old Chinese limestone sculpture and, perhaps, a pigskin map—'

'—but surely hereditary leaders or traditional healers handed down
relics to passing generations?'

'Aha, Credo Mutwa claims that rusted swords of ancient Greek
manufacture, some gold coins, parts of bronze shields, helmets, spears
and Egyptian battle-axes, are among the secret artefacts of sangomas
in southern Africa.'

'Isn't he that controversial diviner?'

'Vusamazulu Credo Mutwa is a *sanusi* or shaman, yes. While a man
of no formal education, he is a self-proclaimed tribal historian of the
amaZulu and calls himself the "Guardian of the Umlando".'

'*Umlando?*'

Mendle nodded: 'It means tribal history. He also refers to himself as "Vasamazulu the Outcast", because he betrayed the secret lore of the Southern Bantu.'

'So he's more of a story-teller than a healer?'

'Can't he be both?'

'Yes, of course. So what does he say about these relics?'

'He claims to have inherited sacred objects from his grandfather, a direct descendant of Dingane, the last great Zulu king. He also says such artefacts prove the story of Zima-Mbje.'

'Zimbabwe?'

'*Zima-Mbje*, yes, which Mutwa describes as a fugitive Phoenician colony that survived the Roman sack of Carthage. He also describes them as the *Ma-Iti*, a red-headed people who landed somewhere near Mozambique. He says the oral traditions of the Mashona, Bechuana, Venda and Varozwi still recall the *Ma-Iti*, or Strange Ones, from over the Great Water. They came long before us Light Ones. Tradition tells how the Strange Ones also chose their wives from the swarthy Lawu and Batwa—generally known as the Khoisan today.'

'But where are these artefacts now? So far as I know, you only have trade items in the museum?'

'Ah, good question. Iron ingots found in the Congo basin and at Falmouth harbour, Cornwall, correspond to an ingot mould found in Zimbabwe. Hold on, let me get Mutwa's book.'

He set down the receiver and reached for his copy of *Indaba*.

'Wait a moment, here, you may find this interesting. Mutwa says the Strange Ones began to spread inland but fever and frequent epidemics killed all who stayed.'

Sonja intervened quickly, knowing others had described the history of expansion and encounter in terms of disease:

'Jared Diamond and Malyn Newitt argue that disease crippled the Portuguese enterprise in Africa and, more than any other factor, ruined their attempts to conquer Monomotapa.'

'Exactly. Yet Mutwa says the Strange Ones amassed great wealth, enjoying fantastic luxury in their cities. Today, Mutwa adds, one can still find rusted swords with bronze hilts among local diviners; swords so old that their blades crumble at the slightest blow.'

Mendle raised the book to read aloud:

There are unbelievably old ornaments of gold and silver and bronze—ornaments that are neither Bantu nor Arabi; worn, pitted and distorted by age—ornaments jealously guarded by the Tribal Historians and High Witchdoctors as the Secret Charms of the tribe. These ornaments are still used in secret rituals today and keep the memory of the Strange Ones fresh in the Tribal Story-Teller's mind.

Mendle continued: 'Mutwa describes the construction of Zimbabwe under an evil leader, called Munumutaba, who revived the ways of the Strange Ones. Munumutaba was a bandit from the Mountains— *Munumutaba*, I think, means "from the Mountains"—and under his direction the gentle Bechuana were enslaved. They built big sleds, big enough to carry a hundred men, which were drawn by a single column of fifty oxen. The Bechuana were forced to collect, load and transport stones for five whole summers. They died in their hundreds of thousands while their beasts were beaten to death. Mutwa explains how, at the crowning moment of the Munumutaba, the great bandit stood on the highest tower, known as the "Eye of Zima-Mbje", but as he came down a stone slipped, causing others to slide apart, so that he fell like a bird to his death. Then—'

'—like the fall of Montezuma?' she said, rhetorically.

'Then the Munumutaba's son rose to power under a new scourge. A race of men never seen before, lean men says Mutwa, who ravaged the land and its people. It was from these Feared Ones, the *Arabi*, that the Munumutaba learnt to make metal very hard. The Feared Ones were thin men of fierce will, adds Mutwa, with noses like the beaks of vultures and hair that grew long—though not as long as the Strange Ones. The Arabi took slaves to mine for gold, gold that was then shipped overseas. In those days many traders came to our shores for this precious metal—and to look for the teeth of the great elephant, which they regarded as sacred. No-well-fine, I guess the Portuguese weren't the first to take Zim's gold...'

'No, and after them Britain took the lion's share, including Shaka's ivory. And all as a consequence of Almeida's murder? Imagine what may have happened if the diamonds and gold had gone to Portugal instead? I think it's been of far greater benefit to the world that this wealth was used to finance the British Commonwealth and, in turn, that these very nations were able to contribute to the Allied successes in World War I. The outcome was a turning point for all Europe, as seen in the Treaty of Versailles, and reset East-West power relations.'

'Indeed, how different our world would be had the wealth helped to rebuild the Portuguese empire. Between 1890–1910, Portugal was a *de facto* colony of Brazil and feebly facing a crisis of mass emigration. Economically, Brazil is the waking giant today, the new China of the Atlantic Ocean.'

'And Africa?'

'Ah, always something new or extreme. While Laurence admits no familiarity with the archaeological record, he was told that Zimbabwe was built around 2000BCE, corresponding to a period of widespread warfare in the ancient Middle East; when the late Sumerian Empire fell under attack and the Hyksôs took occupation of northern Egypt. It was a time of mass migrations, including Abraham's westward trek from Ur to Canaan. Laurence also says the founders of Zimbabwe were Hittite refugees fleeing persecution, and came by way of the Gulf of Aden.'

'By sea, then, not overland?'

'Yes, and hence the Zimbabweans practised human sacrifice and worshipped a phallic god. In time, the priests became more and more brutal and oppressive, especially toward women. The birth rate fell steadily, until 500BCE, when the culture died out. Interestingly, the citadel of Great Zimbabwe was built around an elliptical temple with a spiral interior, supposedly to portray a foetus in the womb.'

'Prof, isn't this all a bit much?'

'Perhaps, but Laurence hasn't had the time to look at this properly. He says more information will be mediated, but not now. Anthropologically, the Hittites appear to have come from Turkey and, later, occupied parts of Syria and the Arabian Gulf. They spoke an Indo-European language while their neighbours, the Phoenicians, spoke a Semitic language. So the Hittites may be seen as Phoenicians, since ancient Phoenicia sat on that narrow coastal strip belonging to Syria, Lebanon and what is Israel today. Laurence's reference to brutality and human sacrifice concurs with Mutwa's view of an evil culture. He suggests that Mutwa's *Ma-Iti* was derived from a word for Hittite. In Hebrew, of course, they were called *Hittim* and their land was known as *Hatti*.'

After a long pause, Mendle concluded:

'According to Faria e Sousa, the Monomotapaians believed in one God, *Mazimo*, who had no idols. Witchcraft, theft and adultery were the crimes most severely punished. Every man was allowed as many wives as he pleased, or could maintain. The Monomotapa himself had a thousand wives, according to Faria e Sousa again, but his first wife commanded over the rest—and only her children were entitled to inherit the title. Their houses were built of wood, their apparel made of cotton (though cloth of a better sort was mixed with gold thread), and their funerals superstitious. Attendance on the Monomotapa was ceremonious rather than grand. His dominions were ruled by numerous governors, often unrelated by birth and, to prevent rebellion, he kept the heirs close to his court. Ironically, women were treated with such respect that even the king's sons would give way when they passed. Equally strange, they had no law-suits.'

'And for weapons?'

'They had bows and arrows, spears, daggers and sharp hatchets. But no horses. They fought on foot.

'And their gold?'

'It seems Arab traders from Magadoxa were the first to possess the mines of Sofala, after which they were seized by the King of Quiloa. Sofala should have been the first Portuguese stronghold in East Africa but, after the overladen *Santiago* sank in Lisbon harbour, Almeida had the fort at Kilwa completed instead. As Kilwa was taken on the eve of Santiago's Feast, the fort was dedicated to St James the Moorslayer... *Oi-vey*, isn't that ironic? Anyhow, speaking of slaves and gold, king Manuel hoped Sofala would supply an amount equivalent to Elmina. There, the rest you know already...'

91

Everything in Africa is in extremes.
Harriet Ward, *Five Years in Kaffirland* (1848)

Their day had just begun and the heat was already unbearable. They kept to the shade under the stone-pines, heading for the homestead. Jason explained that Zimbabwe and Monomotapa were neither the fabled mines of King Solomon nor the biblical Land of Ophir—and certainly not built by blue-eyed Indians or Phoenicians.

'Such attributions were made by a wandering German geologist, Karl Mauch,' he explained, 'who visited the derelict ruins in 1871. Mauch was first to declare that only an advanced, and hence foreign, civilisation could have been responsible for its construction. He even speculated that it was built for the Queen of Sheba herself.'

'She Who Must Be Shebah, not Sabaean?'

'Right, historically, Ethiopia was closely linked to southern Arabia. From the immigrant Sabaeans came the art, language and writing of early Abyssinia, with Aksum as its capital, while in turn, the kings of Ethiopia ruled over lower Arabia. They identified with Arabian culture and inherited the legendary "Makeda of the Azeb".'

'Oké, literally, the Queen of the South?'

'Yes. Mauch and others were eager to transform the Zimbabwe Ruins into the most meticulous mystery in history.'

'But not you, Jason, no, of course not!'

Jason grinned back: 'No, twentieth-century scholars were inspired by this Exotic-hypothesis, despite an Essentialist-theory-of-origins put forward by archaeologists one hundred years before. Today tourists either believe foreigners were responsible for the stone-walls, or that local craftsmen built these structures themselves.'

She understood the importance of Africa's claim to the *dzimbahwe*, including Mapungubwe's iron-age citadel in the Limpopo basin, as it reinforced the Africanist independence movement of the 1960s. And the process was not yet complete.

Jason's friend and colleague, Prof Tom Huffman, had shown that Great Zimbabwe was the economic, political and cultural successor of Mapungubwe—although its new rulers were not part of the same dynasty. The continuity of the royal *mambo* had depended on how well his family integrated with those they met while migrating north.

Leaving Bart at home, Jason had taken Sonja to see the collection of Zimbabwean artefacts at Groote Schuur—the "Grand Granary" on the lower slopes of Table Mountain. Situated in a private parkland, it was built for Cecil John Rhodes and had been the home of Nelson Mandela and other heads of state. Here decisions were taken that shaped the course of South Africa's future. One illustrious visitor was the then UN secretary general, Dag Hammarskjöld.

'If the place where we die is also where we plant a seed for our next life,' she said, 'then I hope Dag Hammarskjöld returns soon. I think you need an African Charlemagne, not a Black Napoleon!'

Jason flinched.

Was the heat that intolerable? Or did his head still throb from last night's drinking bout?

The original barn stood a stone's throw from where Almeida had been ambushed. As they approached, Sonja recalled Stein's idea of a World Granary—an international clearing house for the distribution of food and the exchange of raw materials. Jason was still talking:

'Tom Huffman says Mapungubwe's role as the trade-capital was short-lived, a mere fifty years, after which the population rapidly decreased. Around 1290—'

There was no time to speculate. The curator stood waiting on the front steps. He wore a tailored suit and spoke eloquent English. Jason had obtained prior permission for their visit.

The men shared a joke while she reflected on Zimbabwe's demise. Was it a lack of natural resources, climatic change, or the pressure of hostile tribes moving into the region?

'Coffee?' interrupted the curator, leading them to a deep terrace. Jason nodded. It was getting hotter, his headache almost visible.

'During Mapungubwe's collapse, Zimbabwe's rise to power was dramatic,' explained the curator. 'It became the region's commercial centre for the next one hundred and fifty years, until the 1470s, after which it declined rapidly. By the time the Portuguese first arrived, Monomotapa had already superseded Great Zimbabwe. The political succession of these inland states, including Thulamela, was based on a thriving gold and ivory trade network around the Indian Ocean—'

'—and their exchange items included?' she asked restlessly, holding her Persols up to the light.

'Oriental trade items,' cut in Jason, 'mostly glass beads or ceramic shards, now in Zim's museums. The best fucking artefacts are—'

'—of course,' she said, glancing over her rims at the curator. 'Please continue, Jason is not usually so expressive.'

'Very well then. Rhodes acquired his art collection through mining interests in the region, establishing the Ancient Ruins Company in the closing decades of the nineteenth century...'

But by now Jason wasn't listening, he needed more caffeine.

A half-hour later, the curator took them up to see Rhodes's bedroom. On the stairs they passed a faded Flemish tapestry depicting a metaphorical Africa—with mating snakes, a tortoise and the unicorn. Noting their interest, the curator halted:

'That's the Queen of Sheba. And there the Lion of Judah, emblem of Abyssinia... Please, this way to the master bedroom.'

The room was simple and austere, with a stiff single bed facing the window—something Henry would have liked for himself in Sagres.

Against the far wall stood a glass display cabinet with a pair of iron gongs, a copper ingot, a wooden divination bowl, and the famous Zimbabwe Bird. However, it was Rhodes's death mask that grabbed her attention. He looked like a mummified Egyptian pharaoh.

'Replicated throughout the house,' noted the curator, 'the bird was a sacred ceremonial sculpture and linked to the Ancestral Realm.'

Leaning forward, Sonja noticed it was carved from a solid grey-green soapstone; with well delineated features and a deep patina. It was a precious totem—added their guide—one of only eight in the world, and remarkably like the ibis-head Jason had photographed in Ethiopia. He'd shown this to her and Bart the day before.

Was there a rational link between his archaeological experiences in Ethiopia and Zimbabwe, she reflected, or was it a mere coincidence that he chose to dig where other people had died so violently? Jason seemed drawn to where past and present met in strife and warfare.

The curator continued:

'The first bird from Great Zimbabwe was found on the so-called Acropolis, by big-game hunter Willie Posselt in 1889. The totem was too large to carry off, so he hacked the bird from its pedestal and offered it for sale to President Kruger, but the Afrikaner statesman was out done by Rhodes, who bought it instead. So here it is, along with the last bird to be found. The other six are all in Zimbabwe—'

'—where they belong,' mumbled Jason.

'Of course,' replied the curator, politely, then turning to her. 'The birds are exceptionally rare, unique in fact, as no others have ever been found. As a symbol they may have migrated down from Arabia, via the Great Rift Valley, as a totem of the phoenix, known in Egypt as the Bird of Heaven. This paradisal fire-bird, according to Pliny, came from the island of Socotra at the mouth of the Red Sea.'

'A symbol of transformation and renewal, like the Grail?' suggested Sonja. 'In that case, what's the symbolism behind these soapstones?'

It felt like something Prof Mendle would ask.

The curator turned to Jason for an answer. Jason obliged:

'Huffman argues that the birds served to establish authority after the collapse of Mapungubwe. They legitimized the power invested in a new dynasty.'

'Like the heraldic shields and armillary spheres of the Avis?' she said, nudging Jason with a playful elbow.

'I reckon so.'

He disliked being teased. Sonja glanced back at the curator:

'Could the bird be some sort of guardian or messenger?'

'Sure. It could be a messenger corresponding to the *chapungu*, or fish eagle, which traverses air, water and land, and is thus able to mediate between the ancestral and physical worlds. Each bird is thought to memorialize the spirit of a former king. However, once a centralised political authority had been established, no more totems were made.'

'Why, because they no longer had to prove their sacred kingship?'

'Well, that's what Huffman said after excavating, documenting and researching the site for several years, and it takes you a mere minute!'

'But he had the evidence to back his theory,' she smiled, 'I have only my deductions, which don't prove anything.'

She led the way back to the terrace.

'So, what d'you think?' began Jason, once outside.

'It's easy to make statements about the specialisations of others. I'm usually cautious in my own field. Anyway, what else did they find at Great Zimbabwe?'

'Gongs, ingots, bowls, birds and—isn't that enough?' he asked.

'It's not what I'm looking for.'

'If I may,' volunteered the curator, 'they also found wooden divination tablets, ritual stone cylinders, ivory and brass ornaments, as well as iron hoes and bronze ceremonial spearheads. The latter were kept by the *vahozi*, the king's first wife, in the Royal Treasury. Other items were found in the royal graves and storage bins. Then, of course, there was all that gold…'

With that said the curator retired, promising to send out a fresh pot of coffee. They went and sat out on the lawn, the mountain towering behind them. Jason lay on the grass, shading his eyes from the fierce afternoon sun. The garden appeared to be overtly structured, like a picturesque watercolour, showing ancient nature and modern culture in sublime harmony. Yet the manor was unlike any Soviet, Xhosa or Friesian granary she'd ever seen. She could also see that no amount of coffee would stop Jason's throbbing head now.

'Who knows what the first white men took away? No doubt CJ's Ancient Ruins Company smelted countless items of gold.'

'That's scandalous!'

'Sure, Rhodes was a scoundrel. Mapungubwe's gold was removed in the 1930s and kept at the University of Pretoria, effectively hidden from view until the post-Apartheid era.'

'Why?'

'Why. Because white nationalists didn't know how to explain the existence of black civilisations in pre-colonial Africa.'

'Come on, Jason,' she said, over her rims again, 'that sounds like a conspiracy—'

He sat up, squinting at her through pinched eyes:

'—well, that's how we felt when the National Gallery exhibited the gold a decade ago, on Heritage Day. The show was called *Musuku*, meaning "gold" in luVenda, and included two spectacular artefacts:

the Gold Rhino and a Gold Sceptre. Both were made of a fine beaten foil attached to a carved wooden core; and both from a royal grave on top of Mapungubwe Hill.'

'Hey, I saw the rhino when I visited the Gold of Africa Museum, next to the Netherlands Consulate. Theirs is a copy—'

'—the Gold Rhino may be small, but its symbolism is big. Mandela recognised this when he declared it a cultural treasure. It was also an icon for Mbeki's long awaited African Renaissance.'

'Well, that sums up the difference between your former Presidents. Mandela was a pragmatic leader who acted in the nation's interest and achieved international acclaim; whereas Mbeki achieved little at home but became an all-African ideologue abroad. His Renaissance had more rhetoric than all the gold from Monomotapa.'

'And you can be *so* sarcastic in your summaries. It was actually the cleptocratic Mobutu who coined the term "African Renaissance".'

'Really, is that after he outlawed Sinterklaas and Christmas Day?'

'Sure, sure. Anyway, a revisionist Pretoria University incorporated the gold rhino into its coat-of-arms. The curator of *Musuku* said the rhino symbolises leadership; being a fierce and solitary animal.'

'But also slow, stubborn and short-sighted—'

'—thus appropriate for a university with myopic vision.'

'Hey you are on form today, Jason, despite your headache.'

'No, just too much coffee...'

The curator returned to complete the tour, leading them back to see Rhodes's handsome study. Rhodes had been obsessed with the career of Marcus Aurelius and had his life's work translated, typed and hand-bound in red cloth. The collection dominated Rhodes's library, filling an entire wall, making it his favourite room in the house. It did not escape her attention that Aurelius, one of the four Archons, had visited Groote Schuur as Dag Hammarskjöld.

The Zimbabwean artefacts had since been removed from the walls, as had a tattered Portuguese ensign captured in Manicaland in 1891. The ensign had hung next to an equally tattered Union Jack, carried into Matabeleland when Rhodesian pioneers first seized the territory.

To her mind, the two flags symbolised the intersection of territorial interests in Africa: from Mozambique to Angola, and from the Suez Canal to the Cape Colony. The Portuguese wanted to link West with East, bringing their Atlantic and Indian footholds together; whereas the British wanted to string together their adjacent possessions, all the way from the top to the bottom, North to South.

The flags also symbolised the Portuguese-British trend outlined by Stein, wherein the English fulfilled Portugal's mission in Africa. She would have to look at this matter later. Jason was still talking to her.

'CJ was a short, stocky and egotistical man. An empire-builder of grandiose proportions who wanted to rule Britannia—'

'—publicly, yes, but what about privately?' she stumbled, gathering her thoughts. Her feet were tired and she wanted to leave. It had been enough for one day.

The curator glanced at Jason, answering the question himself:

'His personal life seems to have been a failure. He was probably bisexual and unable to exercise his preferences publicly. Still, as a visionary, he had ambitious plans to link Cape Town with Cairo. His railway was supposed to unite Colony and Empire, but the proposed Red Line ran through Natal, making war with the Zulu inevitable—'

'—and from Rhodes, of course, we got Rhodesia,' added Jason.

'The Portuguese dreamt of reaching Monomotapa from both sides of southern Africa,' concluded the curator, 'but Rhodes's Red Line cut across their land claims. Had he succeeded, the railway may have been the largest man-made structure in Africa, perhaps even more impressive than the pyramids—'

'—and far longer than the Great Wall of China.'

She could stand no longer. It had been a long afternoon and so, thanking their eloquent guide, she led the way back via the shaded stone-pines.

'They say the Zimbabwe Ruins are the most impressive structures south of the Sahara—and that only the pyramids compare,' hollered Jason, catching up with her. 'Others say Great Zimbabwe was built by Africans who first migrated east, across the Sahara, and then came south via the Rift Valley—but that's another debate, and perhaps one for another lifetime.'

'Oké, Jason, then finish this one first.'

He overtook and strutted on, toward the car, making the sound of two half-coconuts banging together.

92

O Guardian of the City by the Sea...
Great Janus of the Southern Seas
Marion de Beer, *The spell of Table Mountain* (c.1930)

The sky behind Table Mountain turned Giotto-blue. It had been another brutally hot day, Heritage Day, of which the hottest part was spent in the Winelands with Bart and Jason. Returning before sunset, Sonja phoned Mendle to invite him for sundowners on the rocks, saying they had a few bottles of chilled wine in the car and were on their way to fetch him. She also wanted to discuss Almeida's skull.

Parking on the curb above Clifton, they tumbled down the stairs looking for an open spot on the flat-topped boulders. Two massive granite outcrops flanked the narrow beach, as if Table Mountain stood with its giant toes in the water. Jason led them to the far corner, beyond the farthest bathers, to where a ring of sun worshippers stood with their glasses already raised.

The shallow water's edge swarmed with activity: laughing children splashed in the surf, barking dogs chased airborne frisbees and agile youngsters played touch rugby. Further back, under their umbrellas, reclining couples pretended to be alone as picnicking families dug into their hampers.

Having reached the huge boulder top, Jason set down the cool-box and declared the spot to be the best still available. From up here they had a commanding view of the sun as it careened toward the sea.

Below, in a secluded passage between the giant boulders, an archer installed his polka-dotted target and backup-board against the rock.

'He wants to hone his skills with practice bolts,' observed Mendle, watching the archer unpack his equipment.

'Let's hone ours with a corkscrew,' said Jason, reaching for the first bottle in the cool-box. Bart handed out four plastic glasses.

Seated with a sauvignon, Sonja spoke of Saint Odilia, the Knights Templar and Stein. As Grail Christians, they all searched for common ground beyond the Mediterranean environment:

'Almeida refused to submit the treatise while his Santiago masters considered submission to be his duty, and disposal to be their right. The Order's leadership was entitled to it according to the vows taken by each knight and, to cut a long story short, they thought Almeida had disrespected the brotherhood's code of conduct—for which, in their view, he needed to be punished.'

'Aha, but why,' Mendle asked, 'why then a clandestine murder?'

'Almeida came from a respected line of advisors and treasurers, so a tribunal would have been scandalous. He therefore paid the ultimate price, here, far from any witnesses and where the Native could be blamed instead. And where all evidence would be washed away.'

To Mendle's delight, she described the semiotics of the beach as a fragile no-man's land between two cultures, between two histories:

'As Greg Dening says, history is born on the beach where Stranger and Native meet.'

Mendle chuckled: 'Indeed, and what will you do now?'

'Actually, Prof,' she said with that Etruscan smile, 'shouldn't *you* be doing something about his bones and memory?'

'Ah, yes, a tricky problem, as no one knows about our skull.'

'No one?'

'Yes, isn't that what we agreed? If not, then who do we tell first: the Portuguese authorities or the South African government? Or should we file a story for the BBC and send a *No Comment* clip to EuroNews? Of one thing I'm sure, it will be taken out of our hands immediately. But the museum is also under constant scrutiny, so we can't conceal the skull indefinitely. I say, it *is* a somewhat tricky problem!'

'It's an ethical problem, and one we'll lose if the public interferes,' said Jason, while Bart passed the potato crisps. 'It will only get worse.'

'I know, I know it all too well,' sighed Mendle.

'Why,' asked Sonja, 'because these bones belong to a Portuguese national hero?'

'Yes, but that shouldn't matter. In death we all deserve the same recognition, the same respect and the same dignified burial—'

'—not everyone,' cut in Jason, 'look at the fuss made when they returned Saartje's genitalia from Paris. She had no dignified burial, instead, they turned her into a sensation. Talk of the Eternal Return!'

Sitting beside him, Bart put a hand on his knee: 'Saartje?'

'Sarah,' noted Mendle, 'like the biblical wife of Abraham.'

'But *who* is she?' repeated Bart.

'Sarah Baartman was a spectacular African Venus from the Cape,' began Mendle. 'After being touted as a freak in Victorian London, she fell into prostitution and died of pneumonia.'

'A sort of travelling curiosity?' asked Bart.

'Worse. Her dismembered body and sexual organs were preserved at the Musée de l'Homme in Paris. When her remains were returned a decade ago, she became a symbol for all displaced Khoisan and all exploited women in the country.'

'I say, Jason,' cautioned Mendle, 'take it easy.'

Bart steadied Jason's knee, but he raged on:

'Jesus! It's a problem of ownership. To whom do Almeida's bones belong? To his family, his country, or to his chivalrous fraternity? Not to the scientific community? And certainly not to us who found him? First and foremost, his remains raise the problem of identity—'

'—you mean identification?' checked Sonja.

'—no, *identity*. Let's assume we actually have the skull and bones of Almeida, well, what then? Various groups will lay claim to him as they did to Sarah, St Elizabeth of Hungary, and the Queen of Sheba. They will say his remains belong to them, and to no other, and their arguments will be emotional, political and ideological while ours may only be scientific. They'll argue against our rational justifications and we'll have to be impassionate. It'll be a diplomatic fiasco with lots of officials breathing down our necks—'

'—then what d'you propose?' said Bart calmly.

Jason shrugged:

'Under the present circumstances? I'd say a minimum three-year moratorium should be placed on repatriating his bones, in case the situation becomes volatile.'

'The debate will need time to settle before impulsive decisions are regretted,' agreed Mendle. 'It's a lesson we've learnt from our past.'

The sun disappeared as they talked, carelessly, about the mountain and how it reinforced changing relationships to the landscape; how depictions of it showed ever-changing attitudes toward the Cape.

'When the mountain appeared wild or brutish, like a pagan giant,' said Mendle, 'the Cape was seen as hostile and inhospitable. But once settlers desired women from back home, the mountain was shown to protect virgins and young widows from the dangers of an untamed hinterland. It isn't the mountain that changed, of course, but their perception of the landscape that shifted: from explorer to settler, from traveller to colonialist, and, ultimately, from occupier to occupied.'

Mendle went on to explain how such perceptions drew on a mix of classical literature and local oral tradition, including Credo Mutwa's legend of Umlindi Wemingizimu: the "Watcher of the South".

'Isn't Mutwa that *inyanga* from Zululand?' she asked, handing out paper plates and plastic forks.

'Yes, the same,' replied Jason, propping himself against the picnic basket. 'A bit like the charlatan Tilana Gcaleka—'

'—who found the skull of Chief Hintsa kaPhalo?'

'Same, same. Mutwa and Gcaleka have been labelled charlatans by their peers,' continued Jason, as Bart shifted his weight against him. 'Mutwa argued against the elemental tribalism of the Zulu, ironically, until he found himself shunned for sharing their arcane knowledge with the Whites.'

'I met Mutwa once,' added Mendle, 'at a conference in KwaZulu-Natal during the mid-Eighties, long after his book was published. He's an impressive and charismatic shaman—despite his complaints about publishers and book royalties—but, alas, I was too arrogant to ask about the secret origins of the amaZulu.'

'But *is* he a charlatan?' pressed Sonja.

'Well, born in the 1920s—out of wedlock too, like Shaka—he fell between a rock and a hard place. He also fell between Zulu tribal custom and Catholic missionary zeal. His father was a catechist who cursed the customs of the heathen—including his mother, who came from a long line of revered healers and praise-poets, but was rejected by his father after she refused to convert. During a traumatic and prolonged illness, Mutwa's maternal grandfather instilled in him the belief that he was destined to become a traditional healer.'

'So he started calling himself a witchdoctor?'

'It's an old-fashioned term, yes, which he's used somewhat naively. After ordinary doctors failed him, he began to question the basis of Western medicine and religion... until he renounced Christianity and underwent an initiation as a shaman. After that, he wrote *Indaba* so white men could understand the Zulu.'

'And what did you find, Prof?' she asked, keeping the conversation focussed while her companions opened another bottle.

They were fast becoming exuberant.

'Ah, Mutwa recalls the myth of Umlindi Wemingizimu where the Mother God, Qamata, created the world. Qamata came from the union between the Sky-god and the Earth-goddess, but was crippled when the great Dragon of the Sea tried to prevent her forming dry land above the water. At that time, the earth was still covered by water. However, assisting Qamata were her four brothers (also giants) who guarded the northern, western, eastern and southern corners of the land; the largest keeping watch in the South. After many battles, the four asked their Great Earth Mother to turn them each into a mountain so that they could continue to protect the land from the jealous sea-dragon—even in death. The greatest of these four giants became Umlindi Wemingizimu, the "Watcher of the South", that is, Table Mountain today.'

'Table Mountain's mythology seems to reveal contrasting attitudes to the landscape,' observed Sonja, 'Adamastor turns into a vindictive giant while Umlindi-whatever becomes a benevolent being.'

With Bart's head on his shoulder, Jason resumed: 'Growing up in its shadow, we likened the mountain to a sleeping giant. It's what you saw from District Six, and local fishermen still call it *d'Klipman*.'

'As a child I heard it called the Old Grey Father,' added Mendle.

'And where does Mijnheer Van Hunks fit in?' she asked.

'Ah, it seems the Cape Muslims began the enigma of Van Hunks, a lone pirate who enters a Faustian duel with a cloaked stranger on the mountain. Usually in the saddle above Vredehoek.'

'The Devil in disguise, smoking a pipe,' said Jason with a careless slur, 'followed by a contest to see who could produce the most cloud.'

'Mephisto-like?'

'Right. Van Hunks is a vagabond-hero willing to sell his soul in order to control the forces of nature. I say, semiotically, he symbolises the vanities of the foolish foreigner.'

Mendle corked the bottle and quietly emptied Jason's glass.

Sonja smiled back as he explained how the mythical Janus was not only the Gate Keeper, but also a Guardian of the Threshold, the one who opens and fastens, begins and ends all worldly things.

'Table Mountain was likened to Janus, god of gods,' added Mendle, 'revealing the true meaning of *Cabo da Bõa Esperança*. As death is a gate through which we pass, in-and-out, so too Hope takes us beyond death's threshold. As does the Cape of Good Hope itself—'

'—and the patron saint of Hope is Sant'Iago?'

Delighted, Mendle concluded:

'Janus is usually represented with two faces, suggesting vigilance. He looks before and behind, seeing the future while knowing the past. In this way Table Mountain is truly the "Watcher of the South" and guards the Atlantic and Indian oceans, protecting those who journey between East and West, old and new, warm and cold, good and evil.'

'As do we all right here, now, between the Dark and Emerald seas. Between the most traversed one before us and there, toward the East, the youngest of them all.'

Sonja had hardly finished when Bart slumped forward—*whoosh*—clutching his neck. A red gash appeared, instantly, as if from ear to ear, the blood spreading between his fingers and soaking his collar.

Lowering Bart's head, Jason turned to the man with a crossbow.

Standing up, Sonja saw him draw a second bolt. *Verdomme*, it was no accident, no stray shot. Like an executioner, he raised the crossbow and calmly aimed for her throat.

She screamed, recognising his ogrish form.

'Goliath!'

There was a flash of light, another *whoosh*, followed by a dull thud.

Then silence.

Only the distant sound of playing children.

She waited for the pain... but her body had no sensation.

Instead, the man sagged to his knees, dropping the crossbow in the sand. The projectile still cocked.

The events that followed passed before her like a film—a strip of film with slow, separate frames.

She heard more voices, yelling voices, as several men ran toward her. They came from a nearby beach bungalow, dressed in uniform, carrying telescopic rifles.

Snipers?

She froze as they approached.

'Stand off! Stand off while we secure the area,' she heard, 'we still have him in our sights.'

The next few minutes seemed to blur as uniformed men ran about shouting at each other. She saw three men reach the Black Goliath and another go over to Bart—now limp in Jason's arms.

Behind her someone radioed for a medic.

Mendle grabbed a towel, bundled it around an iceblock, and placed it against Bart's neck.

'You'll be fine, it'll slow down the bleeding until help gets here.'

'You're lucky to be alive, Miss,' said the same voice behind her. 'We were tipped off by French Interpol when he entered the country and have been following him ever since. He's a suspected assassin, known to us as Moordenaar Mordechai, and sent out here for a hit. We thought he came here today to practice. Our mistake, sorry...'

9ᴈ

In Africa, one dreams about India, just as in Europe one dreams
of Africa: the ideal always radiates beyond our actual horizon.

Gérard de Nerval, *Journeys to the Orient* (1851)

The gash on Bart's neck was superficial, luckily, as the point of the
bolt only grazed his skin. The medics said the shot could have killed
him, especially at such close range, although he wasn't the intended
target. They thought the shot was meant for Sonja.

So far as she knew, Ben Mordechai was wanted for violent crimes
and Interpol had issued a "red notice" for his extradition to France.
However, the South African police had kept him under surveillance,
hoping he'd lead them to his handler, supposedly in Johannesburg.

Two days after the shooting, Jason and her left Bart to rest and
went for lunch at Café del Mare in lower Strand Street; a thorough-
fare once built along the old beach to link the Castle with Signal Hill.
Mendle had invited them to meet Laurence.

The dip in the road indicated where a stream once flowed into the
sea and, like the Camissa, now ran under the city. It could be heard
passing below street level on a quiet night—long after the last rains
had gone.

The café was situated not far from where Dias and Almeida came
ashore: Dias with an astrolabe to calculate the latitude and Almeida
with a carafe of wine for lunch. For Almeida's meal, a table had been
brought ashore and set under some big trees, between the beach and

the spring, making this the first tavern-of-the-seas at the Cape. From his shaded spot, overlooking the bay, Almeida watched his crew carry water casks back to the boats. A tally was kept to ensure no sailor scurried off to the Quena village...

Mendle and Laurence had been meeting at Café del Mare for as long as either could remember. It was a convenient location for Laurence, whose private practice was situated around the corner.

True, he was a short man, much smaller than Mendle, with almond eyes and a short soft beard. His modest demeanour was not what Sonja and Jason were expecting from a psychic—certainly not from a white sangoma.

'I suppose people expect someone bigger, taller, even larger than life, but I really have no need for another body when this one serves me so well.'

Neither knew what to say next. Sonja had prepared questions about Almeida and his reappearance as Walter Johannes Stein. Jason came to press Laurence on Josephus the Arimathean.

Both were anxious to do so before the other started.

Sensing they'd leap in together, Mendle eased the situation.

'Shall we order lunch? Laure and I usually have vegetarian pasta or roast vegetables. Then you can ask all your questions. Meanwhile, Laure, why not tell them how it began in Long Street?'

Laurence nodded, considering the chalked-up *Today's Specials*, then turned and spoke softly:

'I had a dream thirty years ago, in 1982, in which I was browsing around a bookshop and came upon a biography bearing my name. For several months the dream recurred, periodically, and I would awaken in wonder. One day—while in reality browsing in a second-hand bookshop—my gaze unexpectedly fell upon the same name: Laurence Oliphant. I stood transfixed in *déjà vu*. As in my dream, I had found the book and knew at once—this is about me. By the next day I'd read it through, cover to cover, and as the remembrance of that lifetime unfolded, it filled me with pride, pain and pity.'

Mendle inserted: 'Laurence Oliphant was a mid-nineteenth century writer, traveller, diplomat, secret agent and mystic.'

'I couldn't come to terms with the idea, not initially, although I believed in reincarnation and had been curious as to who or what I might have been in the past. But quite frankly, Laurence Oliphant was a disappointment. I was dismayed and disliked what I read about him. I tried hard to deny him, despite a forceful feeling of recognition within. Nevertheless, for a while I didn't know what to make of the matter, until its meaning unexpectedly impressed itself upon me.'

Sonja tried to interrupt, but couldn't find the right words, and so gestured for him to continue. Jason sat motionless, like a stone.

'Aha, here's our meal,' said Mendle, as the waitress approached. 'Please begin while Laure continues. He only has an hour.'

'Thank you, Jos, always the mediator, as your good name implies. Anyway, about transpersonal lives, I felt perplexed and asked myself: "What of this Laurence Oliphant?" At once a voice spoke quietly within, saying:

Laurence Oliphant was your last birth…

'I was astonished, naturally, and yet despite my surprise, wondered: "Who was I before?" And the voice promptly responded:

Before Laurence Oliphant was, I am…

'I then posed a question, "Who are you?" and the voice answered enigmatically:

I am your first memory…

'I felt strange—my familiar sense of self seemed to disappear and in its place stood an ancient being called El Aurenx. Quite simply, he is my higher self and now speaks to me daily, usually late at night when, in fact, I'd prefer to go to sleep, which can be somewhat annoying for us both. I presume Jos told you the rest.'

Mendle lay aside his fork, taking Jason's notepad to jot down two words: 'There's a phonetic similarity. Listen to its resonance.'

L aur en ce

El Aur en x

'What truth there is, or not, to believe in,' began Sonja clumsily, 'how did you receive your messages about Almeida?'

'I usually hear a voice in my head. It sounds just like my own, but I recognise differences in tone and tempo. Most often it's El Aurenx. Others speak to me too—which is common for clairaudients—and they always identify themselves. Over the years I've learnt to identify their particular speech patterns.'

'Like alien abduction or possession?' Jason chimed in.

'Hey,' she nudged, irritated, 'don't be the Fool of the Two-Halved Coconuts.'

'Rather like Sir Percivale, isn't he, going from dullness and doubt to despair and destiny?' said Laurence, before turning to Jason: 'Is there anything you *do* believe in?'

Jason was taken aback. Pushing aside his plate, he responded:

'I believe in the power of words, like Quena or Sonqua, in words that stir something within us. We are what we call ourselves, not what others name us.'

'Like?'

'Cape Coloured.'

'What would you prefer?'

'Dunno, just Capetonian, perhaps?'

'Which is what I am, Jason, so we have something in common— even if we are from mixed families. There's no issue of race when we incarnate into different bloodlines all the time. Our names should refer to something personal, something linked to our own recurring identity. Take your name for instance: *Jason Tomas.*'

'Why, because I'm like Jason searching for the Golden Fleece? Or Doubting Thomas needing proof of a Holier Grail?'

'Well,' replied Laurence, 'Thomas never doubted—that's a mere misconception—rather, he questioned what others simply believed. He put knowledge before faith and, as a Gnostic, preferred evidence to superstition. Moreover, Thomas means *Twin.*'

'Yes, and *Ja-son* is derived from *Son of Ja* or *Yahweh*,' added Mendle with a smile, sliding the notepad back across the table.

Jason was silent. Laurence continued:

'Look at the names we have for the One, for the Ineffable, for the One Too Great To Describe, for the Ein-Sof. Look at the incantatory names—Elyorem, Theloy, Abba Sabanda and Holy Father—various names used through the ages by different cultures. Or all the secret names the Hermit whispered into the ear of Parsifal, which Chrétien de Troyes says should only be uttered by the tongues of man in fear of death. *Chrétien* was probably a nom de plume and veils his true understanding of a secret like the Beatific Vision.'

'A beatific vision?' confirmed Sonja.

'The medieval Beatific Vision is described in some surviving texts as a ritual climax through which an individual achieves direct contact with the ultimate secrets of creation and the mysteries of nature.'

'As if you were seeing the countenance of God,' offered Mendle.

'Yes, a terrible beauty after ecstatic pain. Following twenty-eight days of rigorous fasting and praying, the initiate would undergo a near-death experience, one in which he'd "witness" the awesome face of divinity. Richard Barber observes how this white magic ritual was used as an extension to orthodox Christianity, practiced in secret outside the constraints of the Catholic Church, but with the help of a willing priest. The ritual circumvented years of worship and a lifetime of devotion. It was restricted, then, as it is suppressed today.'

'The act defines *mysticism*,' interjected Mendle, 'namely, where one achieves direct consciousness of God—or truth—through meditation, inspiration and intuition.'

Laurence filled in: 'The ritual culminates in a repetitive invocation of arcane names—Elyorem, Archima, Theloy—which are all ancient Greek, Hebraic and Aramaic variations for *God*.'

Sonja recalled what Volodya had said about the body being taught to react differently to the same stimuli and, ultimately, how it can be used to induce an altered state of consciousness.

Jason listened to the pronunciation of each, adding:

'I had an uncle who could recite the ninety-nine names of Allah.'

'Names which only came to the fore after the mystical teachings of the Kabbalah had been translated into Latin,' noted Mendle, asking a passing waitress for the desert menu. Laurence concluded:

'As Barber points out, the Beatific Vision is at the heart of the Grail legend. As the object of a sacred ritual, this vision is achieved with rigorous self-discipline involving fasting, prayer and cleanliness. There are traces of a lost ritual associated with the Grail in the early literature. For Barber—and this is inspired on his part—Chrétien's unfinished story is completed by this ritual. The quest is about a body of secret lore within the Church, a tradition of ritual magic which was known to a select few, East and West, and which represented a non-apostolic tradition. Chrétien knew it was safe to present this as a romance, since most would read it as a chivalric story with a strong moral code; whereas the initiated would understand the Grail as an allegory for the secret tradition of the Templars and Rosicrucians. Barber is correct when he says the Grail is an archetype for the Mass-chalice. It is a symbol of the Eucharistic Mysteries of Atlantis which, ultimately, were invested in the sacrament of Holy Communion. The question of the contrite seeker has an answer:

Whom does the Grail serve?

He who was, is and will be king
—but is not of this world

'The most authentic versions of the Grail legend appear to be those in which a young hero, on a journey of self-discovery, has to ask one essential question about what he sees, bringing his experience to full consciousness: this usually occurs when experience and imagination meet in a moment of truth. In most versions this question is about the essence of being human. This is the true Way of the Grail.'

Laurence paused, wiping his beard, while the waitress took their order for four coffees and one cheese cake. Mendle's favourite.

'No matter how probable they seem,' he added, 'we can never be certain of claims made about the truth. Behind each recorded event are other interpretations—historical, literary, factual and fictional. Even if there is only one interpretation, we can never be certain and are thus unable to solve a mystery like Almeida's murder. The best we can do is offer an account that seems most probable; the version we believe to be right. The riddle of Almeida's murder, like the Grail legend itself, is based on both historical fact and literary fiction—and therefore not objectively true. In short,' he concluded, preparing to leave, 'it's a subjective story that represents a true history. And, above all, it is a story of spiritual regeneration.'

94

Our child, we who speak to you are Akhnaton and Kublai Khan,
known in world history as the heretic pharaoh of Egypt and the
enlightened emperor of China. We would have that you hear the
unfinished story of our time and its sequel in yours, a story now
unfolding in a country you once knew as your own.

Laurence-El Aurenx, clairaudient dictation (25 September 2010)

The blinds were drawn against the afternoon sun, softening the light and dampening the sound rising from the arcade below. Laurence sat by the window and poured Sonja a glass of water, asking after Bart's recovery and any possible history of involuntary manslaughter.

His consulting rooms were well located in the city-centre: spacious, open, and suitably secluded. He'd invited her to visit him, preferably alone, as he felt still more may be said about her part in Almeida's murder.

She was in mid-sentence when he interrupted, saying there were others who wanted to speak to her.

'There's nothing to fear, I promise, as they may only talk about the things you're willing and able to live with. That's a karmic rule. And I'll be present all the time. Do you want to hear them now?'

'Oké, yes, fine.'

Laurence tilted his head to one side, ever so slightly, and focused on the empty space between their chairs. He seemed fully conscious, breathing evenly as he spoke, his voice unchanged:

'I, Akhnaton, will first review the last days of Egypt's Eighteenth dynasty, from the time of my father Pharaoh Amenhotep III, to that of the last pharaoh of the age, the usurper Horemheb. Kublai Khan would speak to you too, afterwards, if you want, about the last days of his reign in Mongolia. We thank you for this opportunity, kind child, as we have a message of some importance.'

Laurence smiled, his eyes diverting to her. 'Okay?'

'Oké.'

His eyes focused between them again.

'I, Akhnaton, would have you know that Horemheb is none other than your Nelson Mandela. Fourteen centuries before your present age, Horemheb was my military commander-in-chief and had warned me of the weakening political situation in my empire. Regrettably, I ignored his advice and forbade any military action. Withdrawn and out of touch with the populace, I concerned myself only with issues of religious revolution—the monotheist religion of Aton. For his worship I built a new capital, Akhetaton, "citadel of Aton", and moved my court out of Thebes.

'Aton or *Atanu* had evolved from the supreme sun-god Ra, whose face was like the disc of a vernal sun and its life-giving rays of light. The priesthood of On had nurtured this tradition since the fifth dynasty. It is perhaps well to remind you that Francisco d'Almeida had also been initiated here, at On, which you now call Heliopolis.

'Horemheb-Mandela feared that the continuing emigration of our Hebrew slave population—initiated by the Royal Keeper of the Ark of Amen, Osiraes, known to you as the biblical Moses—would set off a rebellion, or worse, an invasion.

'Still, I refused to listen, preoccupied by my grandiose vision of a utopian church-state. Had it not been for the diplomatic initiatives of my minister of foreign affairs, Tutu, the eastern provinces may have seceded their independence. However, my political indifference was counterbalanced by Tutu's tactful foreign policy, for he saved Egypt when I, alas, failed my people. It should be easy to guess that Tutu is the gracious and illustrious former archbishop, Desmond Tutu.

'Coincidently, my minister of art and culture was then Bek, the same as your Thabo Mbeki. He orchestrated under my direction a renaissance in art and architecture to express the religious revolution with which I was obsessed.

'You may find these recurrent names ludicrous, but they are so for good reason, which we shall explain in due course.'

Laurence paused, as if listening to an aside, and then continued:

'My queen-wife, a foreign princess from the kingdom of Mitanni in the Tigris Valley, was called Nefertiti on account of her beauty. Her name means "beautiful woman" and she had been chosen as a new wife for my father, but their marriage was never consummated due to his ill-health. Be that as it may, of our unfortunate union no male offspring was born, although we were to have several daughters. She is known today as Winifred, or simply Winnie, former wife of Nelson Mandela.

'The celebrated Eighteenth dynasty came to an end under the rule of its military usurper Horemheb-Mandela, which was to endure for twenty-seven years. It is in consequence of this that, in your era, he would endure imprisonment for another twenty-seven years, and so become the liberator of his oppressed people.

'Horemheb-Mandela's hatred and execution of Nefertiti-Winifred had to be expiated in his troubled marriage to her in this present life. For the law of karma requires hatred to be met again—as tragic love.

'You are wondering in your mind: *Who was Chief Albert Luthuli?* I tell you, this man of peace was a priest of On and a chief minister of my court at Akhetaton. His name was Aper-El.

'The priesthood of On was affiliated with foreign monotheistic solar cults among the western isles, the Atlantides, and in the east toward Sumeria. While I embraced the worship of Aton, the former state religion of Amen-Ra threatened my throne.

'I must digress to my unfortunate marriage again. Unbeknown to official history, I had a son by a beloved mistress Hareth, who was also my court singer. The child was called Tutankhaton, destined to rule as Tutankhamen. Nefertiti was exceedingly jealous, fearing she would be deposed as queen-wife in favour of the child's mother. She became disloyal and treacherous, abducting Tutankhaton and taking him to Thebes. Here he was raised as a royal priest of Amen-Ra, like Osiraes before him, so when the time came he would be presented as my successor, reclaiming their position as the state religion. Hence I am called the Heretic Pharaoh.

'Tutankhaton's mother was heartbroken by the loss of our son and drowned herself in the Nile. My own heart broke and I never smiled again. As the years passed my health began to fail slowly, then rapidly, so that I knew I was dying from grief and disillusionment.'

'Shortly after this I, Akhnaton, died in despair. Smenkhare, my younger brother, bravely ascended the throne and defended my capital against the onslaught unleashed by the Amenite priesthood in Thebes. But the avaricious regime now seized its chance to regain supremacy in Egypt. I would that you know who Smenkhare was. He returned as General JC Smuts, twice South Africa's prime minister, and similarly failed to stave off the ominous rise to power of a new regime—Afrikaner Nationalism. General Jan Christiaan Smuts had been St John Chrysostom, a link you may want to look at yourself.

'You have no doubt realised that most ministers and officials of my court at Akhetaton, some ever loyal to me, reincarnated as the black leadership of South Africa; whereas the priests of Amen-Ra were the leaders of the old white regime. As you see, karma has a way of turning events around to maintain a balance in the world.

'I should also mention that the cult of Sebek, the crocodile-god of the Amenites, had a high priest called Sebekhotep—better known as the Apartheid state president PW Botha, *Die Groot Krokodil*.'

Laurence smiled again. 'Yes, this amuses them too!'

As easily as he spoke, so Akhnaton continued:

'*Who are these leaders?* I sense your thoughts, so allow me to identify a few more prominent ministers from my court and their incarnations in your era, albeit that some are no longer with you:

'Chief-of-police Mahu returned as Chief Mangosuthu Buthelezi. Chief administrator Maya returned as Roelf Meyer. My trusted royal secretary Hani returned as Chris Hani; whereas the scribe and priest of On, Pa-Aton, returned as Alan Paton.

'You are wondering in your mind about the women? *Were none worthy?* Then, as now, men regrettably overshadowed women. But there was one woman who could have ruled Egypt better than any man, had she been given the chance. She was my dear and revered mother, Queen Ti, who returned as Helen Suzman.

'It matters not who was who, who did what, or who was right and who wrong. What matters are the lessons to be learnt from one another. In the politics of your day, there is no one who is right and all others wrong. There are but those who seek to serve their own self-interest and those who consider the good of all.

'You judge which way is best. Be wise and broad-minded in your judgements; gentle and generous in all your doings. To my former ministers I say: may you remember who you are and heed the lessons taught by my life as Akhnaton. May you fulfil the best of my ideals and triumph over the worst of my tragedies.

'In spirit I, Akhnaton, keep watch over this country to see that the mistakes of the eternal past are not repeated. A great future awaits you in due course, if you heed my counsel and dedicate yourselves to reconciliation. God never takes sides; no one is on God's side who does not first love his neighbour as himself. There is no separatism in God's eyes; no such thing as a chosen people or holy war.

'There is no cause whatsoever that justifies enmity against one another, no ideal worth the exaction of another, for you must live up to your ideals with inner fortitude and not, no, not with outer hostility— as Almeida learnt when he died.

'This is the lesson South Africans must learn and teach the world: that ideals cannot be divorced from the people they serve but must grow in their hearts and minds, not through imposition, but through nurture. Let my people grow.

'I am Akhnaton.'

Laurence halted for more water, and to check on how she was doing.

'Overwhelmed, honestly, but getting used to it,' Sonja responded.

'Shall we continue?'

'Please.'

While Akhnaton spoke, a sombre bank of cloud had obscured the sun, darkening the consulting room. Laurence raised the blind and reseated himself, closing his eyes this time:

'My Child, I who speak to you am Kublai Khan, the enlightened overlord of a cultural renaissance dedicated to the advancement of religion, art and knowledge. My history must speak for itself, for it is not why I come to you. I would speak of my brothers Mongka, Hulagu and Boka, who are reincarnate among you today as Nelson Mandela, Mangosuthu Buthelezi and Thabo Mbeki, respectively. We four were then heirs of the monstrous Temüjin, our grandfather, known to you as the notorious Genghis Khan.

'My beloved spiritual brother, Akhnaton, has already informed you of their ancient incarnations in Egypt's Eighteenth dynasty, and I would show you now how their thirteenth-century incarnations in Mongolia shaped their political roles in your world today. I do so neither to glorify nor vilify them, but to illustrate what lessons life teaches us through karma.

'Genghis Khan bequeathed an empire unparalleled in the history of the world. Established through merciless massacres, his realm embraced almost all Asia and was to expand further east and west under his descendents. After our grandfather's death, his four sons contested the succession. My mother Sorgha, a Nestorian Christian esteemed for her sagacity and dignity, bequeathed to us the highest education among the contending princes.

'Our uncle Batu Khan, who extended the Russian conquests into Eastern Europe, favoured the eldest Mongka for Grand Khanate. This may seem ironic, if you recall that Batu was PW Botha, the president who perpetuated the imprisonment of Nelson Mandela on Robben Island.

'Mongka's own military triumph in the ensuing civil war made him, before all, the undisputed Great Khan. The deposed princes were banished while the ex-regent's mother, Oghul, was executed for her sorcery and treachery. She had striven sorely and bitterly against his ascension. I leave it to your discretion to recognise Oghul in her present-day incarnation, in the light of Akhnaton's disclosure.

'After Mongka-Mandela became Great Khan, we brothers began to re-expand the Mongol empire. Batu-Botha used his Golden Horde to occupy Russia and eastern Europe, Hulagu-Buthelezi conquered Persia while I, Kublai Khan, established the Yüan Dynasty and held my court in Cambaluc.

'Under Mongka-Mandela, the Great Khan's court at Karakorum became the diplomatic centre of the world, receiving embassies from all over Asia and Europe. They were welcomed from everywhere.'

Laurence shifted his weight in the chair.

'It is not of these conquests that I, Kublai Khan, now speak, but of our contrasting temperaments and differing ideologies. Mongka-Mandela believed that his destiny was to keep the Mongolian Empire united under his rule and to bring the world under one dispensation. He believed law and order was the way to create political conditions necessary to unite all peoples under a common welfare of peace and prosperity. He practised no racial or religious discrimination.

'Mongka-Mandela believed in one God, but in no particular form of worship. He attended religious ceremonies of all the great faiths—Buddhist, Christian and Muslim equally—and religious freedom was well tolerated by him. But he never could tolerate dissension and was ruthless with those who pitted themselves against him.

'Hulagu-Buthelezi was more intellectually inclined, dabbling in philosophy and science, but lacked the practical broadmindedness of his eldest and more illustrious brother. He practised no religion himself. Though interested in all, he favoured the Christians in reverence to his mother. In this regard he was further influenced by his chief wife, also a Nestorian, who hated Islam. He displayed such intolerance toward the Persian Muslims that the Caliphs never submitted to Mongol rule. For this they were harshly persecuted and their resistance relentlessly crushed. His partisanship greatly fuelled the feud between Muslims and Christians during the last crusades. He displayed a violent temper and was given to fits of terrific rage. While he never challenged the supremacy of his eldest brother, the Great Khan, Hulagu-Buthelezi clashed with him temperamentally.

'Mongka-Mandela deplored the alienation of the Muslims but, for the sake of expediency, would not risk curbing his brother's despotic rule. When Mongka-Mandela died, campaigning with me in China, civil war broke out yet again and we suffered a crisis of succession. Although I was the rightful heir, our youngest brother Boka-Mbeki usurped the right of succession. Boka had been the Great Khan's deputy at court and (significantly for his future as Mbeki) had the imperial family's support. Hulagu-Buthelezi contested this, not out of loyalty to me, but because he feared losing his Persian Khanate. Boka-Mbeki had already strongly criticized his severe rule.

'Their enmity put me in a difficult position. I wanted to abdicate my succession in favour of Boka-Mbeki, for he was honourable and able, but I knew Hulagu-Buthelezi would never bow to his younger brother, making civil war inevitable. I feared our empire would be irrevocably lost, and thus asserted my claim.

'I became the Great Khan of the entire Mongolian Empire, though effectively ruled only China. Having inherited an empire built on violence, I nevertheless tried to maintain it through non-violence and, if not, by humane righteousness. It was through my merciful and compassionate tolerance of conquered subjects that I emulated the famous Buddhist emperor Asoka. It was this that led to me being called a Buddhist myself but, in truth, I was sincerely as much a Christian and a Muslim and a believer in every righteous religion. To my court in Cambaluc came many envoys—including Marco Polo of Venetian fame. I lit the flame for a humanistic renaissance which, I like to believe, kindled the great European Renaissance of a century or two later.

'From my spirit realm, I advocate the renaissance in South Africa. I know all too well the difficulties of trying to serve spiritual ideals in a world of political contention and religious strife. I also know that it can be done, and done well.

'To my three brothers in this life, and to my spiritual brothers and sisters of the eternal past, I say: help one another. Help each other to live up to your highest ideals as human beings. True humanity lies not in enmity and conflict, but in tolerance and goodwill.

'I am Kublai Khan, the Dalai Lama of your time.'

Sonja watched, waiting for more…

Laurence remained silent, eyes closed, while the expression on his face continued to change. She assumed he could still hear the voices.

When he spoke, he looked directly at her:

'I asked Tenzin Gyatso, the Dalai Lama, to tell you more about his own past lives. To which he smiled, saying: "Before Kublai Khan, I was Altan Khan, the Mongol king who first conferred the title of Grand Lama of Tibet in 1578." He thought you'd like a real date, and then he laughed!'

'So he knows my thoughts, my weaknesses too?'

'Yes, they know everything about me, even the time I go to sleep. That's usually when they want me to work,' he smiled, 'which can be unsettling if you have to switch on the light or don't have a pen to hand. Be that as it may, I was born tired! Anyway, I think you should know that this was an extraordinary session, even for me—'

'—really?'

'Yes, I don't usually receive so much in one session. As you know, Akhnaton's immediate forefathers were the four Archons who—like the four giant brothers of the Great Earth Mother of Africa—strove to free the world and maintain peace on earth. Also, that Horemheb-Mandela, in turn, was succeeded by his trusted second-in-command, Ramses, first pharaoh of the next age: the Nineteenth dynasty. Today

Ramses is reincarnate as Cyril Ramaphosa who, I hope, will become president one day.'

'And Zuma?'

'It appears he was an Amenite priest called Ahmose or Ahmes and partisan to Nefertiti's plot to install the abducted Tutankhaton as a puppet pharaoh. With their success he became vizier of the South, at Thebes, under Tutankhamen, and is remembered as Usermontu.'

'Hence his close ties with Winnie today?'

'Yes, but more importantly, the vizier of the North was Pa-Ramose —that is, Ramses-Ramaphosa—who played a counterbalancing role at Memphis too. It will be interesting to see what happens to them over the next few years.'

She took a sip of water.

'Sonja, as you will expect, Zuma reappeared in Kublai's court. From his name, Ahmad Uzma, it would seem he came from what is now Uzbekistan. He rose to the position of finance minister, taking advantage of his master's misplaced trust and the distractions of civil war. He was reputedly the most corrupt court official and renowned for his many wives. Though he was accused of murder, the Grand Khan sidelined all attempts to impeach him and kept him at court. Despite this, Uzma-Zuma's abuses of power did not stop—nor did his lucrative exploitation of the Kublai's war with Ariq-Boka-Mbeki—as he also faced similar charges for capitalizing on arms-deals. Uzma-Zuma's ruthless story was apparently known to Marco Polo…'

'Wait, so how does Zuma's story end?'

'Good. Uzma-Zuma disposed of his rivals and critics in ruthless ways. Some were demoted or imprisoned, many were executed, others simply vanished. However, he surrounded himself with cronies until he was ambushed and killed by a zealous military commander, Wang Zhu, and several co-conspirators. Kublai had the ring-leaders executed. Before he was beheaded, Wang Zhu cried out: "I, Wang Zhu, die for having rid the world of a pest!" Uzma-Zuma received a state funeral, but when Kublai finally came to learn the truth about him, he exclaimed: "Wang Zhu was perfectly right to kill Uzma!" Everything Uzma-Zuma owned was seized. Everything he had done was undone. Yet you should not despair over South Africa's future, Sonja, as we all have to prove ourselves again in other lives. As did Zuma in his next life, when he returned as Montezuma.'

'Montezuma?'

Laurence smiled, his almond eyes just visible.

'The historical Montezuma was the last Aztec emperor of Mexico. His initial career was as a military leader and priest in the temple of the war god, Huitzilopochtli. In accordance with Aztec custom his coronation was accompanied by mass human sacrifices. As an expansionist, he enlarged his empire through the conquest of the Honduras and Nicaragua. His rule was accompanied by unfavourable omens— notably the predicted return of Quetzalcoatl, a local god, white in colour. The arrival of Cortés and the Spaniards was thought to fulfil this prophecy and so Montezuma, with uncharacteristic diplomacy, did not react aggressively. In return, he was imprisoned by Cortés in Mexico City, precipitating an uprising by his brother and heir. In an effort to divert the revolt, Cortés induced Montezuma to address his people from the Spanish stronghold. The angry mob responded by showering Montezuma with stones and arrows, and so he died, either by wounds inflicted by the mob or, afterwards, at the hands of his captors. We must wait to see how he redeems himself in South Africa. Here, let me give you the notes I made on Zuma's last life, in Shaka's Zululand. It may help explain his arrogance and fears in our time.'

95

The road was new to me, as roads always are, going back.
Sarah Orne Jewett, *The Country of the Pointed Firs* (1896)

September 25. Following through on the lives of Jacob Zuma: After his tragic life as Montezuma, his soul ached with a deep distrust and hatred of white men. This carried over into his next life, recorded in the amaZulu chronicles at the time of Shaka and Dingane, under the name *Jacob*.

Jakob or Jacob was the Christian name given to him by Dutch settlers and British soldiers, as being phonetically close to his isiXhosa name, *Jakoet*. His clan name was Msimbiti.

Convicted of cattle theft on the Colony's eastern frontier, he was sent to the penal colony on Robben Island in 1819, along with the banished amaXhosa king Makhanda (hence the name "isle of Makhanda"). He and several others were involved in the daring escape of 1820—in which Makhanda, tragically, drowned when their boat capsized—and was himself caught and sentenced to hard labour in irons for a further fourteen years. However, Jacob was released soon after into the service of English mercantile traders. They needed an interpreter.

On a sea-going expedition with his new masters, including the notorious ex-lieutenant Francis Farewell, their boat floundered in the surf off St Lucia. Jacob rescued one of his masters from drowning. Nevertheless, he was blamed for toppling the boat, at which he deserted and swiftly fled into the bush. Farewell and others would later catch up and seal his fate.

428

For now, Jacob arrived at the royal kraal of Shaka Zulu who, on hearing his woeful tale, nicknamed him *Hlambamanzi*, the "Swimmer", and retained him as his personal aide, adviser and interpreter. While king Shaka welcomed white traders, Jacob always warned against their treachery.

It would seem that Jacob eventually switched his allegiance to Shaka's half-brother, Dingane, for when the latter assassinated the king it was Jacob who sent foot messengers to the traders, saying they had nothing to fear as the new king invited them to trade skins and ivory. Acting as Dingane's ambassador, Jacob promised them renewed peace and prosperity in Zululand.

His former masters were suspicious, however, as Jacob had openly opposed the presence of white hunter-traders in Natal under Shaka's rule. The English were also wary of his criminal record and widespread reputation as a liar and schemer, even among his compatriots.

And indeed it was that Jacob constantly urged Dingane to avoid association with the Whites. He schemed and plotted, calling them "evil sorcerers" while poisoning the king's mind with lurid tales of their cruelty and treachery.

He was again arrested by the Whites for pilfering, and they pressed Dingane to put him on trial for deceit and duplicitous conduct. Dingane vacillated, half-believing Jacob's insistent claim that the Dutch and British were conspiring to invade and steal his kingdom.

But, after Jacob was caught stealing again from the royal herd, Dingane lost his temper and ordered his execution. Jacob was hunted down by his arch-rival, John Cane, to whom Dingane later gave eighty cows from Jacob's own herd.

Dingane never forgot Jacob's oft-repeated prophecy—echoing Shaka's dying words—that one day the Whites would conquer and rule the land. It was his past experience as Montezuma that had told him so. And surely he was right?

Hamba Gahle.

96

They climb the mountain with their children
To put the symbol of the ancient stone on its forehead.

Mazisi Kunene, *The Ancestors & the Sacred Mountain* (1982)

That weekend the torrential rains finally stopped. While clearing over the Cape, both Central and West Africa continued to experience a deluge of unknown proportions. Across twenty countries—from the Atlantic coast to the Indian ocean—thousands of people were left homeless and unable to flee. They were trapped on islands of bush and rock, caught by the worst floods in living memory.

Sonja had climbed Table Mountain by way of Platteklip Gorge, to see the full moon rise at sunset. The moon, it was said, would appear opposite the setting sun, simultaneously. She'd hauled Jason and Bart (with bandaged neck) up behind her. The fresh air would do them all good. The exercise too.

From the summit they looked east, toward the Bergen van Afrika, to the big range Van Riebeeck believed hid the way to Monomotapa, the southern portal to El Dorado.

Here, seated above the Camissa and the Castle of Good Hope, Jason told the story of Sunaj and Janus:

'Sunaj was the favourite daughter of Chief Quena'choa, a trickster and a trancer. She blossomed as a girl but shied away from the older boys, having fallen secretly in love with a young runaway cadet, Janus van den Kaap. Together they formed a rebellion against the fledgling VOC settlement. It was the summer of the Vanishing Eland and Janus had tried to cut the water supply to the Castle. For this he was brutally punished and summarily banished to Robben Island, where he toiled in the slate-quarry and lime-kilns for several years.'

After a daring escape in a stolen boat—which Jason recounted with dramatic detail—Janus returned to ask for Sunaj in marriage.

'She was now a beautiful woman with fat-plaited hair and aromatic skin. She played a tortoise-harp and sang like the legendary fire-bird.'

Bart tugged his sleeve: 'Get on with the story, Jas.'

'It was a moonlit night above Quena-ku, Land of the Red People, and the stars glowed like the campfires of their ancestors. Sunaj and her father sat beside the fire's lingering embers while he told the clan their favourite story. He had brought them there, many moons ago, from the Mountains of the Falling Waters, having walked for several summers, until reaching the Sea of the White Wings...'

Jason raised his hands to mimic the movement of water and wind, indicating cascading streams and bellowing sails. Sonja remembered how he'd demonstrated fleeing men and stampeding oxen.

'The story, Jas, just tell us the story!'

'Right. Janus van den Kaap stepped forward to offer a springbok to Sunaj's ageing father. He'd taken its spirit while out hunting on the mountain, the one she called Hoerikwaggo. He knew the mountain by another name, that of Tafelberg, because it was as flat as the tables at the Dutchman's Castle.'

Sonja laughed. 'That's not really in the story, is it?'

'Why not?'

'Because. Because it sounds too simplistic.'

'You mean the Quena can't have a sense of humour?'

'No, you cannot r-ridicule events like that.'

'Why not, it's what I imagine and you believe.'

'Then it's not true, you have made it up? Like Gibril Tarik burning his boats at Gibraltar, Jason, that's unfair.'

Bart laughed, amused to see them squabbling again.

'True or not, fair is for the fairies.'

'I don't believe you—'

'—but it's true. My mother was born down there, in Fairyland.'

'Jason, be serious.'

'I am. She grew up in District Six, before her family was relocated to Delft and Heideveld,' he paused, shrugging, 'isn't that ironic?'

'What, that you're from the Land of the Heathens? Where I come from, Delft isn't too far from Leiden,' she added cheeringly, seeing that sullen look again.

They sat side-by-side on a flat rock, waiting to see the first tip of the moon. It was a warm evening and a light breeze brushed her hair against his face. She touched him with the back of her hand, gently, drawing her hair away. Despite it all, she had grown fond of him.

They stopped to listen to the muffled din from the city below.

So this is where North-West joins the South-East? Where the souls of our past meet, including the spirits of Almeida and Gaspar?

She now knew South Africa was heir to the karma of ancient Egypt and medieval China—and that its racial-political dilemmas stemmed from that past. She could accept racism as the karmic consequence of a corrupted spiritual lineage: a lineage going back to when the gods became incarnate on earth and dwelt among men; when the Sons of God married the daughters of men. But that their offspring became the aristocracy of Atlantis and were remembered as the mythical gods of Olympus, well, that was still too much for her.

What she did believe was simple: South Africa had bled from the wounds of its racist past and—as Laurence himself had pointed out—all men bleed red. That adage was plain to see.

'So how d'you see yourself, Jason,' she asked, 'and I don't mean in relation to a national identity, but on your own terms?'

'I've been defined by others all my life: as a race, a class, and as a sexual type. I'm supposed to be a Cape Flats Coloured Moffie.'

'I thought "moffie" meant gay, not bi-sexual.'

'Whatever, either way it implies male deviance.'

'Jason, all that was under Apartheid. Another generation has grown up with democracy since then. Surely it's all changed now?'

'Yes, but we still live with the legacy of Apartheid.'

'Oké, but it's a transitional phase. Do you think Volodya defined himself as *soviet* after the collapse of the Soviet Union? Of course not. Soviet Nationalism was an imposed ideology, just like Apartheid and Nazism. Whatever else Volodya was, he was first and foremost a free Slav with a mixed linguistic background.'

'Sure, so what's your point?'

'Simple, I want to know how *you* define yourself. For instance, I define myself—first and foremost—as a woman who wants to have a child some day. Secondly, I'm a cultural historian with a university background. After that, I guess, I see myself as Dutch. And I mean from the twentieth century, not the Golden Age. In fact, make that fourth. Third is from Leiden, as I relate better to my own town than I do to my country as a whole. Lastly, or fifthly, I'm a democrat who believes in justice, freedom, and the right to choose what I read— especially with coffee on Sundays.'

He paused, counting his figures to mimic her meticulousness.

'Sure, so you *do* believe in Truth?'

'I believe in being true, yes, and that we should be truthful to each other, though I don't always know where to find this so-called Truth. As for God, we can only imagine the existence of a supreme being—'

'—fair enough,' he said, slowly regaining himself. 'Who am I now? First, a bi-sexual man from Cape Town. Second, a research scientist who needs physical proof. Third, an agnostic, a metaphysical sceptic. And last,' he smiled, 'lastly, I'm not a historian. Not like you!'

'Why?'

'Because historians juxtapose European textuality against African orality. I seek oral evidence, while you use the written records.'

She laughed: 'Thank God. I suppose our history is transmitted via reading and writing; yours, Jason, only yours is performative...'

Jason became serious. 'Sure, Africa's past has many forms: from amaXhosa firetales to isiZulu praisesongs, from rock engravings in the Karoo to the illuminated manuscripts of Timbuktu.'

'Like Camões's epic, it's all poetry. Anyway, you're not connected to Africa alone, but Eurasia too.'

'So...?' he said leaning provocatively against Bart.

'Remember what we said about the so-called ash of history? What appears as historical memory in the form of treaties and declarations, that this is merely the ash remaining after an event? If we really want to understand our past, properly, then we need to put the spiritual back into historical writing. We should re-examine individuals in the light of their eternal recurrence and ask ourselves how their lives give direction to ours. Just as our interest in Nearchus-Almeida leads us...'

But Jason was hardly listening:

'Sure, whatever. Remember your name resonates with Sonqua?'

He drew the words with a stick:

$$\text{S o n q u a} = \text{S o n j a}$$

Leaning forward, she took the stick and added:

$$\text{S u n a j} = \text{J a n u s}$$

She watched his reaction, smiling broadly, then reversed the letters in the sand. It indicated a range of possible connections—master and slave, brother and sister, husband and wife:

$$S\ u\ n\ a\ j\ =\ S\ o\ n\ j\ a$$
$$\|\qquad\qquad\ \|$$
$$J\ a\ n\ u\ s\ =\ J\ a\ s\ o\ n$$

She leant against Jason, Bart's head resting on his other shoulder, and peered at the fading foreshore below. She wondered where the untamed sea had rushed against the beach; where the waves had once pounded, relentlessly, until the shore finally disappeared under tons of rubble. Today the line of the bay's former incarnation was hardly visible under the Esplanade.

The moon slid out from behind the mountain, a large yellow disc, and she felt like Galahad before the Grail. However, unlike the young Parsifal, Jason felt no remorse for his lack of faith in God. Nor did Bart, apparently, despite his close shave with death.

She would leave them both behind, perhaps never to see this wind-swept Vlek again. It was their paradisal-fairyland, not hers. Yet she wondered about her ties to this place, having felt at home, like Stein, with each and every step.

Lieve help, but we've been through a lot: a skull, a dossier and a crossbow bolt. As well as a poem, a prophecy and that philosophical treatise.

'Remember Camões's prophecy,' she said finally, 'about how the Cape is destined to preserve Almeida's memory with his bones? Well, it also says that Hope grows out of Torment and now, now I hear they've located some of Kaiser Wilhelm's antiquities in Holland— including an early unidentified manuscript in Aramaic! So then boys, I'll be returning to see the enchanting Frans Luthring again, and I hope he feels that way about me too!'

Below her feet she felt the swirling currents of the Great Outer Sea concur with her.

EPILOGUE

It began in mystery and it will end in mystery,
but what a savage and beautiful country lies
in between.

Diane Ackerman, *A Natural History of the Senses* (1990)

Three months later, despite what they'd been through, Bart included,
Jason was still as jaded as ever. Would he ever change? Did he even
want to? While skyping him about the assassination they'd witnessed,
Sonja received her final message.

From: jmendle@sam.org.za
Sent: Thursday, December 16, 21:07
To: sonja@homenet.nl
Subject: Sonja Haas, from El Aurenx
Dearest Sonja
I gather from your email that you're back at university. I'm
sorry to hear about the exhibition being reduced due to cut-
backs in museum funding. There is no need to feel responsible,
at least not for your withdrawal, please remember that.
Speaking with hindsight is always easy. It seems you were
granted the time to pursue the story behind Almeida's murder.
And now one more message from Laurence, especially for you,
on our national Day of Reconciliation:

Sonja Haas of Leiden

Greetings, my child, it is El Aurenx who comes to you again. You used your voice to settle unfinished business, speaking for those unable to do so because of their untimely death.

You are the same soul as Sunaj Sonqua, the beloved wife of Janus van den Kaap, who witnessed the arrival of early Dutch settlers below Tafelberg. Plucked from your unspoilt mountain paradise, you were both sentenced to the rocky isle in the bay, as a purgatory until your death in chains.

Previously, also in the age of Pisces, Janus and you were young siblings when the Portuguese stepped ashore at the Taboa do Cabo. Janus was simply known as Ja'Nu and, together, you witnessed the execution of Francisco d'Almeida. On that day you were playing in the dunes not far from where the soldiers had drawn their water. This traumatic moment would repeat itself in your present life, but on the other side of the mountain. This was not your first experience of Africa's southerly Cape. Much further back in time, in the age of Libra, you were ship-wrecked while returning from the coast of Antarctica. You had been aboard a cargo vessel for which I, then called Alek the Wanderer, was the navigator.

In this present life as Sonja Haas, set in the age of Aquarius, your two journeys to Cape Town serve to tie several loose ends together. As you already know, the dossier was compiled by Walter Johannes Stein so that his story of Almeida's murder could be told; and via my faithful messenger, Laurence Oliver, you were also told about our eternal past and your own eternal recurrence. Through you we can tell those who will still hear.

Now too, my child, you have the knowledge required to draw together your own knot of karma—the strands of your lives having unravelled after Alexander cut the knot in Gordium.

Reconciliation is your recurrent theme and demonstrates that histories are not carved in stone. I offer you the following keys to your past:

Karmic keys

EL ZANA	Back in the mists of time, around 14000BCE, you belonged to an emigrant clan of Atlantean Israelites from Egypt. You were among a crew shipwrecked off the Cape of Good Hope, a place to which you would return, thrice, many ages later.
ZSUZSANNA	A native from Cordoba, you were captured when the Caliphate moved to Granada at the close of the eleventh century. Of you it was memorably said: "A Moor in blood, she possessed the proudest Christian heart among our Castilian filhas."
ELANA	Taken from Kiev by Batu Khan after the Mongol invasion of 1240, you were adopted by a family of Sufi poets from Persia. It was from Rumi that you learnt to give expression to feelings of loss, longing and love. Forever faithful to your husband Jani, you witnessed the execution of your first-born son.
SU'NA	You returned to live among the Cape Bushman of the fifteenth century. As children, you and your brother Ja'Nu witnessed the ritual execution of Viceroy D'Almeida and his men; but never spoke of it, as you had been told to stay clear of their watering place by the //ammi-î-sa. You recently relived that horror together on Clifton Beach, at the foot of Table Mountain. Today your positive karma allows you to move on.
SUNAJ SONQUA	Reappearing as the daughter of Chief Quena'choa, you married Janus van den Kaap, previously known as Ja'Nu and Jani. Janus was rebellious and his influence cost you your freedom. Sentenced to labour in irons for his misdemeanour, your feet suffered greatly—a fact you are reminded of in this life.

PS: Finally, Sonja, take care who you follow in future. Be conscious of each step, and you will lead the way for others. About these lives we may have more to say. El Aurenx blesses you.

FIN

Lightning Source UK Ltd.
Milton Keynes UK

177472UK00001B/4/P